Ice Blue Eyes

An Alaska Story of Greed, Love, and Revenge

Ron Walden

Ugly Moose AK
Box 1326 Soldotna, AK 99669
uglymooseak@gmail.com

Musk Ox
(mâthi-môs)
Ugly Moose

ISBN 978-1-95-726306-9
eBook 978-1-95-726307-6
Library of Congress Catalog Card Number: 2011928704

Manufactured in the United States of America.

Acknowledgements

Writing a book, any book, is both rewarding and challenging. I would never have finished this one without the help and encouragement of my wife, Betty. She is my greatest help and best critic. My friends have supported me and pushed me to continue. I thank them all. I would also like to thank those real folk who appear in this book. Dianne Dubuq and the Flourette C have been on my list of favorite fishing vessels for many years. She is a great skipper and fisherman—thanks Diane. Another friend I used loosely in this book, Jim Stogsdill, has earned my respect as a friend and a river guide.

My friend and editor, Sheryl Oldham, has contributed greatly to the end product. I value her expertise and advice. She has made me appear much more intelligent than I really am. Thank you, young lady.

And for all my doughnut-shop friends, thank you for the tips, advice and information, all of which is used unashamedly. Thank you.

Character List

Tad Morton .... *Kayaker, bank officer, killed in accident*

Ben Gerlitz .... *Kayaker, bank officer, Survivor*

Colin James .... *Kayaker, didn't make the trip. Boeing engineer*

Milo Thomas................. *Trooper captain, Anchorage*

Rueben Hayes .... *Investigating trooper sergeant*

Dave............................. *FWP officer from Seward*

Aliana Pedersen .... *Deputy Director of Finance*

Mr. Stackhaus .... *SeaFirst Bank official. Gerlitz's boss*

Stan Withers .... *Trooper Captain, head of SCAN team*

Eduardo Sanchez

Ramon Chavez.............. *Operate Sombrero restaurant*

Larry Combs................. *Eddie Sanchez' driver*

Aaron Portman.............. *Ramon's lawyer*

Lyda Carney.................. *SeaFirst Clerk*

Burt Fields .... *CPA*

Molita Juarez................. *Informant, worked at Sombrero Restaurant*

Don Sears...................... *Molita's fiance'*

Jules Steinman............... *Lawyer sent by El Dante for Larry and Eddie*

Sgt Leon Balfore............ *Promoted to Lieutenant after Rube promoted*

<h1 style="text-align:center">Chapter One</h1>

Alaska's grandeur is legendary—Its beauty creates a postcard view in any direction you look. Alaska is a land of contrasts. Sidney Lawrence knew this when he painted his landscapes, painting Mount McKinley bathed in sunshine and at the same time shrouded in swirling snow and mist. Robert Service understood it when he wrote his humorous poetry with tragic endings.

The state is a contrast unto itself, with a landmass one-third the total of the lower forty-eight states, more than twice the size of the next largest state, and a population more than six hundred thousand people, about the number to be found in a good size neighborhood of some of the nation's major cities. The distance is greater from Adak to Anchorage than from Adak to Japan. It is farther from Alaska to Washington, D.C. than it is to Russia.

Winds along the coastal areas of Alaska, if found in any other part of the U.S., would be called hurricanes. On the shores of Bristol Bay, winds of one hundred miles per hour just make it a bad day to go flying or boating.

Alaska has more coastline than all the other states combined. Seas of the proportions found along the coast of Alaska, if found in another part of the country, would be called tidal waves or rogue waves. Mariners plying the waters off Alaska cope with one hundred-foot seas on a regular basis. Yes, Alaska is a land of contrast.

It is this mystique that lures adventurers from every corner of the world. They come to experience what cannot be found elsewhere. The adventure can be as close as the steps of the airplane or the boat which transports you here, or be kept at arm's length, through the windows of a tour boat or bus. There is something for everyone.

It was this spirit that prompted the two young Seattle bankers to come to this place. There was supposed to be a third member of the party, an electronics engineer from Boeing, but labor problems at the plant had caused him to cancel at the last moment.

Tad Morton was busy lashing his large backpack to the deck of his sea kayak. The deck hand on the Kenai Fjords Tours excursion boat was lending a hand. A few yards behind the hundred-foot boat was another sea kayak bobbing gently in the calm water. The second man watched as Morton and his helper slipped the bright blue kayak over the stern of the big boat. The deck hand held the line while Tad eased the little boat into the water. After a final check of his equipment, he slid into the cockpit. Making final adjustments, he waved to the deck hand who tossed the end of the line into Tad's outstretched hand.

The skipper of the tour boat had now appeared on the aft deck. "I'll pick you up on Friday."

"We'll be here. Thanks for everything." Tad waved, then punched his paddle into the frigid waters of Prince William Sound. Almost at once they heard the engines of the tour boat begin to move the vessel on its way up the bay.

The two men were now alone to enjoy the adventure they had planned for three years. Every free moment had been spent practicing their skills in the bays and inlets of Puget Sound in Washington State. They had packed and repacked their gear many times, eliminating unnecessary items and refining the ones they kept. Special electronic equipment was built for the trip by their friend Colin James, using technology and equipment secured through the Boeing company. He had built radios into helmets for communications between the three adventurers. He'd built special GPS, Global Positioning System, navigational receivers into the cockpit frames of each kayak. Finally, he had built remote controls for video recorders that could be mounted on four-foot-tall mounts on the bow of each boat. The cameras could be turned right, left, up or down with the touch of a button on the small screen on the cockpit frame.

The three men worked as a team when in their boats. Everything went as planned and they became expert in the small craft. When all was ready, they booked passage to Alaska. Two days before the trip, there was a labor problem at the Boeing plant and James was forced to cancel. The other two men had considered what to do but decided to proceed with the trip as planned without their friend Colin James.

So, here they were, Tad Morton in the blue kayak, and Ben Gerlitz in the bright orange one; the yellow kayak remained in Seattle with its operator.

The two men had ridden the tour boat from the city of Seward to Aialik Bay. They had spent a lot of time researching where to spend the last week of their vacation. This was the ideal spot. They had been advised that the small black sand beach in Holgate Arm would be a safe place to camp. It was safe from most bears and would make a central base from which to explore the bays and inlets of Aialik Bay.

"Isn't this great?" Tad spoke into the intercom in his helmet. "Did you ever dream that the scenery would be this great right from the time we got off the tour boat?"

A few yards to his left was the orange kayak. "Oh man! This is really something. I can't wait to get this heavy stuff off the boat and explore up there by the glacier."

They paddled directly to the beach they had been told to use. Ten minutes of exploring was all it took to find a good campsite high enough to escape the high tides and hidden enough to protect the camp in case of high winds. They set about establishing their camp, all the while ooing and awing about what they had seen in the short time since their arrival in Seward.

Lunch was a hurried affair of sandwiches brought from town and some hot tea from a thermos bottle. They were anxious to get started. Back at the kayaks some time was taken to mount video cameras and to mark the beach on the GPS. In late July there would be no shortage of daylight for the return, but cautious navigation was one of the things they had practiced which had become a habit.

"Wow! Look at the eagle over there. He's so close." The eagle obliged the tourists by tilting his head back and giving his distinctive call. Satisfied the men were no threat, he sat in a spruce tree and watched as the two boats made their slow progress toward the head of the bay.

As they worked their way up the arm, they began to pass small chunks of ice floating in the water. The farther up the bay they paddled, the more ice they encountered and the larger the pieces. Ben had been taking pictures as he maneuvered the orange kayak toward Holgate Glacier. The video camera was working perfectly. He was filming a pair of seals on a raft of ice when the voice on the intercom interrupted.

"Ben, I'm going to try to get closer to the glacier. See if you can get some good video of me with the ice wall behind my boat."

"Okay. But be careful. There is a lot of ice floating in the water, and these boats won't take much of a hit from an iceberg."

The blue kayak began making its way through the pieces of ice, moving slowly toward the glacier. It was a marvelous sight, seabirds circling, seals in the water. Sun shining brightly. "This is the perfect vacation," Ben thought as he followed his partner with the camera.

It took Tad almost a half hour to paddle the distance to the glacier. It was much farther than he had originally thought. The size of the ice wall was so much larger than he estimated. The murky water splashed against the ice where it met the bay. Water poured from under the glacier on the right side, results of the warm summer sun attacking the 10,000-year-old ice. Tad paddled along the face of the ice wall, overwhelmed by the sheer size of this monster. When he estimated he was about half way across the face, he turned and waved to the camera, then began to paddle backward toward the ice. He backed his kayak to the ice and turned so he could reach up and rub his hands on the blue crystal.

Ben bobbed gently in the water some four hundred yards away, filming first wide angle then telephoto. He captured Tad at the base of this monolith, then zoomed out for contrast until the blue vessel was almost unseen in the panorama. The sight was breathtaking.

"I think you should back off a little, Tad. It may not be safe up there."

"Yeah, in a minute. I can see some sea otters or seals to my right. I'm going to check them out before I start back. Did you get some good pictures?"

"I think so. I…" Ben had zoomed in for a tight shot when something caught his attention. He looked up in time to see a huge chunk of ice falling into the water missing Tad's kayak by only a few feet. "Get out of there, Tad. Get out now."

"Right. I'm getting out now."

The blue kayak was blocked from a direct departure by floating ice. As Tad began to parallel the face of the glacier, there was a low rumble that became increasingly louder and higher pitched. Ben could hear the sound through the voice-activated intercom. He watched in horror as the face of the glacier began to slide downward into the water. There was a huge wave created by the moving ice. The blue kayak rose with the wave, then disappeared behind it only to appear again from behind the wave. Tad was paddling as fast as he could, but he seemed to be moving so slowly.

The ice continued to move into the water, sinking deeper and deeper into the sea. Two smaller waves rolled under the kayak, each time the skill of the operator kept the craft upright. Tad continued to power his little boat with all his might. It looked as though he was out of danger when suddenly the ice which had buried its two-hundred-foot tall pinnacles in the opaque water, broke the surface. It rose from the water like some giant sea monster towering over Tad, the sun reflecting from the blue ice. When it reached a height nearly its original stature, it began to tilt toward the sea and to topple.

Ben watched in terror as millions of tons of ice came crashing down over his friend. His view was suddenly obscured by the spray and the falling ice.

"Tad. Tad." Ben waited for an answer. None came. "Tad, can you hear me?"

In a couple of agonizing minutes that seemed like hours, the dream vacation had become an incident of horror. Ben tried to make his way through the icebergs, but it was no use. He looked through binoculars for signs of his friend, but there were none. With panic setting in, he paddled as quickly as possible to the beach. He ran to the camp and found the portable marine radio.

"Mayday! Mayday! Can anyone hear me? Please, someone answer."

Chapter Two

In Anchorage, Alaska State Trooper Captain Milo Thomas took the call and noted every detail. The instant he hung up the receiver he summoned Sergeant Rueben Hayes. The sergeant was several blocks away in Anchorage traffic when the call came, so it took a few minutes for him to get to headquarters on Tudor Avenue.

Once in the captain's office, he began to take notes.

"I just had a call from the harbor master in Seward," the Captain began. "A fishing charter boat, the Flourette C, relayed a distress call from someone in Holgate Arm. He says his partner was hit by falling ice from the glacier. The harbormaster says Trooper Maddox is launching the Boston Whaler and that he and the Fish and Wildlife officer will head out right away."

"Is the guy dead or just hurt?" Hayes inquired.

"I don't know for sure. The radio call said that, because of the ice in the water, he couldn't get to where his partner was hit. I've called Anchorage Fire Department for two divers. They'll meet you at Lake Hood. I want you to take the 185 with the two divers and fly down there. I've called the hangar and they will have the Cessna fueled and ready for you when you arrive. Take your camera and a video camera. I don't know what you'll find when you get there."

"I'm on my way," Rube said, finishing his notes as he stood. "I'll call you as soon as I come back into radio range."

After contacting police officials, Ben made two more attempts to push through the floating ice in search of his friend, Tad. Each time he was forced back. On the second attempt, while trying to push large pieces of ice aside, the ice had punctured several holes in the hull of his sea kayak. Finally he gave up and returned to the black sand beach where he set about packing up his camp. Once they found his friend there would be no need to spend the night alone here. Besides, he was feeling guilt, fear, panic, remorse and any number of other emotions. He needed something to do while waiting, something to keep his mind off what had happened.

He had just carried the two heavy backpacks to the water's edge when he heard the blast from the horn. It was the Flourette C. He watched as the skipper dropped the anchor a few yards off-shore. Ben was having trouble controlling his emotions as he boarded his little boat to paddle out to the waiting charter boat.

The helpful skipper and owner of the charter boat was a young, energetic lady named Diane.

"Are you the one I talked with on the radio?" she inquired.

"Yes, and you can't imagine how much I appreciate your help. How soon before help arrives?"

"They should be here very soon. The trooper from Seward should be here in twenty minutes or so. They are sending an airplane from Anchorage and he won't be far behind. There are divers on the airplane, so things will move quickly when they arrive." Ben was now on board the Flourette C. "How about some coffee?" Diane offered.

While waiting, Diane offered to take him and his gear back to Seward as soon as the troopers were finished and told them they could leave.

"Do you think there's any hope that Tad survived?" Ben asked the experienced sea captain. He had an iron grip on his coffee cup.

"I don't know. There is always hope. He could be out there clinging to a chunk of ice and we might not see him from here, but you have to be ready for the worst."

"I know. You're right. I just feel so guilty for not being able to get over there to where he is. I wasn't able to help him."

Diane didn't know how to respond, but was saved the trouble by a voice on the radio.

"Flourette C. Flourette C. This is trooper Cessna four-four tango."

"I copy, four-four tango."

"ETA about five minutes. Have you had contact with the complainant?"

"That's affirmative. He is on board now. Do you want to meet him on board or on the beach?"

"The beach would be better, thanks. See you in five."

The deck hand, Mike, had loaded the kayak and off-loaded the rubber skiff. He helped Ben into the boat, started the motor and made for the shore. The blue and white airplane made two passes around the small bay, each time passing close to the face of the glacier. After his second circle, he swooped low and skimmed the smooth surface of the murky water. Close to the beach, he cut the motor and drifted until the floats touched the sand. Immediately the doors flung open and people began to exit. Rube held the plane steady while the divers unloaded their gear. Once that had been done, the plane was turned with the nose facing the sea. After tying the plane to a half-buried log, he said hello to Mike and Ben.

The divers busied themselves with the task of donning their equipment. They checked and double-checked every detail. The radio on Rube's hip crackled. He held it close to his ear.

"Four-four tango, C-27, do you copy?" It was the Seward officer in the Boston Whaler.

"I copy, C-27. What's your ETA?"

"Less than ten minutes. Where do you want me?"

"The divers are ready to go. Come on to the beach and pick them up. We need to get a search going as soon as you can get here. I flew over the area but didn't see anything. The ice is pretty bad up there. I'll see you as soon as you arrive."

"Roger that." The radio went silent.

"Sorry about that," Rube said as he returned his attention to the men on the beach. "Which of you is the victim's partner?" One of the men was wearing rubber kayaker gear and it should have been obvious which man had made the call, but Rube had learned long ago not to take anything for granted.

Ben took a step forward. "That would be me."

The trooper sergeant looked around the beach and spotted a nice log half buried in the sand. The man he needed to interview looked as if he couldn't stand up much longer. He motioned for the man to walk up the beach toward the ready-made seat. Once on the log he took a small tape recorder from his pocket and placed it gently in his lap.

"I know this is difficult for you, but you understand we must have all the facts before we can proceed."

"Yes, I understand," was the reply.

The portable radio beside the trooper came to life. "We're ready to go, Rube. The Fish and Wildlife officer will stay on the beach for now."

"Roger," Rube answered. "I'll be up there in the airplane as soon as I finish here. Keep me posted on any developments." He didn't want to say *body* or *debris* with the victim's friend sitting next to him.

The trooper driving the boat waved toward shore and gunned the 22-foot skiff into action. He made a quick turn toward the floating ice and the face of the glacier. The two divers were busy helping each other with tanks and hoses.

"I'm really sorry. Now, will you give me your name and date of birth for the records?" The recorder was working, but Rube wrote the information on his little note pad for his own reports.

Ben answered all the trooper's questions in a soft voice. He kept looking toward the boat and the searchers, glancing only occasionally at the officer asking the questions. The interview took more than half an hour. When Rube had reviewed his notes and decided he had asked enough questions, he told Ben he could go back to the Flourette C.

"I'll contact you when I get done here," he said. "If we find your friend, I'll let you know right away."

"Thank you for everything. I tried to look for Tad, but the ice was too much and I couldn't get up there. I feel responsible somehow." Emotion was overcoming Ben now.

Rube walked the young man back to the edge of the water and helped him into the rubber skiff to return to the Flourette C. Mike, the deck hand, was handling the little Zodiak. With Ben gone Rube turned to Dave, the Fish and Wildlife officer. He had known Dave for two or three years but had never really worked with him before.

"What now?" Dave inquired.

"Let's take the plane and do some searching from the air. We can cover a lot of area in a short period of time that way. I'll do the flying while you do the looking and handle the radio contact with the divers."

The two men scrambled into the Cessna and strapped in. It was getting late now, and though it wouldn't get dark, the light would soon be too poor to see well and fly safely in this small area close to the face of the glacier.

It was after midnight when the Cessna 185 made its final approach to Lake Hood. The three men on board were exhausted. They had found nothing. Rube had flown over the area until he had only enough fuel for the return to Anchorage. They tied the plane in its slip behind the hangar on the lake and agreed to meet in the morning to complete the reports. The diving gear was put in the back of the white pickup and the trio drove toward town.

<h1 style="text-align:center">Chapter Three</h1>

Rube was in the office before 7:30 AM. Armed with the videotape taken by Ben, he walked to the crime lab in the next building. He asked the technician to make him a copy of the tape then place the original in the evidence locker. He returned to his own office and spent the rest of the morning with the reports of the previous day. He had most of this work completed when the lab technician called to tell him the copy of the tape was ready. The lab guys were waiting for him when he arrived

"Have you seen this tape?" asked Harry Conroy, head of the crime lab.

"No, I haven't. I brought it into the lab first thing this morning. Is it going to be of any value? Can you see anything on it?" Rube questioned.

"Larry and I both looked at the tape. This is the best quality I have ever seen in a regular video. I would give my eye teeth to own equipment that would take pictures of this quality. They're great. Did he say how he got this camera set-up?"

"Yes, he did. He told me there was supposed to be another kayaker on the trip, some Boeing engineer. At the last minute, he was called back to work and didn't make the trip. This guy does electronics for Boeing, and set up the video stuff on the kayaks."

"Come in here and we'll run the tape for you," Conroy instructed.

The trio moved into the electronics room where Larry set up the tape player. Harry and Rube took seats in front of the 25-inch television while the technician completed his task and lit the screen. There were some scenes taken in Seward and on the boat during the trip to Holgate Arm. These scenes were fast-forwarded to the point where the two men were setting out to explore the glacier. The sound quality was excellent, and the voices on the intercom units were fed into the sound track.

The first pictures were of the little beach on which they had camped. The tent and backpacks were visible in the pictures. Harry was right—the picture quality was superb. The picture changed and a breathtaking panorama of Holgate Glacier and the surrounding area was presented. The voice of Tad Morton was heard as he told Ben he was going to the face of the glacier. The next pictures were of Tad paddling along the face of the blue ice. So far the pictures verified what Ben had reported.

The three men watched in amazement when the first large piece of ice tumbled through the air and splashed into the water.

"We did a rough calculation of the size of that falling ice block. We used the length of the kayak as a known measurement and then measured the block of ice. That thing was just a little larger than a Volkswagen bus. It's no wonder these guys panicked when they did. Now watch the whole face of the glacier begin to move. The poor guy didn't stand a chance." Harry was narrating.

The scene was awesome. Rube guessed that the moving piece of the glacier face was more than 150 yards across. It seemed as if it were in slow motion. Ice and snow were falling into the water at each end of the moving slab. The man in the kayak paddled as fast as he could, but barely made headway. He bobbed up and down in the waves created by the slipping ice. The entire face of the glacier seemed to slip away deeper and deeper into the water until it had almost disappeared. The kayak slowed as the paddles stopped moving and the man looked around. He must have thought he was out of danger because when he resumed paddling he had lost the urgency and panic he had shown before. He began to pick his way through the chunks of floating ice.

Suddenly, the ice behind him began to grow up out of the water. It grew taller and taller, dwarfing the kayak and its occupant. Urgency and panic took over his paddling again, but higher and higher the blue ice rose. Then, when it had regained about two thirds of its original height, it began to tilt outward as it continued to gain size. Pieces of ice and snow began to fall from the tilting pinnacle. Soon the splashing water, the rolling waves and the falling ice obscured the kayak. The giant crystal continued to topple and began to come apart. It was breaking up as it fell.

The voices on the tape were in panic, calling to each other. Then, there was only one voice on the tape. A pitiful, frightened voice, calling to his friend who would never answer again. The camera had recorded the entire episode in amazing clarity. Millions of tons of ice had come crashing down on one desperate human soul, ending his young life in a spectacular, yet tragic, moment.

The three men watched the last of the tape in silence. When it ended, the tape was rewound and taken from the VCR and given to the sergeant.

"This is pretty convincing evidence of an accidental death," Rube remarked weakly. "Thanks for your help with the tape. Keep the original locked up for now. The coroner will probably want to see it." With that he left the lab and returned to his own office.

He sat quietly in his chair for several minutes before continuing his final report on the incident. Looking at his watch he judged that Ben would be in town any time now. He would need to have a conversation with his captain before he met with the survivor. This was clearly an accidental death, but final evaluation of the incident would have to be done by the captain and the colonel. These things were above his authority. He gathered the files and the videotape and walked to the office of his captain.

Deputy Director of Finance for the State of Alaska, Aliana Pedersen, was playing with her daughter in a small house in Fairbanks when the call came in. It was early, before 8 AM, when Don Cummings from the governor's office called to give her the message about Tad Morton's death. Information about the incident was still sketchy, but troopers had not been able to locate the body and chances of his survival were almost non-existent. There were few details to be had and up-dates would be given her the moment they were learned.

Aliana was born and raised in Circle, Alaska. Her mother was Alaska native and her father a Swedish immigrant who made a sparse living gold mining, and spent most of his earnings on liquor. When Aliana was eleven and her sister only nine, her father had gone hunting with a friend up the Yukon River. When they failed to return, a search was mounted. The two men were never found, but the capsized boat was recovered about fifteen miles upstream from Circle.

Aliana's mother raised the children as best she could, taking small jobs housecleaning, helping at the fish wheel and clerking at the local store. She had always told Aliana she should go on to college. She wanted her daughter to be someone. Money was scarce during those times. Consequently, she was unable to provide anything toward college. A family friend offered Aliana a place to stay if she wanted to work in Fairbanks to earn money for college. The young girl had never been out of the village except on rare shopping trips to the city with her family.

Her first job came easily. She clerked in the local J.C. Penny store. The pay wasn't much, but she was able to save a little. Then came a break. A local bank was looking for trainees. They would hire and train them as tellers, with the possibility of promotion. The money was far better than she was getting at her present job so she applied and landed one of the positions.

She was well liked at the bank. She was bright and learned quickly. She was also discreet. Aliana kept private things private. The bank officials took notice and offered her a scholarship for the fall semester at the University of Alaska, Fairbanks. This was what she had prayed for. Things were going her way.

She enrolled, studied hard and continued to work part-time for the bank. In her senior year, she decided to go for her Masters in Business. She was seeing a recent UAF graduate who was now working for the same bank. The relationship became serious and she had hopes of marrying the young man.

It was her naïve trust that proved to be her downfall. Aliana was a striking woman, tall by any standard, almost five feet nine inches, with raven black hair that sparkled in the sunlight. Above her high cheekbones was a pair of beautiful, pale blue eyes. They were accented by her black hair and dark skin. She had taken care of herself physically, a fact demonstrated by her long deliberate strides and ramrod straight back. She held her shoulders back and her head high, giving her an air of pride.

She dated her young suitor for almost a year. The two seemed happy until she broke the news that she was pregnant. Aliana was thrilled with the situation until she met with the hesitant attitude of her boyfriend. She was devastated by his reluctance to marry and make a home life. Aliana stormed from the apartment she shared with him and began a life on her own. He vowed to provide for the child, a promise he would fail to keep, but marriage did not fit into his plans.

It was a struggle to finish her Master's, but with the help of her sister, who moved to Fairbanks to help take care of the baby, she managed. The bank promoted her as soon as she completed her schooling. She was a diligent employee with a unique savvy for the financial business.

It was apparent upon the birth of her child that something was wrong. Aliana loved her anyway, but as time passed it became obvious that the little girl could never keep up with the rest of the kids her age. Aliana had made an arrangement with her sister to live with them and to care for the little girl while Aliana earned a living for all of them, an arrangement that continued even today.

Aliana had guaranteed to stay with the bank for a designated period in return for their help with her education. That time was past and her reputation in the local financial world was growing. A large Alaska Native corporation approached her with the offer of chief financial officer for the corporation. The responsibilities were astronomical, but so were the salary and benefits. She accepted.

She soon proved her worth to the corporation. Their fortunes grew and their company diversity improved by leaps and bounds. Aliana was given huge bonuses and incentives by the corporation for her efforts. Everyone was happy.

Fortunes for her ex-boyfriend had gone well also. He had chosen to follow a career in politics. He had made many friends while working in the financial world. Those friends had sponsored him as the party candidate for governor. He ran on a platform of financial reform for the State of Alaska, a reform everyone agreed was needed. He was elected easily. Nearly every woman in the state voted for the handsome young man with the soft voice.

As governor he intended to keep his political promises. He spent long hours studying every aspect of the state budget in an attempt to learn how to streamline it without cutting services to the citizens of the state. He and Aliana had remained friendly if not friends. He knew her strong fiscal management abilities and hers was the first name to come to mind when reform of the State Finance Department began. He had called her to come to Juneau to get a first-hand look at the problem. She spent three weeks studying the problems, flying to Fairbanks to be with her daughter on weekends. After giving it a lot of thought she accepted the challenge, but refused the Commissioner title. She was sure she could do more good as Deputy Director, providing she were given free reign to overhaul the department and institute her own policies. The governor agreed.

Since that time she had been the driving force behind successful financial reform for the state. She went to Fairbanks every week to see her daughter and her sister who continued to care for the impaired child.

Sergeant Rueben Hayes was back in his office waiting for Ben Gerlitz. It was late in the day and Rube was weary. He thought he might try to put off any lengthy discussion with Gerlitz until tomorrow, if that could be arranged. Better yet, perhaps he would like to go to dinner this evening, allowing a chance to relax after his ordeal.

Chapter Four

Rubbing his eyes with the heel of his hands, his private moment was interrupted by the ringing telephone.

"Sergeant Hayes," he answered in a tired voice.

"How is your schedule for the rest of the day, Rube?" It was Captain Thomas.

"I'm waiting for Ben Gerlitz to show, then I think I'm done for the day."

"I know this has been a long day for you, but I just got a call from Aliana Pedersen, the deputy director of finance. You've met her. I've sent a trooper to the airport to bring her to the office. She says the state has some interest in this accidental death."

"This thing just happened last night. How did she find out about it so soon?"

"She told me that the governor called her, that's all I know. Will you have time to see her before you leave?" The Captain was putting the responsibility on Hayes.

"Yeah. Sure. I have the file on my desk. Have reception call me when she arrives." Rube looked at his watch and reached for his coffee cup.

The receptionist escorted the lady to his office. She wore a green business suit and red blouse with a black ribbon about the neck. She was striking. He had met her in meetings on previous occasions, but only casually. When he stood to introduce himself, he noticed that with the high heels she wore she equaled his six-foot stature. Abbreviated introductions were given and Rube offered her a seat at the end of his desk.

"What can I do to help you, Ms. Pedersen?" Rube began.

"Please, call me Aliana," she offered. "I suppose you're curious about why I'm interested in this accident."

"Yes, it crossed my mind."

"As you probably already know, the governor hired me to revamp the department of finance. Without going into long details, one of the things I did was to hire the SeaFirst Bank of Seattle through which to route all verified accounts payable. In its simplest terms, that means the bank writes all the checks for all goods and services for the State of Alaska. Well, to be more accurate, monies are electronically transferred to the accounts of those owed."

"From what I hear, you've saved the state millions of dollars in fees and penalties with your new system," Rube acknowledged.

"Yes, and that brings us to why I'm here." A trace of worry appeared on her perfect face. "The State of Alaska has a special account with the bank. The entire system is very complicated and requires special handling by the bank. The bank has gone to great lengths to accommodate this account. They have bought special computers to account for our money and to transfer receipts to those needing to be paid. They have special check writing equipment for those who do not qualify for wire transfers. In return they have the advantage of a huge cash flow from the State of Alaska, an arrangement that has benefited the State and the bank. The Junior Vice President in charge of all this is, or was, Tad Morton. He and I worked very closely together. Now that he is gone, I have to approach the bank about someone else to head up this account. It's an awesome responsibility for whomever takes the job."

"I can see why you came here now." Rube thought a moment. "Would it help you to have a copy of the incident report? I am not allowed to give you the entire file, but I can bend the rules enough to get you a copy of the witness report, if that would do you any good at all."

"Yes, thank you. That would be wonderful." Her smile was warm and friendly.

"Aliana, did I pronounce it right?"

"Yes."

"Ben Gerlitz was the one with Tad Morton and reported the incident. He did a terrific job with the details. He also works for the SeaFirst Bank and they were vacationing together. Anyway, he will be here any minute to go over some last minute questions before he returns to Seattle. I was hoping to take him to dinner this evening. Since you have a vested interest in the situation, would you be interested in having dinner with the two of us?"

"As a matter of fact, I'm really hungry. I haven't eaten since breakfast. I have been busy since the telephone call this morning. You don't think he'll mind if I intrude?"

"I'm sure he won't mind at all. If you wouldn't mind waiting here, I'll change clothes. Can I get you a cup of coffee or a soda?"

"No, thank you. I would like to have a peek at the statements you mentioned, if that wouldn't be too much trouble." Again she displayed her alluring smile.

The trooper changed clothing in the locker room where he spread some fresh deodorant under his arms and splashed on some fresh cologne. He combed his hair, checked his appearance in the full-length mirror and satisfied himself that he was presentable. On the way back to his office, he stopped to ask his captain to trade vehicles for the evening. The captain's car was an unmarked blue Chevy and better suited to transport his guests to dinner than the white pickup with the trooper shield on the door.

They chose the Sullivan Steakhouse for dinner. It offered a good meal with a quiet atmosphere in which to discuss final issues. Gerlitz would be returning to Seattle tomorrow. With the help of the troopers, his reservations were changed — not an easy task in the summer months.

Rube drank coffee; his guests both drank single malt scotch. During the course of the evening's conversation, Aliana asked Ben how he had met Tad.

Ben seemed to be an average sort of fellow, but he had a razor-sharp wit and a strange sense of humor that made him an instant friend to everyone he met. His story began with a grin.

"Tad graduated from UCLA the same year I graduated from UC Berkley. We had never met until we were each being interviewed for positions at the bank. I had been interviewed and was leaving. I must have looked worried. He guessed right away what I had been doing. He told me he was interviewing too. We agreed to meet in the bar at the Four Seasons that evening. I was staying a block up at the Hilton. We were both young and inexperienced in the job market. We were both nervous about our interview. I guess we just had common interests at that point." Ben sipped his drink.

"We both were hired," he continued.

"You remained friends all this time then?" Aliana asked.

"Yes, we did. Neither of us had family on the west coast. My family lives in Indiana. Ben had no family. His family, his mother, his father and his little sister were killed in a car accident on the freeway in California. Ben almost quit school when that happened. His dad left him enough insurance money to finish school so he decided to stay for the memory of his folks. Of course, all that was before I met him."

"The two of you worked together at the bank from that time?" Rube asked.

"We didn't exactly work together. We were really fierce competitors. We were both in personal banking and we each worked pretty hard. Every time one of us was promoted, the other was not far behind. In the end he outdid me, though. He landed the plum of the bank, the State of Alaska account. It's the largest single section in the investments section of the bank—three floors of people and computers doing business for a single account. Don't get me wrong. Tad worked hard. He had the largest account in the bank, but it was also the most work. He was up to it though, he did a good job for them." Ben sipped his scotch again and fell silent, reflecting on unspoken memories of his lost friend.

The three were drinking a final cup of coffee when Aliana broke the silence.

"Ben, you seem to be familiar with our account in the bank. I am going to Seattle in the morning to confer with Mr. Stackhaus about a successor to head the account. Before I make any commitments, would you be interested in talking with me about the position?"

The answer came without hesitation. "You bet I would."

Chapter Five

Flight time for Aliana Pedersen was 7:10 AM. The alarm sounded at five. She stumbled into the shower, groggy from the short night's sleep. She applied her makeup, fixed her hair and, before dressing, packed her bag. She chose a medium length skirt and blazer in which to do today's business. Most department heads were men, and no matter what their age, they all took notice of a shapely woman in a skirt. Recognizing such quirks of human nature had often given her the advantage in negotiations. She checked the time just before six.

Opal Pedersen answered the telephone. It would be another hour before the twelve-year-old Saundra would be up. Aliana's sister Opal walked with a pronounced limp. She had been riding an ATV with a friend when it skidded out of control and rolled over several times. Both youngsters were severely injured. Opal suffered a broken hip that never healed properly, leaving her with a fused hip joint that made her limp badly. When Opal had finished high school, Aliana asked her to move into Fairbanks to care for her newborn baby girl. She had lived there since, taking care of and loving the sweet little girl with the learning disability.

"How is everything, Opal?" Aliana asked.

"Oh, fine. Saundra is still in bed. Should I get her up to talk with you?"

"No, I'll call her later. I just wanted you to know I am going to Seattle this morning. I have some urgent state business there. I'll be staying at the Hilton; you have the number in the Rolodex. Is there anything you need before I leave this morning?"

"I don't think so. We'll be fine. Have a good trip."

"Thanks, Opal, I'll try to call this evening. Give Saundra a big hug for me."

"I will. Bye."

She had just hung up the telephone when she heard two toots on a horn in front of the condo. The cab was here. She turned out the lights and made a final check of the room before leaving. The ride to the airport was uneventful and traffic was light. Aliana was preoccupied with thoughts of a replacement for Tad Morton. It was going to be difficult to replace him. He had been a key player in her entire finance program. Ben Gerlitz seemed to be the logical replacement; he knew Tad; he had equal banking skill and talents; he was personable; and from her brief conversation with him, it seemed she could work with him. There were special considerations, though. Those were going to be the problem. How was she going to approach him about those? Human nature, she thought, play the averages. Man's weakest points were lust and greed. Did he have these weaknesses?

The cab pulled to a stop in front of the Alaska Airlines entrance. A skycap offered to take her bag, but she politely refused his offer. He opened the door for her anyway, tipping his cap as she passed.

She walked to the departure gate, pausing for a latte at a stand in the lobby. The difficulty of finding a replacement for Tad was foremost in her thoughts. These thoughts were played through her mind, given as many twists and variations as she could come up with. No matter how many times she went over it, she came up with the same conclusion: unless someone appeared on the horizon, Ben Gerlitz was her best option. She had met several of the supervisors at the bank, but none showed the promise of Mr. Gerlitz.

It was almost noon Seattle time when she walked from the terminal building. Mr. Irwin Stackhaus had timed it perfectly, stopping in front of the exit door only seconds after she arrived. He rolled down the window and waved in recognition. He walked around the car, opened the rear door and deposited her carry-on bag. He held the front door open for the lady then returned to the driver's side. He slipped behind the wheel, checked the rear-view mirror and sped away.

"Would you like some lunch on the way to town, Ms. Pedersen?" he asked politely.

"That would be lovely," she replied. "I didn't eat on the plane. I'm rather hungry."

In Renton, a short drive off U.S. Interstate 5, he stopped at a fashionable little place in the heart of town called Mike's. Dinner required a reservation, but lunch served only a small and elite crowd of business people. They found a corner table where private talk would remain private.

After ordering, Irwin Stackhaus looked into Aliana's soft blue eyes.

"Everyone at the bank is just devastated by Tad's death. I want to assure you that the bank will do everything within its power to ensure a smooth transition until a new administrator can be appointed for your account."

"I appreciate that, Mr. Stackhaus. That's why I've come. Have you given any thought to a replacement?"

"We have several names on the desk. No decisions have been made yet. We assumed you would like to be party to the interviews, since you will be working closely with whomever we choose."

"That's very kind of you. If possible, I would like to review the candidate files when we get to the bank." She had made the demand sound like a request. "Our account has been working so well under Tad's leadership; it will be impossible to replace him without some lapses during the change. Are you open to going outside the bank to hire someone if there are no satisfactory candidates on your list?"

Stackhaus thought for a moment. "I'm sure the bank would agree to that if it becomes necessary. I would hope, though, you'll find someone on our list who will meet your requirements. With a staff as large as ours, we should have any talent you would wish for. I hope you will keep an open mind about the selection."

"Of course, I'll start reviewing the files after lunch." The waiter brought lunch, which was consumed without much small talk.

They made a quick stop at the Hilton, only a few blocks from the bank, to allow Aliana to check in and drop her bag.

The black glass and steel bank structure is an imposing sight. When it was built, it was the tallest building in Seattle. Now, however, there are other buildings on the same street that out reach the imposing symbol. It was necessary to change elevators to get to the 44th floor. Once there, Aliana was met by bank employees offering condolences. Eventually she and Irwin Stackhaus made their way into a small conference room where two other bank officials were waiting. She was pointed to a chair at the table and Stackhaus took the seat at the head of the table. There was a leather-bound notebook in front of him and a stack of file folders on the table to his right.

"Let's call this meeting to order. Ms. Pedersen, do you know Bob Winslow?" He pointed to the middle-aged man across the table from her. "Bob is Executive Director of Personnel for the bank."

Winslow held out his hand and said, "Pleased to meet you."

"Next to him is Martha Calbrese, recruitment manager. She screens all personnel for hiring and promotion."

"I'll try to assist you in any way I can during the selection process." The two shook hands.

Stackhaus introduced Aliana to the others. "Now shall we get this process under way?" He looked up to make sure he had everyone's attention. "Each of you has a legal pad in front of you. Please write your questions down and ask them when we complete the review of each file. There are six candidates in all. We will take them in alphabetical order. Any questions?"

"Then let's begin with Kenneth Avery." One by one they went through the files. Each member of the panel asked their questions at the end of each file review.

Aliana had met all the applicants, though she needed to be reminded where each one worked. All worked in this account department. Each was qualified to manage the account, but she wanted someone with whom she could work closely without conflict and someone she could trust.

Late in the afternoon they finished the last file. Aliana agreed to interview two of the candidates, Kenneth Avery and Shirley Townsend.

"Is it possible to add a name to this list?" Aliana inquired.

The question surprised Irwin Stackhaus. "I think we can accommodate another name on the list, Ms. Pedersen. Who did you wish to add?"

"I would like to see the file on Ben Gerlitz."

All three members of the committee knew Ben. Each looked at the other and nodded vigorously.

"We should have thought of him ourselves," Stackhaus acknowledged. "He is one of the bright stars in the bank's future. I'll have his file sent up. Why don't we take a coffee break while we're waiting for the file?"

The file was brought to the conference room and given the same style review as the previous six. At the end of the file review, the same general questions were asked. It seemed to Aliana that the committee members were leaning strongly in favor of Kenneth Avery. She thought him a good candidate, but had her own personal criteria for selection. Avery didn't really meet her needs.

It came Aliana's turn to speak her opinion. "Before I make a final decision, I would like to personally interview Kenneth Avery and Ben Gerlitz."

"We understand your concerns about this account, and with that in mind, we will set the interviews for tomorrow morning. How much time would you require for each interview?" Stackhaus asked.

"I think an hour each," Aliana answered. "Can we do one at ten and the other at one-thirty."

Irwin Stackhaus turned to his secretary, who had been taking notes during the meeting. "Set it up. Use this conference room. See that Ms. Pedersen has all the time she wants." He turned back to the people at the table. "If there isn't anything else?" He paused and glanced around the table. "Then this meeting is adjourned. Thank you."

The secretary and Aliana were the last to leave the conference room. The young secretary was arranging her papers to carry when Aliana asked her if she knew the extension number for Ben Gerlitz. The girl opened her book and gave her the number.

"Mr. Gerlitz is on the 38th floor," the secretary commented before exiting the room.

When she was alone, Aliana dialed the number for Ben's extension. A receptionist answered then forwarded the call to her boss.

"Miss Pedersen, how nice to hear from you," he greeted. "How are your meetings going?"

"Very well, thank you," she answered politely. "Are you busy right now? Do you have time to talk for a minute?"

"Of course. What can I do for you?"

"You know I'm here interviewing for a replacement for Tad," she reminded him. "When we spoke in Anchorage, you said you could be interested in the position. Do you still feel that way?"

"You bet, but the rumor is that my name never made the list."

"You should never believe a rumor unless you started it yourself." This was advice her mother had passed on to her. "Are you busy this evening? Say around seven?"

"I can be free. What did you have in mind?"

"I am leaving the bank now and I have several things to attend to this afternoon. I think we should meet before tomorrow. If you're free I'll buy you dinner."

"Where would you like to meet?"

"Given the nature of what we have to discuss, I think a private meeting would be advised. I have a small suite at the Hilton. If you have no objections, I'll have dinner sent up to the room."

"That would be fine. What's your room number?" She gave it, he made a note, said goodbye and hung up the phone. He stared at the number on the pad in front of him. How did she convince management to put his name on the list? What was so important that she needed a private meeting to discuss it? This meeting bordered on unethical, should he get involved or forget it? He wanted the position badly, and his curiosity had been piqued. Dangerous professional ground or not, he was going to the meeting with the blue-eyed beauty with the raven hair.

It had taken her almost an hour after the phone call to get to her room in the Hilton. She had walked the few short blocks, window-shopping as she went. The air was warm and felt good. The smell of salt water overpowered the usual smells of the city. She liked Seattle, but other matters occupied her thoughts now. She had called the Juneau office from Anchorage and asked for information. That information should be waiting for her when she arrived at the hotel. The walk had helped to clear her mind and she was ready to resume her quest.

There were several e-mail messages on her laptop when she returned to the room. She paged through them, making notes of items to be dealt with when she had the time. Item after item she went down the list, finally coming to the information she had been looking for. She read it carefully. It was exactly what she'd hoped to find.

The next item on her agenda was to call Saundra. She looked at the time, 5:30 PM in Fairbanks. Opal would be making dinner for Saundra now. She dialed the telephone.

Saundra answered. "Hello, this is the Pedersen residence. Who would you like to talk to?"

"Hi, honey. It's Mommy."

"Mommy, Mommy," answered the excited voice on the other end. "Opal, it's Mommy." The girl shouted first at her mother then to her guardian/aunt.

"What did you do today, sweetheart?" the mother asked.

"We had fun, Mommy. Opal took me to Alaska Land. I got to feed the ducks. One bit me a little bit, but it didn't hurt, and he didn't mean to."

"You had fun then?"

"Yes and we saw lots of things to buy, but Opal wouldn't let me have them." The youngster went on telling about her day at the park. She finally asked, "When are you coming home mommy?"

"I'll be home as soon as I can. I love you baby." This was the hard part, being away from Saundra. She spoke with Opal a few minutes and hung up the phone, returning to the urgent business of this day.

It was nearly seven when she ordered room service. She thought a Cobb salad and iced tea with lemon and honey would be good.

She had changed into slacks and a nicely fitted cashmere sweater, and was reviewing her messages again when the knock came on the door. It was Ben Gerlitz, punctual to the second.

"Come in, Ben. Let me take your coat." The suite had a small anteroom with a couch and chair, a large cabinet with a television, and a table with four chairs. Ben dropped onto the couch. He noted the table was covered with a laptop computer and several file folders. A briefcase was standing next to the table leg.

Aliana parked herself in one of the chairs at the table.

<h1 style="text-align:center">Chapter Six</h1>

When the governor had appointed Aliana Pedersen to the position of deputy director of finance for the State of Alaska, he had also endowed her with special powers to accomplish the task of reorganizing the credit side of the state ledger. Although she worked for the director of finance, Aliana reported directly to the governor who gave virtual carte blanche to her proposals.

She immediately set about creating a new system for paying the state's bills. New equipment was purchased and the new accounts established at SeaFirst Bank. She established new rules for local offices to process purchase orders, contract payments, payroll and all other payouts. Not all the supervisors in the state were happy with the new system, but in order for her plan to work she must have compliance from all departments in the state. This gave her a reputation, early in her state career, of being a ruthless administrator.

High on her list of priorities was the hiring of five new clerks who were to be her assistants. She recruited these from the best schools in the United States. She had composed a list of definite requirements to look for in the list of applicants. They were all to be women. They would be striking in appearance. They must hold outstanding scholastic credentials. They had to be ambitious and aggressive. Each was hand picked by Aliana Pedersen. It took several months to acquire the five special people who would be the vanguard of her new administration.

The five assistants, along with Aliana, were likened to the cylinder of a high powered revolver—each was a magnum cartridge ready to fire at any district supervisor who violated the financial rules set down by the governor's new and powerful deputy director of finance.

It was one of these assistants, Pamela St. John, who had done the research on Ben Gerlitz. It was her memo on the laptop that made Aliana certain that she would now have the bank administrator she wanted.

Dinner arrived shortly after Ben made his appearance. The salads were excellent. The only conversation during the meal was some small talk about Anchorage and the recent trip with its fatal ending. After dinner, Aliana cleared the tableware and placed the tray out of the way on a credenza. She refilled the tea glasses and returned to her seat.

"I assume, by your coming here tonight you are interested in the open position at the bank," she began. "Before I start with the questions, I must ask if you have any questions I can answer for you?"

"I have a hundred questions, but none I have to ask now. I expect that what I want to know will become clearer when you're finished here tonight. I am wondering, though, why the meeting tonight? I would think that all this would be settled at the interview at the bank tomorrow."

"That's a good point. I have to confess that what we are going to discuss tonight may not be appropriate during tomorrow's interview."

"What do you mean, *not appropriate*? This meeting itself seems inappropriate."

"Do you want this position or not?"

"Of course I want it, but there are limits to what I'll do to get it. I value my position at the bank and I'm not going to jeopardize that in any way."

"Don't worry, Ben. I'm here to help you, not set you up for a lynching," she tried to reassure him. "I have several key people in my department. Each of them hand picked by me. Tad was one of those people. I think you could be the very person I'm looking for to replace him."

"I'm sorry if I sound skeptical, but I've worked hard to get where I am in the bank and losing it isn't a risk I am willing to take at this point in my life."

She checked the screen on the laptop, thought a moment, and asked, "Isn't it possible you're close to losing that position right now?"

"What do you mean?" was the shocked reply.

"I mean I have information that you're quite a basketball fan."

"Yeah, so what. Lots of bankers follow basketball."

"You seem to favor the Sonics and the Trailblazers."

"They're my favorites, but what's that got to do with my job." Suspicion and irritation were making his words come out like hammer blows.

"Being a basketball fan is no crime. I like a good game myself. On the other hand, owing more than your net worth to a local gambler could be seen as being more than a fan."

His face turned ashen. He started to speak, but the words failed to come. He looked into the glass of tea and tried to compose himself.

"I don't know what to say," he said.

"It's true then? You owe a sizable gambling debt?"

"Yes," he said quietly. "I've been trying to raise the money to pay them off, but things haven't gone well in that respect. Some of my investments lost a lot of money this spring and I haven't been able to put together enough to get this off my back. I've been afraid the bank would find out. I guess now they will."

"I told you at the beginning of this meeting that I was here to help you not hang you. I'm not going to tell the bank about this. Had you lied when I asked you about it, then it might have been different. I have to know. Are you still gambling?"

"No. When things went bad for me in the stock market, I realized I was over my head. I'm done with that. I just have to find a way to pay them off without the bank finding out about this."

"What if I told you that I may be able to help you?" she began to tread on the thinnest of ice. "What if I told you that I could erase that gambling debt, just make it go away? Would you be interested?"

Ben stared into his glass again. The list of questions on his mind began to grow.

It seemed almost too much to ask that this woman could, at the same time, solve his gambling debt problem and give him the new position he coveted. Of course he was interested, but at what price?

He looked into her icy blue eyes. "What's in this for you? I mean you're not going to do this out of the goodness of your heart. What do you get from me?"

"A commitment. All you have to do is the same job Tad was doing. You'll understand if I don't care to say anything more until I have assurance from you that we can work together. What do you say? Are we going to be on the same side?"

"You say this is the same arrangement you had with Tad?"

"Yes, it is. I might add that he profited greatly from this arrangement, and you can do the same."

The thought of having a way out of his debt was overwhelming. If he later felt that he didn't like the deal, he could back out.

"What kind of commitment are you asking?" he inquired.

"The governor has one year left on this term of office and I expect he will be re-elected to another four-year term. That means that I can expect five more years as Deputy Director. The length of this arrangement will be for that period of time. In that time you can become financially independent. You would be free to continue at the bank or to go on to other things. The choice would be up to you. Are you willing to make that commitment?"

"How long do I have to think about it?"

"I'm afraid I must have your answer tonight."

"That's pretty short notice for such a big decision, don't you think?"

"I'm sorry, but I didn't set the timetable. That was done by Mother Nature and the ice in Resurrection Bay. I have to decide tonight whether to use you or Avery. I'm hoping it will be you. Being able to make decisions like this on short notice is one of the attributes I need from you. If you don't feel you can commit to this arrangement, then you're free to leave right now and I'll say nothing to the bank about your other problem." She poured fresh tea into her glass and offered some to her guest. He shook his head. She was giving him time to think. She sipped her tea, but said nothing more.

"How much of this debt can I count on you helping me with?"

"How much do you owe?" she asked, checking the figure on the screen.

"The interest is outrageous and difficult to keep up with, but the total is just a little more than $125,000. I was a fool for getting in this deep." He was shaking his head, disgusted with himself and wondering if he was going from the frying pan to the fire.

"I have a figure of $127,500. That total was good as of 4:30 PM today. Does that sound right to you?"

He was again shocked at her accuracy. "Yes, it sounds right."

"Do you have any other outstanding debts I should know about?"

"No, just a car payment and rent and the usual living expenses. I've tried to be responsible. The gambling just got away from me."

"Are you accepting my offer then?"

"Unless you plan to ask me to rob the bank or murder someone, yes, I'll take your offer."

There it was, the commitment she needed. She pulled a sheet of paper from her briefcase, perused it briefly and handed it to Ben.

"This is not a legal document. It's more like evidence. It just declares that I am giving you a sum of money in return for your loyalty. The details are spelled out more eloquently, but that's the gist of it." She paused while he read the document. "The sum of money I am willing to advance you is $150,000. That should take care of your gambling debt and the interest. It will also give you a small financial buffer until you accumulate your own nest egg. The key word here is loyalty. I expect you to manage the Alaska account to the best of your ability. We'll have some meetings about that. There are some other responsibilities you will assume. These will be financially rewarding for both of us."

He had finished reading and was nodding his head. "I can't see where all this is going to be worth this amount of money to you. What is it that you're not telling me?"

"Are you going to sign?"

He hesitated for only a moment. "Yes."

Scanning the paper again, he reached into his pocket for a pen. This was the moment of truth. It would be either his salvation or his demise. He couldn't be sure which. He signed; there were two copies.

"I hope I won't regret this some day," he commented.

"You won't." She picked up the documents and checked the signatures. "A messenger will deliver an envelope to you at your office in the morning. It will contain the cash. You are scheduled to interview after lunch. I expect you to have that debt paid, in full, by that time. Once that's done, we'll have a deal. I think that's all we can do this evening. I'll see you tomorrow afternoon," she said, dismissing him.

Chapter Seven

After breakfast in the hotel restaurant, Aliana returned to her room to make the usual morning telephone calls. There was the mandatory one to Opal in Fairbanks. Saundra wouldn't be up yet, but she would leave a message for the girl with Opal.

Next she called the office in Juneau. There was a problem with the bills coming in from Soldotna DOT. There were several problem billings there, but the largest by far was for their winter supply of salt product for the roads. Repeated phone calls and faxes had failed to motivate the supervisor there into action. DOT was the area of concern for Pam St. John, the youngest of the team members. She was a graduate of the University of Nebraska. Aliana authorized her to make the trip to Soldotna. It would be up to her to resolve the situation using previously applied guidelines. There were other small concerns on the short list, but nothing that needed her personal touch. She delegated it all to her five assistants and hung up the phone.

The next call was to the governor. Any other department head would be making this call to her commissioner or district director. In the case of Aliana, though, the report was made directly to the governor. They passed pleasantries then got down to the business at hand. They discussed the Soldotna problem, along with some of the other lesser developments within her department. She reported that she had decided to back Ben Gerlitz to replace Tad as head of the Alaska account with the SeaFirst bank. She told the governor she had picked Gerlitz over Avery because she thought he was more capable of acting independently. He was more aggressive and his personality was similar to that of Tad Morton, with whom she had worked well.

The governor seemed pleased with her progress and asked when she planned to return to Juneau.

"I'll be back on Monday," she reported. "I'll be in to see you as soon as I return. There are some things we need to discuss and I'll have a full report for you then."

They said their goodbyes and she hung up the phone. She checked her notebook and laptop. As near as she could determine, she was ready for the day. Picking up her briefcase she rode the elevator to the street level of the hotel. The sun was shining, though it didn't reach the street level of this concrete canyon. The morning walk felt good. She enjoyed the fresh air and the brief exercise it provided. It came to an end at the towering black glass structure, once called the box the Space Needle came in.

Aliana was the first member of the committee to enter the conference room on the 44th floor. Someone had provided coffee and rolls. She poured coffee and sat. It took more than a half hour to review the questions and hypothetical situations she would pose to the morning candidate. She had finished the review and was enjoying the view of Puget Sound through the glass wall when the other members began to arrive. Mr. Stackhaus entered and said good morning to the group. Several members were engaged in small talk when the boss called for the meeting to come to order.

"Mr. Avery will be here in a moment," he began. "Are there any last minute questions or concerns from anyone?" He looked around the table at the shaking heads.

"Good. Ms. Pedersen, do you have any last minute statements or questions?"

"No, thank you. I think the process is proceeding very well and I think we can complete our business today. I want to thank each of you for being so kind and for making this a pleasant process. It's this kind of cooperation that makes our association successful. I am looking forward to many more years of doing business with your bank and its wonderful staff."

"Thank you for the kind words, Ms. Pedersen. The feeling is mutual. Now if there are no other comments...? Alright then, let's call Mr. Avery."

His appearance was impeccable. He was dressed in a dark gray suit with nearly invisible pinstripes. He had been to the barber. Each hair on his head was perfectly matched to the next. His tie matched the shirt he wore. The black wingtips were shined to an extreme gloss. His creases were sharp and perfect and the white line made by the handkerchief in his breast pocket made the thinnest and most perfect white line against the gray suit.

"Good morning," he said in a quiet and confident manner.

One by one the panel questioned him. One by one he answered each question confidently and politely. He was perfect. A little too perfect, thought Aliana.

It was Aliana's turn. The proceeding had run longer than planned and she wanted to speed things up.

"Mr. Avery, I am here representing the State of Alaska, whose account is the sole purpose of this department. Other members of the group have already asked the questions on my list. I must say you have done an excellent job answering them. I thank you for your diligence in preparing for this interview. If you ever decide to leave the bank, I hope you will come see me. I can always use a person like yourself in my department."

"Thank you for those kind words, Ms. Pedersen. I appreciate the offer, even though I have no intention of leaving the bank."

"I will reduce my portion of this interview to one question. It's a hypothetical situation that would probably never arise, but answer it to the best of your ability." She looked at him, and he nodded in understanding.

"It's springtime here in Seattle. Lightning strikes your bank building. A giant power surge burns up your computer banks. It could take weeks or even months to replace the computers. It's the end of the month and you're busy processing the checks and transfers for the month. You have had a busy month and there is no time left for delay. Late payments can result in hundreds of thousands of dollars in penalties and interest charged against this account. The governor and I are in Nome for the finish of the Iditarod Sled Dog Race. We are not available. There is no one in the Juneau office with authority to delay the payments. It is up to you to decide what to do. What are you going to do?"

The young executive was quiet for several minutes. He was clearly considering all the alternatives. He was making marks on the yellow pad in front of him. Aliana could see they were not notes, but the doodlings of a very nervous person.

"You have given me an impossible situation to resolve. With the computers all out, there is no way to continue to write checks and make wire transfers. It can't be done in the usual time because we will have to order new computers to do the work. With yourself and the governor out of town and nobody in your office with authority to respond, then it seems there is no way to continue. We would be shut down until your office can find you or the governor. We, at the bank, could not continue to process payments and could not authorize taking the work to an outside contract facility to complete. We would be dead in the water, so to speak. This may be one of those situations where I must shoulder the responsibility for not completing business as it would normally have been completed."

"Yes, that would be the logical conclusion. You have done very well Mr. Avery. That's all I have. Thank you."

Mr. Stackhaus took control again.

"You are excused, Mr. Avery. You have done well. We hope to have a decision before the end of business today. We'll contact you with our decision."

"Thank you sir," Avery said as he stood to leave.

Once he was out of the room, Mr. Stackhaus asked, "Does anyone have any questions or comments at this time? If not, then we will adjourn until 1:30. Ms. Pedersen, would you care to join me for lunch?"

"Yes, of course. Would you give me a few minutes to make airline reservations for tonight?"

"Certainly. I'll meet you in the outer office when you have finished. Lunch will be here in the bank's private restaurant."

The secretary was the last to leave the conference room. When she was alone, Aliana dialed the extension on the 38th floor, the office of Ben Gerlitz. His secretary put the call through without delay.

"Hello, Ms. Pedersen. How are you this morning?"

"I'm fine. We just finished the interview with Avery and expect to have you in here at 1:30. Are you still of a mind for the job?"

"Yes, and I have taken care of that other issue. The messenger arrived on time and I was able to take care of the problem. Thank you."

"That's why I called. I wanted to be sure you were serious. One last time, are there any other items I should be aware of?"

"None. As of now, I'm clear and intend to stay that way."

"Good. See you this afternoon."

Irwin Stackhaus and the other members of the nominating committee were waiting when she finished her phone business. They rode the elegant elevator car to the 49th floor where the bank maintained an exclusive restaurant for its executives and their clients. The menu was quite extensive, though Aliana ordered only a Cobb salad. There was the usual small talk at lunch, but Aliana's thoughts were elsewhere. She would be glad when this was done and she could return to Fairbanks and Saundra. It would be a short weekend, and back to Juneau on Monday morning.

It was almost 1:30 when the group reassembled in the conference room. Stackhaus reminded the group that the rules would be the same as they were at the morning meeting. He then asked the secretary to call Ben Gerlitz.

The questions asked were identical to the ones heard in the morning session. The answers, too, were nearly identical. Each man seemed to be equally qualified. The differences came in personality. Where Avery appeared precise and rigid, Gerlitz was relaxed and flexible. He wore a dark gray suit, but it didn't have the custom tailored look of the morning applicant. Though he was less formal, his answers were professional and precise. He projected an air of confidence and knowledge.

The questioning moved around the table until it came to Aliana. Her question to Avery had aroused curiosity among the panel members. They had tried to determine what she hoped to get from this line of questioning, so each was listening intently when it came her turn.

"Mr. Gerlitz, I'm impressed with the caliber of executives I have seen here today. You have each done an outstanding job of representing yourself in these interviews. I thank you for your honesty and forthrightness. Both you and Mr. Avery have my respect. I'll keep my portion of this proceeding short. I have only one question. In a hypothetical situation, you are the head of this account. It is early spring here in Seattle. A spring storm has caused lightning to strike the bank building, burning up the computer banks on this floor. It is the end of the month and delays of payments will result in the loss in penalties and interest of hundreds of thousands of dollars to the account. Both the governor and I are in Nome for the end of the Iditarod Sled Dog Race. We are not available, and cannot be contacted. As department head, what are you going to do?"

The answer began to flow in less than half a minute.

"This is a difficult situation. Under normal circumstances it would be required that we contact the client, had there been some catastrophic situation like this. Your question preempts this. As department head it's my responsibility to get the task completed."

"And just how would you go about completing this task, Mr. Gerlitz?" Aliana asked.

"There are hundreds of computers in this building. I would contact the heads of the other departments and determine if there are computers available in some other department that could be adapted to our needs. If they were not available during regular business hours, I would consider using them at night when the regular business is completed. Personnel in this department would be assigned to the time slots available to get this work completed as near to on time as possible. In the meantime, repaired or replacement equipment would be my top priority. All of those expenditures, however, are subject to approval by upper management; in this case Mr. Stackhaus would have the final say. As the client, you and the governor would be contacted and kept abreast of what is happening at each step."

"Thank you Mr. Gerlitz, that's all I have."

"Are there any other questions or comments for Mr. Gerlitz? If not, you can be excused, Ben. We will try to notify you of our decision before the end of the day."

The secretary closed the door behind the exiting banker. "Would anyone like a cold drink or coffee while I'm up?" There were no takers. She again took her seat next to Mr. Stackhaus.

They began by reviewing each of the applicant's qualifications. Ms. Cabrese recited school records, personal data, personnel records, work history and personal history with the bank. Neither applicant had any disciplinary actions in their file. Neither had, in the past, been the object of employee conflicts. On the whole, each candidate was equal and each had all pluses with no minuses on their records. Both panel members who spoke were in favor of Avery by a very narrow margin.

Mr. Stackhaus turned his attention to Ms. Pedersen. "I would like to hear how you feel, Ms. Pedersen. You are the one who will be working most closely with the winner."

Aliana opened her yellow legal pad. "I don't see the need to review this entire proceeding. I agree with the other members of this board. The two men are equal in qualifications. You've asked for my opinion and the choice is difficult. I would compare it to hanging two paintings on the wall, a Rembrandt and a Picasso, and asking me to choose. Both are perfect, but the Picasso would suit my décor better than the Rembrandt. The same is true with these two men. Either is capable of doing the job and I would have complete confidence in either. However, in this case, the Picasso fits the décor a little better than the Rembrandt. Mr. Avery is an outstanding individual and deserves a chance at any promotion available.

"My choice, however, would be Mr. Gerlitz. There are only two discernible differences between these men. One, Mr. Avery is married with a family. This would give him stability in the position, in my way of thinking. Mr. Gerlitz is single, but has been dedicated to his work and to his employer. This makes them equal on my ledger. And two, this being the deciding point for me, Mr. Avery is a by-the-book individual. In many ways this is commendable. The hypothetical question I asked each one about having to make a decision, without benefit of advice, is not an unlikely possibility. Ben found a way to continue to do business, albeit at a slower pace, until the client, we, could be advised. This ability to adapt and overcome is the exact quality I need in this position. I, therefore, strongly request that you appoint Ben Gerlitz to head this department. Avery has experience in the department, but the staff here has enough accumulated experience to allow Mr. Gerlitz a short honeymoon." She closed her legal pad and nodded to Irwin Stackhaus.

"Are there any other comments or questions?" Stackhaus asked.

There were none.

"Then, give me thirty minutes to review and we will re-convene in this office."

Aliana used a phone in the outer office to call Opal. She was baking cookies for Saundra. Everything was fine. Aliana advised her that she would be coming home tonight, but it would be late when she got into Fairbanks.

"Give Saundra a big hug for me," she said before hanging up the phone.

Back in the conference room and seated at the table, it was time for the final word. Stackhaus shuffled his papers and opened the files, appearing, for all the world, like a judge about to hand down an earthshaking decision.

"I have reviewed the files and taken into consideration all the arguments. Ms. Pedersen is correct; it is Rembrandt and Picasso, Cadillac and Lincoln. Therefore, I have decided to grant her request, and to appoint Ben Gerlitz. She's the one who must be satisfied with the person at the head of a department where she is the only client. With the two applicants so closely matched, I feel she should have the right to decide which one would be the best for her.

"This has been a protracted process and your time has been used well. I thank you all for your input. Ms. Pedersen, I assume you would like to meet with Mr. Gerlitz before you leave us?"

"Yes. There are a few things I should go over with him."

"Ms. Cabrese, will you send Ben up right away?"

It was only five minutes until his arrival. Stackhaus offered his congratulations and said he would give the word to Avery. The secretary followed her boss out the door. When the two were alone, Ben broke into a wide grin.

"Thank you," he said. "For everything. I won't let you down."

"I have your word on that, do I?"

"Positively. I don't know how long it will take, but I'll pay you back. You saved my career. I owe you."

"I intend to collect. You have no need to repay the advance."

"It's a debt. I have to repay it."

"You don't understand. It was an advance. You will have the same arrangement and percentage as Tad received."

"Wait a minute. What am I being paid for?"

"This account has a daily average balance of about ten million dollars. This money goes and comes quickly, but there is sometimes a pause between deposit and withdrawal. This account is managed on the interest paid on this account. The difference between the management fees and the interest paid is about 2.5%. This amount is paid twice weekly to a separate account. It is immediately transferred, by wire, to an account in San Francisco. The account is the Alaska Maritime Holding Account. This transfer is crucial. It is done at the beginning of business on Monday and at the beginning of business on Thursday. I have instructions written in this folder, which you will read and shred. Do I make myself clear?"

"You're asking me to perform illegal acts. I don't think I want to be any part of that."

"Would you rather take part or be unemployed? Remember, I just put $150,000 into your hands, which you used to pay off a gambling debt. How do you think the bank would look upon that little item?"

"That was indiscretion, you're asking me to break the law. I've never done anything illegal in my life. Stupid yes, but never illegal."

"You don't have to do anything illegal," she reassured him. "You are merely following orders given by me on behalf of the State of Alaska. These transfers have been going on for some time now, so there should be no suspicions aroused. The names on the account at the other end are officials of the state. This should absolve you of any culpability."

"How much time do I have to think about it?" Gerlitz asked.

"There is no time. You're in, and you're going to stay in. The good news for you is that you are going to become very wealthy by this. Your first paycheck has already come to you, so you'll do it, and you'll keep your mouth shut. Do you understand?" Her blue eyes seemed to pale even more.

"All right. I'll do it," he said angrily. "I don't like it, but I'll do it for now."

"And you'll continue to do it." Her eyes were narrow slits now. "I'll be in touch with you." She began to gather her papers and files, stuffing them into her briefcase. She checked her watch. There was plenty of time to get to the airport.

Ben was not happy about all this news. He had been looking forward to the promotion, but now he wished he'd never heard of Aliana Pedersen. She had destroyed the character of his best friend, Tad, and now his entire career was in jeopardy. The only thing standing between him and unemployment was this raven-haired woman. Now she was about to hold the possibility of jail over him. This was going from bad to worse. Somehow there had to be a way to get out of this without losing everything. But how?

Chapter Eight

The weekend with Saundra and Opal had gone quickly; too quickly. Aliana had slept late Monday and missed the early flight from Fairbanks to Juneau. This made it almost noon when she arrived in her office. After checking in with her assistants and discussing immediate problems, she called for an appointment with the governor.

At precisely 2 PM, she was let into the governor's office. Once the receptionist was out of the office, she began to relate the story of selecting a replacement for Tad Morton. She politely omitted the part about the gambling debt and the $150,000 payment to Ben Gerlitz.

"What's your next move?" the governor asked.

"For everyone's safety and peace of mind, I think I'll order an audit of the account. That will give Ben a clean slate to begin with."

"I can report to the finance committee that this account is balanced and that there are no problems arising from this transition, is that correct?" The governor formed a pyramid under his chin with his fingertips. His jacket had been removed and the muscles in his suntanned arms flexed as he pressed his fingers together.

"Yes, that's correct. There's no reason for me to believe there are any improprieties in our account. The only reason for the audit is assure everyone, the finance committee, the bank, you and me, that the account is being managed correctly. This will give Ben a clean slate from the beginning."

Time had only made her more beautiful, the governor thought. She was pretty when they had met in college, but now she had an air about her, a sophisticated bearing that was difficult to describe. The two were seldom seen together. They appeared at state functions together and were seen in finance meetings, but they never socialized. "Sad," he thought, "we were really happy together."

She broke into his thoughts. "If there isn't anything else, I have work to do at the office."

"Just keep me posted. I want to know if there are any changes in that account. I have my neck way out on this and I don't want any surprises."

"There shouldn't be any," she assured him.

She was on the telephone with Pamela St. John discussing the situation with Soldotna DOT when her secretary pushed her head inside the doorway.

"You have a visitor from the troopers, Ms. Pedersen."

"I'll be off the phone in one minute." She continued to give instructions to her assistant in Soldotna, making it clear that the situation should be resolved by that same evening.

The secretary ushered the trooper sergeant into the office.

"Well, hello, Rube. What a surprise. I didn't know you were in Juneau."

"I have a couple of cases I'm working and had to come down here to do some interviews with witnesses. While I'm here I thought I could give you the final disposition on the accidental death case you came to see me about."

"How long do you plan to be in town?"

"I'm not sure. A couple of days at the most." He was trying to find the courage to ask her out, but he wasn't very good at this sort of thing.

"I'll be working until 6:30. Would you like to have dinner this evening?" she asked.

"I'd like that. Can I pick you up here?"

"Sure. I'll meet you out front at 6:30. Do you like seafood? I know a great place."

"Sounds good to me."

It had rained briefly that afternoon, making the city smell fresh and clean. Rube was parked in front of Aliana's office at the appointed time. She was late and he was about to go inside to check on her when she came out of the building, hurrying down the wet steps.

She offered an apology for being late. They drove off to the restaurant. The dinner was spent with small talk. They left the restaurant early. Aliana suggested they walk the several blocks to her apartment building. Juneau is a city of greenery and the walk was pleasant. At the front of the apartment building, Aliana invited him up for a nightcap. He thanked her for the offer, but declined, citing an early interview with a witness in a murder case.

"One of my trooper friends here has a 32-foot cabin boat. He said I could use it to go fishing while I'm here. How would you like to go out for a couple of hours tomorrow evening?"

"That would be fun. I haven't been fishing all summer."

"I'll bring something for dinner. Can I pick you up here?"

"Yes, I'll be looking forward to it." She enjoyed being with Rube. He seemed to like her for herself and not for her title and position. She was truly looking forward to a fishing excursion with him.

———

Wearing a pair of new blue jeans and a plaid shirt over a white turtleneck shirt, she was waiting on the sidewalk in front of the apartment building when the rental car pulled to the curb. Rube reached across the seat and opened the door.

Peering through the open door she said, "Hi, are we still going fishing?"

"You bet. I have a picnic basket in the back seat. The boat is fueled and ready to go. Come on, let's go catch some fish."

She slid into the seat and took his hand. It seemed a natural thing when she leaned over and kissed him on the cheek. It had been a long time since he felt this way. It was like being a kid again. He felt awkward. Rube looked into her blue eyes, smiled and put the car into gear.

Rube had been to the boat earlier and made it ready. Rods were in the holders. The engine had been warmed up. The picnic basket was on the table in the cabin. He helped her over the rail and onto the deck, then untied the bowline. He untied the stern and stepped over the rail. As he dropped into the seat and started the engine, he smiled and asked, "Ready?"

She shrugged up her shoulders, smiled and nodded yes.

They motored out of the harbor, turning north toward the spot Rube's friend had marked on the map. The water was unusually smooth, though they were moving against the tide. Aliana walked out of the cabin and stood on the rear deck, watching as the scenery passed slowly by. The boat cruised at half throttle for almost an hour. They were in a wooded cove with a rocky shoreline when Rube cut the throttle and ignition. He climbed to the side rail and walked to the front deck where he dropped the anchor over the side. They were in about sixty feet of water. Rube played out plenty of anchor line before tying it off to a cleat. He made his way back to the rear deck where Aliana waited.

"I'll bait up and put the rods out if you'll set the dinners on the table."

"That sounds good," she said, moving back to the cabin. "Who made the dinner?" she called back over her shoulder.

"I know the chef at the hotel. He used to work in Anchorage. I had him fix it."

He busied himself with baiting hooks. His choice tonight was a small herring. He had been told this was a good spot for black sea bass. After baiting up he flicked the switch that turned on the water in the wash-down hose. He rinsed his hands of fish scales and slime. In the cabin he sniffed his hands, which still smelled of herring. He washed his hands in the small galley sink before sitting down. He took the bottle of red wine from the basket. There was a corkscrew in a pocket in the lid of the basket.

"I have to go back to Anchorage tomorrow," he said sadly.

"Do you get to Juneau often?"

"No. In fact, I could have sent one of the other officers, but I took a chance I might see you and came here myself." He laughed. "How's that for a confession?"

"I'm glad you came. I work so many hours, it seems I never get out. This is fun for me." She sipped the red wine. "I'll confess, too," she said, looking into his eyes. "I have been thinking about you. I feel like a dumb schoolgirl on her first date."

Rube removed the dome lid from his shrimp salad, sipped his wine and thought for a moment. "Would you consider going out with me the next time you get to Anchorage?"

"I'd like that."

They were finished with dinner and sipping the last of the wine when one of the reels on the stern began to slowly emit clicking sounds. Rube quickly slid from the small booth to set the hook.

"You had better get out here. You have a fish on. I think it's a big one."

She came out of the cabin, took the rod and began to reel in the fish. He teased her about her technique and they both laughed while she reeled in a nice sea bass. He no sooner removed the fish from the hook and the other rod began to bob in its holder. He took the rod, set the hook, and handed it to Aliana. While she reeled in the fish, he baited the first rod and dropped the heavy sinker back to the bottom. The action was fast and exciting for several minutes and the two laughed and reeled in the fish.

"It's been a long time since I've had this much fun," she said, watching him as he cut filets from the fish.

"Me, too. I hate to go back." He finished dressing the fish. In the cabin he washed his hands, trying to rid them of the smell of fish. Satisfied he had them as clean as they were going to get, he started the engine. It was going to be dark soon and the air was cooling off quickly. She was sitting on the small bench at the table, her legs in the aisle. After starting the engine, he checked the gauges. Satisfied with the readings, he turned around and was staring into her eyes. He paused, cupped her face in his hands and kissed her gently. She wrapped her arms around him and pulled him close.

They sat in the front seat of the rental car in front of her apartment. It was getting late. The two held hands for a short while, just enjoying each other's company.

"I suppose I should go in," she said with reluctance in her voice.

"I won't see you before I leave tomorrow, so I'll say goodbye now. I had a wonderful time tonight." Rube hated to turn loose of her hand.

"I'll try to get to Anchorage in a week or so. I go to Fairbanks every weekend. I have a daughter there. My sister takes care of her for me." This was a test. She wanted to get his reaction to the fact she had a child.

"You have a daughter? How old is she?"

She was pleased he was interested and not shocked. "Saundra is twelve. She has a learning disability and goes to a special school. My sister has been a lifesaver for me. She loves Saundra and I couldn't ask for someone better to take care of her."

"I'd like to meet them sometime," Rube said honestly.

"I'd like that too." She kissed him on the cheek and opened the door.

Rube watched as she carried the plastic bag of fish filets up the walk. These were new feelings for him. He had always been satisfied with dating and leaving. This was different. He thought about how nice it would be to have this lady in his life.

Chapter Nine

In the office, sipping her first cup of morning coffee, Aliana reflected on how happy Saundra had sounded this morning on the telephone. She was happy with Opal and school was going well for her. Summer in Fairbanks was a good time for everyone who lived there. Someday this job would end and she would be able to join her daughter for summer fun.

Aliana also thought of the night before. She had enjoyed the evening spent with Rube on the boat. It had been a long time since she had been that care-free. The isolation of the boat and the secluded cove had given her a feeling of detachment. It had been as though she were living in a fantasy, a fantasy that had ended too soon.

Reality interrupted her when the clerk brought in the mail. There would be a great deal to do today and, she supposed, this stack of mail would be a good place to start. A legal size envelope on the top of the stack caught her eye. It was from the coroner's office in Anchorage.

She opened the letter and scanned the short memo inside. It was the answer to her request for two copies of the death certificate for Tad Morton. The coroner had attached two copies of the certificates. Both were notarized and certified by him. This was what she needed to claim the accounts for which she was the beneficiary. Before continuing with the rest of the mail, she spun her chair around and composed a letter to accompany each of the certificates. These she would post herself. The foreign postage could arouse the curiosity of her clerk. With the letters tucked into her briefcase, she continued with the rest of the daily mail.

Promptly at 10 AM, she picked up the telephone and called Ben in his Seattle office. She had dialed directly to his extension and avoided the receptionist.

"Good morning, Ben," she said when he answered. "How is it going?"

"Ah, Ms. Pedersen. Good to hear from you." He tried to keep the tension out of his voice. "The people in this department are running things right now. I'm trying to catch up on the learning curve and the staff is helping me do that. So far there aren't any problems for me to deal with. Have you encountered any difficulty on your end?"

"Things seem to be running smoothly. I don't anticipate any problems."

"I'm glad to hear that. I'm still getting my feet on the ground and it would complicate things if I had to stop that process in order to deal with something I'm unfamiliar with."

"I understand, Ben. You'll do fine," she tried to be reassuring. "I have something for you to do, though."

"Just name it and I'll do my best."

"I spoke with the governor, and he wishes to have an audit of the account. He has instructed me to have that audit done as quickly as possible."

"Will this audit cause any problems? I mean … well, you know what I mean."

"Go to your files and there should be a copy of an audit done about three months ago. We routinely do this on a semi-annual basis. The one with the latest date should be a good model for yours. Unless there's something I don't know about, everything inside the bank is 100% perfect. Don't worry, it's just a precaution on the governor's part. Any time there's a major change in the account, he'll order an audit to satisfy the legislature. This audit should take no more than three or four days. Call me when it's complete and I'll come down to review it. We'll talk then."

"I'll get started on it right away," he replied.

"One more question. Have the biweekly transfers gone out as scheduled?"

"Yes, they have. And that reminds me. I was going to ask. I see that these transfers are made at precisely 9 AM on Monday and Thursday. Is that time an important item?"

"Yes, it is. It must be adhered to without fail. I'll give you more information when I see you next week." It was time to play the ace that could be trumped. He was going to have to be told of some of the workings of the transfers and his percentages. If he accepted this information and continued to follow her, she would have him hooked. If not, the whole thing could come apart. She would have to be persuasive.

She hung up the telephone and took another sip from the coffee cup. What was next on her list? Thumbing through her notes, she decided the situation with the Department of Transportation, Soldotna office, was the most important. She dialed her secretary on the intercom.

"Get me Pam St. John on the phone, please, and bring in the DOT, Soldotna file."

The system for paying the bills in the State of Alaska had taken a dramatic turn under the guidance of Aliana Pedersen. In the old system, appropriations were made to each department in the government. Large contracts were approved by the legislature, the bills were sent to the department of finance who matched the bills to the contracts and paid them from appropriations from the general fund. Today, all billings have to be matched to their contracts by the local accounting clerks. They are then submitted to the department of finance. Totals for the period are submitted, and that amount is transferred from the general fund to the account managed by Deputy Director Aliana Pedersen. Every invoice in the state was handled this way, with exception of the regular payroll for employees and retirement accounts. These accounts were writing checks as they had in the past. Grievances for that sector of the government, were handled by personnel within the Department of Administration. Aliana and her department had nothing to do with those funds.

In the past the State of Alaska had been lax in paying bills on time. Many contractors refused to do business with the state for that reason. Small contractors, especially, could not afford to wait ninety to one hundred twenty days for payment for goods and services they had provided. By streamlining the system, and using centralized accounting, millions of dollars in penalties and interest had been saved. It took time, but contractors were once again competing for state contracts.

The phone rang. It was Pamela St. John. She was in Soldotna, but had nearly finished doing her review of accounting practices in that locale.

"Hello, Pam. How is it going?" Aliana asked.

"I'm nearly finished here. I plan to leave early this afternoon."

"Did you get the problems there resolved?"

"I think so. This was all for local purchases, and the district manager was less than prompt at getting his clerk to process the invoices. We're going to suffer some penalties on this one, but I've convinced the district manager that it is necessary to be prompt with payment for contracted services." What she really meant was that she threatened to have him back driving a snowplow or on unemployment if this came up again. This bit of authority was one of the stipulations Aliana had demanded when setting up the new payment system. She needed 100% compliance and this assured she got it.

"What were the products he purchased?" she asked. "Were they necessary items?"

"It appears so, yes," was the reply. "The majority of the invoices were for sand and various kinds of salts, calcium chloride, etc. Everything on the list was for winter road maintenance. The supplies, including the stockpile of sand, has been delivered and on site for some time now."

"Do you think he'll keep his word about maintaining his accounts current?"

"I think so. If not, we'll have to get him replaced. He's been warned."

"Is this something I should take up with the Southcentral DOT Director?"

"If it's alright with you, I'd like to let the situation settle out for a while. I threatened him pretty good and he seems to have taken it to heart. The accounting clerk here is great. She had things almost completed. The bottleneck was on the local manager's desk. Once I convinced him I had the authority to have him replaced, he became very cooperative. Let's just see how he responds over the next couple of months. I have a good ear down here, the accounts clerk."

"It's your call. Just finish up and come on back to the office. We have several regional classes to schedule. I'd like you to handle them," she paused, mentally going over her list. "I think that's all I have for now. Good job, Pam. See you some time tomorrow."

Of the five top assistants in the office, Pam was, by no means, the most intelligent. Her scholastic record was probably fourth on the list in ranking. Her natural ability to use her knowledge, however, made her an invaluable asset. She knew how to handle people and to get the job done with a minimum of complications. Pamela was a natural problem solver. On top of that she was fun to have around. A practical joker with a raunchy sense of humor, she was the source of most of the laughter in the office. One by one Aliana went through the items on her list. She was known as an innovator. If a problem presented itself, it would be met head-on by this tall, dark-skinned beauty. Each item on her list was checked off and a note made by each entry to record the time and resolution of the item. It was after seven in the evening when she finally turned out the light in her office. She was the last to leave for the day.

The light mist of the morning had burned itself off and the sun was peeking through the overcast. She draped her raincoat over her arm, took several deep breaths of the fresh air and began her walk home. On the way she thought about Rube and the evening before. It had been wonderful. There weren't enough of those evenings, she thought. Maybe someday.

The first order of business when she reached home was to call Saundra and Opal. She told Opal she would have to go to Seattle again next week. This trip should only be for two days. Then, if things were settled down, she would take a couple of days off to be with her and Saundra. It would be fun to spend time with her daughter. Maybe they would drive up to Circle for a couple of days.

Saundra reported to her mother that she had colored a picture for her and that Opal had praised her for staying inside the lines so well. "This is a really good picture," she said proudly. "It's a moose. I'm going to save it for you, for when you come home. When are you coming, mommy?"

"I'll be home this weekend, Honey. See you then." It was hard being away so much.

Aliana took some of the fresh fish from the refrigerator, sprinkled it with spices and dropped it into a hot fry pan. She wondered what Rube was doing this evening. Would she seem too anxious if she called him…just to say hello? She decided it would be best if she didn't call. She sat down to a plate filled with fresh sea bass, fresh tomatoes, cottage cheese and sourdough bread. CNN Headline News gave her a feel for what had taken place in the world this day. She was tired and by ten was ready for bed. Staff meetings would fill her day tomorrow. She thought of Saundra and her moose picture as she drifted off to sleep.

It was just before seven in the morning when she entered the office. Pamela St. John was waiting for her. She had made coffee and was reading the paper when Aliana came in. The greetings were more grunts than words; neither of them was really awake. Aliana poured her first cup of coffee and carried it into her office. She hung her coat and dropped into her leather chair. The aroma of the coffee was good; she took a long but careful drink of the hot liquid. Taking a yellow legal pad from the desk drawer, she began to write notes, items she wanted to cover in the staff meeting this morning. She was on page three when she noticed a coffee ring on her desk. She cleaned it with a Kleenex, wiping while she read her notes. There was a gentle tap on the door of her office.

It was Pamela.

"Do you have a minute to talk, Aliana?"

"Sure, come in."

Pamela St. John was short, five feet two inches tall. She was blessed with a cupie doll look, which she enhanced by bleaching her rather plain brown hair to startling blonde. She had majored in business, but her real skill was with people. She knew how to handle them, to manipulate them, Aliana thought.

Pamela sat across the desk from her boss, sipping her morning coffee. "I didn't have anything important. It's just that I'd been out of the office for a few days and thought I'd see if there was anything interesting in the works."

"I've been so busy that I haven't had time to listen to the office gossip."

"I know, you've been on the move lately. Is there anything I can do to help out?"

"I was just making a list of things to cover at the staff meeting this morning. Do you have anything you want to add to this list?" Aliana dabbed again at the coffee ring on her desk.

"No, I don't think so. You intend to cover the training schedule, don't you?"

"Yes, in fact with things in Seattle being what they are, I'm going to let you handle the training schedule. I have to go to Seattle again next week. I think it will only be a two-day trip. If things go well there, I'm going to take a couple of days off and spend them with my daughter. Do you think you can handle that alright?" Aliana inquired.

"It shouldn't be a problem," Pam assured. "I'll get out of here and let you finish. I just wanted to say hello and welcome home. Besides, if no one is pregnant or getting married, there isn't any gossip worth hearing."

"Thanks. See you at nine. By the way, good job in Soldotna."

Pamela said nothing, but gave a small wave as she left the office.

It was noon when they finished the staff meeting. The office was running smoothly and no major problems had presented themselves. It looked as though she might be able to leave the office at a decent hour today. Aliana was about to leave for lunch when the secretary buzzed. There was a trooper sergeant on the line for her.

"Did you get all that fish eaten?" Rube asked.

"Are you kidding?" she laughed. "I couldn't eat that much fish in a month. I cooked some last night, though, and it was delicious. Thank you."

"Any time. I had a great evening."

"And so did I," she replied.

"Good. I was hoping you would say that. It makes it easier for me to ask if it would be possible for you to stop overnight in Anchorage on your way to Fairbanks this weekend?"

"I might be persuaded," she laughed again. "I think I'll be able to leave here early tomorrow. What did you have in mind?"

"We'll think of something." It was awkward for him. It had been a long time since he had called anyone to ask for a date. "Call me when you find out what time you're getting into Anchorage. I'll pick you up at the airport."

"That sounds wonderful. I'll let you know what flight I'll be taking."

She didn't go out for lunch but spent the time trying to tie up loose ends and making arrangements to fly out in the morning. She was filled with anticipation. An evening with Rube was exactly what she needed.

Chapter Ten

The two boys had grown up together in the suburbs of Mexico City. They had been born just days apart. They played had together as youngsters and attended the same school. The boys fathers worked together at a small chemical plant only a few blocks from their home neighborhood. The boys were twelve when the explosion occurred. Both their fathers had been killed along with three other men, also from the neighborhood. There were many injuries in the explosion and ensuing fire. Officials from the American company that owned the little plant were sympathetic to the families. They assured them that the company would pay the families for their losses and pay hospital and medical bills for those injured. The neighborhood workers praised the company for their compassion and understanding.

For several months after the disaster, the company kept their word; but the company soon found it was not cost effective to keep the plant running and to support those injured people. More profit could be generated if this plant would close and the chemicals made in India. In only weeks following that decision, the plant closed and the company presence disappeared from Mexico.

Without assistance from the company, the mothers of Ramon Chavez and Eduardo Sanchez were forced to move into the heart of the city to look for work in order to support their families. The families shared a small apartment paid for by the shared income of the two mothers. Midway through the first summer, Eduardo Sanchez's mother fell ill due, no doubt, to the poor air quality in the world's largest city. Ramon's mother did her best to support the two families, but even working three jobs she was unable to meet the rent and buy food. When medical expenses were added to the equation, the income fell far short. Food was the first thing to fall from the list of purchases.

Ramon and Eddie, as he came to be known, searched for ways to help augment the family income. Begging wasn't even considered, and employment was impossible given the scarcity of jobs and the age of the applicants. For them, the solution came quite by accident.

It was early one morning, a typical hot and smoggy morning in Mexico City, when the boys were watching a tour bus driver loading baggage into his bus. The hotel bellman poked his head out of the door and called the driver inside for something. Eddie elbowed Ramon in the ribs.

"Come on, quick," he whispered. "Grab two of the small bags and run."

"We can't do that," Ramon protested.

"Shut up and just do it. Come on, before the driver comes back."

With Eddie in the lead, the two boys ran to the front of the hotel where the baggage cart sat on the sidewalk. Eddie grabbed two small items, both make-up cases, and thrust them into Ramon's hands. He picked two small bags for himself and began to run with Ramon hot on his heels. The two made it around the first street corner and into an alleyway. Eddie stopped running and caught his breath. The two looked at each other and giggled. Eddie ventured back to the corner and sneaked a quick look. No one was following them. They moved deeper into the alley, found a quiet place and opened the cases. Thus began the lifelong careers of Ramon and Eddie.

By accident they had found the perfect way to make money. Tourists were prone to hiding money, jewelry and medicines in small carry cases such as make-up bags. The boys quickly learned that the drugs could be emptied into a plastic bag and sold on the street; such bags were known as a salad mix. The jewelry was sold, usually to street vendors, and the money was pocketed. Living conditions soon became tolerable for the small group. Eddie was to lose his mother to lung disease, the doctors said it was TB, in the late fall.

Soon hotel staff and tour bus drivers were looking for the boys. They had made a name for themselves in the downtown area. One person who had watched the budding careers of this duo was Emilio Cardera. Emilio owned a taxi and spent a lot of time in front of the same hotels the boys were plaguing. He had seen the boys and closely followed the antics of the young criminals. At first he thought it was funny and made it a point to see how many of these jobs they could do before getting caught. Strangely, though, they didn't get caught. Over several weeks his curiosity turned to interest as the boys refined their technique. He had heard that the lads were selling large quantities of jewelry at give-away prices, probably because they had no idea what the stuff was worth.

Organized crime in Mexico is very big business. It is, in some cases, hand in hand with the Mexican government. One local crime figure was the cousin of Emilio Cardera, a man who went by the name of Dante. He was a powerful figure on the local scene and a man you didn't want to offend for fear of terminal reprisal.

The boys had been in business for several weeks when Emilio called his cousin, Dante, with information about these brash young men. Dante told Emilio to keep an eye on the boys, and to find out what he could about them. The illness of Eddie's mother was one of the first things he learned. He was able to find out about the death of the boys' fathers and how the American chemical company had failed to keep their word to the families affected by the explosion and fire.

The more reports he had about the young hooligans, the more Dante admired them. When he heard of the death of Eddie's mother, he told Emilio he wanted to meet the boys.

The two were sizing up a baggage cart when the cab stopped alongside them. The muzzle of a pistol appeared over the edge of the window. "Get in," the driver ordered.

Scared half out of their wits, the boys climbed into the cab.

The meeting was in a small restaurant about two kilometers from where they had been picked up. Dante wore a suit and tie, and didn't seem to mind the heat.

"How about some breakfast, boys?" Dante smiled and looked them over.

"You buyin'?" Ramon asked.

Dante laughed. "Yes, I'm buying."

The boys sat. "Who are you?" Ramon asked.

"My name is Dante. Have you heard of me?"

"You mean *big boss* Dante?" It was Ramon again. This time his eyes were open wide in surprise.

"Yes, that's me. What would you boys like to eat?" Dante chuckled again and gave the waiter the order.

"What does a hot-shot, big-time boss like you want with us? We never did anything to you."

"You could do with some manners, kid," Dante scolded. "I brought you here because I've been hearing about you and wanted to meet you."

"What have you been hearing?" Ramon was still doing the talking.

"Lighten up, kid. This is a friendly breakfast. I just wanted to meet you."

Sitting at the next table and listening, it was difficult for Emilio not to laugh at the two little toughs.

"How would you boys like to work for me? You know, get a regular paycheck. Be able to help your mom with the rent and food. Are you interested?"

Eddie was poking Ramon on the leg with his fist; Ramon was shrugging him off.

"How much you payin'?" Ramon inquired.

"We'll work that out later. There are some things you will have to do, though."

"Yeah, like what? We ain't into kinky stuff with old guys, you know."

The waiter brought the meals, and conversation stopped until he had left the table.

"Anybody ever tell you that you had a rotten attitude, kid? I'm trying to help you out and maybe set you up for a good job. You might just hear what the offer is before you get too tough."

"Yeah, well, ain't nobody done us any favors lately." Ramon was still the mouthpiece for the duo.

"I understand, kid. I know you have had it tough. I know your mother works all the time and that Eddie's mother was pretty sick. I know about the death of your fathers and how the company treated you. Life isn't fair, kid. You won't get many good breaks handed to you, so you had better take them when they come along."

Ramon didn't have anything to say.

"If you think you'd like to work for me, I will pay you a small monthly salary to keep you and your families going. You both have to go back to school. I don't want any dummies working for me. Do you think you can handle that?"

"That's all, just go to school?"

"That's it. No more stealing suitcases. Just go to school. In a few years, when you finish, we'll see about college, if that's what you want. You will have to report to me once a week from now on. I'll give you your paycheck when you report."

"Can Eddie and me talk about it?"

"Sure. Finish your breakfast and I'll have Emilio drive you home. He'll tell you how to get in touch with me. Don't wait too long to answer, though. And no more baggage jobs until I get an answer."

That was how it had begun. The boys went back to school and made weekly reports to Dante. When they finished high school, Ramon opted to go on to college and study business management. Eddie never liked studying. Dante took him in and gave him his on-the-job-training. Eddie was tough. Dante made him tougher. He taught him the nuances of mob enforcement. Eddie was an apt pupil and enjoyed his work. He liked the pay and the social contacts he was making. When Ramon graduated from college, Dante and Eddie were in the audience to witness the event, along with Ramon's mother.

For a graduation gift, Dante gave Ramon a small club that specialized in prostitution. Eddie became Ramon's right hand man, bodyguard and enforcer. For the next couple of years Ramon's business flourished. Dante was extremely happy with his young protégé, and decided it was time for the two young men to move up. He moved the two men to Anchorage, Alaska, where they became restaurant owners. After five years in business together, Ramon and Eduardo applied for, and received, U.S. citizenship. It was another proud moment for the aging Dante.

Ramon and Eddie had opened their second restaurant in Anchorage and one in Fairbanks. Dante came north to see the men once a year. He would fish and drink and talk of the old days. Ramon's mother had passed on and Dante was the only family either of the young men had. New bosses had taken over the daily routine in Mexico, but Dante still had the final word in all the major decisions involving the mob. He knew how to wax the government skids and was a friend of the president. Nothing illegal took place in northern Mexico without the approval of Dante. But Dante had a special place in his heart for the two street kids he had befriended so many years ago. That friendship had blessed him with many pesos.

Ramon and Eddie hired many young, beautiful girls in Mexico. They were provided with work permits and given jobs in one of the restaurants. When they came to Alaska, they would bring with them sealed tins of authentic Mexican corn flour for making tortillas. The tortillas were the best in Alaska because of the imported flour. The girls dressed in brightly colored skirts and white peasant blouses while working in the restaurants. Several times each evening they sang and danced for the customers and encouraged them to join in. There seemed to be a large turnover in girls, but it was supposed, by the regular customers, that they became homesick and returned to Mexico to be with their families.

Ramon had kept his boyish appearance over the years, but Eddie was something different. For several years Eddie thought he was too thin, so he had begun taking weight gain supplements and steroids. He was no longer thin. He was only five feet nine inches tall, but the supplements and steroids had done their job. His upper body was monstrous, with no neck, a barrel chest and arms that measured larger than most men's legs, he was indeed, the intimidating creature he had wanted to be. The price he paid was his health. Eddie suffered from a bad heart, clogged arteries and was now suffering lapses of memory. Ramon had cautioned him about the use of these drugs, but Eddie had said that when they began to affect him that he would quit using them; it was too late now.

As always, Ramon looked out after Eddie. He hired an *assistant* to stay with Eddie at all times. It had been little more than a year since the symptoms began, but the progression of his friend's maladies was fierce and quick. The first signs were his memory lapses and his thinning hair. Within weeks other signs of his failing body began to show. The doctors said there was no way to reverse the effects and that he could last no more than a few months. Ramon vowed to stand by Eddie to the end, and to send his lifelong friend back to Mexico to be buried next to his mother. The best he could do for Eddie now was to make life as simple and easy as possible.

Dante, too, was saddened to hear of Eddie's condition. The mob boss had been like a father to the two boys, a mentor who protected and nurtured his pupils. Emilio had been killed in a traffic accident while driving his cab in the city. The two boys, now grown men, were the only family he had left. Ramon had turned into an exceptional businessman. Every venture he undertook became an instant success. In the old days, Eddie had been a large part of that success, but times change and his skills were needed less today. "Hell, we're almost legitimate these days," he would tell his party guests.

The cash flow from the restaurant business was ample. It had provided luxury for the two immigrants. Both men owned luxury cars. Ramon a Lexus and Eddie a Lincoln, now driven by his assistant, Larry. The restaurant corporation owned a bright red Hummer that was used to take guests on hunting and fishing trips. The two men owned adjoining condos in a new complex on Lake Otis Drive.

The parade of girls coming and going from the condos was long. There was a party, in one apartment or the other, every night. The men donated heavily to local charities. Money flowed like the tide in Cook Inlet. Ramon wondered how his life would change when he no longer had Eddie at his side. "Life goes on," he thought. "Life will go on, even without Eduardo."

Chapter Eleven

The flight time was early; Aliana checked in at the counter at 4:30 Friday morning. A cool mist hung in the air, but the temperature was warm. Her only luggage was a small carry-on bag that contained her make-up, computer and cell phone. Everything she needed would be in her Anchorage apartment. She boarded the plane with a certain amount of excitement. She was looking forward to a day off with Rube.

The trooper sergeant welcomed the early morning call. He had time off coming in return for the overtime he had accumulated during the past couple of weeks of investigations. Rube donned civilian clothing instead of the customary trooper uniform and headed for the office. He stopped at the Great Alaska Breakfast Club for breakfast before driving the final mile or so to the office.

"I'm going to take the weekend off, if you don't mind, Cap," Rube reported to his captain. "I have some time coming and I have a friend coming to town. Tony can finish the paperwork on that murder investigation now. And, unless the world comes to an end this weekend, I'm going to take off today and Monday. Chalk it up to comp time."

The captain flipped the pages of his desk calendar. "Yeah, I think it's going to be okay. Just let me know if you're not going to be in on Tuesday. We have grand jury on Friday."

"Right," Rube answered. "We're ready. Like I said, Tony can finish the paperwork and we'll be ready." He thought a moment before continuing. "This guy and his lawyer are going to take a look at the evidence and witnesses and decide that pleading out will be the best thing for everyone."

"I hope you're right, Rube. It would save the State a lot of money. See you on Tuesday."

"I may drive to Fairbanks this weekend," Rube informed his captain. "I'll have the cell phone if anything comes up. See you on Tuesday."

In his office once again, he was busy putting the final touches on the stack of work on his desk. The phone rang. It was Aliana.

"Hi, I'm at the airport. Can you come to get me?"

"You bet. I'll pick you up in front of the baggage claim in fifteen minutes."

She was waiting on the sidewalk, her carry-on bag in her hand. The Jeep Grand Cherokee eased to a stop in front of her. She stooped to look inside and gave a friendly smile to the driver as soon as she recognized him.

She leaned over and kissed him on the cheek. "It's really good to see you. I don't know when I have looked forward to a day off like I have this one." Her broad smile confirmed her feelings.

The shiny white station wagon/SUV eased away from the curb and merged with the traffic going toward the city center. "Is there something special you would like to do?" Rube asked, just hoping she wanted to spend the time with him.

"I haven't planned anything. I just wanted to spend some quiet time away from responsibility. I have to fly to Fairbanks tomorrow," she reminded.

"I know." He wasn't sure what the answer was going to be to the question he was about to ask. "I thought, if you don't object, I might drive you to Fairbanks today. Just take a nice drive; spend some time together on the way, see some sights. Hell, just spend some time with you. What d'ya think?"

"How much time off will you have?" Aliana asked.

"Until Tuesday, anyway."

Now was as good a time as any to break the news. Either he accepts it or now would be a good time to quit. "I have a daughter in Fairbanks. I go there to see her every week. I've told you that. My daughter's name is Saundra. I promised to take her to Circle this weekend." She watched him for his reaction.

Rube liked this woman. He knew how hard it must be for her. "I don't want to come between you and your daughter," he began. She felt the big letdown coming. "But, would I be in the way if we all drove to Circle in the Jeep?"

The urge to cry was almost overwhelming. She stretched across the console between the seats and kissed him on the cheek again. "Oh, Rube, I would love that."

"Good, is there anything you want to do in Anchorage before we leave?"

"I just have to go by the apartment and pick up a few things." She was instantly relaxed. "This is going to be wonderful. You are going to love Saundra. She's twelve."

They drove to her apartment. She invited him up to show him pictures of Saundra and of Opal. Leaving there, they went to his place in south Anchorage where he packed a small bag with shaving gear and a change of clothing to last the weekend.

They drove north, stopping in Wasilla for fuel and refreshments. The Parks Highway is a wide, mostly two lane, well-traveled road that winds north through Denali National Park and on to Fairbanks. The scenery is spectacular along the entire route, but by far the most impressive is *the mountain*. Mount McKinley is truly a wondrous sight. It can be seen on a clear day for more than a hundred miles. Its gleaming glaciers shimmer in the sunlight; wisps of clouds dance around the summit 20,320 feet above the valley floor—the tallest mountain on the North American continent.

The couple made frequent stops to view the mountain and stopped for lunch at the Mountain View Lodge. They drove at a tourist's pace, stopping and looking, talking and laughing. They stopped at several scenic viewpoints and walked to the stations to see what was offered, holding hands like a couple of newlyweds while doing so. It was good for them both, just being together, alone.

The Jeep climbed the long grade to the divide that drops off to Ester and Fairbanks. Rube had been silent for a long while, daydreaming about his relationship with his new companion. Aliana had been quiet too, but had reached across the console to hold his hand while he drove.

He looked at her and smiled. "Can I ask you a question?" he began.

"Sure," she replied. "What do you want to know?"

"In the course of my daily business, I meet a lot of people. Some of them are poor, without two nickels to rub together, people without prospects. They always talk about life and how they want it to be better. Most of those people don't have any idea how they can do that."

Aliana nodded in agreement but continued to listen without commenting.

"But, some of the people I meet are movers and shakers, people with a lot of money and influence, rich and powerful people." He concentrated on the road while talking, not looking at his companion. "Whenever I'm with those people, even if it's just for a cup of coffee, all they want to talk about is money and how to make more of it. They don't seem to have any other interests. You, on the other hand, deal with large amounts of money every day. You make a living dealing with money. You deal with bankers and financiers every day, and yet, when we're together you never mention finance or budget. You never talk business. I was wondering, why is that?"

She chuckled.

"Am I missing something?" he asked.

Again she gave a small laugh. "I've been sitting here wondering why you never talk about police business. I've known some policemen in my time and I've never known one that could talk about anything but police and criminals."

"Yeah, you're right about that. Cops are pretty boring, really. When they get together, all they can talk about is the job. Most outsiders find it exciting and interesting, but the truth is that cops live in a different world that they aren't allowed to discuss except within their own fraternity. I've always tried to keep a life away from the job. Sometimes it works and sometimes it doesn't."

"It's sort of the same for me and what I do. I'm not allowed to talk about my work with anyone outside the department. I deal with bankers and businessmen all the time and, you're right, their conversation is usually limited to money matters. I'm like you; I try to keep a life outside that world. Saundra helps me to do that. I spend so much time traveling that I seldom have time to make conversation with anyone outside the office."

"I hope you'll let me meet Saundra. She sounds like a really neat little girl."

"She is," the mother said proudly. "Mentally, she can't keep up with the other kids her age, but she tries her best and I love her dearly." There was some sadness in her voice.

"I know I'll like her," he said, then changed the subject. "When we get to town, I'll drop you off and go find a motel. You're going to want to spend some time with Saundra and Opal this evening."

"I was hoping to have dinner with you before going home. They don't expect me until morning." She was sincere. This was a day she was reluctant to end. It had been a long time since she had been this comfortable with anyone.

"I'd like that," he answered.

It was 7:30 the next morning when room service brought coffee, fruit, sweet rolls and orange juice to their room. The morning was already warm and the fresh air coming through the open patio doors felt good. They said little while finishing their breakfast. By 8:15 they were gathering their belongings and returning to the car.

Aliana leaned on the front fender. "How would you feel about driving us to

Circle today and coming home tomorrow? There's a big cabin up there with room enough for all of us. Saundra and Opal haven't been home for a long time and I promised them we'd go this weekend. Would you like to go with us?"

"Are you sure you want me along?"

"Oh, yes, I'm sure," Aliana giggled like a schoolgirl. "Besides it would give you a chance to get acquainted with my family. We'll take you fishing in the Yukon River."

It was only a few blocks to the family home from the motel where the two had spent the night. Before arriving she had persuaded him to make the trip. The house was a small ranch style with a fenced yard. The grass was neatly trimmed and summer flowers bloomed along the borders. She hopped from the jeep as soon as it stopped, opened the gate and walked to the front porch. Before she could climb the steps, the door opened and a small, lively little girl ran from the house.

"Mommy, Mommy," she shouted. The girl gave a giant leap and nearly knocked her mother from her feet. Aliana swung the girl in a circle then held her tightly. The little girl hugged her back just as tightly. They kissed and made cooing sounds at each other. Rube thought it to be a long established ritual. It was obvious that the girl had missed her mother as much as she had missed the girl. He enjoyed seeing such a loving reunion.

"I colored a picture for you mommy. Opal hung it on the refrigerator. Come in and see it."

"Okay, honey, I'm coming." She turned and motioned for Rube to follow.

Inside the house, Aliana introduced Rube to Opal and Saundra. "This is my friend Rube. He's an Alaska State Trooper."

"Do you have a gun?" Saundra asked, in the way of any child.

"Yes, but I didn't think I'd need it today so I left it home."

"Can I see it sometime?" She was full of questions.

"Saundra, don't be a pest. Go help Opal." Aliana rolled her eyes and grinned at Rube.

"Okay, Mommy. Are we going to Gramma's today?" she asked as she walked toward the kitchen.

"If you're good," was the short answer before the girl disappeared through the kitchen door.

"Well, do you think you can stand to be with us for a couple of days?"

"Yes," Rube answered. "I think I'll like it just fine. You were right, she's a terrific kid."

It had been a long time since Rube had made the four-hour drive to Circle City. The road was much better than he remembered. On the way they stopped to inspect the rusty pipe of the Davidson Ditch, an 80-mile pipeline used to run a gold dredge in the early days. In later years the dredge was shut down and the water used to run a power plant. Today the pipe is rusted and vacant, a monument to gold mining history in the area. Stops were made at Eagle Summit and other landmarks along the way. At each stop Saundra would get out and run around looking at everything. At one point she was wading in a small stream when she fell and soaked herself. The trip was interrupted for several minutes while she was dried off and a change of clothing could be pulled from the small suitcase in the back of the Jeep. Everyone laughed and had a good time. It was late Sunday evening when the group returned to Fairbanks. Rube found a room in the same motel they had used the first night.

"I had just a wonderful weekend, Rube." The two were standing on the front porch.

"Me, too," Rube admitted. "I can't remember when I have been so relaxed. You seem to have that effect on me. Thanks for inviting me."

"I'll see you in the morning," she said. "I'll ride back to Anchorage with you and fly out to Juneau on Tuesday. I have to go to Seattle on Thursday, so I'll be busy in the office for a couple of days. This trip has been special for me. You're the first person I have ever brought here to meet Saundra and Opal. I hope you aren't too disappointed."

"Disappointed? Hardly. This has been great for me, too. Thanks." He kissed her on the cheek. "See you in the morning. What time?"

Rube was in front of the house again promptly at eight in the morning. The drive back down the Parks Highway would be long, but would seem all too short. They shared the strong feelings that were growing inside each of them. They would share one more night before Aliana went back to her work and Rube went back to his.

Chapter Twelve

Alaska State Trooper office is a busy place, especially the headquarters offices on Tudor Avenue in Anchorage. Rube had taken two extra days of leave time for his four-day weekend, but criminal activity had not ceased. It was business as usual when he returned to his desk. The in-basket was piled high with new cases for him to review and assign. The pile had shrunk to about half its original height and he was finishing his first Diet Coke when the intercom buzzed. The woman at the reception desk asked him to come to the front to meet a possible complainant.

His long muscular frame made a rhythmic swaying motion as he strode down the long hall. It felt good to get out from behind the desk for a few minutes.

The young girl, maybe 22 or 23 years old Rube guessed, seemed nervous. She kept looking over her shoulder toward the front doors. There was a foreign look about her that Rube couldn't quite put his finger on, but she looked Spanish or Mexican, he really couldn't tell. She dressed American enough, in jeans, sweat shirt and running shoes.

"Hello there, I'm Sergeant Rueben Hayes. What can I do to help you?"

She spoke with a definite accent. "I am so glad to meet you. My name is Molita, Molita Juarez." She again looked nervously toward the front door. "Can we talk in private, Sergeant?"

"Of course. Come with me." She followed him back down the long hall to his office. Once inside, Rube closed the door.

"Can I get you something to drink: coffee, tea, water, anything?"

"No, thank you, I'm fine." Once in the confines of the office, she seemed to relax a little.

"Just take it easy and tell me what I can do to help you."

"I am from Mexico. I work at the Sombrero Mexican Restaurant. Do you know where that is?" Rube nodded. "I have a work permit from INS. All the girls who work in the restaurant have permits. We come from Mexico to make money. They pay us well. We wait tables, tend bar and things like that. It is honest work."

"I've been in there. It's a nice place," Rube noted.

"Si, it is a very nice place."

"Is there a problem at the restaurant?" the trooper prodded.

"No, not with the restaurant," she hesitated, looking down at her shoes, then looking up again. "I don't know how to tell this story," she began. "In Mexico I answered an ad to come to America. It was for three months. They said if I liked the job I could go home for a while and then come back for another three months. This is my second trip here, although last time I worked in the Fairbanks restaurant. It is also owned by Senior Chavez. I made good money there and I met my boyfriend there. His name is Don Sears. He works on the North Slope for an oil company. Don and I want to get married, but there are some complications."

"I have to tell you right now, Miss Juarez, that I can't help you with immigration's problems. Those things are out of my hands."

"Oh no, Sergeant. This is not about immigrations. I am here because I want to marry Don and I don't want anything on my record that might stop me from coming back to Alaska."

"Are you involved in anything illegal, Miss Juarez?" Rube was now taking notes and noted the time and date at the top of the page of his notebook.

"I'm not sure if I am or not, but I think maybe yes." Again she was looking at her feet, thinking.

"Perhaps you should just tell me the whole story and we'll see if we can get it straightened out for you." More notes. "Just what laws do you think have been broken?"

"I think Mr. Chavez is using the girls to bring drugs into the United States."

This got the trooper's attention immediately. "Why do you say that, Miss Juarez?"

"Please, call me Molly. Everyone does." The ice had been broken and she now seemed to trust this trooper in the blue uniform.

"Okay, Molly, what makes you think the girls are being used to bring drugs into the U.S.?"

"Each girl comes here with one suitcase and one 25-pound tin of fresh ground Mexican corn flour. Every girl must bring one of those tins. When we arrive, we give the tin to Eddie Sanchez when he picks us up at the airport.

We never see the tins again. Last week one of the girls forgot to bring the tin of flour, and Mr. Sanchez was very angry. He sent the girl right back to Mexico. I heard from a friend that when she got back to Mexico City she was met by Mr. Dante's men, and that they beat her up really bad."

"Who is Mr. Dante?" Rube asked.

"I think he is the biggest gangster in all of Mexico. Some people say he is the one who helped Mr. Chavez start his restaurant business. He comes here sometimes in the summer to fish. I saw him once the last time I was here."

"Miss Juarez…Molly, this is becoming very complicated. Do you mind if I use a recorder to take your statements?"

"I don't mind if you keep them to yourself. I wouldn't want Mr. Chavez or Mr. Sanchez to know I was here."

He took a small recorder from the desk drawer. "I think that what you have to say may be very important and I want to be sure I have all the information correct." Rube switched on the recorder. "Before we continue," he gave the date and the time. "I have to ask if this interview is of your own free will and do you wish to have a lawyer present?" He went on with the necessary legalese before asking her to continue her story.

She answered all his questions with an ease that suggested she was telling the truth. Molly admitted that she was more at ease in the small office, out of view of those who entered the building. Since no one could see her, she felt she could talk freely.

"I am getting very thirsty. Please, could I have a soda?" she asked quietly.

"Certainly. You just sit still and I'll get one for you. I'll be right back." With that he stood and left her sitting in the office.

On his way to the machine to get her a Coke, he poked his head into the office of Captain Milo Thomas. "I think I may have something for the drug team, Cap. I'm doing the interview now. It looks like we may have a major drug importer and a witness. Can you have the drug team commander come to my office in two hours?"

"Is this information that good?" the captain asked.

"I think it is. This witness seems pretty genuine. I'm going back to get the whole story now. I'll let you know as soon as I've finished."

"I'll call Stan and have him come over this afternoon. I'll let you know the time." Stan was Captain Stanley Withers, head of the Southcentral Area Narcotics team, commonly known as the SCAN team.

Back in his office, Rube gave the plastic bottle of Coke to Molita Juarez. She was shuffling her feet and had once again become nervous.

"Relax, Molly." Rube assured her. "No one can see you here and what you say is confidential." She looked at him and smiled. "Do you think you can continue now?"

"Yes. Thank you for the soda." She took a long drink from the bottle. "What do you want to know?"

"First of all, what made you suspect that there were drugs being sold in your restaurant?"

"When you work there, no one thinks you hear anything. They talk openly and pay no attention to the girls. If you listen you soon learn which of the customers are workers and which are criminals. I first noticed these people in the restaurant when I worked in Fairbanks. They would come in and have dinner and then meet with Mr. Chavez and Mr. Sanchez. They would go into the office and close the door, but sometimes they would call out for drinks. I never actually saw the drugs, but I saw paper boxes and sometimes an athletic bag on the desk. When these people left the restaurant, they always took these with them. The same thing goes on today in the restaurant here in Anchorage."

"Let's go back to the beginning. You say the girls are bringing the drugs into the state in tins of corn flour, is that correct?"

"Si, that is correct. The corn flour is for making tortillas. The restaurant is famous for them."

"Do the girls know beforehand there are drugs in the tins?"

"No. The other girls are like me. They just come here to work and make some money. I only recently became really suspicious when they beat up on my friend."

"How do you think these tins escape detection by Mexican and U.S. Customs?"

"The tins are sealed and have a registration paper that says they have been passed and inspected by Mexican Customs agents. The paper says that the tins contain processed corn flour and have been inspected. They are sealed and numbered there. I think the Mexican Customs officials have to be on the payroll of Mr. Dante. He has lots of money to do that."

"Just what kind of drugs do you think are in the tins?"

"I think it must be cocaine. The packages are small and there really is corn flour in the tins. I have seen it."

"You say that the drugs are dealt through Mr. Chavez right there in the restaurant, is that correct?" Rube was trying to pin down exact locations now. He wanted specifics, if there were any to be had.

"Yes, that is correct. Most of the time Mr. Sanchez is there, but he is sick a lot lately and he has someone help him."

"Do you have any idea when there will be another shipment brought in?"

"It will be soon." Molly was looking down again. "They have told me that I will be going back to Mexico in two weeks. They will have to replace me and the other girl who will be going home at the same time." There were tears coming to her eyes now. "Please, Sergeant, will you help me? I want to get married and come back to Alaska. I don't want anything to stop me from being able to do that. Do you think it will be all right for me?"

"If you have told me the whole truth, then there is nothing for you to worry about. I'll start an investigation right away. I'll see what can be done to help you stay here for a while if you like. I can't promise anything, though. That's out of my hands." His words seemed to cheer her a little.

"Thank you, Sergeant. I thank you for everything. Don and I want to live here in Alaska and to raise a family here. I thank you for your help."

"How can I get in touch with you, Molly?" Rube wanted to know. "We can't just come to the restaurant and see you."

"If you have a pencil and paper, I will give you an address and a phone number where you can contact me. I would ask, though, that you be careful what you say to the girl who is my roommate. She might say something to Mr. Chavez."

"We'll be very careful to protect you. And, thank you for coming. I'll be in touch with you soon." He walked around the desk. "Do you need a ride somewhere?"

"No, thank you. I will catch the bus at the corner. It will be safer for me. I don't think anyone followed me, but I am very nervous about being here."

He opened the door and walked her to the front desk. "Here is my card. Call me if you have any problems or you want to talk again. I don't want to put you in danger, but if you can get me any names of the people picking up the drugs, I would like to have them."

"I will try. I will call you soon." She gave a small wave of her hand as she walked down the stairs to the front doors.

He turned and walked directly to the Captain's office. Captain Stanley Withers was waiting in Milo Thomas's office when Rube arrived. The sergeant gave the two captains a rundown on the interview he had just completed.

"We knew there was a major supplier operating here, but I never would have suspected Ray Chavez. How certain are you that this information is good and not just a ploy for the girl to stay here?" Withers asked.

"I guess there isn't any way right now to be 100% sure, but this girl isn't planning to stay. She told me she plans to return to Mexico before she marries this Don Sears. I think that she's telling the truth, and she's trying to avoid any charges that would prevent her from coming back to get married."

It was Milo's turn. "We can speculate all we want, but unless we check it out and come up with some hard evidence, we really don't have anything. The ball is in our court. We're going to have to do some digging and spend some time and assets on surveillance. Personally I think the information is solid enough to warrant spending the effort to confirm. The girl… what's her name… Juarez, says she is going to attempt to get us names of the local dealers picking up the merchandise from Chavez. I say let's spend some time on it."

It was Rube's vote. "I agree. If this proves to be even close to accurate, then the sheer volume is staggering. This one guy is bringing in two kilos of cocaine each week. Break that down into dollars and it amounts to a lot of money for somebody. Again, I agree with Milo. I think this needs to be investigated right away."

"Alright. I'll assign some people to it." He had already decided to go ahead, before the final arguments by Milo and Rube. "I have one problem, though."

"Is it something I can help with?" Captain Thomas asked.

"I don't know. Do you have a good video camera?" Captain Withers tried to explain. "Ours were ruined two weeks ago in that crack house fire that destroyed our surveillance van."

Thomas thought for a moment. "We have a couple of video cameras, but they're just off-the-shelf stuff, not very good for this kind of work."

"I might have an idea about this," Hayes put in. He looked at his watch and shook his head. "It's too late today. I'll have to make the call in the morning."

The meeting began to break up. Withers stood to leave. "Call me if you can come up with something. Our camera equipment burned up and we can't afford another on our budget. We've asked for special funding, but that's going to take a while."

It was late when the SCAN commander left. Rube turned to his captain.

"I was thinking that we might get the use of that equipment in that kayak incident. That Gerlitz fella was going to sell everything, and I think he left it all in Seward. If it's still there, he might let us use it."

"Never thought of that," Milo commented. "Good idea. Call him in the morning. And, find out how much he wants for the equipment. I might be able to find a little funding in our budget."

Rube returned to his office to end his day. Folders and files had to be returned to their proper place before the office could be closed. He made a final calendar note reminding himself of the call he needed to place first thing in the morning. He thought about Aliana and the weekend he had spent with her. Little Saundra was a really nice little kid. It was a shame that she wasn't like other kids. Even worse was the fact that her chances for a long life were very slim. Rube admired the child's mother for spending so much time with her. He thought again of his time with the raven-haired beauty with the ice blue eyes. It would be easy to become attached to her.

Chapter Thirteen

The finishing touches were being put on the morning chores piled on his desk when he checked the time. It was an hour later in Seattle. He reached into the center drawer of his desk to retrieve the business card left behind by the banker. Rube put the card on his desk and stood to stretch. It had already been a long morning. Custom dictated there were still a few minutes before a banker would go to work. He took his coffee cup down the hall and filled it before walking outside to enjoy the morning air. Somehow it was relaxing to walk around the grass, sipping his coffee, and greeting the other officers now coming into the office. Checking the time again he returned to his desk to make the call.

"Ben Gerlitz, please." He waited while the connection was made.

"This is Ben Gerlitz. Who's calling, please."

"Ah, Mr. Gerlitz. This is Trooper Sergeant Rube Hayes. Good morning."

"Oh, good morning, Sergeant." The banker had recognized the name immediately. "How are things in Alaska?"

"Just fine, Ben. Say, I heard you got a promotion. Congratulations."

The voice that answered was sad.

"Yes, thank you. I'm just sorry it came about the way it did."

"Me too, Ben. Me too," Rube consoled.

"Anyway, what can I do for you this morning?" The voice was more cheerful now.

"I come begging. I have a problem I was hoping you may be able to help me with," Rube began. "I want to know if you sold all your equipment from the kayak?"

"You know, Sergeant, I've been so busy I honestly don't know. It won't take long to check though. Is there anything there you need?"

"As a matter of fact, there is. And call me Rube, everyone does."

"Whatever it is, it's yours. You were really great during the time of the accident, and I can never adequately repay you."

"Nonsense, Ben. What happened was a real tragedy. Not many men could have remained as calm as you were able to do. You showed a lot of courage, especially trying, as you did, to reach your friend with the glacier acting up the way it did. I'm just sorry we were never able to find any trace of him."

"I suppose. I wasn't thinking very well at the time, just reacting. Tad was a good friend. It was pretty traumatic to lose him like that." There was a short pause. "Anyway, what is it you need from me?"

"I was wondering if you still owned the camera equipment you had on the kayak? Our department's video equipment is out of commission right now, and we need something better than we can buy off the shelf. Our problem is that we don't have much money left in the budget for purchasing the equipment. I thought if you still owned it, perhaps we could make some kind of arrangement for payment. That equipment was some of the best I've ever seen."

"I think it's still in Seward. The kayak sold, but I don't think the rest of the equipment ever did. I can call and find out." Ben made notes on a legal pad. "Can I check and call you right back?"

"Of course." Rube gave him his office number and extension before hanging up.

He was deep in concentration when the phone rang. It was Ben. He checked the time. It had been less than twenty minutes.

"I talked with the owner of the shop in Seward and he told me that everything is in his back room. He's had a couple of bites, but no serious offers. If you want any of it, it's yours."

"I really do need the video equipment. Like I said, I'll have to make some arrangement for paying you," Rube again told the banker.

"How about we do this? I'll donate all that video equipment to your department. You send me a receipt so I can deduct it on my taxes as a legitimate item. I'll probably get more out of it that way than if I sold it outright," Ben declared.

"Are you serious?" Rube asked. "You have a lot of money tied up in that stuff."

"I know," Ben explained, "but, with this promotion, I need all the deductions I can come up with. I'll never use that stuff again, so you may as well get some use out of it."

"There's no way I can thank you, Ben," the trooper was overwhelmed.

"Can you use another unit like that one?" The question was unexpected.

"Sure, like I said, we're out of video equipment for the entire detachment." Rube wondered what was coming.

"Before I called Seward, I called Colin James. Colin was the third member of the party who had to cancel. He works over here at Boeing as an electrical engineer. He has an identical unit on his kayak. If you can use it, he'll donate it the same way as I have done mine. Just send him a receipt for his tax accountant. Do you want it?"

Reuben Hayes didn't know what to say. "What can I say? That's wonderful. Give me his address and I'll get you the receipts as soon as the equipment arrives." With the notes completed and the arrangements for shipment made, he leaned back in his chair to think about what had just happened. This was great.

Captain Thomas invited his sergeant to lunch. The revelations of the past two days were discussed on the trip to and from the café. Milo was ecstatic to hear about the donation of the two video cameras. This would save his budget a great deal of money and provide state-of-the-art equipment for the officer's use.

When they returned to the office, the receptionist told Rube he had a long distance call holding. He said he would take it in his office and went there directly.

"Sergeant Hayes here, who am I speaking with," he answered.

"Sergeant, Colin James here. I'm a friend of Ben Gerlitz."

"Oh, yes. Say, I want to thank you for the generous donation. You have no idea how much this will help our department. We were in quite a bind," Rube explained. "We have a major drug case developing and our video equipment gave up."

"Maybe I can help you out even more, Sergeant." He went on to explain that Boeing had done some testing with adapting video cameras to the lenses and controls used in the U-2 and SR-71 spy planes. The testing was now completed and bids submitted for a contract to produce the hardware. Boeing was in the process of surplusing out the test equipment. Which meant that Boeing had no further use for it and would be glad to part with it for any reasonable sum. He had talked to the project engineer and had been given permission to donate it to the Alaska State Troopers. It would be a nice goodwill gesture, they thought.

"The difference is in the lenses and controls. These lenses will take beautiful digital images in almost total darkness. The controls on this model can be set up remotely with the camera on any kind of mount. Light settings are automatic; zoom is wireless remote; sound is parabolic and can be aimed in a wide or narrow beam. Are you interested?"

"This thing sounds like magic for our work. How soon can we get our hands on it?"

"I'll ship you two boxes today. With luck you will have them tomorrow afternoon."

Rube was impressed. "How much training will it take to ensure good images? We don't want some defense attorney saying we rigged the pictures."

"I'll send the handbooks, but operation is really simple. Basically the same as an off-the-shelf video camera." The engineer was being very helpful. "If you need further instruction, I'll fly up there and give you a class."

"I owe you, Mr. James. I don't know how I can ever repay you and Ben. If you ever get up here, though, I'll see you have the best fishing trip of your life." Rube laughed.

"I'd love that," Colin chuckled. Then his mood changed. "Can I ask you something? Something rather personal?"

"I'll answer anything I can," Rube stated with a certain amount of curiosity. "What is it you want to know?"

"I'm worried about Ben. He was shook up when he came home after the accident, but that seemed normal. Later, after he was promoted at the bank, he changed. He seems sullen and never talks about work anymore. He's different now. It's nothing I can really put my finger on, but something's wrong." There was strong concern in his voice. "Is there something about this accident that I haven't been told?"

Rube thought back on the earlier phone conversation with the banker. "I don't know Ben that well, but now that you mention it, when I offered my congratulations on the promotion, he changed the subject right away. I remember being curious about that at the time. As far as the accident, it was just that, a tragic accident."

"I'm glad to hear that," James said with relief in his voice. "Tad and Ben were really close friends. I was lucky to have been able to kayak with them. I really hated missing the Alaska trip. But, something is bothering Ben. I'm glad that's not the reason."

"If I can help, let me know."

"Okay. Call if you have trouble with the new photographic equipment. Good luck on your drug case." They said goodbye and hung up.

Something was wrong with Ben Gerlitz. Rube had sensed it this morning. It was nothing solid, just one of those things that tweak the instincts of a career cop. Now, that sensation was back, brought home by the call from Colin James. *It may be nothing, but I'll check it out…soon.*

Down the hall he shared the good news with Captain Thomas. After a short discussion they called Stan Withers, whose office was in an adjacent building, and asked him to join them in Milo's office. The mood of the three men was good. It wasn't often things worked out as well as they had this time. Rube volunteered to drive to Seward in the morning to retrieve the donated equipment from the operator of the small booking agency who dealt in sea kayaks and kayak trips. He thought he would be back in Anchorage by noon, if all went well.

With this business finished, it was time to quit for the day. He would eat dinner and call Aliana at home later.

They talked of many things, like a couple of kids whose parents were keeping them apart. Finally he got around to mentioning that he had spoken with Ben that morning. He also mentioned that Ben's friend, Colin James, was worried about him.

"I'll be with him tomorrow afternoon," she said. "I have to sign off in an audit of the account. Would you like me to find out what's bothering him?"

"No, I don't think that's necessary. It really isn't my affair. But, I agree with Colin, something is on his mind."

"Well, don't worry about it. It's probably nothing. He's been under a lot of stress, what with his promotion to head of the department and then having an audit dumped on him," she rationalized. "I think he'll be all right."

"I suppose you're right," Rube conceded. "Not much I can do about it anyway. And, if I'm going to waste away the hours worrying about someone, it will be you, and not Ben Gerlitz, I'll worry about. You're prettier." He laughed, said good night and hung up. He went to sleep smiling.

Chapter Fourteen

The flight from Juneau to Seattle arrived a few minutes early, but the heavy traffic from the airport to the downtown offices of the SeaFirst Bank made her arrival late. It was 10:45 when she entered the building and 11 by the time she reached the floor occupied by the administrator and staff of the Alaska Fund. Exiting the elevator, she walked directly to the desk of Ben Gerlitz.

She smiled and offered, "Good morning, Ben."

"Ah, Ms. Pedersen. How was your flight?"

"It was as usual, long." She hadn't eaten breakfast before leaving this morning and airline food was no way to start a day. "How would you like me to buy you lunch?" He looked at the clock on his desk. "It is getting to be that time, isn't it? Where would you like to go?"

"Would you mind having lunch at the Hilton? I could check in and we can eat in the coffee shop. The early time should allow us to beat the regular lunch traffic." She wanted some time alone with him before the business day began. She needed to know if she had made a mistake in judgment by supporting him for this position. She wanted to know if he was having second thoughts about continuing this relationship.

He picked up the telephone and dialed a four-digit number. "Just let me tell the secretary where I will be."

Upon leaving the building for the short walk up the block, Aliana began to test her new protégé. "Last night I had a call from Sergeant Hayes of the troopers. He said he had talked to you."

"Yes, I talked with him on the telephone yesterday."

"Did he mention anything about our arrangement?" she asked.

"No!" was the startled answer. "If he had, I'd be on a plane for Brazil this morning."

"You aren't making any plans to abandon our arrangement, are you?"

"No, I'm in for the duration. I can't say I like it, but I'm in and there's no way for me to change that now."

"I'm glad to hear that." She thought it was time to reinforce the relationship. "The first payment has been made to your numbered account and those deposits will continue to be made for you. The governor has another year on this term and he will most certainly be re-elected. That means that I am assured this position for another five years. I calculate that by the end of that time, given the economy of the state stays on course, your share of this venture will be somewhere in the neighborhood of $1.3 to$1.8 *million dollars.* That's a lot of Supersonics basketball tickets." They were approaching the Hilton Hotel.

Inside, they went directly to the check-in desk. Aliana dropped her carry-on bag with the concierge. The two found a quiet table and ordered lunch. They discussed the conversation with Rube the previous day, including the donation and the referral to Colin James. By the time lunch was finished, Ben seemed more relaxed. She thought, *it's funny the effect a million dollars or so will have on a person.*

There was little conversation on the walk back to the bank. The sun was high and reached the bottom of the concrete canyon. They could smell the salt air that gave Seattle its character. The return walk was much less tense than the one before lunch had been.

Another cab took them back to the Hilton. They agreed to begin at 9 AM the following morning. Ben walked back to the bank parking lot in the basement of the building. During the walk back, he couldn't stop thinking about the money. He made a generous salary, but even with good investments he had never dreamed he would be able to accumulate this kind of capital. On his way home he stopped at the Shamrock Club and downed four vodka gimlets.

The following morning the audit review went on. By late afternoon every aspect of the account had been verified. He checked to be certain one item was carefully omitted from the final copies. There had been the matter of the administrative costs for the account. These costs were deducted from the interest paid on the account. Since that excess interest was not used to pay scheduled account balances, it was transferred to a separate account: Alaska Maritime Savings. The address for this account was a private post office box to which only Aliana had access. She checked the box every month. The only mail delivered to the box was the monthly statement from SeaFirst Bank for the account of Alaska Maritime Savings.

Funds were transferred to the account semi-weekly. On Monday and on Thursday there were deposits made to the account. Later the same day an electronic transfer would empty the account, transferring the balance to Peoples Bank in San Francisco. That account was in the name of Alaska Maritime Investments. Again the same day, the balance of this account, minus service charges, was transferred to the account of the Maritime Investment Group at National Bank Of Panama in Panama City, Panama. Funds in that account were immediately transferred electronically, minus service fees, to the account of Investment Group Ltd. The new account was in the International Investment Bank of the Bahamas. Again an immediate transfer was made under the same conditions to International Investment Group at National Bank of Commerce, Sao Paolo, Brazil.

In Brazil the system changed somewhat. The transfer, less fees, was made to a numbered account in Hong Kong on Monday and to a numbered account in Lucerne, Switzerland on Thursday. Monthly this account was emptied, by transfer within the bank to three separate accounts, also numbered. Agreements with the banks made Aliana's account the parent account and the beneficiary of the other accounts in the event of the death of either of the other account holders. This option had been recently exercised in the death of Tad Morton.

The address for each of the accounts was the same, a blind box in the same Seattle postal service. This box, too, was checked at regular intervals. This complicated arrangement was made to confuse anyone attempting to trace the original interest money out of SeaFirst Bank. The system had worked well for more than two years now. Aliana expected it to continue to function well as long as Ben kept his head.

By late afternoon the final touches were put on the audit. Copies were made for her to file in her own offices. Copies were also made and notarized for the office of the governor. These copies were certified correct with the signature of Mr. Stackhaus. This was done during a short meeting with him. She assured the banker that Ben was doing a fine job. She expected that the governor felt the same. Irwin Stackhaus offered to drive her to the airport, but that arrangement had already been made with Ben.

It was almost 2 AM when the cab dropped her at the front door of her small home in Fairbanks. She tried to be quiet and not wake anyone when she unlocked the door and made her way to her own bedroom.

Friday had proved to be another beautiful summer day in Anchorage. Rube was in the office early, just after six. The usual paperwork awaited him, with more accumulating as the morning went on. He had stopped for a short break and a Diet Coke when Don Sears came into his office. He refused a seat and said he only had a minute to spend.

"What can I do for you this morning, Don?" They had only just met, but Rube thought that, through Molita, he already knew the man.

"Molly gave me this note to give to you. She thought it might be safer for me to deliver it than for her to do it herself," Don explained.

Rube took the note, removed it from the small white envelope and read its contents. "Did she tell you what this contains?" he asked.

"Yes, I'm the one who encouraged her to come here in the first place. We don't want any trouble with the law when it comes time to apply for permanent entry into the U.S. I don't use drugs and I have no use for those who do. I've had friends that used drugs. Any pleasure they got was more than offset by the grief they suffered from it. One friend I worked with used cocaine every day. Two years—two years is all he lasted. He died of a heart attack. He was only thirty-two years old. Personally I've never been that bored with life." He looked up to see Rube studying his face. "Sorry, didn't mean to get on a soapbox."

"I'm glad you feel that way, Don, and I wish you and Molly the best," Rube said sincerely. "Tell her I'll make good use of this. Thanks."

"Thank you, sergeant. Molly was really apprehensive about coming here, but she said she felt a lot better after talking to you, and frankly, so do I."

"I hope everything goes well for you and Molly. Let me know if I can help you in any way."

"I appreciate that, sergeant. Thanks. We'll be contacting you." He gave a little thumbs-up sign and walked from the office.

As soon as Don left the office, Rube was on the phone to Stan Withers who said he would be right over to see the list of names Molly Juarez had sent. They met in Milo's office.

"The guys are really having a good time with the camera equipment you got us," Stan reported to Rube when he walked into the office. "The CIA doesn't have anything this good. The pictures and the sound are perfect, studio quality stuff. I never dreamed this kind of equipment existed. Thanks for your help in getting it for us."

"I just got lucky, Stan. Glad I could help. That spy camera must be as good as advertised then?"

"Come over this afternoon and we'll give you a demonstration," he offered.

"I'll do it. Around three all right for you?"

"Great."

"Here is the list of names from Molly Juarez." Rube handed the list to Withers. "I didn't count them, but I think there are eight names there. I recognize most of them. How do you want to handle it?"

Withers looked the list over and nodded. "Everything seems to be on our side on this one. We have inside information. We have an importer who thinks he's out of the loop and can't be caught. We have a list of dealers and distributors, and we have some brand new surveillance equipment. My metro team has just finished up on another case, so I'm going to assign this one to them. They're a five-man team with a lot of experience. Lieutenant Randy Austin is the team leader. This team has a good track record and a lot of brains. They'll handle it."

"Just remind them that we have an informant who could get hurt if things go bad," the trooper sergeant reminded.

Stan Withers stood. "We'll protect her, Rube. Call me if you get anything else. I'm going back to the office and get this started. I'll keep you posted on the progress of the case. Thanks again. See ya."

"Don't worry, Rube," Milo advised. "Stan's a good man and I know his metro team. They're good men, too. Just leave it to them."

"I know, Cap, but usually informants are druggies wanting to make a deal. In this case the informant is a good citizen. I'd hate to see her get hurt in the crossfire."

"I'll be seeing Stan and I'll mention your concerns to him. He'll understand. I'll have him give an extra word of caution to his team."

"Thanks, Milo. I appreciate that." Rube studied the yellow legal pad on his lap for a moment. "I think I'm quitting for the day. See you on Monday."

Milo had another hour's work to finish, then he too would quit for the weekend. He had a charter lined up in Homer. He was looking forward to this halibut fishing trip with his teen-age son.

Chapter Fifteen

The metro team wasted no time in getting started on this new project. Captain Withers had briefed his team as soon as the first information came in. Lieutenant Randy Austin was the team information specialist. His responsibility had been to gather any information available on the suspects, Ramon Chavez and Eduardo Sanchez. Other names associated with these two were being checked both here and in Mexico. It was late Friday when the six names on the list were handed to Austin who immediately began a search of known activity for the names on that list.

Of the six names on the list, two stood out as having crossed paths with the team on other occasions. The first name on the list was a nickname: Stroker, an alias used by a dealer whose real name was Elwood Stokes. At age 23 he was young and aggressive. Rumor had it that he had partnered with the son of a local preacher to buy and sell drugs. When business began to boom, Stroker decided he couldn't stand the moral outrage from his partner when he did business at the local high school. The partner went missing and had never been found. Once again the rumor grapevine within the drug community became active. It was said that Stroker had driven his partner to a remote gravel pit and shot him. It was also said that Stroker had taken a three-carat diamond ring from the victim's finger as a souvenir, had it remounted and now wore it in his left ear as an earring.

Another name on the list that got immediate attention was Byron James Miller. He had served time for burglary and armed robbery. While in prison he had made some new friends and learned a few new tricks. After his latest vacation in the Alaska prison system, he had become a runner for a local cocaine dealer. It was his job to deliver and collect money for cocaine used by crack house operators. He had been very good at it. He had also been able to stay out of the prison system for almost four years now. B.J., as he was known on the street, had taken over the distribution to crack houses. That segment of the business in Anchorage was his alone. A couple of up-and-comers had tried to enter the market but were discouraged when B.J.'s goons shoved a 10mm Smith and Wesson automatic up a nostril. On each occasion the new-comers had left the city suddenly.

The other names on the list would have to be researched. They, no doubt, had criminal records but were not known to Lt. Randy Austin.

Electronic surveillance was Sergeant George Kennedy's specialty. He was anxious to try out the new spy camera and sound recording equipment he had recently been issued. George was a product of the U.S. Government. He had spent his college years at Stanford Law School. Upon graduating he applied to the F.B.I. and was accepted. They were the ones who discovered his aptitude for electronics and sponsored him for two years at MIT. A year after he took active duty as an agent, he was involved in a high-speed pursuit on a Florida freeway. The agents were attempting to box the perpetrator's vehicle and to stop him. One of the suspects fired a shotgun into the rear tire of Kennedy's car. The tire blew out and sent the car tumbling and rolling down the freeway. It finally came to rest in the median. George had been riding in the passenger's side, seat belt fastened. During the rollover the door sprung open. The young F.B.I. agent's leg was flung out the open door. The car continued to roll over, smashing his leg bones to splinters. The doctors wanted to remove the leg, but George insisted they attempt to repair it. The bones were rebuilt around steel rods. Two years later he was able to walk and to run on the shattered leg, but the bureau decided he should be retired anyway. He applied to the Alaska State Troopers and was accepted after proving he could pass the agility tests. His training and education moved him up quickly within the ranks of the troopers.

The team had rented a run-down apartment above a pawnshop across the street from the Sombrero Mexican Restaurant. Kennedy carefully set up his equipment in the window. He used Windex to clean a small space on the glass to ensure clear pictures. A tear was made in the pull-down shade to allow the camera a view of the restaurant without being visible from the street. Chavez's office was on the second floor of the restaurant. A window in the office overlooked the street. There were curtains on the window, but they were lacy and pulled back from the center. This made for good pictures and allowed the listening device to function reasonably well. There seemed to be a lot of street noise, but by narrowing the beam of the receiver Kennedy was able to shut most of it out.

A rusted, unmarked van was parked on the street near the condo where Chavez and Sanchez lived. The video equipment taken from the kayaks was adapted to use here. George had done the work of mounting the equipment in the van. It was a skillful and tidy job. The rest of the team would man this stakeout only when the two men were at home.

It was coming together nicely. Each man knew his job and had done it many times before. This time, however, they knew who they were looking for. It was a matter of photographing them coming and going, and following them to see where they went from here. It was the team's duty to dig into the suspects' lives to learn everything they could about the men whose names appeared on the list. It had begun.

After dropping Aliana at the airport, Ben made his way through the Friday traffic toward his apartment in Seattle. As he neared home, it seemed like a good idea to make a stop at the Shamrock Club for a short drink. He called Colin to ask if he could join him for a drink. There had been no answer at Colin's home phone or on his cell phone. So, here he sat alone at a small table in a dark corner of the bar drinking vodka gimlets, dealing with the guilt that seemed to grow exponentially each time he met with Aliana Pedersen.

While waiting for his third gimlet to arrive, he pulled the cell phone from his breast pocket. Colin James number was listed in his speed-dial; therefore, he had no trouble with the number. His friend answered on the fourth ring.

"I'm down at the Shamrock. How about coming down for a drink with me. I'd kinda like to talk." Ben was beginning to slur his words slightly.

"Sure, buddy. I just got out of the shower, so it'll be at least twenty minutes before I can get there. Is that okay?"

"Sure, come on down." The girl brought his drink. "I'll be here waiting."

Colin wasn't much of a drinker. He found he could nurse one drink through an entire cocktail party by adding ice to it every few minutes. His usual drink was club soda with a twist of lime. Ben's drinking habits had been much the same in the past, but recently he had taken to stopping at the bar almost every night as he made his way home from the bank.

The Shamrock is a businessmen's bar. Stockbrokers, insurance men, retail managers and bankers were common among the crowd that assembled here each night to brag about a big deal made or cry about one lost. Colin stopped at the bar and ordered a club soda. While waiting for the drink he spotted Ben, alone at the small table in the back of the bar. The cocktail waitress tapped him on the shoulder and said she would bring his drink. Colin thanked her and made his way to the back of the crowded tavern.

"Hey, old buddy," Ben greeted. It was obvious that the empty glass in front of him was not his first. "Come on... Sit down... I'll buy you a drink."

Colin sat. "I have one coming." Ben had loosened his tie and his suit coat was not buttoned. "What's the occasion, Ben?"

"I just finished the first audit of the one account my department handles and it came out to the penny. Isn't that a good enough reason to celebrate?"

The girl brought Colin's club soda. "Would you like another vodka gimlet, sir?" Ben ordered another.

"Hitting it pretty hard tonight, aren't you, Ben?"

"Hey, man. I got promoted, got a raise and I got a new savings account. I can afford to have some fun."

"Maybe you should take it a little easy," Colin cautioned.

"I'm in the big time now, Colin. Nobody can tell me what to do any more."

"I'm not trying to tell you what to do, Ben. But that vodka is going to kick you in the head in the morning. Why don't you let me drive you home? We can come back for your car in the morning."

The banker took a sip of his fresh drink. "In a while, buddy. In a while." Another drink.

"I thought you had gotten over Tad's accident."

"I have. This has nothing to do with Tad. I'm going to be a millionaire," Ben bragged. "Isn't that worth a celebration?"

"You're not making any sense at all, Ben. You had better let me take you home."

"I'm making perfect sense, Mr. James," he said with a haughty twist of his head and a laugh.

"Not to me, you're not." Colin was losing patience.

"I'm not allowed to explain it to you, but the State of Alaska is going to make me a lot of money. That woman I work with did it for me. Tad was doing it and now it's my turn. Ol' Tad didn't tell us everything, old buddy. Now I have his job and his benefits."

"You've had enough, Ben." Colin stood and took Ben by the arm. "Come on, I'll take you home."

Ben was unsteady on his feet. "Okay, but remember, you have to keep it secret. You can't tell anyone what I said." He was giggling and waving his index finger in Colin's face.

It was late when the Boeing engineer helped his friend up the stairs to his condo. Ben supplied the key, but Colin opened the door. He supported the wobbly drunk through the apartment and into the bedroom. He pulled the shoes from his friend's feet and covered him with a blanket. He looked back before turning out the light. *This isn't like Ben. I wonder what brought this on. And, what was he rambling about.* He shook his head, turned out the light and left the apartment.

It was late Saturday afternoon by the time George Kennedy, along with his partner Don "Paddy" McGuire, completed the fine tuning of all the new equipment. George had encountered some difficulty with the sound and recording system. As it turned out, the problem wasn't with the equipment sent by Boeing, but with a cable connector used to plug into AST's recording devices. Once this problem was repaired with a new part from Radio Shack, things came together quickly. It then became a waiting game for the two troopers. With the equipment in place, and working to advertised specs, the afternoon was devoted to learning the capabilities of the science fiction electronics.

The surveillance revealed nothing new. Chavez was in his office approving supply orders for the coming week. He was interrupted several times by the restaurant manager who, it seemed, was unable to make any management decisions on his own. The first problem was with one of the chefs. He wasn't using the prescribed garnish on the dishes he prepared. Chavez showed a great deal of patience in dealing with the young manager and gave him several options from which to choose a solution. Several similar problems arose during the afternoon, and each time the same tack was used by Chavez to address the problem. It was later learned that this was the club manager's first day in his new job after being promoted from headwaiter. As the afternoon wore on, it appeared the new manager was taking command of his new position. By early evening the visits consisted of reports of what he had done to resolve whatever problem had arisen. Chavez seemed to like the young man and with each step in his progress gave him a verbal pat on the back.

Saturday night was a good night for the dinner crowd. Chavez had walked through the restaurant several times during the evening, greeting patrons and visiting with regular customers. It was late and he was back in his office when the telephone rang.

"Ramon Chavez," he answered.

There was a pause then, he replied in Spanish, "Hola, Senior Dante."

The conversation lasted several minutes. George and Paddy were both frustrated by the fact that the entire conversation was conducted in a language they couldn't understand. It was further complicated by the fact that they only heard one end of this intercourse. A note was made to have the Captain procure a warrant for a wiretap on this telephone. George cursed himself for not making prior arrangement for an interpreter. That problem, too, would have to be addressed by Captain Withers.

Kennedy and McGuire remained in the apartment until well after closing time at midnight. Chavez stayed in his office checking the daily receipts and balancing the cash. This would prove to be a daily ritual for the conscientious club owner. This man, George thought, was a good businessman and would have been successful without dealing in drugs. It was amazing to him that some men couldn't resist the lure of easy money.

It appeared that everything was in place and working. It was now a matter of waiting until the next shipment came to the restaurant. That was supposed to happen some time this coming week if the information in hand was accurate. The metro team would now settle into the routine of watching and waiting.

The sun was shining brightly in the Seattle area on that Saturday morning. Ben Gerlitz awoke with a throbbing headache. His mouth tasted like a herd of camels had spent the night in there. His shoes, suit jacket and necktie were off, but he was still dressed. He started to sit up then fell back on the bed, his head throbbing like a hundred jackhammers. Drinking wasn't one of his usual bad habits. Slowly he arose again. This time cautiously standing, trying to remember how he got home. Shuffling into the bathroom, he brushed his teeth, trying to obliterate the taste in his mouth. It was no use.

A hot shower and four aspirin helped a little. His head pain was abating, but his stomach was on fire now. He opted for two glasses of milk and a piece of toast instead of the usual coffee and cold cereal. The night before was a fog. He sort of remembered Colin being there, but wasn't sure. He was still trying to put it all together when he opened the living room drapes to squint at the bright sun. It hurt his eyes and he turned his head away. Gradually his eyes became accustomed to the day. With a slice of toast in his hand, he walked through the patio doors to a small deck overlooking the condo parking lot. It was then he noticed his car was missing. First it was panic, thinking someone had stolen his car, then uncertainty. He didn't remember driving home. *Colin. Colin was there, I'm sure of it.*

"I wondered what time you would get up and around. How are you feeling this morning?" Colin asked when he heard his friend's voice on the phone.

"I've died and gone to hell," he replied. "Were you there last night?"

"Yes, I drove you home. I've never seen you drink that much, Ben."

"I don't think you'll see it again, soon. I'm too young to feel this bad." Both men laughed lightly. "Do you have any idea where I left my car? It's not in my parking space here."

"I drove you home. Your car is still at the Shamrock. I'll come get you and take you to it when you feel up to it. I'd like to talk with you anyway. I came to talk last night, but you were having too much fun," another small laugh.

"I'll be ready when you get here," Ben said. "You can fill me in on what I said last night."

Just over an hour later the two were on their way back toward the downtown area. They stopped at Denny's for some breakfast. Colin ate, but Ben had only juice. His stomach wasn't ready for anything else. The two men sat in a corner booth away from most of the morning customers.

"Do you want to tell me what set you off?" Colin asked his friend.

"What did I say last night?"

"You said a lot of things that didn't make much sense, but I was able to get enough to know you're in some kind of trouble. I'm your friend, Ben. If there's anything I can do to help you, all you have to do is ask."

Ben was looking into the bottom of his orange juice glass. "I can't talk about it, Colin."

"You had better talk to someone, Ben. You can't go on like you were last night. Whatever you say will be between us." Colin was genuinely concerned for his friend. "I know you wanted to talk last night, that's why you called me."

Ben didn't remember calling him. "I'd really appreciate it if you could keep last night just between us. It was a mistake." He looked out the window and muttered in a low tone, "Right now my whole life seems like a mistake."

"Well, you had better get a grip on it, buddy. You can't take many nights like the last one." Colin didn't know what to say that would help. "I'm here for you, anytime."

They left the café and drove to the Shamrock, parking alongside Ben's car. The banker opened the door to get out, then turned back to Colin.

"Thanks for everything, Colin. If I can't work this out on my own, you'll be the one I talk with." He climbed from the car and unlocked his own. He started the engine, gave a small wave of his hand and drove off in the direction of his condo.

Chapter Sixteen

The Alaska legislature had not met since the end of the session the first of May. That, however, didn't mean the governor had nothing to do. His schedule was filled with executive duties from early morning until late in the evening. This governor believed in being active in the affairs of the state. This meant meeting with individuals and groups, each of whom believed their cause was the most important one in the state. But that was, after all, his job. Don Cummings, his chief aide, managed this busy schedule. His was the voice on the phone when Aliana called.

"Good morning, Don," she greeted. "Can you work me in this morning?"

"Aliana! Good to hear your voice." It had been two weeks since he had spoken with the deputy director of finance. "Let me check…" a pause. "Can you make it at 10:15?"

"I'll be there." She checked the clock on her desk. It was now 8:05.

She consulted the yellow legal pad filled with notes of items she wanted to attend to today. In the margin opposite the item marked *call the governor's Office,* she made another note, *10:15.*

Several file folders were stacked on her desk. Each one had a cover sheet held to the front by a paper clip. One by one she reviewed each one of the files, making notes about action to be taken in each case.

The Soldotna office of the DOT was at it again, she found as she reached the fourth folder in the stack. She set this file aside, found a fresh page on her pad on which to make some notes for Pam St. John. Both Pam and Marge Dawson would be in the office this afternoon for a conference. These notes made, she dealt with the final two folders on her desk. It was almost time for her to walk to the office of Paul Talmadge, Governor of the State of Alaska.

Her briefcase contained the certified copies of the latest bank audit. This meeting would be short; its only purpose was to deliver the audit and a report on its contents to Paul, thus saving him the time of reading the columns of figures. He had better things to do, and it was her job to make sure everything in the audit was verified and correct. Her assessment had been checked and certified by Mr. Stackhaus of SeaFirst Bank. The governor would be pleased. She dropped a fresh yellow note pad into the case and closed the lid.

Light rain met her as she walked from the accounting office and headed toward the governor's neatly appointed sanctum. Don would have sent a car for her, but she liked the walk, even in the rain. She shook the water from her umbrella as she reached the top of the steps. Outside the door she closed the parasol and removed her damp coat. Don was waiting for her in the anteroom and ushered her into the boss' office. She refused an offer of coffee before he left her and the governor alone.

"You look wonderful this morning, Aliana," the governor greeted.

"Well, thank you, sir," she replied, opening her briefcase.

"And how did things go in Seattle?" he asked curiously. "Is this new guy going to work out for us?"

"He's not a Tad Morton, but I think he'll do fine." She put the folder containing the audit on his desk, closed the lid on her case and placed the legal pad atop it. "I had a talk with him and he understands the importance of the account. His people are the same ones that did the work when Tad was there, so I don't anticipate any serious problems."

"Are the accounts running smoothly?"

"Do you mean the checks and the transfers being made on time?" she asked for clarity.

"Yes." He flipped open the folder, looking inside. He really didn't know what he was looking for, just that it contained a thick volume of figures and totals.

"We're well within our parameters." She confirmed. "Less than two percent of the contracts are dropping outside the criteria. I have reviewed every one of those cases and found that, in each case, it was the responsibility of the contractor and not the contracting agency that caused the lapse. With one exception, we have paid no interest or penalty during the past quarter. A pretty good record, don't you think?"

"You and your gang have done a splendid job, Aliana. I want to congratulate you on turning the department around, especially in this short period of time." The governor was now making a note on his note pad. "Please, pass along my appreciation to your group."

"I'll do that, Paul. They'll be pleased that you noticed."

"I plan to do better than that. I've made a note to give your unit a special award for their good work."

"Like I said, they'll be pleased."

"I don't want you, or them, to think that this is just a carrot to keep them working hard. I'm sincere with this. Your group has saved the state many millions of dollars. With tight money and the legislature unwilling to pass an income tax, this has been my best source of added income. It was always there, but you and your little band of shepherds have managed to keep us from losing it through mismanagement." He grinned. "After all, that's why I hired you. I knew you could do it, if it was at all possible."

"Maybe I should buy a silk slit skirt," she joked. "The department heads all call me the *Dragon Lady.*"

"Maybe I can cure some of that. I'll have each of the commissioners advise their department heads of just how much you have been able to add to each of their budgets. I don't think they realize how much money we were losing. Perhaps the facts will change their attitudes."

"I really don't care what they think of me personally, just as long as you know I'm doing the job you pay me to do." She had written nothing on the new pad atop her briefcase. "Do you know of any area we've been weak in? Anything we've missed?"

"No, as far as I know, things are going well."

"I'll get back to it, then." She opened her case and dropped the pad inside. "I'll try to keep us on track." He stood, they gently shook hands and she walked from the office.

The rain had almost stopped, making the walk back to her office very pleasant. Her mind drifted away during the walk. She thought of Rube. It had been nearly a week since she had talked to him. She vowed to call him after lunch.

The staff meeting was scheduled as her first item of business after lunch. Lunch today consisted of half a sandwich and an orange eaten at her desk. The receptionist was showing Pam St. John and Marge Dawson into the office when Aliana came out of the private washroom. She was drying her hands on a paper towel as she walked.

"Pam, Marge," she acknowledged with a nod of her head. She dropped the paper towel into the wastebasket. Each of the guests had a handful of papers and file folders with her.

"Good to see you back, Ms. Pedersen." The first greeting came from Marge Dawson.

"Yes, it is, Boss," Pam added. "We don't have anyone to blame for our mistakes when you're out of town." The pair giggled. "Did you do anything raucous and obscene in Seattle?"

"None of your business, but if I had, you'd be the first one I'd tell." Aliana opened a fresh bottle of Diet 7UP that had been sitting on her desk. "Marge, I had a call this morning from the Commissioner of Fish and Game. He and some of his managers attended your class last week. He was impressed. There were only positive responses from the attendees in his department. He wanted me to tell you that biologists aren't fiscally oriented as a rule, but they reacted well to your insights and how they related to their scientific budgets," she chuckled. "You pierced the void, to use his words."

"Thank you. I was really apprehensive before the meetings. This is the first one of these I've done alone. Once I got started, though, it seemed to smooth out." Marge was the organizer of the group. She knew how to cover the most information in the shortest period of time and with the least amount of confusion.

"I'll expect to see the written review by Friday."

"I'll have it by Wednesday, if the office stays quiet."

"When is the next training seminar?" Aliana asked.

"Two weeks, in Fairbanks," Marge said after checking her notes inside the top file folder. "Do you want to do that one?"

"I'll let you know, but right now I'm leaning toward letting you handle it. I'll have an answer when you bring me the report on the Anchorage meeting."

"I have two cases I'm working on right now. They don't seem to be problem cases, just routing problems—one in Nome and one in Cantwell. Again, I don't think these are personnel problems, only processing difficulties due to the remoteness of these two stations," Marge advised her superior. "If you have nothing further for me, I need to contact these managers this afternoon."

"Go ahead and do what you need to do. And, good job on the Anchorage training seminar." Aliana took a drink from the soda. "Keep me advised on Nome and Cantwell." She made a note to follow up on this one.

Pam waited for her co-worker to leave before beginning. Aliana found a fresh page on her note pad.

The tiny blonde shuffled through the file folders to come up with the one she wanted to discuss with her boss. "That DOT guy in Soldotna must not have gotten the message. I had a call from the secretary. She told me that her boss is delaying payments on four local contracts. She also told me that everything is on his desk and that he's locked it in his file cabinet and refused to give her the final billings to approve and forward to us. I think this guy has too much bureaucratic DNA." Pam was frustrated because she had just returned from Soldotna with assurances from him that the delays would no longer be a factor. However, if the problem could be dealt with right away, there would be no penalties to be paid.

"What, exactly, is the problem up there?" Aliana was writing while talking.

"I don't have facts, only suspicions sprinkled with some information provided by the secretary. The secretary tells me that the manager has a guide business. He takes fishermen on the Kenai River. He can make a lot more money during the summer being a guide than sitting in his office doing contract completion verifications," Pam provided.

"I asked you, when you came back last time, if I should contact his supervisor. You said at that time you thought the problem was handled. It's only been a couple of weeks and his office is back on the list." Aliana reviewed the situation to assure that the two were operating with the same facts. "What are your feelings now?"

"I've looked up the four contracts we're dealing with. If these go into default, we're liable for penalties amounting to almost 50% of the total contract. That's unacceptable by any standard. The penalties and interest are going to be generated by the neglect of one man. Unless he can explain his actions differently from my assumptions, I recommend that you have him replaced by the Southcentral Director."

"Give me the files, and show me the contracts we're dealing with."

Pam opened the folder and placed it on the boss' desk for her to read. "I've marked the four contracts and provided a thumbnail review of each one."

Aliana checked the clock. "Give me an hour to contact DOT in Anchorage. I'll let you know what action the Director will be taking."

"I'll be at my desk, just give me a call." Pam St. John picked up the rest of her papers and left the office.

The boss-lady thumbed through her Rolodex for the number of the Southcentral Director in Anchorage. He was in.

"Fred, Aliana Pedersen. How are things in the other Capital City?" She had dealt with him enough to greet him by his first name.

"Aliana, good to hear from you." He liked this lady, but knew she would not have called if there weren't a problem somewhere in his jurisdiction.

"How's the wife. I hear she's been in the hospital. Was it anything serious?"

"Just doing some tests. She took a couple of nasty falls. And, she had a spell of being dizzy and disoriented, but it turned out that it was her new glasses. We had them replaced and she's fine now, thanks for asking. What can I do for you?"

"That Davidoff fellow you have in Soldotna, what sort of person is he?" There was groundwork to be laid before getting a man replaced. Supervisors usually protected their kingdoms.

"He's a nice enough guy. A little short on personal initiative and deep into personal objectives, but a good personnel manager." Fred knew his man well. "Why do you ask?"

"We're coming up on the end of he month and he has four contracts to review. We have word that he has locked up the paperwork and won't have it done. I've checked the fine print and we're going to lose close to $80,000 in penalties and interest in the event we don't pay on time, and time is running out."

"Have you talked to him about this?"

"I had one of my assistants in his office for a few days. She thought at the time that the problem was solved and asked me to give him a chance. That doesn't seem to have worked. We're only two weeks down the road and the same situation has come up again. Only this time it amounts to a lot more revenue loss."

"Do you have the contract numbers handy?" Fred was taking notes of his own now.

She gave him a rundown on the contract numbers, the amounts, the participants, dates and the penalty figures. He had copies of the papers in his files, but this saved him a lot of time.

"I'll get back with you this afternoon," he assured her before breaking the connection.

It was nearly 5 when Fred returned her call. He had talked with the secretary who had been instructed to locate her boss, no matter where he was, and to get those contracts reviewed and out by fax. Fred was unable to justify the actions of his subordinate. This amounted to two cases of administrative action directed at him in the last couple of weeks. Fred had information that the man had falsified his time sheets and claimed he was working when, in fact, he had been on the river, guiding. This action coupled with his disregard for departmental protocol in dealing with his assigned duties had prompted the DOT Director to replace him at once. Fred had not decided on a replacement, but had a short-list from which to choose.

"I apologize for not picking up on this problem before now," Fred offered. "I hope we've taken care of the immediate and the long-range problems. You should have what you need, by fax, today."

"I thank you for your prompt response to the problem, Fred. Say hello to your wife for me."

It was well past normal office hours now. Aliana pressed the numbers for Pam's desk. She was still in the office.

"What did you tell Soldotna?" Pam asked. "I just got the fax with everything on it. That was quick."

"Is everything there?"

"It looks like it. How did you get him to respond so fast?"

"I told Fred what was going on. He checked it out and replaced him. It seems the information you had was good and that the assumptions you made were accurate. Good work."

"Did they replace him or fire him?"

"It seems he's been falsifying his time cards, taking checks for working when he was with clients on the river, guiding. Fred terminated him."

"Sorry about that, but I guess he had it coming. The secretary will be happy." Pam stood and started for the door. "I'll get this off the to the bank by fax right away. See you tomorrow." She danced out the door, waving a handful of papers as she went.

It had been a long day. Aliana checked the time. After dinner she would call Rube. She was out of the office in a matter of minutes. The streets were wet from the intermittent rain, but it had stopped now and the sun was trying to peek through the clouds. It was a welcome walk after a long day spent in her office chair.

Chapter Seventeen

Summertime in the city of Anchorage is an interlude of scenic splendor unmatched anywhere in the world. Late July produces more than eighteen hours of sunshine for those who choose to enjoy it. North America's tallest peak is visible from the heart of the city on days when the mountain is clear of clouds. For tourists, the long days make vacations seem a little longer. For those who live and work in the city, it means driving to and from work in the daylight.

It was straight up 8 AM, and Rueben Hayes had been in his office for more than two hours. His morning ritual was interrupted by the ringing intercom. Milo summoned him to his office with some urgency in his voice. When Rube arrived, Captain Stan Withers, as well as Captain Thomas, greeted him.

"Morning, Stan," Rube greeted. "What's up, Cap'n?" he asked, turning to Milo.

"How's your schedule look for the next couple of days, Rube?" his supervisor asked.

"Just the usual stuff, mostly administrative. Why, what's going on?"

"Stan and I have been on the phone with DEA and Customs in Seattle. We got their attention right away when we started making background checks on Chavez and Sanchez. The feds have an investigation of their own underway. They've assured me that they don't want to interfere with what we have in progress here, but they don't want us to blow their investigation either. They want me to send two people to Seattle to meet with them. My first choice is you and Stan."

"I'll check my calendar, but I can't think of anything that would stop me. Lou Balfore can cover the daily stuff," his mind was running over his calendar. "I don't have any court dates for two weeks; grand jury a week from Friday."

"Check it out and let me know. I'll get you two on the airline to Seattle this afternoon. Is that satisfactory with you, Stan?" Milo asked.

"I just have to pack a bag. How long do you think this will take?" the other captain responded.

"I don't know for sure. I think I'd plan for at least Friday, maybe Saturday."

Rube stepped to the door. "I'll go check my schedule. Be right back."

He found nothing on his appointment book or in his daily activity log that couldn't be changed. While in his office, he had the dispatcher notify Sergeant Balfore to come back to headquarters as soon as possible. Balfore, as it turned out was just pulling out of the headquarters parking area. He made a U-turn and returned to the office. By telephone, Rube notified his boss that he was clear to go to Seattle.

Sergeant Hayes was busy writing telephone numbers in his notebook when the other sergeant poked his head through the door.

"Hey, Rube. What's up?"

"I have to leave town for a couple of days. Can you cover the office until the end of the week"

"Sure," Balfore answered. "Can I ask where you're heading?"

"Nothing mysterious," Rube replied. "Stan Withers and I have to go to Seattle for a couple of days for some kind of meeting with the feds. We didn't know about it until this morning. This isn't going to hurt your schedule, is it?"

"No, the corporal can supervise the road troopers and I can take care of any personnel problems from here."

"It makes me worry that I can be replaced that easily," Rube joked.

By 3 in the afternoon, Milo had dropped the two men at the Ted Stevens International Airport. Each of them had a small bag to check and a carry-on. Reservations had been made at the Edgewater Inn, Stan Withers' choice of lodging. A rental car was reserved at the Hertz counter. Like all good Alaskans, the two men exchanged fishing tales on the three-hour flight, just to pass the time. Airline seats didn't allow the privacy to discuss official business, though they each had questions to ask the other about the up-coming meetings in Seattle. It was past 9 when they met in the hotel dining room.

The two men met again, in the dining room, early the next morning.

"How'd you sleep?" Captain Withers asked.

"Great. How about you?"

"Me, too," Withers answered as the two were seated near an ocean-facing window. "What do you think the feds want us for? I've been thinking about that, and I think we may have tripped onto something of theirs. This Sombrero case is getting muddy."

"I've thought about it too. You're right. You'd have a better handle on that than I. I guess we'll just have to wait and see."

The restaurant began to fill and conversation moved to other things. Breakfast was good and the coffee excellent while the view, with ferryboats and ships coming and going, was breathtaking.

"I need to make a couple of calls today," Rube mentioned. "I should personally thank the two guys who donated the video equipment to us."

"That's a great idea. I can't make it this evening, but I'll buy dinner for all of you. I owe you, and them, that much. George Kennedy tells me the equipment you got from Boeing is the best he has ever seen, even when he was in the FBI."

It was 9 AM sharp when the two walked into the Federal Building. They were issued visitor passes and escorted to the fourth floor. Three men were waiting in the small conference room when the troopers entered. At the head of the table sat a short, stocky man with salt and pepper hair. When he stood it was plain that he wasn't overweight but had the physique of a weight lifter.

"Come in gentlemen," his voice was surprisingly shrill. "Can I get you anything before we begin?" The troopers declined. "I'm agent Brownfield, Fred Brownfield. Most people call me Fritz," he introduced himself with a friendly smile.

Captain Withers shook his hand, "How do you do. I'm Captain Stan Withers and this is Sergeant Rueben Hayes."

Another handshake, "Just call me Rube."

The other men in the room were introduced. One was Cal Bennett, an FBI agent. He was a tall, thin man with deep-inset, almost black eyes. The other was Tom Simpson of the DEA. There were more handshakes.

Simpson was young, not yet 30, blonde, and despite his friendly smile he seemed to have a no-nonsense personality. Each wore the federal law enforcement uniform: dark suit, white shirt and conservative tie. The troopers wore their own version: blue blazers with brass buttons, white shirts, blue tie and gray pants.

"First of all," Fritz opened, "let's dispel any hostilities between agencies here. This meeting is for the benefit of everyone involved. Local departments sometimes get shortchanged by our agencies, and I don't want that to happen. I hope you feel the same way and we can get on with business without jurisdictional frictions."

"I don't have a problem with that," Withers replied, caution flags already jumping up in front of him.

Brownfield had a thick folder on the table in front of him. Opening it he removed a stack of fingerprint cards. "Your agency recently asked us for information on a list of men who now reside in Alaska. Two of those men are subjects in an ongoing investigation by the FBI and the DEA. We'll give you anything you want and need in this case; however, in return we ask that you help us to protect our investigation which, by the way, is not in your state."

Withers looked at Rube. "Then I can't see how we can affect anything in your case."

It was Tom Simpson's turn. "None of this is to get out of this room." He paused for a sign of agreement from the two troopers. "You asked for information on Ramon Chavez and Eduardo Sanchez. These two men are in the employ of a Mexican Mafia Don by the name Alejandro Romano. Romano is probably the most influential criminal in all of Mexico."

Again Stan looked at Rube. "We've never heard of this Romano. At least I can't ever recall hearing his name." Rube nodded in agreement.

Simpson went on, "You may have heard of him by the name of Dante. He has his hands in every dirty enterprise in Mexico. He controls the street thugs in every major city in the country. He has a piece of all the drugs grown in, or transported through, Mexico. The Minister of Customs owes his position to Dante and in turn does him a lot of favors. That's how the drugs are shipped out of the country so easily. In the case you're working on, drugs are coming from Mexico, right?"

Captain Withers provided the answer. "Chavez hires girls in Mexico. He brings them to Alaska to work in his two restaurants. They rotate out at a rate of two girls a week. Each week two new girls arrive to take their place. The word we have is that the girls don't know they are carrying drugs. We suspect that they're being transported in 25-pound tins of ground corn flour, hand carried by each of the girls. The tins are sealed and have inspection stamps and paperwork from the Mexican Department of Customs. They are never opened because of the inspection certifications and the fact that it is food-stuffs. The girls deliver the tins to the restaurant when they report to work."

"You guys know more about this than we gave you credit for." Simpson meant this as a compliment. "We want Dante. We're working with DEA in Mexico, and with the new President there, to dismantle his entire crime network. But, he's like an octopus with a hundred arms, it's impossible to tell if you've cut them all off. You may not be aware that he is the head of the syndicate smuggling immigrants into this country. Almost 25% of those people he brings are dead when they arrive. This guy is guilty of mass murder. He's into prostitution, murder, drugs and who-knows-what. Hell, he even buys stolen cars. He has a network of thieves working in the big cities down south. They steal high-dollar cars and ship them to Mexico; there they repaint them and sell them. Like I said, if it's illegal and it's happening in Mexico, then probably Dante is making money on the deal."

It was Bennett's turn. "If he kept everything in Mexico, we wouldn't be involved, but, like your case, his business keeps spilling over into the U.S. of A."

"What is it you want from us," Rube asked in a quiet voice.

Brownfield again. "We want to work with you on this. We're offering you all our resources and access to our files. We'll lend you any manpower you require. We will assist you in any way possible. You will maintain control of the case. Anything that happens in Alaska is yours to handle, unless you say differently. We reserve the right to prosecute anyone arrested on federal charges, but in addition to the charges you file."

Brownfield paused a moment to allow the two visitors to digest what had just been said. "The truth is, we need your help to nail the lid on Dante's coffin. We can do that with the help of Chavez and Sanchez. The other sad truth is that we plan to make a deal with them, but only on federal charges. You nail them on drug and racketeering charges and they go away for those, we won't interfere."

"We're going to need some time to think about this," Stan answered. You understand that anything I agree to will be subject to approval by my department and the attorney general of my state."

"We understand that," Brownfield replied. "And, we agree to those terms. I suggest that you take this file and look it over. Can you have an answer for us by tomorrow?"

Stan Withers took the file folder. "I'll do my best."

Arrangements were made to meet again the following morning, same place, same time. In the parking lot, before starting the engine, the two men could only look at each other. Each had questions, which, as it turned out, were the same questions.

Withers handed the file folder to Hayes. "It can't be this easy, can it? Do you think we're getting the whole story?" he asked the sergeant.

Rube grinned. "My past experience says no, and this story has red flags all over it. The only reason I give any credence to it at all is the fact that they seemed to be negotiating from desperation."

"That's the same feeling I got." Stan moved the car out of the lot and pointed toward the hotel. "Let's go back and give the file some study. Maybe we can find some clue as to what they really want."

Rube checked the time. "Stan, if you don't mind, I want to call Colin James, the Boeing engineer who got us the video equipment. If he's free I want to buy him lunch. You're welcome to join us, if you like."

"I appreciate that, Rube, but I think I'll stay here and go over this file. I'd sure like to know where these guys are coming from. Somehow I feel like we're about to become the butt of some enormously cruel joke. I'd like to avoid that if I could."

"I'll use the car, if it's okay with you." Stan assured him it was. The two men went into the hotel where Rube called Colin James.

The restaurant was at the south end of town in the business park area. Rube parked the rental in front of the place, which was made from long-ago retired railroad passenger cars. Inside was also a railroad motif. The waiter asked if he was here to meet with Mr. James, then led him to a table in the adjoining area, another railroad car.

They introduced themselves and shook hands. Rube studied the pictures on the walls as he sat.

"Nice place," he said.

"It's usually quiet here and the food is good. Most Seattle visitors like the atmosphere."

Rube studied the menu. "I want to thank you for the equipment you sent us. We have the spy-camera at work right now. In fact, one of the kayak cameras is out on the same case. Our department was in a real bind and you saved our bacon. I want to thank you personally for what you did."

"You're more than welcome. My company likes to help public agencies whenever possible. If there is ever anything I can do in the future, please don't hesitate to call me. Besides, I owe you for what you did when Tad was killed. That was such a tragic and unexpected accident. It devastated Ben. In fact he's still having some problems with it."

"Oh, what kind of problems?" Rube put his menu down. A waiter took their order.

"It's nothing I can really put my finger on, but last weekend he got drunk and called me. I drove him home. That evening he made a couple of comments that just didn't seem to fit." Colin sipped his coffee. "Ben doesn't usually drink very much. We used to kid him about it."

"Do you remember what the comments were about?"

Colin considered what he was about to say. He didn't like talking about his friend.

"I hate gossip, and I hope you don't think that's why I brought this up, but he made a comment about *that woman I work with.* I took that to mean the woman in charge of the Alaska account his department deals with. I've never heard him make a statement like that. There were a couple of other innuendoes, too. They didn't make any sense to me because they were out of context, but they seemed to refer to his job. Maybe all this is my imagination, but it just didn't seem like Ben."

"I know the lady in charge of that department, and she's really a super lady. I find it difficult to believe he could have a problem with her." Rube realized immediately he had just made a statement based on personal feeling and not the facts. "Would you like me to talk with him to see if I can find out what's bothering him?"

"Would you do that?" James asked. "It may be nothing, and I hope that's true, but something seems to be eating at him. I'd like to help him if I could."

"I have some official business this afternoon, but I'll see about having dinner with him tonight. I'll call him."

Lunch was paid for by the State of Alaska. Rube drove back to the hotel, thinking about his lunch conversation with Colin James. Something had triggered the suspicions about Ben Gerlitz. Everyone has a little voice inside that speaks whenever something is wrong. Colin's little voice had spoken to him. Years of police experience had taught him that your little inner voice is seldom wrong. The cause may not be apparent, but one should never ignore the little voice.

Rube tapped on the hotel room door. It opened and Stan invited him in.

"Have you found anything in the file?" Rube asked.

"There isn't much about Sanchez and Chavez," Withers began, "but this Dante fella is a really busy person. He has his hands in every kind of dirty enterprise you can name. His operations extend all over the country of Mexico and to a couple of neighboring countries as well. They have a pretty good case against him. It doesn't say what evidence is available, but the facts are all here. I think the feds have someone in the organization, probably DEA. I also think that, whoever it is, is pretty close to Dante. This information comes from inside the management circle of his organization."

"Do you think we should go along with them?" Rube asked. "If they deal it all away, it could be a wasted effort."

"We've both been down that road before, haven't we?" The Captain gave a cynical chuckle. "Remember that gal from Kenai? The one with all the dogs."

"Yeah, we spent a lot of resources on that one and had it dealt away in court by the DEA. *To catch a bigger fish,* I think was the term they used. The judge was going to throw you in jail for contempt on that one, as I recall." Rube was laughing.

"Don't remind me." Stan laughed with him. "I don't really trust them, but we're already investigating our case. I say let's go ahead. I don't know why they want us to work with them, but we really don't have anything to lose at this point. If they want to snatch our case and deal it away there really isn't much we can do about it in any event. It looks like they need us worse than we need them on this one."

Rube thumbed through the file. Stan was right. Cases were pending in every part of Mexico, as well as California, Arizona and Texas. A charge against Dante for arranging shipments to Alaska would only be redundant and costly, and in the end not be of much benefit to the state. If the federal government wanted Dante, then they could have him. The two troopers agreed to cooperate with them, if for no other reason than to acquire a huge trump card they could play at some future date. It could be fun to own the hammer being held over a couple of federal agencies.

Chapter Eighteen

The Seattle banker had agreed to meet Rube for dinner. The trooper had showered and changed clothes and was waiting in the lobby when Ben arrived. Rube spotted him as he entered and was walking across the carpeted lobby when the banker recognized him. The two men said hello and shook hands.

"Good to see you again, Ben."

"Good to see you, too. What brings you to Seattle?"

"We have some meetings at the Federal Building," Rube informed his companion. "I thought as long as I was here I should buy you dinner and properly thank you for the generous donation. The equipment you donated is already in use. I can't thank you enough. You and Colin James really pulled us out of a dilemma."

"You're more than welcome. Your department may as well get some use out of it. I'll never use it again," Ben hung his head modestly. "Anyway… do you have a preference for dinner?"

"The food's pretty good here," Rube replied.

The two men moved to the dining room where a waiter seated them. Close behind him came another waiter with water, menus and an inquiry, "Would you like something besides water to drink?" Ben ordered a double vodka gimlet. Rube settled for the water.

"Is it okay to ask what you are using the video equipment for?" Ben asked, sipping his first drink.

"We're investigating a big drug case. I can't say much more than that. The investigation is underway right now." Rube never liked discussing cases, even ones long closed, with anyone outside the department.

"I understand," the banker replied, taking another long drink.

"I'd like you to know that I've flown down to Holgate Glacier several times to check for any signs of your friend. There's nothing. I haven't seen a life jacket or any other debris in the water or on the beaches. I'm sorry. There was just too much ice. I doubt we will ever see anything."

Ben was ordering his second vodka gimlet. "Thank you for looking. I've dealt with it. His death was an accident and there was nothing anyone could have done. I try to think of the good times we had together. Tad was a good friend."

"How's the new job?" Rube nudged.

"The department is running smoothly. That's more to the credit of the staff than to my abilities. I didn't realize how much responsibility this account required. Everything about the account is computerized, but data must be constantly updated. Every day there are new contracts and contractors to be entered. Did you know that the annual cash flow through this account is now more than two billion, with a B, dollars annually? Of course, the summer contracting season is, by far, the busiest time of the year. There are four major highway projects in progress this summer. Those projects alone account for almost $200 million. Daily, we accept funds from the state's general fund to pay for completed portions of contracts, payroll and project commodity purchases. If we move a decimal point, right or left one position, it can mean an error of tens of thousands of dollars." There were shorter intervals between sips now.

"It sounds like an incredibly stressful job." Rube commented. "You work with Ms. Pedersen, don't you?"

"Hmph, yeah, I work with her." There was a new tone in his voice.

"You don't sound too happy about it. When I met her in Anchorage, I thought she was really nice."

"Yeah, well don't turn your back on that blue-eyed barracuda." The vodka was working now.

"I thought she helped you to get promoted," Rube prodded.

"She did that alright." Ben's attitude was bordering on anger. "Promoted to boot-licking lackey," he raised his glass in salute. "But, the money's good."

"Does that mean things are not well down at the bank?" Rube was deeply interested now. "Is something wrong with the account?"

"Sergeant, we just had an audit that came out to the penny. Things are perfect." Ben maintained his cynical tone. "But, like you, I can't ethically talk about what goes on in the bank."

Rube judged he had carried this conversation about as far as it was going to get tonight. So far dinner had consisted of water for him and vodka for his guest.

"I think I had better drive you home," Rube suggested.

"Okay, just let me finish this one."

Rube used Ben's cell phone to call a cab for the return to the hotel. During the ride back he tried to make sense of the ramblings of the banker. Clearly, something was eating at the man. What had happened to cause him to make insinuations like this about Aliana? She had gone out of her way to get him the position as head of this department. He claimed the work was going smoothly. Aliana had been to the bank several times in the past few weeks, but she gave no indication anything was wrong. But Ben was definitely stressed to the breaking point. Colin had noticed it, and it had surfaced tonight with a little gentle prodding from Rube. It was something he would have to look into when he returned to Alaska. There was a Red Robin about a mile from the hotel. Rube had the cab drop him there; a bleu cheese burger would make a great dinner.

It was late when he returned to his hotel room. Inside he turned on the television. With the sound muted, he flipped the channels until he came upon a program on Fishing The Northwest. A local guide was fishing for salmon in Puget Sound. He and his guest were hooking and releasing Coho Salmon with incredible frequency. Rube walked down the hall to the soda machine and purchased a Coke. His thoughts were on Aliana. Setting the open can on the nightstand, he dialed her number in Juneau. On the fourth ring, the answering machine delivered its message.

After the beep… "Hi, Aliana… Rube. It was nothing important, I just wanted to say hello. I'm in Seattle tonight and I hope to finish with business tomorrow. With luck I'll be home tomorrow evening. I'll call you then. Bye."

He sipped his Coke and watched the muted television. It was difficult to concentrate on the show. His mind kept returning to the ramblings of Ben Gerlitz. How could he say those things about Aliana. Was he just in over his head with this promotion? Was he blaming her for his own shortcomings? He had no answers, only more questions. His head was scarcely on the pillow when his mind fled to the arms of Morphius.

The sun was shining and the air fresh and crisp as the men drove toward the federal building. Rube rolled his window down to breathe in the fresh salt smell in the air.

"Do we still agree that we should accept this offer from the feds?" Stan asked.

"It's impossible to know if they're telling us the whole truth, but assuming they are, we might find them useful. Remember, our witness is a Mexican National who is about to leave this country. It would be nice to have some clout if we had to bring her back. I don't think she'll refuse, because she wants to marry a U.S. citizen, but we have no control over what will happen when she goes home to Mexico. The other thing is that, if the feds want to take our case out of state court, they can just do it. We don't have much in the way of leverage with them." Rube's view was cynical.

Stan wheeled the rental car into the spot marked *Visitors, U.S. Government Property, Official Use Only.* Inside the building they were subjected to the same ritual as the day before. The receptionist signed them in and issued them visitor passes. She allowed them through the electronically controlled door where they were met and escorted to the conference room on the fourth floor.

Fritz Brownfield greeted them as they entered. Simpson and Bennett held their greeting to a nod of recognition from each. Brownfield asked if the newcomers wanted something to drink or a sweet roll. They declined the offer.

The group shuffled around until they were seated in the same manner as the previous day. Stan Withers held out the manila envelope containing the file folder. Brownfield recognized it.

"You keep that. It may have information inside you can use in your case."

"Thank you," Stan said. "We can use this."

"Are there any new questions I can answer before we continue?" Brownfield asked.

"No, I think you covered everything pretty well yesterday," Stan replied.

"Well then, may I ask if you have made a decision?" Brownfield asked. "About working with us, I mean."

"We talked about it. It will have to be approved by my colonel and by the attorney general, but as long as you stay within the parameters you have outlined, I think you can count on our cooperation."

"Don't hesitate to call us if there is anything we can do to assist you in this investigation." Fritz reached into his jacket pocket and handed each of the men a small notebook. "These contain the numbers for the Bureau. I've written our numbers," he pointed, indicating the three of them, "on the inside cover of the notebook. Please keep these numbers confidential."

Stan and Rube each gave business cards to the three federal officers. "I'd appreciate it if you would stay in touch with us. We have some innocent folks out there we are trying to protect. We may ask for your assistance in accomplishing that. I'll make it a point to keep you informed on a regular basis of the progress in this case." Stan couldn't think of anything else that needed to be said. He turned to Rube with an inquiring look. Rube shrugged. "Then, if that covers it, we need to get back home and go to work."

"I want to thank you for your cooperation, gentlemen. We'll be in touch.

If there are developments, in other states that affect your case, we will be sure to let you know. Thank you for coming."

With that, the meeting ended. Handshakes were exchanged and the two troopers headed for the parking lot, leaving the three federal officers in the conference room. Hayes and Withers knew the three feds would be discussing the results of the meeting. Rube used a cell phone to call the airline to confirm their return trip.

Little conversation passed between the two on the return ride to the airport, but each of them was anxious to know what was happening back in Anchorage.

It was late when Rube got to his condo. After dropping his baggage on the bed, he went to the refrigerator for a Coke. He took a long drink while walking to the living room. Flopping his tired body into his favorite chair, he picked up the telephone to dial the now familiar number in Juneau. She answered on the third ring.

"Hi, it's me. Got time to talk?" Rube asked.

"Oh, Rube, it's so good to hear from you. Where have you been?" She seemed excited to hear from him. "I got your message last night, but it was late. I was at one of those schmoozing parties. Greasing the wheels of the State's economy," she explained.

"Just got in from Seattle. We had a meeting with some federal people there." His talks with Ben had been forgotten in the excitement of talking with her. "How are things in the Capital?"

"You know how it is down here; everyone chasing the carrot. Our office has a tremendous workload this time of year because of all the construction projects coming to an end and all the contractors wanting their money. We'll be busy for about another month, that's when things will begin to get back to normal. How about you, have you been busy?"

"Yes. I have been involved in a new investigation, but it's been handed off to the metro unit. That's what this trip to Seattle was about." Rube didn't want to talk business. "How are Saundra and Opal?"

"They're doing great. They ask about you quite often. Saundra thinks you're just the cat's meow." She laughed.

"You tell her I love her, too. You were right, she's really a sweet kid."

"I'm going to call her in the morning. I'll tell her what you said."

"Are you going home this weekend?" Rube asked.

"I have an early flight on Saturday morning. I have a 40-minute layover in Anchorage. I'll buy you a cup of coffee, if you can make it to the airport."

"I'll call you from the office tomorrow and let you know. It would be really nice to see you again, even if it's only for a few minutes."

"Do you have any time in your schedule for us to get together, soon?" Rube asked.

"As a matter of fact, I am going to be in Anchorage for several days. The dates aren't set yet, but I think week after next. They want me to do some seminars and classes for contractors and accountants. The class is scheduled to be at the University. UAA wants me to instruct. It's an 80-hour class, so I would have to be there for two weeks." It wasn't the first time she had been in the city to teach one of these classes, but it was the first time she was looking forward to being in Alaska's largest city for a two-week period.

"That sounds great. Let me know as soon as you have the dates. I'll try to find something for us to do while you're here."

"Being with you is special for me, Rube," she said sincerely. "I'm looking forward to some time with you."

"Me, too. I'll call you tomorrow about meeting you at the airport. Hope to see you then."

Hanging up the telephone, he turned on the local news. He finished his Coke and waited for the score in the Arizona Diamondbacks baseball game. They won. He turned off the tube, took a shower and went to bed. His last thought of the day was the pleasant remembrance of Aliana's voice.

Chapter Nineteen

Things had been busy during the time Rube and Stan were gone. There
had been an injury traffic accident involving a trooper. The trooper had been
responding to an alarm at a liquor store near Eagle River. It was just past ten
at night, driving with lights and siren. He exited the freeway and turned left.
As he approached the first street on the other side of the highway, an intoxi-
cated driver ran a stop sign, hitting the trooper car in the passenger door. The
trooper, a rookie named Gene Lorenzen, suffered a broken wrist caused by
the deployment of the airbag. The driver of the other car was hospitalized
with internal injuries, a broken neck and two broken legs. His face was cut
severely when his head hit the windshield. The alarm, it turned out, was a
false alarm.

The troopers, as well as the Anchorage Police Department, would investigate the accident. Rube studied the report and decided that, since
Sergeant Lou Balfore had started the investigation, he should continue it to
its completion.

The other immediate matter, and one that would require he fly to Tuxedni
Bay, was a shooting in a fish camp. Tuxedni Bay is located about 100 miles
south of Anchorage on the west side of Cook Inlet. There are several commercial fishing sites in and near the bay. Rube was familiar with this site. It was
located on the northern tip of Chisik Island in the mouth of the bay. The call
had come in during the night. The other fishermen at the site had locked the
shooter in a shed. The victim was definitely dead. Rube called the hangar and
requested they ready the Cessna 185 for a trip to Chisik Island. They assured
him the plane would be ready by the time he arrived.

Captain Thomas was, as yet, not in his office. Rube put a note on his desk and gathered the investigative equipment he would need to take with him: cameras, recorders, plastic bags, etc. An investigator, Tim Brighton, was in his office when Rube buzzed. Brighton said he could leave the office and accompany the sergeant on the flight. They piled gear in the back of the plane and climbed in. Rube filed a flight plan and the two men took off for Tuxedni Bay, a flight of about 45 minutes, depending on winds.

Rube taxied the small floatplane to the floating dock at the fish site. Two young men caught the plane and tied the lines to the dock. Rube and his companion were hardly out of the plane when the two began to give an excited account of what had taken place. Rube listened to the story for the first time while Tim brought the equipment from the plane.

Yesterday had been a record day for the nets, the first fisherman related. There had been a big party last night. Someone had brought out several bottles of vodka. As the evening went on, and the party became more raucous, an argument broke out between one of the new men and the beach foreman over what his share would be. The new man, Ivan Moreseth, was drunk and shouting. The foreman, Mitch Sabitini, ordered Moreseth to go to his cabin and go to bed. Moreseth left, but in a few minutes came back with a rifle. Without saying a word he shot Mitch in the chest. The other fishermen wrestled the gun away from Moreseth and locked him in a gear shed. He was in there now.

"Where is Sabitini's body?" Rube asked.

"In the ice house," Burt Clausen replied.

"I need to see it first," Rube told the men.

The sergeant instructed his aide to bring the camera equipment and follow. They were led to a shed where a gasoline-powered ice maker was running. Inside was the body of the foreman, shot through the center of the chest. There was only a small hole in the front of his shirt, but when Rube rolled the stiff cadaver over, a gaping wound was visible in the center of the man's back. A pool of gelled blood lay under the body, which had been placed on a blue plastic tarp. Rube lay the body back in its original position and asked the men to tie the tarp around the victim. They would need to load it on the airplane when they left.

Next, they went to the shed where the shooter was locked inside. One of the fishermen opened the door while Rube cautiously stood by. When the door opened, Rube peered inside. There, sleeping on a pile of gillnets, was Moreseth. The shed reeked of vomit and urine. Rube unsnapped the retainer on his holster and put his hand on the butt of his stainless steel Smith and Wesson automatic. With his toe he nudged the sleeping fisherman. It took four tries to get the man awake. Tim Brighton stood by the door of the shed with his pistol in his hand.

"Hey, man," the young man protested. "Can't you let me sleep?"

"Sit up and listen," Rube instructed.

He attempted to lie down again. "Go away and leave me alone."

Rube motioned for Brighton to come in and give him a hand. The two troopers rolled the groggy Moreseth over and put the handcuffs on his wrists. They stood him on his feet and led him into the sunshine. He squinted and tried to turn his face from the sun.

"Is your name Ivan Moreseth?" Rube asked.

"Yeah, why?"

"Pay attention while I read you your rights. You're under arrest for the murder of Mitch Sabitini. You have the right…" Rube read the warning from a card. "Do you understand these rights?" the sergeant asked.

"I didn't kill nobody," he protested again.

"Do you understand your rights as I've explained them to you?"

"Yeah, yeah. I understand. What happened to the boss?" Moreseth asked.

"I have six witnesses that say you fought with him and then killed him."

"Me? I killed him?" Moreseth sounded shocked. "I couldn't kill nobody last night. I was too drunk."

Videotape was made of the scene and the body. Rube interviewed everyone on the fish site. After more than four hours at the scene, the body was loaded into the small Cessna. Brighton sat in back, next to the body. With Rube in the right seat and Moreseth, handcuffed, in the left front seat, the plane taxied out and took off for Anchorage. Once airborne, Rube reported a flight plan for the return trip. He used the trooper frequency to make a short report to his Captain. An hour later they were unloading at the dock on Lake Hood. The body bag was loaded into the trooper pickup to be taken to the crime lab, where the Coroner would do an autopsy. Brighton transferred Moreseth to his patrol car and transported him to jail for booking.

It was now mid-afternoon. Rube reported to Milo and returned to his office to complete his reports. Evidence was logged and a formal complaint filed with the court. By the time he was finished, it was nearly 8. He hadn't eaten since breakfast. On his way home he stopped at the Burger King and picked up a double Whopper with fries.

Inside his apartment he loosened his duty belt and dropped it into a chair. He was about to open the bag containing his supper when the telephone rang.

"Hello."

"You sound grumpy this evening," the soft voice on the other end said.

"I'm sorry. I didn't know it was you. I thought it was the office." Rube was tired and hungry, but a call from Aliana was always welcome. He dug the hamburger from the bag.

"Have a tough day?" she asked.

"Just long. How about you?" He took a bite of his sandwich.

"The usual. I have the dates for those classes. Are you still interested?"

"Can you come tonight?" he laughed.

She, too, laughed. "Not for another week. I'll be there a week from today."

"How long will you be in town?" The two talked for almost an hour. Rube picked at his fries and ate his sandwich while talking. Saundra and Opal were fine and said to tell him hello. Things around her office were expected to begin to slow down in about another week, maybe two. They talked about the trip to Fairbanks and of the fishing excursion in Juneau. Both were reluctant to hang up, but fatigue ruled and they said good night.

Rube slept later than usual the following morning. Stan Withers was waiting in the office when he arrived.

"You look a little frazzled this morning, Rube. Tough night last night?" he asked.

"Just long. Tim Brighton and I went to Tuxedni Bay yesterday to investigate a shooting. By the time we got back last night, it had become a long day." He sipped his first cup of coffee. "How are things at your end of the hall?"

"Action down at the stake-out is picking up," Withers began. "You remember Stroker?"

"Yeah, wasn't he one of the names on the list Molly gave us?"

"That's the one. While we were in Seattle, two new girls came to the restaurant. They had the usual tins with them. That night the surveillance team recorded Stroker in Chavez's office picking up his weekly supply. The boys called Randy Austin and let him know. He hot-footed it down there and caught Stroker on his way from the restaurant. He posed as a dealer and flashed a roll of bills. He told Stroker that his supplier had been busted and that he needed to make a buy. Randy told him that his customers were dry and that he needed it right away. Stroker sold to him right there on the street, in the back seat of his car."

"Did they get this on tape?" Rube asked.

"Live and in color."

"Great. What happens next?"

"The team is waiting to see what other fish rise to the bait. We'll probably let them distribute this load and start making arrests with the next shipment. We think we can get Stroker to testify against Chavez and Sanchez by making a deal for a reduced sentence on the sale to Austin." The metro team was putting a case together. Withers had confidence in his men; they had done this many times before.

"Is there anything I can do to help your team?" Rube inquired.

"Not right away. We might need some of your men when we make the final arrests. I just wanted you to know that we were making some progress and that your photo equipment was being put to good use. The team wanted me to relay their thanks to you. They're really thrilled with the quality of the equipment."

By mid-afternoon Ramon Chavez was on the telephone informing the local distributors that the new shipment was in the office and ready to be picked up. His buyers would know already, but Ramon had always paid attention to details. The owner of the Sombrero Restaurant called Eddie to be sure he would be at the restaurant on time. Larry answered the phone.

"Yes, Mr. Chavez. Mr. Sanchez is getting ready now."

Chavez drove himself to the restaurant. Inside, the cleaning crew was busy making the place ready for the evening crowd. In the kitchen, the cooks were frying fresh tortillas. The aroma from the kitchen was wonderful and Ramon couldn't resist making a stop for a taste of one those warm tortillas. He made a quick inspection of the restaurant then went to his office.

Eddie was not far behind. He moved slowly, but he was an imposing figure nonetheless. Eddie's faithful assistant, Larry, followed behind. It was sad, Ramon thought, to see such a strong man wasting away, his vitality gone, his mind failing; but Ramon would stand by his friend, no matter what.

Ramon checked the time. "Eddie, B.J. will be here in a little while. Stick around. There may be some trouble when I ask him to pay his tab. He got behind when they raided those crack houses last month and I fronted him some inventory. I suspect he may want to get another buy without having the cash. That won't happen."

"You can count on me, Ramon," Eddie said. He tried his best not to show any weakness, but it was difficult to disguise. That's where Larry came in.

"Be careful. This bozo is loco. I don't trust him. I think he is crazy enough to try to kill the golden goose."

"We'll keep an eye on him, Mr. C," Larry said confidently.

By four in the afternoon, the restaurant was coming alive. Bartenders were busy stocking their bar, waiters were checking reservations and inspecting tables. The cooks were busy preparing fresh vegetables and salads for the evening meal. Ramon made another inspection tour of the Sombrero making sure everything was in place. His new manager was now taking care of most of the daily staff problems. After his initial insecurity, he had settled in to the job nicely. The staff liked him and performed well under his supervision.

The dinner crowd was beginning to fill the tables when B.J Miller and his party arrived. B.J. was a flamboyant character. Like many cocaine dealers, he had many friends. Two of the three men with him were his employees, the third was a sometimes associate and frequent companion, Tyrone Bystead. Also in the group were three over-painted and underdressed young ladies. The group was loud and demanding.

The club manager disliked the entire group, and B.J. in particular. He tolerated them only because they were friends of the boss. Tonight, however, they were disturbing the other customers. He called Mr. Chavez to report the situation. Ramon said he would handle it.

He turned to Larry. "Larry, would you go downstairs and ask Mr. Byron J. Miller to come to my office?"

Larry nodded and disappeared out the door. Eddie reached inside his coat to loosen the retainer strap on his shoulder holster.

"Take it easy, Eddie. I don't think we'll need to go that far. I don't want it happening in the restaurant anyway."

Eddie nodded. It was plain to see he was in pain, but he said nothing.

Larry returned with B.J. "Mr. Miller to see you, sir."

"Thank you, Larry." Mr. Chavez said. Larry returned to his station beside Eddie. "Now, B.J., I assume you have come to settle your account."

"Not really. I came to pick up some stuff. I can pay you in a few days." B.J. was a brash individual. "You know you can trust me. Haven't I always been a good customer?"

"Yes, you have. But, in the past you have always paid cash. And you, of all people, should know that this is a cash business. I helped you out the other week because you had some bad luck. You've had time to recover from that situation and now it's time to pay me. You understand?" Chavez was looking directly into the eyes of the drug dealer across the desk. Chavez's voice was cold and lacked any sign of compassion.

"Yeah, but I need a little more time and I need some more stuff. They hit my customers awfully hard. They're back in business, but they need a little time to recoup their losses. I'm into them and you have to help me out. I'm out of stuff."

"You don't seem to understand, B.J. I want what you owe me. I don't run a charitable organization. I run on cash. You should have been paid for the shipment you purchased on credit. For that shipment I want my money." Ramon's eyes narrowed. "I helped you in good faith and I expect to be paid in the same way."

"I don't have it yet, Mr. Chavez. It'll take a few days. You'll get your money."

"When, exactly?" Ramon demanded.

"Soon," B.J. offered.

Ramon flipped the pages of his desk calendar. "Soon isn't good enough. I'll give you two days. You get nothing further until you pay up."

"I can't do it in two days."

"I think you had better find a way to do it. Now, get out of here." Ramon motioned for Larry to escort B.J. out the door.

"Two days, Eddie. If he doesn't pay, he's yours."

Eddie nodded; he understood.

———

Across the street, the surveillance team was dumbfounded. This was a revelation they hadn't counted on. It was time to call Randy Austin.

"Let's put a tail on him for now. We have to keep him alive. Put Steve Hirsch on him, for now. I'll try to get us some help." Austin knew the team was being spread too thin.

Chapter Twenty

Tour boats filled the harbor and tourists filled the streets of Juneau. The summer season was winding down and bargain rates were in effect. Tourist business is the mainstay in the Juneau economy. While the tour boats are running, everyone prospers. Politicians see the boats and their passengers as the golden goose with an endless supply of golden eggs. The move to tax the tour operators is fierce. Those in favor of taxes say the city needs the money to pay for services needed to accommodate the influx of touring public. Those opposed to the tax say the city is already collecting the tax from the local business operators, afraid new taxes will drive the tour boasts to another city or stop them all together.

The morning newspaper, The Juneau Empire, was filled with the controversy. The good Governor, Paul Talmadge, issued warnings to the city officials that state subsidies to the city would be dwindling during the next few years and that alternative funding of city-based projects would have to be found. Declining oil revenues were to blame for this and, unless there was a miracle, the state was simply unable to continue to fund those projects.

Aliana read the articles and statements with interest and tried to imagine how they might impact her department. It was early and the sun had yet to reach the front of her apartment building when the telephone chirped.

"Hello," she answered in a pleasant tone.

"Hi, it's me," Rube replied.

"Oh, hi. I've been thinking about you. I've been so busy I haven't had time to set those dates. I'll try to get to it today. How have you been?"

"I've been fine," he answered. "I've missed you a lot."

"I've missed you, too." This was silly, she thought.

"I didn't have anything important to say. I just wanted to hear your voice before the day got out of hand. It's been really busy here. The summer is getting away and I haven't done much; no fishing, no camping, nothing fun."

"Me either," Aliana replied. "It seems as though I spend all my time traveling. I just move from one crisis to another. It should begin to taper off next month. I try to delegate as much as possible, but it seems the more I delegate the more things tend to return to my desk. Are you ready to take me away from all this?" she laughed.

"Can we leave today?" he was laughing with her. "I hope you can get here next week," he said seriously. "I want to spend some time with you."

"I'm looking forward to that, Rube. I miss you."

"Well, I just wanted to say good morning. I'll call you in a couple of days."

"Thanks for calling, Rube. You're so sweet. I'll call you this week with my schedule. Bye." She was reluctant to hang up, but she had nothing more to tell him.

Although he could never admit it, he felt the same. He had called with nothing to say, but wanting to hear her voice. He was behaving like a high school kid—a not-too-mature high school kid at that. He chuckled at this image of himself.

It was not yet 7. Rube was scheduled to fly to Soldotna to meet with several young troopers. The detachment had only one pilot left on the staff and they had recruited Rube to talk to a group interested in pilot training. He would answer questions about what the state would provide in the way of training and aircraft. He could tell the young men how much monetary incentive the state was willing to pay to up-grade their educations. The sergeant had spent the morning making notes and looking up the regulations he would need to quote. Snatching his jacket from the hanger, he gathered his papers and headed toward Lake Hood and his Cessna floatplane.

Administrative Assistant, Marge Dawson, was admitted to her boss' office. Aliana offered Marge coffee and poured one for her self.

"Is your mother coming to visit you this fall? As I recall, she makes an annual trek to Juneau about this time of year." Aliana didn't usually deal in office small talk, but she liked Marge and her energetic mother.

"Yes, she'll be here in three weeks," the assistant remarked. "I hope to have all my contract reviews completed by the so I can take a couple of days off while she is in town."

"We'll manage. You just enjoy her while she's here. I know how hard it is to be away from your daughter. Just plan to take some time off while your mother is here."

"Thank you…Gosh, I almost forgot why I came to see you." She fumbled through the file in her lap. "I see some problems developing with the contractor on the new ferry dock in Ketchikan."

Aliana opened a file cabinet behind her desk. "Which contractor is it?" she asked.

"Merideth Construction," Marge Dawson replied.

The Deputy Director took a file from the drawer. "I made some notes on this file some time ago. I think the company underbid the contract in hopes of getting additional funding at the end. I asked the DOT commissioner about it at the time."

"I think your suspicions were justified. We're getting to the end of the season and the contractor is starting to submit cost overruns. DOT is approving them and passing them on to us for payment. I think we're being set up to take the blame for paying on under-bid expenses. It's my opinion that this bid was let in an unethical manner. Someone got this contract approved without verifying the cost figures. If we pay the bills as submitted, the end-of-contract costs will be at least 25% over bid."

Aliana was nodding her head in agreement. "What do you suggest we do?"

I think you and I, along with the DOT commissioner, have to go to Ketchikan to see exactly what's happening there and to get an explanation from the contractor."

Thumbing through the file on her desk, Aliana compared the figures on the bid with the ones submitted on the re-cap sheet just given her by Marge Dawson. "I agree. I'll call on the commissioner and see what he has to say. If he concurs, we'll schedule a flight."

Marge left the office, satisfied with the result of the visit. Once she was alone in the office, Aliana called Commissioner William Riggins.

When he answered the telephone, she explained the problem. She wanted to know if he had time to see her this afternoon. He checked his appointments and agreed on a time right after lunch.

She drove to Riggins' office, climbed the steps and was admitted to the office. The two were in a conference for almost three hours when it was decided the figures warranted a personal inspection trip by the people paying the bills.

A charter flight was scheduled for 8 the following morning. Bill Riggins, Marge Dawson and Aliana Pedersen would be on the flight. The Commissioner asked his secretary to make an appointment for them with the contractor. This would not be a pleasant visit.

The trio went to the offices of Merideth Construction, which were housed in a temporary building at the job site. When they arrived in Ketchikan, they learned that the project superintendent had, just this morning, been called to Seattle for consultation and that the project site foreman would be assisting them.

A mini audit was conducted on the site. They found the files incomplete and in an undecipherable mess. Enough information was gathered to warrant calling the Alaska State Troopers. A court order was obtained and all files and records at the site were impounded. An on-site-audit would begin as soon as personnel could be flown from Juneau. It was too early and premature to issue criminal warrants for anyone, but a "locate-only" bulletin was sent out for Guff Rumley, the project superintendent.

On the flight back to the Capital, Bill Riggins began to wonder who in his department had been responsible for letting this contract. He wondered if there was complicity in the irregularities he suspected were attached to the letting of this contract. It was hard for him to believe one of his own people could be involved in what appeared to be a conspiracy to defraud the State of Alaska out of millions of dollars. "I don't know what to say," he had told Aliana. It was dark when the charter plane arrived in Juneau.

In the period of one day, Marge Dawson's workload had gone from hectic to furious to frantic. It was 9 the following morning when the first call came in. Bill Riggins must have worked all night. He had researched his files to find the one place in his command that could have allowed this contract to be approved. He had checked all the competing bids for this contract.

"Ms. Dawson, Bill Riggins here. I think I've found the DOT link to the ferry dock contract. Do you have a re-cap of the expenditures for this contract?"

"Yes, Commissioner. They're in my file. I can make a copy for you, if you like."

"It's important that I get a copy as soon as possible. Can you look in your copy and tell me who approved the final draft and who has been approving the expenditures on this contract?"

Marge opened the file and began to search the pages. "Ah, here it is…" Another pause. "That's strange; both items are signed by the same person."

"What name do you have, Ms. Dawson?" an anxious Riggins asked.

"All of these bid sheets and contract expenditure approvals are signed by Matthew Buffett. I wonder why we didn't pick up on that one before? Either the bid sheets or the cost sheets are in violation of policy."

"Thank you, Marge. I just wanted to confirm that you had the same signatures as the ones in our files. I'll get back to you and Ms. Pedersen on this." Riggins had what he needed. Now he had to confront Matt Buffett.

Marge dialed her boss' intercom number. It was important that she relay this information as quickly as she could. Once in Aliana's office, she opened the thick file.

"I can't imagine us missing this," she said, after explaining her conversation with Commissioner Riggins. "The Commissioner didn't elaborate on what he was going to do, but he was in a hurry when he hung up the telephone."

"Bill Riggins runs a tight ship over there. I think we can count on him to resolve this crisis. In the meantime, will you give me a report on this and include the figures comparing the bid and the approved costs?" Aliana asked, making notes on her legal pad while talking.

"Of course," Marge answered. "It will take some time to pull all the figures together. I'll have it in a couple of days. I can have an outline sooner, if you need it."

"I don't think that will be necessary. Bill has all the figures, but when we get to court we'll need all this."

A few specific items were discussed and added to the list of figures to be gathered. Marge made her notations and returned to her own office and began the task. Her plan was to personally write the report while having two of her assistants pull out and document the figures she needed.

In the DOT Commissioner's office, things were tense. The Deputy Commissioner and the Director for Southeast Operations were summoned to Bill Riggins' office. They had been instructed to clear their calendars for the rest of the day in order to devote full attention to this matter. Bill Riggins was a short, overweight man with a cherubic face. His stern face now lacked the angelic and friendly look that was his political trademark. Above all else, Bill Riggins was a brilliant administrator. When a fight was on, he could root with the pigs and didn't mind the dirt, as long as none of it stuck to him. He had formulated a plan of attack.

His next call was to Major Timms, Commander of the Alaska State Troopers, Southeast Division. He explained the situation to the Major and asked to have two troopers on stand-by. It was likely that at the end of this meeting Matthew Buffett would be under arrest. Once there was proof of wrong-doing, a warrant would be issued for Guff Rumley, Project Superintendent for Merideth Construction. There would, undoubtedly, be charges filed against some of the officials in Merideth Construction.

Next on Bill's list of things to do was to call Aliana Pedersen. He asked her to come to the meeting and to bring Marge Dawson along with the files on the

Merideth contract. He explained that he possessed all the files, but that Ms. Dawson would be able to locate the discrepancies much quicker and more efficiently than he. They would be in the office within a half hour, she told him.

Commissioner Riggins was notified that the plainclothes troopers were in the building before he called Engineer/Architect, Matthew Buffett. They would remain out of sight until the meeting concluded. He had called them as a precautionary measure in case Matt Buffett decided to leave the meeting prematurely.

The receptionist in the outer office notified the Commissioner that Ray Donaldson and Moses Cobbett were here. Bill Riggins stepped out of his office and told the two men to come in.

Moses Cobbett had to duck his head to enter the office. In college he had played center for the Duke Blue Devils. Duke had taken the national championship two of the three years he had played. Cobbett was one of the few black administrators in the Talmadge administration. Years had added pounds and inches to his body and gray to his hair, but he could still beat most of his challengers in a one-on-one game of basketball. It was Riggins who had selected him to be his Deputy Commissioner.

Close behind him was Ray Donaldson, Southeast Area Director. Ray had never been athletic. His prowess lie in his accounting abilities. He was an outstanding administrator with a knack for getting his subordinates to give 110% on every business day. He was known for protecting the people under his command from anyone above him. He never allowed anyone above him to reprimand one of his people. On the other hand, his people knew who was boss and respected him for it.

Bill Riggins took the seat at the head of the conference table, Donaldson and Cobbett to his left. The commissioner briefed the two men on what was taking place and informed them that he would handle the specifics of the charges. They were told that, once Buffett arrived, Ms. Pedersen and Ms. Dawson would be called to give cost comparisons and specifics. Commissioner Riggins had talked with Major Timms, and a list of probable charges had been set down. This list of charges could be modified once the final audit was complete. At this time it was important to see that Matthew Buffett was held within this jurisdiction.

The two newcomers were also advised that the Project Superintendent had fled the state. It was not known if further charges would be brought against Merideth Construction Company.

The Commissioner was just completing his briefing when the receptionist notified him that Matthew Buffett was in the outer office. "Show him in," the Commissioner ordered.

Matthew Buffett had been to the Commissioner's office many times before. This meeting seemed no different from the others, DOT officials present and the table covered with blueprints and files.

"We're expecting a couple other members of this panel, Matt, so would you please take the seat at the other end of the table?"

"Sure, what's this meeting about?" he asked.

"Some problems have come to light. We need to discuss them and decide what course of action to take. Riggins opened the thick file folder in front of him. "This meeting is in regard to some problems at the new ferry dock construction project. You are the Architect and Project Engineer on that job, is that correct?"

"Yes, I am." A curious look crossed Matt's face. "That project is on schedule and going very well."

"Yes, we see that. What we have come to question is some of the expenditures being submitted."

"I think that, if you check, you will find every expenditure was outlined in the original bid and in the contract," Buffett explained.

"Again, you are correct." Riggins was about to go on when there was a tap on the door. He stepped over to answer it.

At the door with the receptionist were Aliana and Marge. He showed the ladies to their seats and again made his way to the head of the table.

"Before we go any further, Matt, have you met everyone here?"

"Yes, I've met everyone except for the lady with Ms. Pedersen."

Aliana handled the introduction. "Mr. Matthew Buffett, this is Marge Dawson. She is one of my assistants. She's here because of her knowledge regarding your project in Ketchikan."

"Pleased to meet you, Ms. Dawson," he acknowledged.

"All right then, let's get on with the specifics of this meeting…" One by one the charges were explained and the figures quoted. Comparisons were made between the competing bids and the Merideth bid. Actual costs were compared with other bids, Merideth's bid and the final submitted expenditures. The list became so long that it was impossible to justify their numbers as simple cost overruns or price adjustments.

Late in the day, after Matthew Buffett admitted he could not explain the differences, the troopers were called in to read him his rights. The meeting had been so intense that none of the participants had taken notice of the time. They had worked through lunch and through the dinner hour.

Once the arrest had been made, they began to reassemble their folders. The Commissioner volunteered to buy dinner for the group.

Chapter Twenty One

Dinner had taken the time to past midnight before Aliana made it home. A long, hot shower had relaxed her enough to sleep. The sound of the alarm was not a welcome sound this morning. She stumbled out of bed and into the kitchen. She had just poured water into the coffee pot when the telephone rang.

"Hello," she said sleepily.

"Did I call too early?" Rube laughed.

"Oh, Rube," she instantly became more alert. "No, I'm glad you called. I'm getting a late start today. We had a late meeting last night," she explained. "How are you?"

"Doing fine," was his reply. "If I've caught you at a bad time, I'll call back another time."

"Oh, no. Don't hang up. The State owes me lots of comp time and I can't think of a better way to use it than talking to you."

"I really miss you. I can't remember ever feeling this way. Have you given any thought as to when you will be coming to Anchorage. I need to see you."

"I feel the same way," she admitted. "I've been so busy I haven't had time to make arrangements for those classes. I'll put Pam St. John on that project this morning. I thought I might bring Pam and Marge with me. I can let them run the classes and I can do the politicking with the department heads. That would leave the evenings free for us to enjoy."

"That sounds good to me. How are Saundra and Opal?" This wasn't an idle question, he was genuinely interested.

"They're fine. Both of them ask about you all the time. Saundra asked if she could send you a picture she had colored. I told her it would be all right. I hope you don't mind."

"I've never had a picture pinned to my refrigerator. It would be really nice," he laughed. "You tell them both hello for me when you talk with them again."

"I will." She paused a moment. "I was just looking at the calendar. I'll try to set those meetings in Anchorage for a week from Monday. Is that good for you?"

"That will be great. I wish it was sooner, but I guess I can wait. They say absence makes the heart grow fonder. In another week I should be pretty fond."

"I think you had better get back to work before I have to have you arrested for making an obscene phone call." Now she was laughing. "Besides, I have to get ready to go to work. If I don't show up soon, they will think I'm AWOL."

They said goodbye and she finished getting ready for work. She took the time for an extra cup of coffee this morning. The events of the last few days had planted a seed of regret within her. Her blossoming relationship with Rube was something that had not been calculated when she set out on this life plan. The last couple of days were something of a revelation to her. Would she be called to one of those meetings at some date in the future? She couldn't afford those thoughts.

<hr>

Randy Austin was short of people to cover all the avenues he was now being presented. He had two men on B.J. Miller when there should be six. Since learning about the threat to B.J.'s life, there had been a tail on him 24 hours a day. His crew was being spread too thin. It was time to ask Captain Withers for help.

The meeting took place in Captain Withers' office.

"I know the budget is tight, but this guy may be our best witness. We have to keep him alive. I have two men on him. They're working two twelve-hour shifts and are alone. That situation is putting my men in jeopardy. With manpower like this, we can't guarantee the life of B.J. Miller, and some of my troopers may get hurt for lack of backup. It's a serious situation, Captain." Austin was pleading for more help.

Stan Withers had his chin on his knuckles, listening intently. "You know how it is this time of year, Randy. Everyone is overloaded. I agree with you that you have to have more help, but I can't just take people from another detachment. Give me until this afternoon. I'll call the colonel and see if he will authorize some help for us."

"Thanks, Cap. My team is getting pretty tired. I'm afraid they will start to make mistakes if this situation goes on much longer. I don't want anyone hurt."

"I'll call you as soon as I hear from the colonel." With that the morning meeting ended. Austin was headed back to relieve one of his team to give them a few hours break.

The colonel's office was in the main headquarters building next door to the building used by Stan Withers and his SCAN team. It was mid-morning when the commander of the troopers returned his call. Stan was invited to the office for a short meeting.

At age 42, Norm Gilbert had 21 years with the troopers. He had served in nearly every area of the state. As a pilot he flew the state's Beechcraft King Air, a job that allowed him to see even more of the remote parts of Alaska. There was a soft spot in his heart for the SCAN team because he had served as its leader for almost seven years. Now, as boss of all the troopers, the team could count on him for little favors. More manpower was not a little favor.

"Good to see you, Stan. Have a seat." The colonel pointed to a chair. "I've been following this surveillance on the Sombrero. This is turning into a big case. What can I do to help?"

"Have you read the report about the threat to B.J. Miller?" Stan asked.

"Yes. I can't believe we have this on video. I see you have someone following him. Do you think you can turn him? He'd make a powerful witness."

"That's why I'm here. Randy was just in my office to ask for more men. He has two of his team tailing Miller on a 'round-the-clock basis, but he only has two men for the task. He's afraid, and I agree with him, that he needs more people. He's afraid for the safety of his team members." Stan could see the colonel was sympathetic to his appeal. "Even if nothing happens, the team can't keep this pace for a long period of time. They need some rest, too. Randy made the point that a weary team could begin to make mistakes. Those mistakes could cost us the case, as well as get people hurt."

Colonel Gilbert sat, thinking. "Do you have any idea how long your team would need extra help?"

"I don't see any way to predict that. All I can do is give you an educated guess."

"What's your best guess, then?"

"We need to turn Miller and at least one other good witness before we can file on the rest of them. We're turning up good evidence every day. Chavez is importing four and a half pounds of cocaine every week. We want to shut him down as soon as we can."

"I understand, but I'm asking for your opinion as to how long you will need the extra help." The Commissioner would ask him this question and he wanted an answer he could use to justify reassigning personnel.

"No guarantees, Colonel, but I'd say four weeks. It might be only three, but I'd count on four." Stan hoped his numbers were accurate. He didn't want to come back in a month to do this again. Next time it would be much more difficult.

"I'll call you this afternoon with an answer. I'll try to get you six men, but if I were you I wouldn't count on more than four." Stan had stood to leave when Norm spoke again. "Your team is doing an outstanding job. I know how hard it is to work shorthanded. Tell them I'll do my best with the Commissioner."

Stan thanked his commander and left the office. On the first floor he walked down the hall to Rube Hayes' office. It might be a good day to take the Sergeant to lunch.

In Seattle, the business week was coming to a close. Colin James picked up the telephone and dialed his friend at SeaFirst Bank. The voice on the other end sounded tired.

"Ben Gerlitz, how may I help you?"

"Ben? Colin. I just called to see if you could get away for lunch."

"Good to hear from you, Colin. Yes, that sounds great. Where do you want to go?"

The same railroad-car restaurant was selected. It was about the same distance for each man to drive. Colin arrived a couple of minutes before Ben. He got a table and ordered coffee for himself.

When Ben arrived, Colin could hardly believe his eyes. Ben looked terrible. His eyes were red; he needed a haircut; and, as he picked up the menu, his hands were shaking.

"Are you okay, Ben?" Colin asked.

"Yeah, fine." The waiter was asking Ben what he wanted to drink. "Vodka martini," he replied.

"I don't mean to preach to you, Ben, but it seems to me that you have been drinking an awful lot lately."

"Bankers are expected to drink a lot," he answered. "If I drink enough, I could be Bank President." He gave a dry laugh and returned to the menu.

"I have to ask, Ben. Something has been bothering you for a while now. What is it? Is there something I can do to help you?" Colin voiced his concern.

"Nope, I'm just fine." The statement came with a large amount of sarcasm attached.

"I'm worried about you. In the past few weeks, you have been drinking every day and you don't get out to do anything. Since you got that promotion, you've really changed. What's happening, Ben?"

"Nothing that concerns you, Colin. Leave it alone." The waiter delivered his drink. "Bring me one more," he told the waiter.

"I'm just trying to be your friend. I wish you would let me help you." Colin's worries for his friend were deepening.

"You don't have to worry about me, Colin. I have a black-haired angel, with ice blue eyes, to look after me. I'll never have to worry again."

The waiter came with another drink for Ben, and the two men ordered lunch. The silence was thick as the two men ate. Colin couldn't imagine why Ben refused to confide in him. In the past they had found it easy to use each other as a vent for building frustrations. Colin noted that, once again, Ben had made reference to the lady from Juneau. He didn't know what significance that held, but he knew that she had something to do with what was happening to Ben. The silence continued for the rest of lunch. Ben picked up the check.

"I'll get it." He pulled some bills from his pocket and placed them in the leather book with the bill.

Outside in the sunshine, Colin waited. As they walked to their cars, Colin tried once again.

"I wish you would allow me to help you, Ben. Call me if you change your mind."

"I will. Don't worry, though. I'll call you this week."

Colin watched as his friend drove away in the direction of downtown Seattle. The same questions kept entering his mind as he drove back to his office at Boeing. What was bothering Ben? What did Aliana Pedersen have to do with it? Why wouldn't Ben talk about it? Why had he shut himself off from the rest of his friends? The questions kept coming as he drove back to his office.

———

It was just after two when Colonel Gilbert called Stan Withers. Although the Commissioner had once been a cop, and a good one, he was now a politician. He had to justify the political aspects of all his decisions. It had always been difficult for the cop on the street to understand why he couldn't get a positive response from the administration when he needed something that required monetary backup. Stan Withers had been a unit commander long enough to know that the budget was the determining factor in almost every decision made, even in law enforcement. He remembered a case a few years ago when the State of Alaska tried an individual for multiple homicide; some of the victims were children. He was tried three times and had a hung jury or mistrial each time. The attorney general determined that it would cost too much to bring him to trial again, and so he got away with murder, for the sake of budget.

"I was able to get you five men," the colonel said. "You can have them for one month. I expect to see results within that time."

"Thanks, Colonel. You'll get results." It was more than Stan had hoped for. "How soon can I expect to see the new men?"

"Two are coming from the academy and will report to you on Monday. The other three will come from Metro Traffic in the Anchorage bowl. They will be in your office before the end of the day."

"Thanks again, Colonel." Stan hung up the phone, feeling relief. His next move was to call Randy Austin. He asked the Lieutenant to come to his office.

The two men spent the rest of the afternoon mapping a strategy and scheduling relief for the members of the team who hadn't had a day off since this thing began. They decided to schedule a new man with one of the current team in order to spread the expertise to all the shifts. Randy, too, was relieved at the thought of giving his men some well-deserved rest.

Pressure was being put on all the crack house dealers in the city to come up with cash to pay B.J. Miller. He had systematically made the rounds of each of his customers to demand payment for merchandise they had already received. Subtlety was not one of B.J.'s better qualities. At each stop on his route there was shouting and threats. On two occasions the trooper following B.J. saw the dealer slip a handgun from its shoulder holster. The trooper couldn't hear what was said, but it was plain that threats were being issued. Each of these events was being recorded on video through a small window in the side of the van.

Two men accompanied B.J. the entire day. Both these men were dressed in worn-out jeans and sweatshirts. Don Hillman, the trooper assigned to follow Miller, wasn't able to hear what was being said between the men, though he could faintly hear voices as they walked back to the car. What he could hear was the voice of the taller of the two men with B.J. The man had an irritating laugh that reminded Hillman of a mule braying. Each time the man laughed, it struck Don as funny and he began to laugh. It was a ridiculous sight, the trooper sitting alone in the van, laughing at another man laughing.

The radio in the van crackled to life. "Where are you, Don?"

"Muldoon and Fireweed, moving north," he answered.

"Want a day off?" Austin asked over the secure frequency.

"I'll take it," came the reply.

They agreed to meet at a coffee shop in the Muldoon area. It was Hirsch and one of the new men who came to take over the tail on B.J. Miller. Instructions and information were passed. The new man was introduced as Jerry Leber from Anchorage Metro Traffic Division. The new man was a welcome sight to the tired Hillman.

"The boss gave you two days off, you lucky stiff," Hirsch laughed. "I'll let you know where I'll be. See you in two days."

The rest of the day went pretty much the same as Hillman had experienced earlier. The team expected Miller to spend the night partying, but he must have been worried about collecting. He went home early and never came out the rest of the night. His two stooges stayed in the house with him.

The two troopers in the van decided it was a good time to get some rest and split the stakeout up into two hour shifts, one man sleeping in the front seat while the other watched. The men inside the house made no attempt to leave. At 7 the following morning, Leber walked the three blocks to McDonalds for coffee and Egg McMuffins. The breakfast was brought back to the van where the two settled in for a long wait.

Just before noon a beat-up, early 70s model Buick stopped in front of the house they had been watching. Recording equipment was turned on and license plate numbers were called in. When a lone occupant got out of the car, Hirsch recognized him immediately. The Scan Team had arrested him in a crack house raid only one month ago. The man, Hirsh couldn't recall his name, walked as though he were keeping time to music, swaying, almost dancing as he moved toward the yellow house. He knocked; the stooge with the weird laugh opened the door. Only minutes later the door opened and the crack dealer came out again, got into his car and drove away.

Less than a half-hour later, another car, almost a twin to the last one, stopped in front of he house. Hirsch recognized the driver as another crack dealer. The dealer was known on the streets as Beans. He had brought a man with him, presumably for protection. Again the video was operating. As before, the door opened, the visitors admitted and, a few minutes later, they left.

This same scenario was repeated four more times during the day. Hirsch remarked to Leber that whatever B.J. had said to his customers, they had taken it to heart and were here to pay their debts. The diamond earring in his ear was proof that B.J. didn't make idle threats.

Chapter Twenty Two

The staff in the Alaska Account office had a very low turnover rate. Consequently nearly all the employees in the office had been there for a very long time. One of the core staff, Lyda Carney, had been with the unit since its first days. As a senior clerk, she was responsible for the final printouts of the computer-generated data for the entire department. The responsibility was immense. She was familiar with every bit of legitimate paper within the unit. During the latest audit, something had caught her attention. Something she had never seen before. With the tenacity of a bloodhound, she had begun her search.

It had taken several days of searching files before she came to the right drawer. It was usually locked, but on this day Mr. Gerlitz was working in the file and had left the drawer unlocked while he had folders out of the file. Lyda easily found the folder containing the audit figures. To her amazement, inside this file jacket were two folders, one marked SeaFirst Bank, the other marked State of Alaska. Checking to be sure Mr. Gerlitz hadn't noticed her, she took the file to her desk. As quickly as she could, she compared the pages; they all matched. She was about to give up and put the file back into the drawer when she turned the final page of the report. In the back of the report there should have been an index noting the page numbers for certain items. In front of the index of the SeaFirst folder, however, was an extra page. One not included in the file marked for the State of Alaska. This last page contained interest rates and accumulated amounts. The page also gave computer codes for a file she had never seen. She wrote the numbers on a sheet of paper and returned the files to the drawer, once again checking the whereabouts of Mr. Ben Gerlitz.

The clerk hurried back to her desk. She was nervous and felt like a thief. Never before had she presumed to look inside her boss' files. She had no idea what all this meant, but it had piqued her curiosity; she couldn't quit now. Lyda sat quietly at her desk for several minutes, feeling guilty and afraid of being caught. It was her job to know what was in the files and she had the right to inspect any file in the department, but this was different. Something here was not right. As her nerves began to calm, she took a deep breath and removed the paper from her pocket. Entering the password and subsequent file numbers, she came to an account she had never heard of, Alaska Maritime Savings. The account had a Seattle post office box number.

Interest from the Alaska Account was being paid, with service charges deducted, into an account within this department. The account was emptied twice each week. Lyda found this to be very strange indeed. Checking the dates she found that the account made electronic transfers on Monday and Thursday of each week. These transfers left a zero balance in the Alaska Account, interest column. The more she read, the more curious she became. At first she thought Mr. Gerlitz might be taking the money for his own use, but then she realized this had been going on since the opening of the account and had been approved by Mr. Morton before him. She was becoming nervous again. With a flick of the electronic mouse, she pointed and clicked, printing out a copy of this document. She didn't know what it meant, but it wasn't something she wanted to study here at her desk.

Many of the clerks carried briefcases and laptop bags. Lyda was one of those. She stuffed the stack of printed sheets into a manila folder and placed the folder in her laptop bag. The tension was so heavy she had to go to the ladies room to wash her face and regain her composure. Several minutes went by before she felt she could go back to her desk.

Looking across the open office floor, she could see Ben Gerlitz preparing to leave for the day. He took the files from his desk and locked them in the cabinet she had just finished pilfering. He closed the drawer and locked it. Returning to his desk, he looked at his calendar and locked his desk drawer. He dialed a number on the intercom; Lyda thought it was to inform his secretary he was leaving for the day. The young executive lifted his topcoat from the rack and walked to the elevator.

Being as cautious as she could, she walked to his desk and opened the Rolodex. It took a couple of minutes to find the two numbers she wanted. Closing the lid of the Rolodex, and trying her best to appear calm, she returned to her own desk. Chief Clerk Lyda Carney had a lot of thinking to do. She closed her desk and rode the elevator to the garage. Driving directly home, she could scarcely contain her anxiety. She wanted to see what was in the folder hidden in the bag on the seat beside her.

With the Friday traffic being what it was, it took her almost an hour to cross town to the north end of the Aurora Bridge. Once she exited the freeway, it was only a short drive home. She kept an eye on the rear-view mirror to be sure no one was following her. There was no way for anyone to know she had the papers in her car, but she was paranoid nonetheless. She felt a certain sense of relief when she reached home.

Lyda Carney had graduated from high school right here in Bothel. She had gone to college in Tacoma, attending Pacific Lutheran University. Her accounting degree had landed her a position at Seattle First National Bank, now SeaFirst Bank. Now 32 years old, she lived alone with her dog McGyver. Lyda wasn't an attractive girl, but her personal image of herself was far less than reality. She mixed well with others at office parties, but seldom socialized anywhere else. She could be found almost any evening, with McGyver, sitting on a bench, reading or walking near the Lake Union boat locks.

She parked her car in the short drive. The house was in an old, but well-kept neighborhood. Carrying her coat and laptop bag, she climbed the five steps to the porch.

"McGyver," she began to call as she unlocked the front door.

The dog, half Terrier half mixed breed, yelped in response to her calls as she turned the key in the lock. After being in the house alone all day, he was happy to see his mistress. He knew this was his time to be petted and fed. It also meant he would have a chance to run and sniff and investigate new and old smells. For a city dog, the life wasn't bad. Tonight, however, the little dog would be disappointed.

Lyda fixed a sandwich for herself. She put fresh feed and water down for the dog. By the time this was done, the teakettle was whistling on the stove. The hot tea was taken to the living room where she opened the computer bag. She pulled the thick manila file folder from the bag and began to sort through the files.

It took her all evening, with McGyver curled up on the couch beside her, to compare the two files. What she found was what she had suspected in the beginning. Both files were the same except for the pages entitled Interest, Withdrawals and Transfers. These pages were included only in the bank copy of the files, and carefully excluded from the State of Alaska files.

She found that the bank had received their fees for handling the account. Those fees had been paid out of the interest accumulated by the account. The remaining interest was transferred regularly, semi-weekly, to an account outside the bank. This account was in the name of the Alaska Maritime Savings. The money trail ended there except for an address to where the Alaska Maritime Savings was receiving notification of the transfers. On the surface there was nothing illegal or improper involved in the account. What was strange and had drawn her attention was the fact that only one file had a record of the transactions; the SeaFirst Bank file. This file had been signed and certified correct by Mr. Irwin Stackhaus, Senior Vice President. These same pages were missing from the Alaska file and yet, these too, were certified accurate by Mr. Stackhaus.

It was all very confusing to the Senior Clerk. Was Mr. Stackhaus involved? Was Mr. Gerlitz involved? Did Ms. Pedersen know what was happening? Was it all her imagination? Was all this legitimate and taking place after it left her jurisdiction? Questions, questions and more questions. So far she had no answers.

Who would she turn to for answers? Mr. Stackhaus? He had certified both copies of the files as accurate. Mr. Gerlitz? He had kept the files locked up and never allowed her to see them. Who else in the bank was involved in the cover-up, if that was, indeed, what this was. Who could she trust?

The two numbers she had taken from her boss' Rolodex were those of Ms. Pedersen and of an Alaska State Trooper who had come to visit Mr. Gerlitz. He seemed to know Ms. Pedersen, too, but it seemed unlikely that he was involved in anything to do with this account. Since she didn't know if there were officers in the bank involved, and in fact, if there was really any wrongdoing, she didn't want to go to the State of Washington Banking Commission. The more she thought about it the more confused she became.

Finally, after several hours of study, she decided to wait until Monday and call that trooper sergeant. After all, this was an Alaska account, and it appeared as if someone was taking monies rightfully belonging to the State of Alaska. He would be able to advise her on a course of action. She thought she had found something wrong; it was up to someone else to find out what it was and what to was to be done a about it.

A blue and white cab pulled to a stop in front of the yellow house in the Muldoon section of Anchorage. Three young women in tight dresses slid out of the back seat. One of B.J.'s stooges came out of the house and paid the driver. The ladies went inside while the man who had paid the cab driver brought a new Lincoln around to the front of the house. The door of the house opened and a parade of people, giggling and talking, walked to the car. Last in this line of party goers was Mr. Byron J. Miller, himself. B.J. slid into the back seat with the three women. The driver pulled slowly from the curb, turning toward the downtown area.

Steve Hirsch was driving the van; Jerry Leber was on the radio to George Kennedy.

"They just left the house, Sarge. Steve thinks they're headed for the restaurant." Leber was talking to the stakeout in the apartment across the street from the Sombrero.

"We'll be ready for them," Kennedy said. "I'll call you as soon as I see their car."

"Roger that."

The shiny Lincoln stopped in front of the restaurant. Everyone but the driver stepped out of the car. The girls were laughing and clinging to B.J. as they made their way into the Sombrero. The driver pulled around to the side of the building where the parking lot was located.

Kennedy called Leber and told him to keep the van out of sight a couple of blocks up the street. The two men in the van agreed. George had his team watching the restaurant. Hirsch told his new partner to try to get some sleep while they waited.

The stooge with the weird laugh was carrying a black athletic bag. George Kennedy was wishing he could see inside the restaurant. Soon, though, the night manager knocked on the office door where Ramon Chavez and Eddie Sanchez waited. Eddie's companion, Larry, was by his side. The young manager brought the message that B.J. was here to see Mr. Chavez.

"Send him up," he was told.

Two men came to the office, B.J. and the man carrying the black bag.

"Do you have my money, Mr. Miller?" Ramon asked politely.

"Yeah, man. I got your money," B.J replied.

"Good." He turned to Larry. "Would you please take it? I know Mr. Miller wishes to get back to his guests." Without a word, Larry stepped forward to take the bag.

"I'm going to need some stuff, Mr. Chavez." B.J. said.

"Can you pay?"

"Not today, but you know I'm good for it." B.J. was almost whining.

"Then, I'm sorry. I cannot operate on credit. Feel free to come back when you have the cash."

"You can't treat me this way, Ramon. I've done business with you for a long time and I've always paid. Things have been tight since the raids last month.

My dealers need some time to catch up. Hey, man, I paid you what I owed you, didn't I?"

Ramon Chavez had heard enough. "If you want to finance your crack house friends, that's up to you. But until you can pay me in cash, get out of my office."

Miller opened his mouth to say something then thought better of it. He turned to his associate and motioned him to the door.

Ramon called after them before they could close the door. "Don't forget to pay for your dinner tonight. My manager will bring you the bill you forgot to take care of last night, too. And, please, leave the waiters a tip."

In the restaurant, B.J. was furious, throwing three $100 dollar bills at the manager.

"Get the car," he ordered. "We're getting out of here."

Eddie watched out the window as the entourage climbed into the Lincoln.

Ramon leaned back in his chair, shaking his head. He had thought about it for several days.

"Eddie, I think it's time to take care of B.J. Miller. He's too dangerous a man to leave out there. We can cut off his supply, but I think he will be back to retaliate. Make him disappear. Do it soon."

"Sure thing, Ramon. I'll take care of it." Eddie answered calmly.

In the apartment across the street, George Kennedy nearly panicked. Using the hand-held radio, he called the men in the van parked only a few blocks away.

"Steve, crank it up. They're leaving," he said into the secure frequency. "Ramon just told Eddie to hit B.J. You had better stay close."

"We're on it," came the reply.

Kennedy's next call was to Randy Austin. It took a few minutes to relay the entire conversation to the Lieutenant.

"Okay," Austin acknowledged. "Can you handle the surveillance alone for a while?"

"Yes. No problem."

"Then, have Paddy and the new guy follow Eddie Sanchez and his friend when they leave the restaurant. What do you have for a vehicle?" Austin inquired.

"We've been using that old green pickup."

"Good. Tell Paddy to stay with him and to keep in radio contact. I'll call Don Hillman to come in and sit with you," Austin advised. "We have to keep Miller alive and get him to testify against Chavez. Tell everyone to be careful. I'll be down as soon as I can get there."

"I can handle things here, Lieutenant. If Eddie and his partner leave, Ramon will be the only one here to worry about. If he stays with his usual schedule, he'll work an hour or two after the restaurant closes then go home. Use the men on the other end. I'll be okay here. I'll get some shuteye as soon as Ramon leaves to go home."

"Thanks, George. This may be coming to a head whether we're ready or not. I'll be talking with you."

Paddy and his new partner were in the old Chevy pickup waiting for Eddie to leave the restaurant. They didn't have long to wait.

Larry had been instructed to find a car, one not traceable to Eddie. A half-hour later he parked an old black and red Eagle station wagon in front of the Sombrero. He parked in a loading zone and went inside. Only minutes later he and Eddie climbed into the car and drove away.

Following at a safe distance was the green Chevy pickup. Paddy was good at this, he had done it many times before. The AMC Eagle drove to a convenience store where Larry purchased a plastic gas can. At the pumps in front of the store, he filled it with gasoline and screwed the lid on tightly. He took a handful of windshield towels and put them in the back of the station wagon with the gas can. The two men stopped for coffee at a small all-night café in Muldoon. Paddy could see the pair checking the time frequently. He presumed they were giving their victims time to get to sleep.

It was just after one in the early morning when Larry stopped the car around the corner from the yellow house. He opened the back of the car and began to stuff rags into the open lid of the can. Paddy picked up the radio and advised the rest of the team of what was taking place. He told Steve Hirsch to use the cell phone to call the fire department and to have them respond without lights or siren. They also called for backup from the trooper Metro Traffic Detachment. Everyone was out of their vehicles now. Larry was sneaking through the shadows of the twilight with the can of gasoline. Paddy went after him.

Steve Hirsch climbed from the van and followed Paddy while Jerry Leber joined the rookie at the Chevy. Leber saw headlights a block down the street and caught a glimpse of the approaching fire truck. He pulled the phone from his pocket and dialed quickly. He told the night dispatcher to have the fire truck hold where they were for now. Leber saw the truck stop and turn off its lights.

Paddy and Hirsch were less than 10 yards behind Larry when he stopped to light a match to the rags stuffed into the can. It had begun to burn when they stepped from the shadows.

"Hold it right there. Police officers," Paddy ordered.

The startled arsonist looked up to see two men with guns aimed at him. He turned to see how far he was away from the window on the side of the house. Again he looked back at the men with the guns. He grimaced, grabbed the can and ran toward the window. He held the heavy, burning can behind him as he ran.

"Stop, NOW!" Paddy ordered, but the man kept running.

Larry put all his muscle into the throw. At the same instant the can left his hand, Steve Hirsch fired the first shot. Larry was moving and the shot was low and off center, striking him in the left arm, and knocking him to the ground. The can had been launched, however, and made a wobbling, end-over-end arc disappearing inside the broken window. Flames instantly erupted inside the yellow house.

The phone line was still open and the dispatcher on the line when Paddy shouted into the speaker. "Get that fire truck up here now. We have flames inside the house."

The shot had startled Eddie, who was sitting in the car, waiting. He opened the door of the Eagle to be met by the rookie, gun in hand.

"Police. On the ground, now," he shouted. Eddie started to face the officer. "On the ground, NOW," the order came again. "Hands on your head, lock your fingers."

Eddie could see two men with guns standing over Larry. It took a great deal of physical effort on his part, but Eddie Sanchez put his hands on his head. He sunk to his knees. Jerry Leber came around the car to join them. He holstered his weapon and took his handcuffs from the pouch. He was snapping the locks on the handcuffs when the fire department arrived.

The gunshot had awakened the residents of the house. Flames met them as they entered the living room. Two men ran out the back door in their shorts, followed a couple of minutes later by B.J. Miller who was carrying an arm load of clothing.

By the time the firemen burst through the front door, the house was unoccupied. Foam fire retardant was used to put out the burning gasoline. Little damage was done to the home. The fire crew was picking up their hoses and equipment when the homeowner, now dressed, approached Paddy McGuire. An ambulance had been called to transport Larry to the hospital for treatment of his gunshot wound.

"What the hell is going on here?" B.J. asked Paddy.

"Mr. Miller, I think you had better ride downtown with one of our officers. We have some things to discuss." Paddy motioned to one of the uniformed officers on the scene to come.

"I'm not going anywhere." He was now fully awake and, recognizing Eddie and Larry, started to put things together. Anger was welling up inside him.

"Mr. Miller, we have just apprehended two men trying to kill you. You could show some gratitude for that," Paddy said facetiously.

Another car pulled to a stop at the curb near the yellow house. It was the unmarked car belonging to Randy Austin. Paddy watched as the Lieutenant purposefully strode across the yard.

Austin greeted McGuire. "Mornin', Paddy. What we got here?"

"Mr. Miller here was asleep in his home when someone threw a large Molotov cocktail through the window. Luckily we were in the area and saw this happen. We called the fire department who put out the fire and saved his house."

"You're lucky my men happened to be in the neighborhood, Mr. Miller."

"Go to hell." B.J. blustered.

"You are going to have to give us some information about the house," Paddy continued speaking to B.J. "We will have to know who owns the house, who the insurer is and things like that."

"I own the house and there ain't no insurance, anything else?"

"Would you have any idea why these men came here to do you harm?" Austin asked. "This could have killed you."

"What can I say? It was just a random act of violence." B.J. answered, evading the real answer.

"I'll tell you what it looks like to me," Austin explained. "It looks to me like you have made some powerful enemies. Ruthless enemies. Someone sent two men here to kill you. If my men hadn't seen this happening, that burning gas can probably would have trapped you inside and you and your buddies would now be dead. And burning to death isn't a pleasant way to go."

"Just don't worry about me. I'm capable of taking care of myself."

"Do you know the men who did this? That's Eddie Sanchez over there." Austin pointed to the back of the patrol car where Eddie was now sitting. "Larry is the only name we have on the one Paddy shot."

"Don't know 'em." It was plain that Miller was not going to give the trooper any information. It was also plain to see that he was planning revenge. He was known to be a very violent person. This situation could spark a series of killings in the city. It had happened before.

"Mr. Miller. We are going to ask you to come to Trooper Headquarters," Austin looked at his watch. "Let's make it 1 PM. You will have to fill out some reports for our records. I will warn you that any attempt on your part to avenge this action will get you arrested. Got that?"

"Yeah, okay." B.J. turned and called to his men. The three marched back into the house.

"What do you think, Lieutenant? Should we keep an eye on him tonight?" Paddy asked.

Austin thought about for a minute before answering. "No. Eddie and Larry are in jail. Ramon will be at home by now. I'm sure Eddie will call him to let him know what has happened. I expect the lawyers to be at the jail first thing in the morning. B.J. knows he can't get to Eddie and Larry. I don't think he'll try to do anything to Chavez tonight. You guys might as well get a few hours sleep. I'll see you in the office around ten.

That was welcome news to the men who hadn't had a good night's sleep in the last two weeks. The rest of the weekend would be spent preparing court complaints and other details. Paddy instructed the uniformed trooper to take Eddie to the pre-trial jail and book him on arson charges. Other charges would follow, but this would hold him for now. A uniformed guard was assigned to the hospital where Larry would be undergoing surgery.

It was 3 AM when Ramon Chavez received the call from Eddie Sanchez.

Eddie gave Ramon the short version of what had happened at B.J.'s house. He told Ramon about Larry's gunshot wound. "What do you want me to do?" He asked.

Ramon thought a few moments before answering, then said, "Just sit tight. Don't say anything to anyone. I will have a lawyer down there by morning." Again a short pause. "I will have to call Dante and let him know about Larry. We don't want this to become unmanageable. Get some rest and I will take care of it in the morning when offices are open. Remember, don't say anything."

Chapter Twenty Three

Trooper Sergeant Rueben Hayes was used to the twelve-hour days of the summer schedule. He was, as was his rule, in the office about 6 each morning. Late summer presented him with another beautiful morning, but it was evident that the days were getting shorter. The sun was low in the eastern sky as he drove to work this morning. By the first of next month, tourists would begin to make their way south once again. Once the big motor homes had vacated the parking lots of the big box stores in the city, winter could not be far behind.

Rube was deep in concentration, sorting the morning pile of files and papers on his desk when the phone on his desk jingled.

"Sergeant Hayes," he answered.

"Sergeant Hayes, you don't know me, but we have met. My name is Lyda Carney. I didn't know if you would be in the office this early."

"Yes, Ms. Carney. What can I do for you?"

"I'm the head clerk in the Alaska Account Department of SeaFirst Bank. I work for Mr. Gerlitz. That's where we met." She was hesitant to come to the point.

"Oh, yes, Ms. Carney, I remember you. What prompts you to call me? Is there something wrong in the bank?" The question was meant to be facetious. He made the remark to lighten the conversation. It didn't.

"Do you have any suspicions about the Alaska Account, Sergeant Hayes?" she asked timidly.

"Please, call me Rube. I apologize for trying to be funny. I can see you have a problem. Let's start again. Now, exactly what can I do for you?" he asked.

"I guess I should begin at the beginning." she said quietly. "For some time now, I've had the feeling that something within our department was not right. I had no idea what it was, but something just didn't sit right for some reason. Have you ever had one of those feelings, Sergeant?"

"Yes, I have. And they're usually right," Rube admitted.

"I have to tell you that I did something that was totally against bank policy. I took some papers from the locked files belonging to Mr. Gerlitz. I copied them and put them back. I felt like a burglar."

"I have no authority in Seattle, Ms. Carney. If you're looking to confess to a crime at the bank, I suggest you call your local police department. I should tell you that what you did probably violates bank policy, but not state laws."

"You don't understand, Sergeant. I copied these files and took them home to see if there was anything wrong with them. I think I found something very wrong."

"Okay, let's try to get this all sorted out. Take a deep breath and relax a minute. I'm on your side. But before I can help you, I have to know what the problem is."

"I know, Sergeant, and I'm sorry for making this so confusing. I'll try to explain properly." She paused and Rube heard her take a deep breath. "I told you that I was suspicious about the account. Well, I really had no idea what was going on, and quite frankly I still don't. That's why I called you. I know something is wrong with the account, but I don't know who is involved."

"Are you saying there are funds missing from the account?" Rube began taking notes. The feelings he had while talking with Ben Gerlitz were now coming home to haunt him. These were the same feelings Colin James had experienced. "Always listen to that little voice inside you, always!"

"When I took the file from the drawer in Mr. Gerlitz's office, I found two file folders inside, one for SeaFirst and one for the Sate of Alaska. Mr. Stackhaus had notarized both sets of files. Mr. Gerlitz and Ms. Pedersen had each signed them also. The trouble is that the files are different. The SeaFirst copy has a few extra pages. The pages itemize the interest payments made to the account. Those pages are missing from the State of Alaska copy."

"So you think someone is taking the interest money from the account, is that correct?" Rube was writing as fast as he could.

"Yes, that's correct. The problem is I don't know who is responsible, or if the three of them are in it together. That is why I can't go to the officers in the bank or to Ms. Pedersen. I just don't know who to trust. There may be nothing wrong. Perhaps there is an arrangement for doing what they are doing, but I couldn't find it. The other thing is that the interest money is transferred twice each week to an account outside the bank, Alaska Maritime something-or-another. The statements are sent to a post office box here in Seattle. I thought that to be a little strange, too."

"All this sounds suspicious all right. Is it possible for you to send me a copy of the files?"

"I've already done that. I sent them express mail on Saturday. I took the address from your business card in my Rolodex. You should have them some time today. Would you look them over and let me know what you think? I need someone to tell me what to do." Tension was again mounting in her voice.

"You go back to work and try not to let anyone know about your suspicions. I'll take a look at the files when they arrive. If I find anything wrong, I'll let you know right away. Is it safe to call at the bank?"

"I may not be able to talk very much on the office phone, but I can call you back on another one. Just call me here, at the bank. My home number is in the envelope I sent to you." She seemed to be more relaxed now. "Did I do the right thing, Sergeant?"

"We will soon see, Ms. Carney." Rube was checking his notes to be sure he had all the information he needed. "What time will you get home this evening?" he asked.

"I should be home by 6 o'clock our time." Alaska time zone was an hour earlier.

"If I get the files today, I will try to call you by 6:30"

"Thank you for your help. I just didn't know where to turn."

"I'll do what I can." They said their goodbyes and hung up.

Leaning back in his chair, deep in thought, it was impossible for him to imagine Aliana being involved in something illegal. Ben Gerlitz seemed like a nice enough guy when he was here, but he had changed the last time they had met. Colin James had noticed it, too. How could they skim off the interest money from the account without anyone becoming suspicious; without anyone finding out about it. More questions. He would have to wait for the files to arrive in the morning mail.

He filled his coffee cup and went back to the regular morning routine. It had been a busy weekend and there was a huge stack of files on his desk. Rube was about to finish reviewing the stack when, again, his telephone rang. It was Stan Withers.

After checking to be sure Rube was in his office, Captain Withers made the walk from the neighboring building to headquarters. He looked as though he hadn't slept in days. He stuck his head through the doorway and Rube motioned him in.

"Looks to me like you've had a rough weekend," Rube commented.

"It was busy all right. Have you heard about the team making an arrest early Saturday morning?" Withers asked.

"No. What happened? Who did they arrest?"

"They followed Eddie Sanchez and his driver from the club. Ramon Chavez had put a hit order on B.J. Miller. Eddie and his friend tried to burn B.J.'s house. Randy had our team members following them. When they lit up the Molotov cocktail, one of them shot Larry Combs, Eddie's driver. He threw the bomb anyway and set the house on fire. We had a fire truck on the scene right away. B.J had some people in the house with him, but they all got out okay. We tried to get B.J. to roll over on Chavez, but he was too angry to negotiate. I think he'll come around today or tomorrow, though. I'm having an audiotape made that will let Miller hear the hit order for himself. We need him as a witness against Chavez and Sanchez."

"Sounds as though you had a really busy weekend."

"Yeah, my team is really getting tired. I hope we can wrap this up in a couple of days. You know how it goes; people start to make mistakes when they get fatigued. I borrowed some men from Metro, but they don't have any experience in this kind of work."

"Sorry, I can't help you out with personnel. If this had been a month from now, I could have loaned you some troopers. Right now, with all the tourist traffic, my men are spread pretty thin." Rube laughed. "Makes you glad to see the snow, doesn't it?"

"I don't know if I'm quite ready for that yet." Stan, too, was chuckling. "I'll get out of here. I just wanted to give you a rundown on what was happening, since originally, this was your case."

"Thanks, Stan. Keep me posted. Call me if you need an extra hand. I might be able to get out of this office for a while." Stan waved as he left the office. Rube stared after him for a moment, then went back to the folders on his desk.

He was just finishing the daily reports when the receptionist came in with a large blue and white envelope. She dropped the packet on his desk and wet back to the front. Rube saw the return address was that of Lyda Carney. He walked around the desk and closed the office door before opening the envelope.

Inside was another manila envelope. It, too, was sealed. Opening the envelope he withdrew two file folders. They had been carefully marked to identify one as the July audit, SeaFirst Bank copy, the other was marked July audit, State of Alaska copy. Also included was a letter from Lyda Carney. She had meticulously outlined the pages and line numbers that were different in each of the two copies. Rube found her outline easy to follow and soon came to the section of the audit dealing with the interest payments. There were several pages of columns of numbers reflecting the total interest paid to the account. There were itemized figures dealing with the expenses assessed for management of the account. At the end of each page there was a positive balance of several thousands of dollars. The bank copy showed those funds were paid to Alaska Maritime Investments account on Monday and on Thursday of each week. This entire section was missing from the State of Alaska copy of the audit. No mention of Alaska Maritime Investments in any other part of the audit. No mention of the company appeared anywhere in the State of Alaska copy.

Not being an accountant, Rube found it difficult to analyze what he was reading. He had no trouble realizing why Lyda Carney had become suspicious. Although there was no evidence, that he could discern, of any wrongdoing, there was certainly probable cause for investigation.

Like Lyda, Rube wondered where to turn for help. Under other circumstances he would have called Aliana. It was a thought he didn't enjoy, but she may be involved. He was having trouble making himself believe that. It seemed more likely that, since the Alaska copy contained no information about the payments, Aliana had no idea this loss was taking place. Another scenario would be that Alaska Maritime Investments account was a legitimate State of Alaska account.

Looking at the clock he realized he had worked right through the regular lunch hour. He punched the numbers for Captain Milo Thomas.

"Got a few minutes to see me?" he asked when the Captain answered.

Rube carried the files down the hall to the Captain's office. He spent several minutes giving the boss the Readers Digest version of the files. At the end he presented a list of what he considered viable possibilities, both legal and otherwise.

Milo stared at the center of his desk and blew out a long, deep breath. "Do you understand what implications you've got here?" Milo asked.

"Yes, I do. And under ordinary circumstances I would just take this to the department of finance, but I can't do that with this information because they have signed off on this report. I see only two options. We don't have the expertise within this department to deal with this. So, we can either go to the private sector for accounting assistance or we can go to the FBI. The feds deal with this sort of thing all the time. They should know how to investigate this one. I have thought of going outside the department with this, and the attorney general may not let us do the investigating anyway."

"What's your recommendation," Milo asked.

"Can I take a few days, let's say the rest of the week, to find out if there really is a crime involved here. If not, we can relax. If there appears to be one, we can either get authorization from the AG to investigate or turn it over to the FBI." Rube knew the dangers of his personal involvement with one of the principals in the case. Blinded by personal feelings, he rationalized he could take care of this initial investigation. That way he might be able to protect Aliana from unnecessary embarrassment if it turned out there was no crime.

"I'll give you until Monday morning," Milo instructed. "I think we should find out just who Alaska Maritime Investments really is. If it is a state agency, we can forget the whole thing. If not we'll have to decide where to go from there."

"I agree. I'll get started right away."

Aliana was planning to be in Anchorage next week. Rube wanted to resolve this situation before she came back to town. He didn't want any of this to come between him and this lady for whom he was beginning to develop strong feelings.

Chapter Twenty Four

It was nearly 3 in the morning when Ramon's phone awakened him. Groggy and half asleep he answered. "Hello," he said gruffly.

It was Larry, Eddie's driver. "Boss, don't say anything. This phone may be recorded. Eduardo and I were arrested tonight." He waited, but there was no comment. "They brought us to the Post Road jail and booked us. During the booking process Eduardo became very ill. He was throwing up and looked awful. His face was red and he seemed to be choking. They wouldn't let me help him. They called a nurse to look at him. That's when they took me to a cell and I never saw him again. They won't tell me how he is." Again he waited for Ramon to speak. Nothing. "What do you want me to do?" he asked.

"Nothing." Ramon said in a calm tone. "Do nothing and say nothing. I will have a lawyer there sometime this morning. Have they told you the charges?"

"Sort of, they said we had been arrested for arson and attempted murder. I would have called earlier, but I got shot in the arm and have been in the medical office until now. I'll be alright, but I don't know how Eduardo is doing."

"Okay, sit tight and wait for the lawyer. I'll call Dante right away and see how he wants me to handle this. Thanks for the call."

Ramon hung up the telephone and thought. This was serious and his boss needed to be called right away. It was a call Ramon was not looking forward to making. He checked his watch and calculated the time difference. Two hours later there. He dialed the direct number for Dante.

"Hola!" came the brusk answer. The entire conversation would be in Spanish.

"Dante, this is Ramon in Alaska. I hope you have a bed full of beautiful women."

"Did you call me this time of the night to chit-chat or do you have business?"

"I have a situation here, Dante. It is one that I think will require your advice." Ramon spoke solicitously.

"I should have known this was not a social call. Hold on a minute while I turn on the lights and get a note pad." There was a long pause. The voice once again came on the line. "Now, tell me what is happening in Alaska that can't wait until a decent hour."

"A very bad thing happened tonight. Eduardo and his driver, Larry, were arrested. Larry called me a few minutes ago from the jail. He said they were charged with arson and attempted murder. I will call a lawyer this morning. Larry was shot in the arm, but says he is going to be okay. However, Eduardo got sick. He has been getting much worse lately. Larry said he was choking and his face was red. When the nurse came to look at him, they took Larry to a cell and Eduardo wasn't able to learn any more. Larry called from the jail and was afraid the line was monitored, so he didn't want to talk much. I just wanted to let you know what the situation was like and ask how you want me to go ahead."

"It was a wise thing you did." He seemed to be pondering the problem. "It is too early in the day to call anyone now. When our lawyer opens his office, I will call and have him make arrangements for a lawyer to come to Anchorage. Get your local lawyer to ask the judge for two weeks to prepare a plea for both Eddie and Larry. The attorney we send you will be well versed in how to handle this situation. You will be able to speak openly with this person, but let him handle everything, and I do mean everything. Don't contact Larry or Eduardo yourself. Do you understand?"

"I understand." He knew there would be no further discussion on the telephone.

"Good night, then. I will call you tomorrow." The conversation ended with a click in Ramon's ear.

Unable to get back to sleep, Ramon walked down to the refrigerator, poured a glass of orange juice and sat in the dark kitchen, thinking. An hour later the phone was ringing again. He turned on the light and answered. This time it was the shift supervisor at the jail.

When he learned who was calling he asked, "Yes, Sergeant, what can I do for you?"

"You may already know that two of your employees were arrested tonight. One Larry Combs and one Eduardo Sanchez. Both these men gave your number as a contact. Is this the correct number?"

"Yes, these men work for me. Is there a problem I need to be concerned about?"

"I was asked by both prisoners to contact you to inform you that Larry Combs was shot in the arm this evening. His wound has been treated and the nurse on duty says the injury is superficial. Mr. Sanchez, however, became ill during the booking process. The nurse was summoned and recommended we transport him to Providence Hospital by ambulance. He is being examined at the hospital at this time. There will be a guard with Mr. Sanchez all night. I have no further information on his condition."

"I thank you for your call. If there is any further information about either of the men, please feel free to call me at once."

Ramon finished his juice. He sat at the kitchen table contemplating his next move. Eddie had been sick for a long time and was getting worse. It appeared that it was only a matter of time before his friend would no longer be there for him. The two had been friends all their lives and Ramon had always looked after Eddie. It would be difficult to leave him in the hospital and not contact him. The lawyers had to get him out of jail. When he was released Ramon would send him to Mexico City for medical treatment. There was nothing he could do now but wait.

It was not quite 8 AM when Ramon contacted Aaron Portman at home. He explained the situation to the lawyer, giving him details of the charges and the injury to Larry as well as the health of Eduardo. He agreed to represent the pair until a criminal lawyer could get here. Ramon said he thought the new lawyer was coming from San Diego. He also agreed to meet with Larry Combs within the hour. He would call when he returned from the Post Road Annex.

Rueben Hayes was at his desk and had nearly finished the stack of paper the night shift had generated. With a fresh cup of coffee in his hand, he walked outside to stretch and enjoy the clear, warm morning. He sipped his coffee, trying to clear his mind. It made it easier to cope with any new developments the day may bring. He felt good and wished he had time to fly his airplane for an hour or two. He drained the last few drops of coffee and walked back to his office.

The Captain passed him in the hall, "Good morning, Rube."

"Morning, Cap. Going to be a nice day."

"Good. I will be out of the office this morning. Have you got time to cover for me?"

"Sure. I have a lot of catching up to do in my office, and I have that call to make to the CPA."

"I'll be back after lunch. I would like to see you this afternoon when you have some time."

"I'll have time. See you later today." Milo waved and walked on down the hall.

Rube rinsed his cup and returned to his office. He searched the Rolodex for Burt Fields. Burt looked like a bookkeeper, down to the bow tie he habitually wore. He was a wiry little guy with a sense of humor you would not expect from him.

"Hi, Burt. Rube Hayes. Can you talk a minute?"

"Hello, Rube. Haven't heard from you since tax season. How has your summer been going? Been flying a lot?"

"It's been a busy one, but it's winding down now. I might even get a day off this weekend." Rube didn't want to take too much of the man's time. "Burt, can I come by your office for a minute this morning? I have an accounting problem I would like you to take a look at. You can bill this to the state."

"Sure thing, Rube. What time did you want to come over? I'm pretty open this morning."

"This may be urgent, so the sooner the better. I have an audit I want you to look over."

"Bring it over. Shirley isn't in yet, so just come on into the office."

"Thanks, Burt. I appreciate it. See you in a few minutes."

He hung up he telephone, dug the SeaFirst file from his cabinet and walked to the receptionist's office. He told the woman at the desk where he would be and how long he expected to be gone. He would have his radio, he told her.

Driving to the CPA office, he couldn't help wondering who could be involved in this scheme, if indeed, it turned out to be a criminal act. Traffic was light and he made it there in less than ten minutes. The front office door was unlocked, but Shirley was not yet at her desk.

"Anybody home?" Rube called.

"Come on back, Rube. Just finishing a report for a client." He closed the green file-folder and set it aside.

"Good to see you, Rube. You look well and healthy. What is this audit you wanted me to look at? Is this Trooper business?"

"I guess that's what I need to have you tell me. I must preface this with a note of confidentiality. There may or may not be a crime here. In either case this file contains confidential state information. This information cannot go further than you and me. Do you agree to this?"

"Of course. All my client information is private and confidential."

"I know, Burt. But it would look bad if any of this file turned up on the front page of the Anchorage Daily News," he said, sliding the manila envelope containing the file-folder to Burt's desk.

Burt opened the envelope, scanned the accompanying letter, then began to look at the files. He looked again at the cover letter. When he had sifted both files, one page at a time to the final pages, he stopped, blew out a long breath and gave Rube an intense look.

"Wow, Rube. I have been an accountant a very long time and this is the first time I have ever come across anything like this. It will take me some time to read this in detail, but there is most certainly unauthorized activity here. You were right, as was Ms. Carney. There is no way, at this point, to know who is responsible and certainly not who is involved. This could include the bank President, the guy in charge of the Alaska Department, department of finance personnel, and maybe even the governor. How much time can I have to look at this?"

"I have to report on this to my Captain on Monday. Can you give me a summary and an opinion by then?"

"I can, but it will all be based on these files. I won't have time to investigate the details."

"Thanks, Burt. Like I said on the phone, bill this time to the State of Alaska. I will have to wait for your report before opening a full investigation." He stood to leave. "I'll let you get at it, then. You have my cell phone number. Call me when you get finished." He waved and closed the door behind him. Shirley was at her desk. He said "hi" and left the office.

Rube told the receptionist he was back in his office. He had just taken his seat at the desk when there was a light tap on his open door.

Rube waved him in. "Good to see you, Stan. How is the drug business these days?"

Stan Withers chuckled. "We took two big players off the street last night, Larry Combs and Eddie Sanchez. Just in time, too. We tried to renew the warrant for listening to Ramon's office, but the judge got huffy. He said this wasn't an open-ended warrant and if we hadn't found probable cause by now we would have to do it some other way. The warrant expires at midnight on Monday. It will make my troops happy. They will finally get a day off." He grinned, waved and left the office.

Chapter Twenty Five

Sergeant Hayes had been working on his time sheet and daily log. He was totaling his monthly flying hours when Captain Milo Thomas returned. The intercom brought his attention back to the office.

"Sergeant Hayes. How can I help you?"

"Rube, it's Milo. Do you have a few minutes to come to my office?"

"Sure. Be right there."

Five minutes later Rube was in the Captain's office. "Close the door, Rube. I want this to be private."

Rube closed the door and took a seat across from his boss. "Am I in trouble, Cap?" he inquired.

"No, but I just came from the colonel's office, and I have some things I need to discuss with you privately. First off, I will tell you that the meeting with the colonel was to inform me that I had just been promoted to Major in charge of all Southcentral personnel."

"Congratulations, Cap, er, I mean Major."

"Yeah, but keep this under your hat until it's announced by the Commander. I wouldn't have told you about this, but it has to do with what I am about to ask you next. In the past you have turned down promotions in order to keep flying fishery patrol. I need to know if you would give that up for a new position as Captain? The colonel asked who I wanted to replace me in this office. I didn't have to think twice; I want you. But it would mean that you would have to find someone to replace you during commercial fishing season." He paused a moment to evaluate the puzzled look on Rube's face. "Do you think you could consider the job?"

Rube took a long drink of his coffee before answering. "Whew! This is quite a shock. How much time do I have to make up my mind?"

"How much time do you need? I would like an answer early next week. Are you going to consider it?"

"I'll let you in on a little secret," Rube confessed. "I have someone in my life right now who is causing me to re-evaluate my priorities. I can't say who right now, but if there ever was a time to make a change, now would be it. I'm going to have to give it some thought. I have a question for you, though. Did you tell the colonel you wanted me specifically?"

"I told him I was going to ask you." Milo gave a wry grin. "How long have you had this new girl, and why haven't I heard about it?"

"I'm not certain she feels the same way, but I hope she does."

"I know it's not fair, but you won't be able to discuss this with her. This won't be made public until late next week."

"I understand, Cap. I'll try to have an answer for you by Monday. And, by the way, I should have something for you by then about that other issue. I am having my CPA look at the file. At first look he indicated that there is probable wrong-doing." He stood, picked up his cup and walked to the door. "Thanks for the vote of confidence, whatever I decide." He opened the door as the Captain saluted.

Rube returned to his own office, trying to assimilate what he and Milo had discussed. This was totally unexpected. There was one person he had to confide in before he could begin to make this decision. He got out of his chair, walked around his desk and closed the door. He wanted privacy for this call. He had no idea how he would approach Aliana about this, but no guts no glory.

Marge Dawson answered the telephone. "Is Ms. Pedersen in?" Rube asked.

"Yes, she is. Who shall I say is calling?"

"Tell her it's Sergeant Hayes with the Alaska State Troopers."

He was on hold for a few seconds, then Aliana's voice filled his ear. "Sergeant Hayes, this is a surprise. To what do I owe this call?"

"I have something very important to discuss with you. Can you talk a few minutes?"

"For you I'll make time. It's so good to talk to you, Rube. I've missed you." She gave a short giggle. "What important thing do you need to discuss with me?"

"Aliana, I miss talking to you. This isn't something I planned to talk to you about on the telephone. It's something better done with candlelight and wine." He still didn't know how to approach this.

"This sounds just yummy. Is this an obscene phone call?" she giggled again.

"You're not helping. This really is serious." Here goes nothing, he thought. "I know we haven't been going together long, but I have to tell you that I feel about you like no other person I have ever been with. Something has come up and I need to know if you have any feelings for me, as well. I guess I need to know if you think this relationship is going anywhere. Do you think it has a chance of lasting?"

"Oh, Rube, I'm sorry. I didn't mean to make light of your call. I was just so happy to hear from you. To answer your question honestly? I just don't know, but I hope it will last. I like you more than you can know. Most men I meet run like the wind when they find out about Saundra. You embraced her and treated her with love. I could never forget that. As far as me personally, I can't say how things will turn out, but I have hopes that we will be together a long time."

Neither of them spoke for several moments. Rube broke the silence.

"Aliana, what I am about to tell you is not to go public just yet. I have been offered a promotion to captain, commander of the Anchorage detachment. Somehow, it seemed important that I know how you felt; that I include you in the final equation. You have become that important to me. I know this is a poor way to announce all this, but my decision will include my feelings toward you. Does that make any sense?"

"Rube, I can't, at this point, say how long we will last. The thought of living happily-ever-after is very appealing to me. Will it work? I don't know. Do I want it to work? Oh, yes, very much. My job takes so much of my time and Saundra takes most of the rest, but my time with you has been the most en-joyable of my life. My contract with the state will last as long as the governor, perhaps five more years. After that, I can't say. Please don't ask me to be more definite than that."

"The best I could hope for is that you be honest with me, and I guess that is where we stand. We can talk more about it next week when you get here. I am really looking forward to seeing you." Rube didn't know what to say. "You still want to come, don't you?"

"Rube, you can't keep me away. I have to hold you tight."

"I'll call you over the weekend and let you know what I decide. I miss you and wish you were here now."

"I miss you too, you dear man. Good luck. Please, call me soon."

They said their good-byes and hung up. He wasn't any more at ease than he had been before the call. The good news was that Aliana had the same strong feelings he was enjoying.

Rube was still thinking about Aliana when someone tapped on his office door.

"Come in," Rube announced.

It was Stan Withers of the SCAN team.

"Got a minute, Rube?"

Sure, Stan. What's happening at your end of the building?"

"I just came down to fill you in on a couple of developments. They just called from the courthouse to say that the judge won't renew or extend the surveillance on the Sombrero Restaurant. The judge said this wasn't an open-ended warrant and if we didn't have probable cause for arrests by now we would have to get it some other way," Stan was shaking his head. "Disappointing to say the least."

"Too bad. Seems like it was just beginning to pay some dividends. Do you thank you will be able to turn B.J.?"

"We are working on that now," Stan said. "All this will have an effect on your witness, Rube. I'm sorry it hasn't worked out better. The good news is that I have more bad news. The two we arrested for arson had a court appearance today. Larry Combs was there with his lawyer and Eduardo Sanchez was represented by the same lawyer. They asked for a two-week continuance because of the illness of Mr. Sanchez. The judge granted it. However, he denied bail for both; said they were both a flight risk. The Judicial Services Trooper that brought Larry combs to court overheard him talking with his lawyer. He said Ramon is having a big-time attorney from San Diego come up to defend them. I'll send you the dates and times when I get them from the courthouse."

"You're just full of happy information today, aren't you, Stan?" Rube thought a moment. "Do you think we need to call Seattle and tell our friends there what is happening? They may have information about the attorney being sent, who he is and what he is like."

"Hadn't thought of that, but it might be a good idea. I'll do it when I get back to the office." Stan sauntered out of Rube's office.

Rube pulled a file from his drawer, opened it and found the contact number for Molita Juarez and her soon-to-be husband. Molita answered the telephone. After pleasant hello's, the sergeant told Ms. Juarez what was happening in the case. He apologized to her for the lack of progress, but told her there should be progress in the case, soon.

He checked the time. It was late in the day and he was getting tired. He usually didn't think about such things, but he thought, this must have been a stressful day. Checking his calendar he found nothing on it for the rest of the day. He reached for the phone and called his old friend, a retired trooper, now a Kenai River Guide, Jim Stogsdill. Jim said if he could come down that afternoon he would take him out on the river for some great silver salmon fishing. With his cell phone in his pocket, he checked out with dispatch and drove to his airplane at Lake Hood checking the weather, he was looking forward to a relaxing flight to the Kenai Peninsula.

Chapter Twenty Six

The drive to the office at this early hour was usually pleasant; however, the dark skies overhead mirrored his mood. Rube had made his decision. Was it the right decision? He wasn't sure. He had come to law enforcement by accident. In college he had dreams of a law degree and a career as a trial attorney. His senior year at the University of Idaho had finished off his savings. He had taken a Criminal Justice Degree and looked for a job in a police force somewhere. It was the check and not the job that had his interest. In just a short time, he realized he was becoming a good cop. When he read of openings in the Alaska State Troopers, he applied and was accepted.

Shortly after finishing the trooper academy, he began flight training. It seemed a natural step when living in Alaska. The rest, as they say, is history. His log book indicated he had averaged 22.5 hours flying time each week since May. This was in addition to the hours spent with his administrative duties.

He parked in his usual place, got out of the car and looked at the dark sky. The days were getting shorter. The dark skies were a harbinger of the approaching fall season. His fishing trip to the Kenai River had been great and the relaxing time with Jim Stogsdill had helped clear his mind and allowed him to contemplate the future. He gave a shrug of his shoulders, climbed the steps to the office building and was looking forward to his first cup of coffee of the day.

The sergeant's desk was piled high with reports from the previous weekend. None of the files were marked for his immediate attention, so he began with the top file and slowly worked his way to the bottom of the pile. By 8:30 AM the administrative staff were in their offices. After retrieving his second cup of coffee, he dialed Captain Milo Thomas to schedule a time for a meeting. 10 AM.

His telephone rang as he took the first sip of his hot coffee.

"Sergeant Hayes," he answered.

"Rube, Burt Fields. Can you talk a minute?"

"Burt. Thanks for calling. You were the next item on my list. Were you able to discern anything from the files I gave you?"

"Yeah, we need to talk right away. Do you want to do this in your office or mine?"

Rube thought a moment. "I have a 10 o'clock meeting with the Captain. The meeting should last less than an hour. Can this wait until then?"

"In fact, that would be better for me. I'll be in your office at 11. This is important and we need to do it without disruptions. Can we do that?" Fields asked.

"I'll see to it, Burt. See you at eleven." The uneasy feeling hit him immediately. His early morning feeling of depression was back. He closed his files, closed his office door and walked to the Captain's office.

"Mornin', Cap. You ready for me?"

"You bet," he said while closing a file folder on his desk. I was hoping you would be in this morning. Have you made your decision?"

"Well, I think so. I thought about it all weekend and finally came to what I hope is a good decision. At least for me and my future. It's a big step and a big change in my life."

Milo stared into his eyes. "Am I reading you right? You decided to take the promotion?"

"Yes, sir. That is my decision, though I'm not certain I will do well at it."

"You will do just fine. You have been doing most of the job for years. You have done it as a sergeant because you wouldn't let me promote you to lieutenant. The colonel will send you to some administrative training, most of that will be right here at the University of Alaska Anchorage. You and I will have to go over some things before I move to the new office. That move is scheduled for Thursday. We have a lot to do before then. Thank you for accepting, Rube. I have always enjoyed working with you and look forward to more of the same." Milo reached across the desk to shake the hand of his soon-to-be Captain.

They discussed a few items that occurred over the weekend and Rube told him that Burt was coming with his report on the SeaFirst files.

"I will call the colonel right away to let him know of your decision. Until he contacts you, this should remain just between us. Okay?"

Rube nodded his agreement. "Thanks again, Cap."

He had just returned to his office when the receptionist notified him that Burt Fields had arrived. Rube met him at the front. "Want some coffee?" he asked.

"No thanks, Rube. I've had my quota for the morning."

"Come on back to my office then, Burt." He motioned for Burt to follow.

Rube pulled another chair to the front of his desk beside the one Burt Fields had taken. Burt took a manila folder from his briefcase and placed the contents, two files, on the desktop. Inside each folder cover, a typewritten outline was stapled. He checked to make sure the door was closed.

"This is a hot potato, Rube. Your clerk at SeaFirst was right to get outside help. I have been over this and, if I worked in that office, I'd be scared, too."

Rube nodded his understanding. "Then there really is evidence of wrongdoing indicated in these files?"

"Big time. My research ability is limited to what I can find in the computer, but Ms. Lyda hit the nail on the head. The SeaFirst file and the State of Alaska file don't match. The SeaFirst file has several pages dealing with operational costs and administrative fees. They also deal with the interest paid by the bank to something called Alaska Maritime Investments. I have searched everywhere I can think of and cannot find any company of that name. I searched all 50 states to find a corporate registry for the company. I couldn't find one. It appears that the company is only camouflage." He paused to make sure Rube was still following.

Burt continued. "It appears to me that this is a dummy company to which a bank account somewhere is assigned. The bank forwards the proceeds from interest to that company name twice weekly. Bare in mind, more than two BILLION dollars a year pass through this account. Though the daily balance is much less than that amount, the bank is paying interest on an average daily balance that stays in the MILLIONS. At two and one half percent annually, less administrative fees and service charges, we are talking a lot of money. Once it has been paid to Alaska Maritime Investments, it never appears again. Do you know of any such agency within the state?"

Rube got out of his chair and opened the bottom drawer in his filing cabinet. He pulled out a small book. The official state office registry. He thumbed through the pages and found nothing.

"I don't see it listed in the state registry." He made a note. "I'll have it checked out." He returned to his seat beside the CPA. Can you tell who is involved in this? Mr. Stackhaus from the bank? Ben Gerlitz, our friend Lyda, the governor, the department of finance? How deep does this go?"

"I don't know, Rube. It has to be someone with knowledge of finance. It appears to be an ingenious scheme. The banking and investment authorities will be very interested in this. Who do I think is involved? I don't know, couldn't even guess. Be very careful how you deal with this. Since high state officials could be involved, I think the attorney general would be the logical point to start. I can't tell you much more, only details, but you have the general theme. Like I said, this thing has the potential to turn around and bite you." He stood. "I have to get back to my office, but if you need anything else, just call me."

Chapter Twenty Seven

Ramon had spent the past several days worrying about his lifelong friend, Eduardo Sanchez. His health was deteriorating quickly. Eddie's condition was self inflicted, but that did not make the result less heartbreaking. Eddie had protected Ramon his entire life. It was a good friendship. Ramon supplied the brain power and Eddie did the muscle work. El Dante had given the young boys employment and an education. He had taken care of their mothers, as well as caring for the two lads. Now Eddie was surely dying and Ramon could do nothing to prevent it. It was sad.

Ramon was on the way to the Ted Stevens International Airport to pick up the lawyer Dante had sent. His name was Jules Steinman. His office had called and told Ramon what time Mr. Steinman would arrive. He didn't know how he would recognize the lawyer, but once at the baggage carousel, Ramon found him at once. Steinman was a very large man in a dark suit, carefully tailored. Ramon introduced himself and offered to carry his large suitcase. They said little on the way to the parking garage.

"Is there somewhere we can get a bite to eat and to discuss this? Someplace quiet and private," Steinman asked.

"Of course. I own a restaurant. We can have food and privacy in my office."

"Have you talked with Eduardo since he was arrested?" the lawyer asked.

"No, Dante said I shouldn't contact either him or Larry until you arrived. I must admit I was tempted to go to the hospital to see Eddie. Do you want me to contact my attorney and have him meet us at the restaurant? I would be happy to make the introductions." Ramon wanted to help.

"No, that won't be necessary. I have spoken with him and once I go to meet our clients I will be very busy. I won't have time to socialize." Steinman was all business. "I don't want you to contact either of these clients without asking me first. I know they are your friends, however, they are my clients. At this point, I want to keep you distanced from them for the benefit of both you and the clients. Do you understand that?"

"Yes, I understand, but you get this. These men are my friends and employees. I want you to keep me informed every step of the way. Do you understand that?" Ramon used a calm, but firm tone.

"You are paying the bill. You can have it your way. But remember I run the legal defense. Don't get in my way," the lawyer countered.

The rest of the trip was made in silence. At the Sombrero Restaurant, the lawyer gathered information and laid out plans for the defense. He called the hospital and the jail to speak with his clients. He had nearly filled a legal pad with names, dates, and case numbers. He inquired into the general facts of the case. He then called Ramon's lawyer to schedule a meeting.

"I would prefer a car and driver. If you cannot arrange that I will use cabs. I find that, in the end, a car and driver are less expensive," Steinman said, still trying to be in control.

"I'll have a car and driver for you in front of the restaurant in about ten minutes. He will know the addresses of most places and people you wish to visit. If there is nothing else, I have a business to run. Thank you for coming, Mr. Steinman."

Rube was busy studying the letters on the inside covers of the two SeaFirst files. He was beginning to acquire some understanding of the differences in the files. This was not his field and it was difficult for him to follow, not knowing what was allowed and what was done, or which was legal and which was not. He had been at it for a couple of hours when someone entered his office.

It was Milo Thomas. Milo smiled and, as he neared the desk, opened a small black box and placed it on Rube's desk.

"The letter of promotion is being drafted in the colonel's office as we speak. Congratulations, Captain Hayes. You can wear the new bars tomorrow." Milo reached over the desk to shake Rube's hand.

"That was quick, Milo. And thanks for the vote of confidence. I guess I should think about my own replacement now," Captain Rueben Hayes said, shifting mental gears.

"Do you have anyone in mind for the job?" Milo asked.

"I am thinking about Sergeant Leon Balfore. He has always done a good job of replacing me when I had to be out of the office."

"He would be my choice, too. You realize that your replacement should be a lieutenant. You would have been one if you had taken the promotion."

"I'll talk with him when he gets back to the office this afternoon." Looking at his watch he realized it was already afternoon.

"Congratulations again, Rube. Supply will fix you up with new uniforms. See you tomorrow."

Back in his own office, he dialed the intercom for dispatch. He asked to have Leon Balfore sent to his office when he returned before going off shift. He then returned to the question of what to do about the discrepancies in the SeaFirst report. He picked up the telephone and dialed Juneau.

"Department of Finance, Ms. Pedersen's office. How may I direct your call?"

"This is Sergeant Hayes of the Alaska Troopers. Is it possible to speak with Ms. Pedersen?"

The call was transferred and a friendly voice filled his ear. "Hello, Rube. To what do I owe this call?"

"I could tell you that it was just because I miss you, but I'm afraid this is business."

"Oh, Rube. You aren't going to try to get out of being with me this weekend, are you?"

"Oh, nothing like that. In fact, I was calling to see if you could make it earlier. I have some papers I want you to look at. It has to do with your department. It's very important. I am tied up here because of some things in this office."

She was curious. "What is so important it warrants a trip from Juneau? Are you that lonesome?" She giggled a little.

"As a matter of fact, I am. But I have some disturbing information about your department of finance and I need some professional advice. I don't know anyone more qualified to answer my questions than you." There was silence on the other end. "This really is serious, Aliana, I need you here in your official capacity. Can you come?"

"Of course, Rube. I'm sorry I took your call lightly. I thought you were teasing. Can you tell me what this is about?"

"I'd rather not do that on the telephone, but I have some information that indicates a crime has been committed and I really do need your advice. Besides that I have some good news. I just received word that I have been promoted to Captain and made Commander of the Anchorage Detachment. That won't be official until tomorrow, so keep it under your hat." Hayes wanted to talk more, but his intercom line was blinking. "Can you come?"

"I'll be on the first flight in the morning. I should be in Anchorage a little after noon. It just moves my schedule up one day." She was very curious now. She couldn't imagine what would have prompted this call. "See you tomorrow."

"Call me and let me know your flight number and I will pick you up at the airport. Gotta go. See you tomorrow."

"Congratulations on the promotion. I'll kiss the new Captain tomorrow. Bye."

He answered dispatch. "Sergeant Balfore will be here in ten minutes."

Rube cleared his desk and waited.

Balfore tapped at the door. He looked like a Mountie. Tall, slim, dark wavy hair. The creases in his uniform looked as if they could cut you. He was a man of detail. "You wanted to see me, Sergeant?"

"Yes, Leon, come on in and close the door. We have to talk. Do you want a cup of coffee or a soda?"

"No thanks, Sarge." He closed the door and took a seat. "Am I in trouble for something?"

"No, but we have a serious matter to discuss." Rube tried to put him at ease. "First of all, I want you to keep this conversation confidential for a day or two."

"No problem, Sarge. Is something wrong?"

"Not really. You will be the first to know I have been promoted to Captain and made the Commander of the detachment," Rube announced.

"Congratulations, Captain. Can't think of anyone I would rather see in the job. Where is Milo going?"

"He is the new Major in charge of personnel for Southcentral. Works directly for the colonel. Which brings me to why I called you in here. I want to know if you would be interested in taking my job in this office. It would mean a promotion to Lieutenant with the appropriate wage adjustment. Are you interested, Leon?"

"Wow, this is a surprise. Are you sure I can do the job?" Leon inquired.

"No one knows the job when they get promoted. That goes for me, as well. You have done the job in my absence many times, and done it well. There is no question in my mind you can do it. The question is, do you want the position." Rube watched as Leon looked at his feet, thinking. "Do you want to sleep on it, and give me an answer tomorrow?"

"I think, Captain, that I can do the job. If you want me, I will be glad to give it a try. Thank you. Will it be alright to talk about it with my wife?"

"Sure, Leon. She should be proud of you. The colonel is supposed to have a letter out to the departments by tomorrow. It will be public knowledge then. I'll get on the phone and let Milo know of your decision. The men like you and I like you. It should be an easy transition. Thank you for accepting. Once you get the official word, you can go to supply and get new uniforms—without stripes. I think all this will be official by the end of the week. Congratulations, Lieutenant."

Rube called Milo to inform him of Leon's decision. Suddenly he was very tired.

Chapter Twenty Eight

Major Milo Thomas was in Rube's office at 8. The new leaves on his shoulders told the news of his promotion.

"I'll be out of my office by Friday, Rube. You can move in Friday morning. The colonel has approved both you and Leon. The notices are being sent this morning. You are the new detachment commander. I'll be in the office on the other side of the building, but if you need anything from me, just let me know. It's been a pleasure working with you all these years. I expect that to continue. I will be moving my office today. It will probably take most of the day. Good luck to you, Rube."

"Thanks, Milo. I guess we did work well together, didn't we?"

"Yeah," Milo said, smiling.

"I'll get Leon in here this morning and give him the rundown on what is expected."

"It's all yours now, Rube. Good luck." With that Milo turned and left the new captain's office.

Leon came to the office shortly after Milo left. He was a little adrift as to his responsibilities and wanted to discuss it with Rube. Now Captain Hayes had him sit and the two spent the next two hours mapping details. Leon knew the daily routine, but was unsure about some of the details. They were just finishing when dispatch called.

"We just got an e-mail from the colonel. It says you are now the Chief, and Sergeant Balfore is now the Lieutenant. I guess that makes you our new boss," the dispatcher said, half serious and half in jest.

"Maybe I can get a little respect from that office now," Rube quipped.

"About as little as before, Sergeant--pardon me, Captain. For what it's worth, we like it."

"Thanks. Try to be nice to Leon for a while."

"Yeah, right," she said as she hung up.

The rest of the morning was taken up with facilitating the change. Before he realized it, the phone was ringing and Aliana was telling him she had arrived in Anchorage.

Leaving the duties with Leon, he quickly drove to the arrival gate where she was standing on the walk, waiting. She tossed the small carry-on into the backseat of the car. She, in her bright yellow business suit, seemed to brighten his whole outlook.

"Do you think anyone would notice if I were to kiss you right here?" Rube said as he put the car in gear. They drove to the Sea Galley where they each ordered salad and iced tea. Lunch was a quiet affair, but once back in the car all that changed.

"I am dying to know what the mystery is all about. Can you tell me now?"

"I will show you all the details and paperwork when we get to the office. I think you are going to be shocked" He looked into her eyes to see a puzzled look. "How much faith do you have in the banker, Gerlitz?" Rube asked.

"He lacks some of the skills his predecessor had, but as far as I can tell he is doing an adequate job. We just had an audit and everything came out fine. Why do you ask?" She was very curious now.

"Like I said, you will see the files when we get to the office, but I have had them looked at by someone who knows accounting and he tells me there appears to be some criminal activity in his department. I don't want to influence your judgment about this. I want you to see the files first." He tried to leave it there. "Are you going to stay at my place tonight?"

"I had planned on it if you asked me." They were close to Headquarters now and personal conversations would have to wait.

As they entered Rube's office, he pointed her to the chair in front of the desk. He turned and closed the office door. Aliana was still standing. He turned her around and kissed her passionately.

"That's a first for this office since I've been here," he remarked.

"Do I get a certificate for my wall for that?" she snickered and hugged him.

"Okay. Let's get serious now." He unlocked the file behind him and removed the envelope containing the SeaFirst files. "These are the files I want you to look at. You read them, and I won't interrupt. Can I get you some coffee or a soda?" he asked.

"Thanks, Rube, but no. I had enough at lunch. I would like a few minutes with these files, though. Where did you get them? I recognize them as copies of the latest audit. These are confidential. How did you get them?"

"I'd rather not say right now. The source wishes to remain anonymous, at least until we can determine whether there is wrong-doing or not. That's why I need you to look at them." His tone was very official.

"Since I am familiar with the files, just give me a few minutes to review them and then I will try to answer your questions." She was becoming very nervous. Had her plan been discovered or was this something else all together? She began by reading the cover letter from Lyda. Her name had been removed from the letter on this copy.

Rube found a legal pad and pen for her, then sat back to await her comments. It didn't take long. She reviewed the files with great efficiency, comparing the files as she progressed. When she ended the state copy, there were several more pages in the bank copy. She read these, and when she finished, she looked up with a perplexed look on her face.

"I can't believe this, Rube. The files should be the same, but they are definitely not. You were right to call me. These files indicate there are interest monies being paid out by the bank that are not accounted for in the state copy. I don't understand this." She was thinking as fast as she could. "I am going to have to contact my office, the bank and the governor. It will take me a few days to gather the facts I need, but by early next week I should know all the answers. Will that be soon enough?"

"Of course. I can't call the attorney general until I know what I am talking about."

"May I have copies of the files, Rube?" she asked quietly.

"Certainly. Take those copies. I made them for you." Rube saw the worried look on her face. "It's late in the day, and since I'm the boss now, how would it be if I closed my office, went home, changed out of the uniform and took you to a victory dinner. I did get promoted, you know."

"Yes, I know, and I'm very proud of you. It is a little early for dinner, can we find something to do for a couple of hours?" she asked with an impish look.

"The SCAN team is having a little barbeque tomorrow afternoon. Kind of a promotion celebration and the end of a long surveillance ordeal. How would you feel about going to that with me? Sort of introduce you to the crew. And, it is a chance for me to show you off to the guys I work with. Are you up for that?"

"I will be working on this SeaFirst file all day, but I hope to be done early. What time?"

"Captain Withers told me 4:30. This will be at his place in south Anchorage. Will that be good for you?" Rube was excited about her going with him.

"Yes. I should be done by then."

"Good, let's get out of here. Will you need to go by your place before we go to mine?"

She held up her briefcase. "All I need for now is in here. Will you let me take a shower at your place?"

"I will help you with that if you want."

He called dispatch to tell them he was leaving the office for the day.

Chapter Twenty Nine

They had a quiet dinner at the South Side Bistro. Venison cutlets, spinach salad and a decent red wine. Not much conversation passed between them during dinner, but longing filled their eyes and their hearts. Rube vowed to himself to spend as much time as possible with this beautiful woman. He had never felt this close to another person; it felt good. Back in the Jeep he held her hand. He could tell she was feeling the same as he.

"It will take me a couple of minutes at my place. I have to take time to call Saundra, and she will be going to bed soon." she said. "Is that okay with you?"

"Of course it is." He smiled at her. "I can wait in the car—give you some privacy with your daughter."

They climbed the stairs to his condo. Rube carried her bag. He could think of nothing else but holding her and being with her tonight. The night passed all too quickly. When he awoke there was a smell of toast and bacon. He put on a robe and went into the kitchen to find Aliana, looking marvelous in a fresh beige pantsuit. The stark white of her blouse contrasted nicely with her dark complexion and raven black hair. Her glacier-blue eyes met his as he entered the room.

"Good morning, sleepy-head," she said, turning the eggs. "Have a seat and I'll pour you some coffee. You look as if you could use it."

He sat. "Do we have to go to work today?" he asked. "Can't we just stay here? I think I want to hold you all day."

"If you want me to review those bank files, you will have to leave or I won't get them done," she snickered. "Unless, of course, you want to carry on from last night."

"I'd love to, but I do have things to do at the office. If I don't go into the office, the big gun at the department of finance may eliminate my position. Can't have that happening, can we?"

"I've heard the dragon lady is sweet on you. I think you could get away with it." She gave him a coy look and went back to removing the eggs from the skillet.

An hour later he was in his office beginning the chore of removing his personal items for the move to his new office. He walked down the hall to inspect his new quarters. He was surprised to see a new nameplate on the door reading, Captain Rueben Hayes, Commander.

Jules Steinman was scheduled to meet with Ramon in his office this morning. Ramon would not be happy with the news he would receive. The two exchanged pleasantries, earlier tense conversations appeared forgotten. The attorney refused coffee.

Ramon looked across his desk and asked, "Well, where do we stand?"

"I'm afraid I don't have good news." Steinman began. "First of all, Eddie is in bad shape. The doctor told me that he probably won't live to see trial. His brain is irreparably damaged from long-term steroid use. He is only intermittently conscious and seldom lucid. I would expect the worst within a few days at most." He waited for Ramon's reaction.

Ramon's eyes were filled with sadness. "Have you contacted Dante? He will need to know right away."

"I thought you would want to be the one to pass this news on to Dante. You will also need to know about Larry Combs. I saw him in the jail and read the case file. The legal term for his position is *screwed*. Somehow the troopers knew what they were up to and followed them. When they bombed B.J.'s house, troopers were already at the scene. I don't know who passed the word to the troopers, but they knew about it. And, to make things even worse, my guess is that the troopers will try to turn B.J. I can't advise you what to about all this, but it looks to me like they will soon be knocking on your door."

"Is there any chance Eddie and Larry will be allowed bail?" Ramon inquired.

"Under Alaska Statutes, virtually everyone is entitled to bail. My guess is that it will be a very high amount, but that amount has not been set by the judge. I will try to get a hearing today or tomorrow." The lawyer was gathering his papers and returning them to his briefcase.

"Call me the minute you find out about bail. I want both of them out," Ramon said impatiently. "I will call Dante right away and let you know how he wants to proceed. Call me immediately when you hear from the judge." He waved his hand in dismissal.

When the lawyer was out of the office, Ramon dialed Dante's direct number. "Hola!" he said when the old man answered the phone. His entire conversation was in Spanish as he gave Dante all the details. Dante loved both Ramon and Eduardo. This was heartbreaking news.

"Call me back as soon as you learn about bail. Get them out, no matter the cost. I will send the jet. Eduardo must die here, at home. I will see him buried near his mother." There was much sadness in Dante's voice.

"How do you want me to take care of Larry? He is a good man."

"Bail them both. I think it is time for you to come home also. It is time for you to try on my shoes. Is there someone who can run your operation in Alaska?" Dante asked.

"Yes, my manager in Fairbanks can do it. He is familiar with all the business. He has run the Fairbanks end for a long time."

"I trust your judgment, Ramon. Get it done quickly."

"Are you sure you want me to stay in Mexico with you?" Ramon asked.

"I am getting old, these days. It is time to turn the business over to someone young. Someone I can trust. I had planned to split it with you and Eddie, but it appears that is no longer an option. Come home, Ramon. I need you here."

"I will come, Dante. It is difficult for me to believe you will be giving up all you have spent a lifetime building. We will talk more when I return. I will call as soon as I hear from the lawyer." Ramon said good-bye and broke the connection. He didn't really want to return to Mexico; he was happy here. He was comfortable with his life here.

Rube had finished moving to the new office and Leon Balfore was now in his old office. His administrative duties found him almost immediately. He was pleased that Leon was able to take over the new position at full stride. Rube had skipped lunch, but by mid-afternoon wished he hadn't. He had been to the vending machine down the hall for a Coke and a package of cookies. Stan Withers followed him back to his office.

"Having the low cal, low cholesterol lunch, I see." Both men laughed. "The festivities will start about 4:30 this afternoon. Are you planning to be there?" Stan asked.

"I plan to be. Is anyone bringing a wife or girlfriend?"

"They usually do. Why, do you have a wife I don't know about?"

"No, but I have a lady friend in town for a couple of days and I would like to bring her, if that's alright."

Stan was curious, but didn't ask. "Bring her along. We have enough steak and beer to go around. See you later."

As Stan left the office, Rube reached for the phone and called Aliana. She answered on the second ring. "The barbeque starts at 4:30. Will you be ready to go?"

"Oh, yes. Are you sure you want to be seen with me?" she asked.

"It's seldom I get to escort the prettiest girl at the party. How are you doing with the files. Have you found anything?"

"I'm not sure, but it looks as if I will have to go to Seattle. It looks like Ben Gerlitz is up to his eyebrows in a fraud. I can't believe it, but something is not right. You were right about one thing, I can't tell who is involved. I can't imagine Mr. Stackhaus is involved, but he could be. I just don't know at this point. Will you trust me to investigate this, at least for a few days?"

"I can't see any harm in that for now. Go ahead." Rube wanted to be with her. "I'll be there to pick you up just after 4:30. My first day in this office, I should put in a full day." After hanging up he thought about it. It seemed odd that Gerlitz could have established all this, what appeared to be an elaborate system, in such a short time as he had been in the office. That little voice again.

Rube left the office and drove home. Aliana met him at the door with a warm smile, a close embrace and a passionate kiss. Rube thought he could get used to this in a very short time. He changed clothes and drove in his Grand Cherokee to South Anchorage. Even with the heavy traffic, it was a short trip. They parked, walked down the side of the house and entered the backyard through the gate. All eyes greeted the pair as they came in. Most of the eyes remained on Aliana.

Stan Withers spotted them and came to introduce himself. He handed each of them a cold Alaska Amber. Rube took Aliana by the arm and escorted her around the yard, introducing her to all his crew. Two wives and one girlfriend came to her rescue.

Wither's wife explained to Aliana that these men had not had a day off for a very long time, and with a look around she could tell by the happy faces it was going to be a good party.

After everyone had eaten all the steak and salad they could hold, and washed it down with a considerable amount of beer, Aliana stood near a group of party-goers, listening, drinking a 7UP, grateful for the relaxed atmosphere. The group near her was talking about the surveillance they had just completed. Rube was in a huddle with Stan, drinking coffee. The other women had their own little huddle. The conversation near her was interesting. Without realizing it, the men had discussed and laughed at almost every aspect of the case they were working on. She made mental note of the Sombrero and Ramon Chavez.

She was sitting at a picnic table, sipping her soda, when Rube found her.

"Have you had enough?" he asked, quietly.

"Yes," she replied, "but I have to say thank you to our host and hostess." The laughter was getting loud now.

Traffic was much lighter now. "Is there something you would like to do?" Rube asked.

"Can we just go back to your place and relax this evening?"

"You bet." He looked at her a moment. "You were the hit of the party this evening. I expect I will have to explain you to everyone who met you." He grinned. "It won't be an unpleasant task."

She squeezed his hand and put her head on his shoulder.

Chapter Thirty

Jules Steinman called Ramon at 11:15, Friday, with news from the judge. Bail was set for both Larry Combs and Eduardo Sanchez. For Combs bail was set at $1 million. For Eddie bail was set at $500,000. Steinman had arranged with a bondsman to post the bond. It would cost $100,000 for Larry and $50,000 to free Eddie. The lawyer was processing release papers now.

Ramon sighed with relief and called Dante. He explained the current circumstances to his boss. Dante said he was relieved to know the two men would be out soon.

"I will see that Eddie stays in the hospital until the airplane is ready to take him home," Ramon explained. "How soon will it take for the jet to arrive?"

"The pilot told me he would leave early tomorrow morning and be in Anchorage in the afternoon. They will fuel the airplane and be ready to leave Sunday morning. The time of departure I will leave to you." He paused, then added, "I want you to be on the plane, Ramon. It is time for you to come home. I need you here."

"Thank you, Dante. I appreciate your concerns. I will be on the plane with Eddie. I will see you Sunday night. I have things to arrange now. Please forgive me for being short."

He had scarcely hung up the telephone when it rang. It was Larry Combs.

"Get cleaned up and come to the office, Larry. We will talk and have some lunch."

Now he called his manager in Fairbanks. Without giving much detail, he told the man he was now in charge of all Alaska operations, though Ramon would remain his boss. Ramon explained he expected to be away for an extended period. It would be up to him, as the new manager, to determine how things should be run.

Ramon sat at his desk attempting to organize his departure. Cash, investments and his condo must be ready to close. There was a lot to do in a short period of time. Again the telephone was ringing.

"Sombrero Restaurant, Ramon Chavez speaking," he answered.

A pleasant female voice was on the line. "Mr. Chavez, you don't know me, but I need to meet with you. Not at your office. I will meet you in the food court of the Fifth Avenue Mall. One hour. I wish to give you information that is important to you. Say nothing, someone may be listening."

He did not have time for unnecessary conversation, but this woman had already told him much when she warned him someone may be listening. A frightening thought, considering all that was happening at this time. He checked the time and decided to meet with her.

Aliana didn't know what Ramon looked like, but had a general description. The food court was not crowded. She was alone at a table waiting. At the appointed time, Ramon stepped off the escalator and began to eye the patrons at the tables. Aliana stood and walked toward the man. She was striking and he watched her approach.

"Are you Ramon?" she asked.

"Yes," he answered and pointed toward the table she had just left.

As they sat she looked around to see if there were familiar faces in the sparse crowd. There were none.

Ramon looked into her blue eyes. "Miss, I am very busy. Tell me what you have to say and I can get back to my business."

"Mr. Chavez, I am willing to give you this information, but I want something in return. I understand you have access to a private jet."

Ramon was startled. "You seem to know a lot about me and my business. How is it that you know these things?"

"You are right. I do know a lot about you and your business, even though we have never met. My information, you will find is accurate." She let him think about this a moment. "In exchange for this information, I want you to arrange passage on your jet at the earliest possible time for me, my sister and my daughter. My destination is Costa Rica, but Mexico or any other Central American country will suffice. It will be up to you to judge the value of the information I have." Again she paused while he assimilated her words. "Do you understand my terms?"

"Of course, I understand them," he answered, irritated. "You still have not answered the original question. How is it you know these things?"

"Do you agree to the terms I have laid out?"

"Yes, yes, yes." He was getting even more irritated. "If what you have to say is useful to me I will fly the three of you to Mexico. Now get to the point."

"Mr. Chavez, I work for the State of Alaska and within the scope of my duties I have learned a great deal about your business. For instance, I know you are dealing drugs, cocaine, through your restaurant. I know the waitresses you bring from Mexico bring the drugs here for you. I also know that the troopers have been listening to your business —with a warrant—for quite a while. They used this information to arrest your friend and his man. I know you are in very deep doo-doo. Are we on the same page now, Mr. Chavez?"

"We cannot talk of this here. We must have some privacy." Ramon was totally shocked. "Can we continue this in my car? It's in the parking garage. Don't worry, Miss, you will be safe."

Aliana slid into the passenger side of the dark blue Mercedes. The white leather interior made it a nice place to talk.

"Who, exactly, are you?" he asked.

"Like I said, I work for the state. At the moment I have some issues that could come to light and embarrass me and my family. I want to be out of the state when that happens. I have a broker in Costa Rica who has purchased a small villa for me. I just want to get there as quickly as possible."

"And your name, again?"

"My name is Aliana Pedersen. That is not important. I just want to know if you can, anonymously, get me and my family out of the United States. I am trying to protect my daughter and sister."

He studied her for what she thought was forever, saying nothing. Finally, he said, "I will take the three of you to Mexico. My jet will be at the Security Aviation hangar Sunday morning. We will depart at 7 o'clock sharp, with or without you. I must insist that, on the flight, you must tell me everything you know. There will be others on the flight, but I will have it arranged that you sit beside me, for us to talk."

She sighed with relief. "Thank you, Mr. Chavez. We will meet you at the airport on Sunday morning. My daughter has mental disabilities, but she will not be any trouble to you."

The two talked for another hour. Ramon gleaned as much information as he could think to ask from her. He would have to warn Kevin Bullard, his manager from Fairbanks. All this was very unsettling. He had always tried to avoid this kind of surprise. His cell phone jingled. It was Larry Combs. He and Steinman were on the way to the restaurant.

Aliana wrote her cell phone number on the back of her business card and gave it to Ramon. "I will see you on Sunday," she said as she slid out of the plush leather seat. She had come in a taxi and would leave the same way.

During the cab ride back to Rube's condo, she dialed her sister, Opal.

"Hello." Opal answered.

"Hi, Opal. It's me. Is everything okay at home?"

"Oh, yes. Saundra is just fine. We just got home from shopping. I'll let you talk to her."

"Yes, I want to talk with her, but first I have some news for you. We are going on a long trip. You will have to bring your's and Saundra's passports. Pack one bag for each of you, a big one. You will need to bring all her medications. We may not be coming back soon. I can't say more than that now, but one other thing. Get a real estate person to list and sell the house. Have them give the money to Momma. Do you understand all that?"

"How much time do I have to get this done?" Opal inquired.

"None. You have to be here in Anchorage by tomorrow afternoon. I know this is sudden, Opal, but I can't explain now. I will tell you everything when you get here."

"It sounds exciting." Opal said. "I'll get Saundra now."

Aliana talked for several minutes with Saundra. Saundra told her about school and her best friend there. She told her mother about the pictures she had drawn that now hung on the refrigerator. She told her mother she loved her. Aliana told her she loved her too and that she would see her soon.

The cab stopped in front of Rube's condo. Aliana paid the driver and went inside. She was feeling very guilty about the way she would be leaving Rube. She went to the bedroom, undressed and showered. She found her slinkiest gown and best perfume, then went to the kitchen to prepare dinner. Something simple, she thought.

Looking in the refrigerator she spotted a bottle of white wine. That should go well with a tuna and noodles casserole and a green salad. She was setting the table when Rube came home.

"A fella could get used to this," he commented before kissing her.

"Don't get used to it, big boy. I'm not housebroken yet." She kissed him again and went back to setting the table. He doffed his duty belt while she poured the wine.

"I tried to call you earlier, but there was no answer."

"Yes, I had a couple of errands to run. Was it something important?"

"It was. I had a sudden urge to tell you how much I was looking forward to seeing you tonight. Since you weren't in, I told a dispatcher—and she hit me!" He laughed.

"Oh! You didn't." Now she was laughing.

He put an arm around her waist and held her tight.

"I have some bad news for you, sort of good for me." She looked at him with sad eyes.

"Do I have to hear the bad news?" he asked.

"I'm afraid so. Tonight will be our last night together for a while. Opal and Saundra will be here tomorrow afternoon. I will have to stay home tomorrow night. You can come and have dinner with us, though. Saundra would love to see you again."

"I would love to see her again, too. I'll be there. Just let me know what time." He gave her a devilish look. "There is tonight."

"There is that," she replied. "By the way, how was your day? Did everyone call you *sir*?"

"I haven't been fired yet. Nobody tried to shoot me. I guess it was a good day."

"What about those two men they arrested, that Larry and Eddie somebody. Are they still in jail?" She hoped her inquiry didn't seem out of place.

"Stan came by my office this afternoon to tell me they both made bail. Larry left the jail with his lawyer, but Eddie is still in the hospital. The doctors say it's only a matter of days for him. He is in bad shape." He sipped his wine. "Did you get a chance to work on the files today?"

"Yes. Next week I will have Ms. St. John instruct my classes here and I will have to go to Seattle. My first meeting will be with Ben Gerlitz and Mr. Stackhaus. I have to find out who is engineering this mess. Come sit down, we'll eat, and then relax." The lies were coming much too easily.

She put her two arms around his neck and squeezed. To assuage her guilt, she kissed him hard, and held him tightly. If things could only be this simple, forever, she thought.

Chapter Thirty One

Rube had been up for nearly an hour before he heard the shower come on. It was his cue to begin breakfast. He re-assembled the newspaper and placed it on her side of the table, and proceeded to prepare breakfast. Omelets were his specialty.

She appeared in the kitchen wearing only her robe. Her hair was wet and she had not yet applied make-up. To Rube she was still the most beautiful woman he had ever seen. His feelings for her were growing by the day. Those pale blue eyes had a certain sparkle to them this morning. He motioned her to her chair and retrieved the coffee pot. He kissed her lightly before pouring her coffee.

"Sleep well?" he asked.

"Like a hibernating bear," she commented. "How about you? You're up awfully early this morning."

"I've been waiting for you to roll out." He checked the skillet and buttered the toast. "What time are Opal and Saundra due to arrive?"

"Not until this afternoon. Will you be able to drive me to the airport to pick them up? I want to spend all day with you." It was the truth. She was enjoying her time with Rube.

"Sure. Happy to do it. And spending the day with you seems like a good idea. Anything special on your mind?" He used a plastic spatula to spoon the omelet onto a platter.

"No, I don't care if we don't leave the house. I just want to be with you." She had her chin on her folded hands, looking at him. She wondered how he would feel if he knew this would be their last breakfast together. It was a thought that saddened her.

"Dig in," he said, filling her glass with orange juice. "I think I can be very happy spending the day here in the condo. I don't get much chance to relax like this."

They ate without much conversation. When finished, Rube began to clean up the kitchen while Aliana returned to the bathroom to finish dressing and combing out her hair. When she returned she was wearing jeans and a cotton shirt. The wide beaded belt at her waist was a nice touch. When they finally turned the TV to a sports channel, they found the Mariners and the Yankees tied at three in the fifth inning. Seattle was high in the standings for a division pennant, their first. Aliana worked the crossword while Rube tried, unsuccessfully, to watch the game. He fell into a light nap with his head on her lap. He was awakened by Aliana's cell phone.

"Hello," she answered. A pause. "Okay, Opal. Rube and I will pick you up in front of the terminal at 2:15. Did you do everything I asked?" Another pause. "Alright, that's good. See you both in a little while."

"Is everything okay?" Rube asked.

"Oh, yes." She checked the time. "We have about an hour, would you take me to the store for some dinner supplies?" She needed to talk to Opal before she saw Rube. "Or, perhaps better yet, could I borrow the Jeep? I can go to the store and shop while you finish the game. I'll pick up Opal and Saundra, drop them at my place and come get you. How does that sound?"

"That's fine. I should call the office and see what is going on, anyway. Just don't stay away long. I like having you around." This was good, he wasn't much for shopping. "Say hello to Opal and Saundra for me."

It took only a few minutes for her to gather her purse and the car keys. She kissed Rube on the cheek. "After I take them to my place I will come back and get you."

It had taken longer in the check-out line than she anticipated and when she arrived at the airport terminal Opal and Saundra were outside with their luggage. Aliana could see immediately that Saundra was restless and impatient with waiting. The young girl was at once excited upon seeing her mother. Aliana hugged her daughter and greeted Opal. They loaded the luggage and started for home. Once in traffic, Aliana began to explain what was happening. Opal seemed surprised, but was accepting it well. "So," Opal said, "we will be leaving Alaska in the morning. Will we ever come back?"

"I can't answer that for you right now. This has all come about suddenly and I haven't had enough time to make a total plan. I was hoping it would be five more years before we moved. Please, don't ask me too many questions about it all. I really don't have all the answers yet." She looked at her sister. "And remember, Rube doesn't know anything about this, and we can't tell him. Please, we have to keep this secret from him."

"You are in a lot of trouble, aren't you, Aliana?"

"I'm afraid so, Opal." The two spent the rest of the drive in silence, but Saundra made up for it. She was excited to be with her mother.

At home they unloaded the luggage and groceries. Saundra ran through the apartment reacquainting herself with the place. It didn't take long for her to find toys and other things that were hers. Each one she discovered she brought to show her mother.

"Saundra, what would you like for dinner tonight?" Aliana asked the girl.

"Mac and cheese," she replied.

"How about some meatloaf to go with that?"

"Yeah, I like your meatloaf," she commented and was again off to play with her newly found toys.

She and Opal busied themselves in the kitchen. It was after 5 in the afternoon when she called to tell Rube she was on the way to pick him up.

When she arrived she kissed him. She returned his car keys and walked through the condo gathering personal items she had left behind. The sadness mounted again as she walked around the apartment. It was difficult to hold back the tears.

She stood in the living room, reflecting, when Rube slipped his arms around her waist. "What's got you so deep in thought," he asked quietly.

"You," she said. She turned to face him, placing her face on his chest. "I don't know if this is the right time to say this, but there may not be another opportunity in the near future." She held him tightly. "I want you to know that, no matter how things turn out, I love you. You may not feel the same way, but I love you. Please, always remember that." She looked up at him with tears in her brilliant blue eyes.

He bent to kiss her. "Why do I get the feeling you are about to tell me to get out of your life?"

"Oh, no, Rube. It's nothing like that. Please don't think that." Again she had tears in her eyes. "I meant it when I said I love you. It's been a lot of years since I was able to say that to another person."

"For what it's worth, I have been having the same thoughts recently. And, since we both seem agreed on our feelings for each other, why don't we think about making this arrangement more permanent—something with a future?"

The tears were streaming now. "I'm sorry, Rube. I just can't talk about that now, please."

"Okay, whatever you say." He tilted her face up and wiped away her tears. "Do you still want me to come for dinner?"

"Oh, yes, Rube. I especially want you to come for dinner tonight."

It was after 10 when Rube returned to his condo. There had been no further mention of their earlier discussion. He had spent most of the evening talking with Opal and playing with Saundra. He especially enjoyed being part of the family life. He had been very young the last time he was included in this kind of an evening. He was unable to determine what Aliana's meanings were. In the same breath she had pulled him close and immediately shoved him away. It confused him. He wanted to be with her, but she seemed to be putting him out of her life. He wasn't able to make heads nor tails of any of this. At home he took a Coke from the refrigerator, turned on the news and sat in the darkened living room. An hour later he was in bed, tossing and turning, unable to sleep. This morning he had been full of happiness and hope; tonight he was full of confusion and uncertainty. He got out of bed, got another Coke and watched the Science Fiction Channel.

Chapter Thirty Two

At 5 in the morning Rube was scanning the front page of the Anchorage Daily News, waiting for the coffee to finish perking, when the telephone rang.

"Hello," he answered.

"Hello, Rube," the soft voice replied. "Are you speaking to me this morning?"

"I'll always speak to you. I meant it when I said I love you."

"Oh, Rube. I know I have hurt you, but I also hurt myself. I love you, too."

"Then can't we put all this behind us and start fresh?" Rube asked. "I need you in my life."

"I have thought of nothing else since yesterday. I want to be with you, Rube, but I don't know if I can do that at this point in my life." There was sadness in her voice. "Please believe me when I tell you that I want nothing more. Being with you makes my life complete, but I am dealing with issues in my life now that can only hurt you. I have to take care of them alone. This has nothing to do with you or how I feel about you. It's the things in my life I must deal with." There was a soft sigh. "I have to go to Juneau and then to Seattle to investigate those files you gave me. Perhaps we can work this out when I return. I just wanted to call and let you know I will be leaving this morning. Please try not to hate me. I love you."

Before he could comment, she hung up.

———

Aliana had called a taxi and carried all the luggage to the street. Opal had readied Saundra and the three were standing inside the front door when the cab arrived to take them to the airport. Light traffic at this time of day made it a short trip to Security Aviation. A uniformed employee opened the door and held it while Aliana and the cab driver unloaded the baggage. A young man with four bars on his epaulets came from the hangar bay to greet them.

"My name is Jorge," he said. "I will be your pilot today." He looked at a small notebook. "Are you the Pedersen party?"

"Yes."

"The others have not yet arrived, but it will speed things a bit if I can get your names for the manifest. We will make one stop in Phoenix for fuel. We could make it all the way to Mexico City, but if there are weather problems it could catch us short, so we will refuel and go on from there. You will need to have your passports when we get to Mexico City. Do you have them with you?"

"Yes, thank you. May I ask, how long a flight will this be?" Aliana asked.

"We will be almost four hours to Phoenix and another three and a half hours to Mexico City." The young pilot displayed great efficiency and poise. "There is food and beverages in the galley. You can help yourself to them at any time. We do not have a flight attendant on the flight today. Leave your luggage here; I will have someone load it for you. Mr. Chavez and his party will be here in a few minutes." He checked his wristwatch. "We will start the engines in 58 minutes."

"What kind of airplane is it?" Aliana asked.

"The aircraft was manufactured by Dassault-Breguet and is designated the Falcon 50. This aircraft was manufactured in 1982 and was factory up-graded last year. We have eight seats, a galley, and restroom. We will have two pilots on board today. There is an intercom so that it is possible to talk with the pilots," Jorge recited. "It is a very nice airplane."

"Thank you for the information. Which way to the airplane?" she asked.

Aliana judged the seating and had Opal and Saundra sit in the rear two seats. She took a seat in front of them, leaving a seat for Ramon. She was nervous and apprehensive. This was a gigantic lifestyle change for her. She felt fortunate to be getting out ahead of the legal consequences that were soon to follow. Ben Gerlitz would surely by arrested within a few days. She had made a great deal of money with this endeavor and, she guessed, it had been worth it. Her only regret at this point was leaving Rube. He was the best thing to happen to her since Saundra was born.

She spent a minute affixing Saundra's seat-belt and making certain Opal was settled in for the flight. She was slipping into the seat in front of Opal when the rest of the passengers began to enter the cabin. Ramon was first.

He instructed Larry and Eddie to take the rear-facing seats at the front of the cabin, which contained eight seats total. Ramon spoke with the pilot and copilot, then took a seat next to Aliana.

"Is everything suitable for you?" he asked in a pleasant voice.

"Yes, thank you for asking."

"When we are airborne, we will have headphones. These will allow us to talk without shouting, although this is a pretty quiet airplane."

"I will be happy to tell you anything I know, though, you know most of it already."

"I want to know every small detail," he said. "I am curious about why you are leaving Alaska. It would seem you have a good job here. Why would you want to leave all that?"

"Let's just say things aren't working out, and let it go at that," she said in a cold voice.

They conversed for most of the flight between Anchorage and Phoenix. The flight was smooth and comfortable. They cruised at 33,000 feet in sunshine. Once she got out of her seat to get a cold drink and to check on Saundra. As they approached Phoenix, the pilot advised the passengers to fasten their seatbelts. The landing was uneventful and when the air stair was lowered she felt the need to get out and stretch her legs. As she walked around on the ramp, she couldn't stop thinking about Rube.

Ramon was on the telephone the entire time they were on the ground. Once they were in the air again he spoke to her over the headset. "Ms. Pedersen, I have been on the telephone with my boss in Mexico. We talked about you and your information. It is very useful to us and will save us a great deal of money and time. We thank you for that. El Dante, my boss, is grateful. In way of thanks he wishes you to spend the night at his villa. I will be there tonight also. And tomorrow," he continued, "El Dante would be pleased to furnish the Falcon for you to continue on to Costa Rica."

Aliana was astonished. "That is very generous of you and El Dante. I will accept both your invitations. And I thank you. It will save me a great deal of time and inconvenience. Please pass this on to El Dante."

"I will be happy to do that, but you can thank him yourself tonight at dinner. He will be our host this evening. You will, of course, bring your daughter and sister."

A private Mercedes limo met the group at the private hangar in Mexico City. All their luggage was transported with them to the villa. The place was magnificent. They were shown to their rooms where Aliana showered and changed for dinner. Opal and Saundra had another room and were soon knocking on her door. They chatted and giggled for a while until it was time to go down to dinner. A servant met them and guided the little group to the dining room. Ramon was on the right hand of El Dante. Aliana sat next to him and then Saundra and Opal. The table was huge and could accommodate at least 30 guests. Eduardo Sanchez was absent.

El Dante was an impressive gentleman in his early seventies, she guessed. His white mustache contrasted against his Spanish complexion. Even at his age he was a handsome man. He stood and offered a toast.

"Welcome to my home. Larry, I thank you for all you have done for Eddie. You will be rewarded for your kindness. Ramon, it is good to have you home again. This time, I hope, to stay. And to Ms. Pedersen, I owe you a great debt. I understand you have accepted my offer of use of the airplane. In addition to that, I wish to tell you that my influence is felt throughout Central America. If you ever need my help with anything, please feel free to ask. And now, let us drink to friendships both old and new." He raised his glass, bowed slightly at the waist and sipped his wine. The buzz of the conversation began as the waiters served one of the most elegant dinners Aliana had ever experienced. She was told they would take her to the airport in the limo at 11 AM.

By the time she was ready for bed, she was so exhausted that sleep was almost instantaneous.

Chapter Thirty Three

The past several days had been lonely and depressing. He had not heard from Aliana since Sunday morning when she said she was leaving town. Rube had tried to reach her on her cell phone on several occasions with no luck. Activity in his new office had been hectic to say the least, for a man with his lack of experience. Rube had been coping well with work, but couldn't help longing for Aliana.

Late afternoon on Thursday, his phone rang, the receptionist said he had a call from an FBI agent named Brownfield. He instructed her to put the call through.

"Agent Brownfield, Rube Hayes. How are things in Seattle?"

"We win some and we lose some. At the end of the day, I think we are about even," he quipped, unusual for a federal agent. "Heard you got promoted. Congratulations."

"Thanks. Sometimes I wonder if this was a wise decision, but I'm learning. What prompts your call today?"

"Let me back this story up a bit. You remember I told you we had an informant inside the Dante organization?" Brownfield began. "Confidentially, that informant is a lawyer named Steinman. He has just returned from Alaska. He said Dante, himself, had called and ordered him to go to Anchorage and represent two of his employees. They had been arrested for arson and attempted murder. Their names are Eduardo Sanchez and Larry Combs. Are you familiar with these names?"

"Yes, we had been doing some surveillance on Ramon Chavez's restaurant when we came up with information about a hit on one of the local drug dealers. Our drug team staked it out and caught these guys tossing a firebomb into the dealer's house. Our team took them down, shot one of them in the arm. Sanchez is very ill and was put in the hospital, under guard. When that lawyer arrived he got them bailed. I haven't talked to Withers about it, and I can't tell you where they are now."

"That gets us to the reason for my call," Agent Brownfield said. "Our informant told us Dante sent his little Falcon business jet to pick them up. They left Anchorage Sunday morning, bound for Phoenix and on to Mexico City. On board, according to Steinman, was Ramon Chavez, Eduardo Sanchez, Larry Combs, and three women, one of them a young girl. We have no information about the females on the flight. It's not like Ramon to take a girlfriend with him when he on his way to see Dante. Do you have any idea who these women could be?"

Rube was shocked. It sounded as though Aliana, Opal and Saundra could possibly have been the ones on that plane. He refused to allow that thought to linger.

"Are you there, Captain Hayes?" the FBI agent asked.

"Yes, I'm here. I was just trying to think who they could be. I will have to ask Captain Withers about that. He may know who they are."

"I would appreciate it if you would get back to me as soon as possible with regard to them. Is there anything else I can do for you?" Brownfield asked. "If not, just get back to me as soon as you learn anything. Thanks again for cooperating."

Rube hung up the telephone, stunned. He picked up the receiver again and dialed the offices of the department of finance, Juneau. Ms. Whitehorse answered the phone with a cheery tone.

"How do you do, Ms. Whitehorse. This is Captain Rueben Hayes with the Alaska State Troopers. Is Ms. Pedersen in today?" he inquired.

"I'm sorry, Captain, Ms. Pedersen is in Anchorage conducting some classes. Her cell phone must be out of order because we have tried to reach her for two days without any answer; the phone appears to be shut off. That's very unusual for her. She is always available, day or night"

Rube's anxiety level shot up again. "If she checks in will you have her call my office? She has the number."

"Of course, Captain. And if you talk to her, will you ask her to call the office? We are worried about her."

"Certainly, Ms. Whitehorse. Thank you for your help."

Rube leaned back in his chair, rubbing his eyes, attempting to overcome the building headache invading his skull. He sat up in his chair and checked the time. Lyda Carney should still be in her office. Checking the Rolodex, he dialed SeaFirst bank.

"Lyda Carney," the business-like voice answered.

"Ms. Carney, Captain Hayes of the Alaska State Troopers. How are you today?"

"I'm fine, Trooper Hayes." A short pause. "Do I need to use another phone?"

"No, this one will be fine. I have a question for you. Have you heard from Ms. Pedersen this week?"

"No, she hasn't called all week. I would have taken the call if she had," she answered. "Is she supposed to contact us this week?"

"I'm not sure, Lyda. I just had a hunch she might show up there sometime this week. If you hear from her, please, give me a call."

"I'll do that, Captain. Do you want me to have her call you if I hear from her?"

"That would be nice." Then, Rube added, "I will be talking with you soon about that other item we discussed. It appears you were right. Thank you for your help, Ms. Carney."

Again he leaned back in his office chair, trying to accurately recall their last conversations. Had he been a fool? Had she used him to gain information? Was he acting like a teenager? Was he jumping to conclusions? Questions, questions, questions. No answers.

Lacking a better avenue to pursue, Rube called his old boss, Milo.

"Can I have a few minutes this afternoon, boss? I think I need to talk with you, face to face. It could take a half hour. Can you fit me in?"

"Sure, Rube. Come on. I'm mostly open the rest of the day."

Rube grabbed a Coke and walked to his boss' new office in a separate building a short distance from his own office building. The fresh air felt good and helped to clear his mind.

Rube gave Milo a Readers Digest version of recent events. There were no immediate answers to why Aliana had disappeared or how she was acquainted with Ramon Chavez. Rube could not explain her involvement in the possible bank fraud case. He explained to Milo that he felt like a fool allowing her to have access to information about that case. He had done almost everything wrong.

Milo listened without interrupting, but when Rube ended this confession Milo smiled and leaned forward on his desk.

"Rube, you are not the first trooper to be taken in by a pretty girl. And, be honest with yourself, it's possible she has done nothing wrong. She may be a victim in all this, just like you. Deal with the facts. The first fact I see is that you can't be sure there was a bank fraud. There may be an explanation for what you have seen. Investigate. If you find evidence of a crime, pursue it. As I see it, right now all you have is suspicions. I have to advise you that your personal involvement is enough for me to take you off this investigation. I think I know you, and I believe you can be objective, so if you want to investigate, then do it. I'm giving you a lot of latitude, in return I want results. Do you think you can handle it?"

"I'll do my best, Major," Rube said, his hands clasped in his lap. Where to start, he wondered.

Back in his office, checking the time, he still had time to contact the attorney general's office. He retrieved the little book of numbers and dialed. The secretary put him through to Woody Parsons, the attorney general for the State of Alaska. He had dealt with Woody on many occasions in the past.

"Hi there, Rube. I hear you are the commander in Anchorage now. Congratulations."

"Thanks, Woody. How are things with you?" Rube asked. "Ready to go fishing?"

"You bet. When?" he asked, laughing.

"As soon as you help me solve a little problem. And, Woody, for now, I would like to keep this between us. Can you do that?"

"Can't answer that until I know what we are talking about. You still want to tell me?" Woody asked. He was curious, Rube was not given to idle chatter.

"I think someone in SeaFirst Bank in Seattle is dipping into the state's account. I'm not sure who is involved, but it involves a lot of money. My problem is that I have no experience in this field and it involves a corporation outside the state. I just don't know how to go about pursuing this and I need your advice," Rube explained.

"Wow, Rube. I'm glad you called me. Can you tell me if there may be state employees involved? If there are, I'm going to be required to have my office investigate."

"At this point I don't know. My thought is this: have the banking commission in Washington investigate. This may all be done by one person in the bank, or it may be done with several officers of the bank and even members of our own finance department. My gut says let Washington investigate the bank. If it reveals collusion with someone from the state finance department, then you and I would become involved at that point. Am I thinking along the right lines?" Rube let Woody think about it for a few moments.

"Not knowing more about the situation. I think you have the right idea.

I'm going to have my secretary get me the number for the Washington State Banking Commission." Rube was put on hold. When Woody returned, "Here's the number." He read it to Rube. "I want you to keep me in the loop on this. We may have recourse against the bank, assuming there is a theft. Rube, this could turn out to be a major scandal. If you have any documentation on this, I would like to see it as soon as possible."

"I'll send you copies of what I have, if you promise to sit on it until we learn who is involved. I don't want a big media spread about something that may or may not involve state employees. Will you agree to that?" Rube asked.

"Yes, of course. I don't want to see anyone unjustly accused of anything, but I won't cover it up either."

"That's all I ask, Woody. Thanks. I'll get this stuff to you in the morning."

Rube checked the time. It was too late in the day to call Olympia. He opened his file cabinet and set about making Woody a copy of the SeaFirst file.

In desperation he tried Aliana's cell phone one more time without success.

Chapter Thirty Four

The following morning, one hour before local business started, Rube placed a call to Olympia, Washington. He explained to each of the three people to whom he had been forwarded, he wished to speak with the head of the banking commission. Each of the minions wanted to send him to another minion screening calls for the Commissioner. Finally he reached the office of the Commissioner and asked to speak with Commissioner George Findlay.

"You certainly have a battery of bulletproof secretaries," Rube commented when the Commissioner came on the line.

"I guess I do. But that's their job," Findlay said, laughing. "What can I do for you?"

"I am Captain Rueben Hayes with the Alaska State Troopers. I command the Anchorage Detachment," Rube explained. "I have information that may indicate there has been fraudulent activity in an account with SeaFirst bank in Seattle. The account is exclusively for the State of Alaska. I have called you because I need your help. The simple facts are, (1) I don't know who is involved, it could be anyone from a bank clerk to the president of the bank or the Governor of Alaska. (2) This is outside my area of expertise, and (3) It occurred outside my jurisdiction. Are you with me so far?"

"Good Lord," Findlay remarked. "Do you have documentation for any of this?"

"Yes, I do." Rube said. "My first question is, do you think I should meet with you, personally, and bring the files to you? I really don't feel comfortable sending this information electronically."

"Absolutely," George Findlay replied, shocked at what he was hearing. "Question; do you think Irwin Stackhaus could be involved in this case?"

"I can't answer that, his name is on some of the documents, but I honestly don't know who is involved. Again, that's why I'm calling you."

There was a short pause. "How soon can you be in Olympia?" he asked.

"If I can get a flight today, I will be there late this afternoon. Hold on just a minute and I will have my secretary check on flights." He called the front desk and asked the receptionist to book him a flight to Olympia in the first available seat, State Priority. "I'm back, they're checking on a flight for me."

"While you wait, can you give me any particulars about this case? You mentioned that it may go as high as the governor of your state." Findlay was fishing. "How did you come into possession of this information?"

"An informant sent me a copy of some bank files. She didn't know what to do with the information. She thinks her immediate boss is involved, but didn't know if other bank officials could be in it also. As a matter of fact, I have the same questions about some Alaska officials." The light was blinking on his desk phone. "Hold just a minute, they may have a flight for me." Again he put the banking commissioner on hold. When he came back on the line he said, "I will be in Olympia by three this afternoon, your time. I fly into Seattle and catch a shuttle flight to the capital."

"Good, give me your flight number and I will have my driver pick you up at the airport."

Rube read the flight number and time. "I'll see you later today."

His next call was to Milo. He explained the situation and reported that he would be out of the office for a couple of days. Milo instructed Rube to leave Lieutenant Balfore in charge while he made this trip.

Rube went to his condo and packed a bag. He hoped he was doing the right thing. Leon Balfore had sent a nearby trooper to chauffeur Rube to the airport. They rode in silence and Rube was let out at the departure gate for Alaska Airlines. The flight was on time and his security check-in went quickly.

In Seattle he had only 30 minutes to change planes. His commuter flight was in a nearby concourse which allowed him plenty of time. The flight was smooth and as they taxied to the terminal Rube could see a uniformed officer waiting at the gate.

The Commissioner has some stroke, Rube thought. Walking to the terminal, he waved at the Washington State Patrolman. The officer waved back.

"I'm parked in front of the arrival gate," he told Rube. "Commissioner Findlay asked that I take you directly to his office. Is that okay with you?"

"My name is Rube Hayes. Yes, it is." Rube said, enjoying the ride. "This is my first trip to Olympia. I get to Seattle pretty often, but I've never been here. Looks like a nice place."

"My name is Fred, by the way. Yes, I like it here. I was raised here. My folks still live on the south end of town." He paused, thinking up some small talk. "Are you acquainted with the Commissioner?"

"I've never met him. What sort of fellow is he."

"You will like him," the patrolman said. "He's tough and gets the job done, but he is friendly and personable. I get to work with his people quite often."

It took more than twenty minutes to get to the commissioner's office. When they arrived the patrolman gave Rube a card. If you need anything, just give me a call. And if you have a chance before you leave, I would like to talk with you about a trip to Alaska next summer."

"Be happy to do it." Rube took his own card from his shirt pocket. "This has my office phone in Anchorage, and it has my cell phone number. I have the cell with me."

The patrolman gave Rube directions to the proper office and waved good-bye. Rube returned the wave and started up the walk. It was a typical 1920s government office building; neatly kept. As he entered the building he was met by an, also neatly kept, middle-aged lady who asked who he was, and once she determined she had the right man, asked him to follow her down the first floor hallway.

At the far end of the first floor hall, she ushered him into an office, went to the receptionist desk, sat, and dialed the phone. Almost immediately a door opened and a short, stocky man in his early sixties came toward him.

"Captain Hayes, pleased to meet you. How was your flight?" Before Rube could answer, he said, "Come into my office. Can I get you anything?"

"Thank you. I could use a bottle of water," Rube said, following the Commissioner into the office.

At his desk, Findlay picked up the phone. "Ruby, bring a bottle of water for my guest and come in with a steno pad."

Before Rube had all the files out of his small bag, Ruby was there with his water. She took a seat beside the commissioner's desk.

"Ruby is here to take notes, that's all, Captain."

Rube spread the files on the edge of the large mahogany desk. There was no more small talk. The two men went into the files and discussed what they found. The Commissioner seemed to know every rule, regulation and law pertaining to his area of responsibility. Almost immediately he saw what Lyda Carney had found. He also surmised that Ben Gerlitz was "in this up to his eyebrows." For nearly two hours the two men went over the files. Ruby had filled one steno pad and started a second.

Finally, George Findlay, looked at Captain Rueben Hayes. "What are your plans for this evening, Captain?"

"I came directly here from the airport. I haven't even made a hotel reservation. Can you recommend someplace?"

"If you have no plans, I would like to take you to dinner. We can stop at a hotel on the way. In the morning I will assign two investigators to this case. With any luck, Mr. Gerlitz could be under arrest by this time tomorrow."

"Sounds good to me," Rube replied. "And, if it wouldn't break too many rules, I would like to go to the bank with your investigators. If it comes to light that someone from the State of Alaska is up to their eyebrows, I would like to know about it first hand."

"I think we can arrange that for you." George looked at Ruby. "Take the rest of the day, Ruby. I know it's late. Go home and take it out on Frank." They both laughed.

Findlay set about closing his office for the day. Rube had given him these copies of the files, which George locked in a cabinet drawer. The two men walked out the front door and, at the end of the walk, were met by a new Chrysler and its driver. The driver opened the rear door and the men climbed aboard. They took Rube to a hotel near the downtown business district where he was issued a room key. He left his bag with the desk and returned to the car.

Dinner was excellent, prime rib and prawns with fresh strawberry shortcake for dessert. George paid for the dinner and informed Rube that the State of Washington was picking up the tab on his room also. Nice, Rube thought.

Back in the hotel, he showered and fell into bed; travel, stress and that huge dinner had worn him out, completely.

In the morning, in the middle of his shave, the hotel phone rang. Ruby was on the line. The commissioner was sending his two investigators to pick him up. He would have time for breakfast in the coffee shop.

Chapter Thirty Five

The two plain clothes investigators met Rube in the coffee shop. They explained that, though it was early, it was a two-hour drive to Seattle. They introduced themselves as Ray Culp, the taller and thinner of the two, and Hank Fisk, a young black man with a muscular build and broad smile.

In the car, Fisk was driving on the I-5 moving north at 75 miles per hour. Culp was conversing over the seat-back. He had copies of the files and began asking questions and taking notes as the car sped along.

"I met Ben Gerlitz when he called in a rescue mission while on vacation in Alaska. His friend was killed when a glacier calved off and fell on top of him. Tragic accident. Tad Morton was his name. I learned later Morton had been the head of the Alaska account with SeaFirst Bank. During the next couple of days, I also met Aliana Pedersen, the one responsible for the account." Rube continued, "Ms. Pedersen eventually appointed Ben Gerlitz to replace Morton. Personally, I liked both of them."

"Have you discussed these files with Ms. Pedersen?" Culp inquired.

"Yes, I have. That may have been a mistake on my part. I was trying to figure out what was going on with the account and asked her to look at the files." Rube was feeling guilty. "A couple of days later she disappeared. No one has seen her since. Her office hasn't heard from her, and the clerk, Lyda Carney, says she has not contacted the bank. And before you figure it out, I was personally involved with this lady. I really liked her and had no reason to believe she was involved with the case other than being the Alaska contact for the bank. My boss, Major Milo Thomas, is aware of all this and you can check it out with him, if you have any doubts about me."

"We did that this morning," Culp said, matter-of-factly. "For what it's worth, you have a clean bill with us. Everybody gets snookered every now and again. Now, I see Irwin Stackhaus and your governor have signed off on the files. Do you suspect that either of them are involved?"

"You have already checked me out?" Rube asked, somewhat incensed.

"Just answering questions that arose when we looked at the files. We weren't sure, at first, if we should let you come with us or have access to information we might get. Sorry if we offended you, but we needed to cover our own butts," Culp confessed.

"I guess I would have done the same thing," Rube said. "In fact, it looks like I should have done that before letting Aliana look at the files."

"Do you have any idea where she may be now?" Fisk interjected.

"No," replied Rube. "She has a mentally-affected daughter and a sister who takes care of her. Both of them are missing also. I had a call from an FBI contact who suspects she left the country. He thinks she went to Mexico on a private jet that belongs to a major drug dealer from there. I have tried to contact her without success. I think he may be right. She's gone."

This line of conversation went on for the rest of the drive. Closer to Seattle Culp began to map his intended strategy for interviewing Ben Gerlitz. Rube agreed to stay in the background and to let them handle the interview. Culp let Rube know he was welcome to ask questions if he thought of something they had missed.

Rube thought of something. "Gerlitz has a friend, Colin James. I have spoken with James a few times. He has been concerned that something was bothering Gerlitz. He told me that Ben had been drinking a lot and behaving strangely. He was friends with Morton, too, but I don't think he knows anything about all this."

Hank Fisk wheeled the car into the underground parking garage of the fifty story, black glass and steel bank building. From the basement parking garage, it required two elevators to reach the 38th floor where Ben Gerlitz had his office.

When they entered they were met by Lyda Carney. She immediately recognized Rube and said hello. He greeted her and told her they were there to see Gerlitz.

Without consulting Gerlitz, she asked, "Would you like me to set you up in a conference room?"

"That would be wonderful, Lyda." She showed the three men into the conference room just a few steps from her desk. She offered refreshments, which they declined.

"Will you ask Mr. Gerlitz to come in now?" Culp asked. "And, please try not to tell him who we are."

Ben Gerlitz came into the room looking harried. "Hello, I'm Ben Gerlitz, manager of the department on this floor. Who are you and how can I help you?"

Both Investigators Ray Culp and Hank Fisk provided him with identification credentials. "I believe you know Captain Hayes of the Alaska State Troopers." Ben nodded. "Have a seat, Mr. Gerlitz. We have some questions for you, but before we ask them we are required to read you your rights." He read the Miranda Rights from a card and asked if Ben understood his rights. He said he did.

"Is there a problem, officers?" he asked. "Have I done something wrong?"

Fisk took the lead now. "We just have some questions for you. Some questions have been raised with regard to the Alaska Account which you manage. We thought you would be able to answer our questions and set this whole thing straight. Is that okay with you, Mr. Gerlitz?"

"Of course, I'll be happy to answer any questions you have. Am I suspected of doing something wrong?" Ben was obviously very nervous now.

"Not that we are aware of, Mr. Gerlitz. Just have a seat and relax." Fisk sat, too. He reached under his chair and lifted the two files to the tabletop. When Hank opened the cover of the first file, Ben instantly turned stark white, recognizing the files at once. "Are you alright, Mr. Gerlitz? Is something wrong?" Fisk was toying with the man's guilt. "You don't look well. Can we get you something?" There was a long silence while Gerlitz tried to compose himself. Fisk thought there were tears in the man's eyes.

"I'm sorry, this comes as a shock. I knew it could happen, but not so soon." Culp and Fisk, as well as Rube, were completely amazed at this turn of events. "Will you allow me to call Mr. Stackhaus, my boss? He should hear this from the start. I don't want to go over it any more times than necessary. I am so ashamed." Tears were streaming down his cheeks now.

"Of course, use the phone on the table, though," Culp said.

It took nearly a half hour for Irwin Stackhaus to arrive. He was used to conducting most of the meetings he attended. He was not happy about this not being on his terms. "What is this all about, Ben. Who are these men? I know Officer Hayes, but I have no idea who the others are." Introductions were made and again credentials were shown.

"Mr. Stackhaus, we are here to interview Mr. Gerlitz. With both your permissions, I will be recording this meeting to assure the accuracy of all statements being made. Is that agreeable with the both of you?"

"Of course," Stackhaus agreed, while Gerlitz only nodded.

The recording was orally prefaced and the interview began.

"I think it will save all of us a lot of time if I make a statement at this time," Ben offered.

"If this is in any way a confession, Mr. Gerlitz, you may want a lawyer present," Fisk informed him. "Do you want to call one before we start?"

"That won't be necessary. I have been expecting this moment since I was first recruited." Ben wiped his eyes and gave a huge sigh. "Mr. Stackhaus, I apologize to you in advance for what you're about to hear. I don't think I could have lived with this guilt much longer." He took a deep breath, interrupted by a sob, and began his tale.

"After Tad was killed, I thought I might have a chance to fill this position. That's when I became better acquainted with Aliana Pedersen. She found out, I don't know how, that I owed a lot of money to a local bookey. She called me to her hotel and offered to pay my debt. In return she wanted me to continue with a scheme she and Tad had been operating. I never knew anything about all this until she offered me the position." He had calmed a little, sighed again and continued. "She and Tad had been taking the interest money from the Alaska account and twice weekly sending it out of the bank to fictitious accounts."

"Would that be Alaska Maritime Investments?" Culp interrupted.

"That's the one. I tried to follow the money, but that is a numbered account and it disappears right there. The money is forwarded to some other account the same day it arrives. I was never able to follow it any further." He paused, attempting to gather his thoughts. "It was my job to move this money twice weekly. It was also my job to keep two files on the account. One for the bank and Mr. Stackhaus. The other for the State of Alaska. The two files are identical except for the last pages containing the interest monies paid to the account. That information is in the bank copy, but is eliminated from the Alaska copy. Ms. Pedersen kept a close eye on the transactions."

Irwin Stackhaus was mortified by what he was hearing. "Are you saying you helped Aliana Pedersen steal the interest monies from the Alaska Account?"

"Yes, sir," Ben replied, again with a sob.

"You realize, Ben, this will mean your immediate termination." Stackhaus said.

"I know, sir." he said quietly.

Irwin Stackhaus stood. "I will need a copy of this entire report, if you will be so kind as to furnish me one. I will have to leave this meeting now to confer with the bank's lawyers. This is going to be an outrageous scandal." He was addressing the investigators. "Now, if you will excuse me." With that he left the conference room.

"Mr. Gerlitz, At this time I am placing you under arrest for bank fraud, a felony. Do you understand?" Fisk asked. "We have many more questions for you to answer before we end this interview. Do you feel like continuing?"

"Yes. I just want to get all this out in the open." He reached for the telephone.

"Miss Carney, come to the conference room, will you please?" Ben asked. When she arrived he instructed her to make a computer copy of all the data in the Alaska Account files. "These gentlemen only have the information from the last audit. They will need the entire account. Make two copies, one for these two gentlemen," indicating Fisk and Culp, "and one for Trooper Hayes." Looking at Rube he said, "I am assuming your governor will be interested in this."

The interview went on for several more hours before the two banking commission officers escorted Ben Gerlitz from the building. Once in the parking garage, he was handcuffed and placed in the backseat of the Chrysler with Captain Rueben Hayes. It was a long, silent journey back to Olympia.

Chapter Thirty Six

The following morning, Saturday, Rube found the home number for Lyda
Carney. It rang five times before the lady answered. It was a beautiful, sunny
morning. Lyda had been on the front porch of her home, reading the newspaper and working the crossword.

"Good morning," she answered pleasantly.

"Good morning, Lyda. It's Rube Hayes. Can you talk a minute?"

"Oh, yes. I'm glad you called. I needed to thank you for yesterday. I didn't
want anyone to know I had sent you those files. I was terrified when those
bank investigators came in. Thank you for keeping my name out of all this."

"I have been thinking about all this. You are the one who made it all happen. You should be very proud of what you did. In my opinion, you saved the
reputation of the bank." Rube gave her this verbal pat on the back, then added, "I've been thinking, would you like me to talk to Mr. Stackhaus about you
taking over the management of the Alaska Account?" He waited for a reply.

"Oh, my, Captain Hayes. I never considered that possibility. I don't know if
I can do that job. I'm the head clerk in the department, but—perhaps I could
do it, but—it's just that it is such a big step. I guess I'm not sure if I can do
it, do you?"

"Of course, you can, Lyda. You have passed that test. I just wanted to thank
you for bringing this to my attention. The investigation is just beginning. I
suspect you will be interviewed many times before it's over. No one else may
ever know, but I know you are a hero."

"That is so kind of you, Captain." She paused an instant. "Can you tell me?
Is Ms. Pedersen involved in this?"

"I wish I could tell you, but the investigation is still in progress," Rube pointed out. "Between you and me, though, it looks like she is involved. Please keep this under your hat for now."

"I won't tell a soul, Captain. By the way, I made those DVD copies of the Alaska Account files. Mr. Stackhaus asked me to send a copy to the banking commission and a copy to you. I will mail them on Monday."

"Well, I just called to thank you for everything you did. If you ever need a favor from me, just ask. I owe you a big one."

"All this has been very stressful for me, and I thank you for helping me. Good bye, Captain. I will talk to you again soon." There was relief in her voice now. She had been vindicated.

Culp and Fisk were both working when Rube called. He had breakfast in the coffee shop and returned to his room. He couldn't think of any good reason to remain any longer.

"Ray, Rube Hayes. Have you learned anything new?" Rube spoke into the phone.

"Good morning, Rube. No, nothing new, but we have firmed up an awful lot of information we had. Your suspicions were dead-on. We will send you all the interviews and, I think, about everything you will need to prosecute Aliana Pedersen—if you ever find her." He laughed.

"That will make it the easiest felony case I ever had." Rube was laughing now. "Do you need me for anything else, Ray? If not I am going to go home."

"We know where to find you. Thanks again for your help," Ray Culp said. "When do you plan to leave? Do you need a ride to the airport?"

"I'll call to confirm a return flight, then call you back with a time." By 11 AM he was on his way back home to Alaska.

Before boarding in Seattle, he called the office and told the receptionist he would be in the office on Monday. He told her he was coming home today, and gave her the flight numbers and time. She told him she would send a car for him upon his arrival. Once back in Anchorage and at home, he called Milo to let him know he was back and to report on the arrest of Ben Gerlitz. He unpacked his bag, turned on the TV and watched the end of the Mariners game. They lost to the Yankees seven to five in a home game heart-breaker.

Rube was settling into his new routine very swiftly. He was catching up on the learning curve and his duties were becoming habitual. Once he had completed his morning duties, he called the attorney general. The two men discussed in detail the events of the past several days. Rube informed him of the DVD file Lyda Carney was sending and promised to have it forwarded to him. Then, Woody Parsons, the attorney general, let Rube know he should call the governor and discuss this with him, since all this was, ultimately, his responsibility. He said Rube should call him because he had the most current and most accurate information. They said goodbye with Rube saying he would stay in touch on this case.

Rube's call had been expected, by way of a call from Woody Parsons. The governor's aide asked him to hold for the governor. A few moments later a strong, friendly voice came on the line.

"Good morning, Captain Hayes. This is the governor on speaker phone with my aide and a stenographer. We will tape this call, too." He explained the procedure. "I've been informed by the attorney general that one of my department heads has become an outlaw. Is that true?"

"I'm afraid it may be, governor. Circumstances suggest Aliana Pedersen is involved in a scheme to take the interest monies earned by the Alaska Account from SeaFirst Bank. Monies that should have gone back to the account have been diverted to what appears to be a private numbered account. At this time we cannot locate Ms. Pedersen and have been unable to interview her. She was in Anchorage, but she shifted all her scheduled duties to Miss St. John, also of the finance department. It appears Ms. Pedersen has disappeared, along with her sister and daughter. I have information that she, along with her sister and daughter, boarded a private jet and left the country. They have not been located since. My source says she went to Mexico."

"Good Lord," the governor's aide interjected. "How could this happen? We had an audit within the last month and everything was fine. Was the bank covering this up?"

"No, sir." Rube continued to explain what he knew. "A bank employee, Ben Gerlitz, was involved in the theft. Investigators from the Washington State Banking Commission have arrested Gerlitz. He has confessed, but at this time the commission has been unable to trace the path of the money. It was sent out to a disguised account and, they tell me, transferred several more times to cover the trail. This has been occurring twice weekly. I don't have the beginning dates yet. I'll give you updated information as I get it."

"Thank you, Captain. I want to be kept current on this. I can't have any of this linked to me personally. It could, conceivably, destroy the credibility of my entire administration." The governor was understandably anxious.

"I will keep you informed, sir."

The governor broke the connection.

Rube lit up his computer. He had been trying to keep a log of all events pertaining to this case, but it was becoming difficult.

Late in the day, he called Burt Fields. "Just wanted to give you an up-date on those files, Burt. They arrested Ben Gerlitz. He is singing his little heart out."

Burt snickered, "I don't suppose any of this is for publication?"

"Not now, maybe sometime down the road. I can see it all now, your new business card will read—BURT FIELDS—TAXES DONE—WILLS WRITTEN—SCANDALS VERIFIED.

Should do wonders for your business," Rube joked.

"It doesn't seem right somehow, you making fun of a guy who wears a bow tie."

"See you later, Burt." Rube hung up the phone

Bits and pieces of information trickled in to Rube over the next few weeks. This was something Rube had early in his career learned to live with, but this time his personal involvement was making him impatient.

Miss St. John had been named as interim administrator in her department. There was no word from Aliana; she had simply disappeared.

Captain Withers called to offer him a beer after duty hours. Rube accepted.

It was late. Rube had just finished a sandwich and a Coke. He was reading the newspaper when the telephone rang.

"Captain Hayes," Rube answered out of habit.

"Hello, Rube." The soft voice said.

Rube sat bolt upright and dropped his newspaper. "Aliana, is that you?"

"Yes. I have missed you terribly. I had to call you." She sounded genuine.

"Are you back?" he asked.

"No, I don't think I can ever come back. But I miss you so much I had to call," she said quietly.

"Are you still angry with me?"

"Angry? I don't know if I'm angry, but disappointed, yeah."

"I'm sorry, Rube, I didn't mean to hurt you, I never expected to fall in love with you. I wish all this would just go away, but I know it won't. Please don't hate me, Rube."

"I can't hate you when I still love you, but you left my world terribly empty. Can you tell me where you are?" Rube asked.

There was a short pause before she answered. "Costa Rica," she said. "Opal and Saundra are with me. It's very hard on them. It is very nice here, but it's lonely."

"Is there anything I can say that would bring you back?"

"You don't understand, Rube. I have done things, bad things, and I can't come back. When everyone finds out what I've done, they will be looking for me and trying to arrest me. I can't let that happen. Saundra needs me."

"I need you, too." Rube didn't know if he should tell her, then decided there was nothing to lose. "Have you heard what is happening here?"

"No, we don't get any news from there."

"Ben Gerlitz was arrested." As he paused he heard her gasp. "The Washington State Banking Commission is looking for you." Again he paused. "Is it true, Aliana? Did you really take all that money from the bank?"

"I'm afraid it is, Rube, but all that was before I met you. You changed my life, but this plan was in motion by then and I couldn't stop it. It all began to unravel when Tad was killed. And when I met you, my life changed. Saundra loves you, Opal loves you, and I love you. I can't change any of those things now. It's too late to correct my mistakes." She was sobbing.

"Exactly where are you, Aliana? Will you allow me to come see you?"

"What good would it do, Rube. You have a career you care about; you love Alaska. I will still be wanted by the authorities. If you come, nothing will change."

"Give me an address where I can reach you. Do you have a telephone?"

"I shouldn't tell you this. I know you will have to tell someone. Costa Rica won't allow extradition, so I'll tell you. I have a lovely home in a planned community near the capital city of San Jose. There is a new development here called Los Reyes. I can't give you my telephone number because you will have to pass it on, I'm sorry. I promise to call again, though, if you will let me. I love and miss you very much."

"Call again soon. Please. I still love you, too."

She hung up.

Chapter Thirty Seven

He was in his office attending his daily routine when the receptionist rang his phone. As was his habit, he checked the time and made a note on his desk pad.

"A Mr. Hank Fisk for you on line two. He said it was important."

Rube punched the button for line two. "Hello, Hank. How are things in Olympia?"

"Great, Rube. Glad to see you are still on the job. How are you doing?"

"I stay busy," he replied. "They keep me locked in the office and give me nourishment through the key hole." He was curious about the call. "Anything new in the investigation?"

"As a matter of fact, there is. I need to meet with you, in person and off record," Fisk said.

"How do you want to do it?" Rube asked. "Do you want to come here or should I go there?"

"I have several items I need to check out in Alaska, so, I think I will come to you. Can you make me a hotel reservation?"

"Sure, but I have room at my condo, if you would like to stay with me," Rube offered. "It ain't much, but it's home. Will you have time to spend a day fishing? I have a friend on the Kenai River, a great guide. I'll see if he will take us fishing, if you have the time. They have been doing well with the coho fishing."

"How far is that from Anchorage?" Fisk asked.

"By road, 150 miles, but in my airplane it's only 35 minutes. Bring some warm clothes and plan for a fun day. We have all the gear you will need. Call me with your flight number and time. I'll pick you up at the airport."

"I'll call you back with that information, Rube. Thanks for the offer. Are you sure your friend will take us out?" Fisk inquired.

"He doesn't guide that much any more. He usually makes time for me."

"Say, have you ever heard of a fella from Oregon by the name of Herb Goode?" Fisk asked. "He's a fishing guide and does cooking demonstrations at sport shows. Nice guy. He spends the summers on the Kenai River. I've fished the Rogue River with him a few times."

"I've met him. He fishes with his sponsors mostly. I don't know if he is still here, but if he is we can look him up while we are down there."

"Okay, I'll call you back as soon as I make arrangements."

Now his curiosity was in high gear. What information could be so important as to warrant a trip to Alaska? Had they learned something about Aliana? Did Ben Gerlitz implicate someone else? There was no point speculating; he would find out soon enough.

Rube called Jim Stogsdill. Jim said he didn't have a lot going on and would take the two men fishing. He offered an upper river rainbow trout fishing expedition, if the men had time. Rube thanked him and said he would call when he knew the date of arrival.

An hour later Fisk called again. "I'll be there just before noon tomorrow. Is that okay with your schedule?"

"Great, I'll buy lunch." Rube told him. "We're on for fishing. Can you get an extra day?"

"I think so. What's happening?"

"We are scheduled for a coho fishing trip, but Jim said if you want to go rainbow fishing, he'll take us the next day. The upper Kenai River has been really good. It turned on about a week ago. I'll call Jim and let him know we will be fishing both days." Rube smiled. "You aren't going to ruin these plans with your message, are you?"

Hank Fisk chuckled. "I guess that depends on your politics. See you tomorrow."

Rube was parked in front of the Alaska Airline arrival gate when Hank came out the door. He was towing a small suitcase on wheels. Rube stepped out of his Jeep and waved to him. Hank tossed the suitcase in the backseat and climbed into the front, smiling as he did so.

"It used to be fun to fly," Hank said. "It's not much fun these days. How are you, Buddy?"

"I'm doing well. You aren't going to ruin it are you?" Both men laughed. "What do you want for lunch?"

"I'm not particular; I'll eat about anything."

"The Sea Galley has some good fresh salmon and halibut. Will that do?"

"Oh, yeah. I love halibut," Hank said, smiling, "after lunch we need to find somewhere private to talk. I don't think you want anyone else hearing what I am going to tell you."

Lunch was excellent. They passed small talk during lunch, never mentioning the case. Rube could hardly wait to hear what Hank had to say. After lunch they drove to Rube's condo.

Inside, Rube pointed to a door. "You can have that room. It has a private bath. Mine is at the end of the hall," he said flipping a thumb toward his right. "When you get settled we can go into the kitchen and do some business."

"I'll just be a couple of minutes," Hank said.

While he waited, Rube brewed a fresh pot of coffee and cleared the kitchen table.

Hank returned before the coffee was perked. He had a large bundle of papers which he placed on the table. Both men sat and Hank began to spread out the papers.

"I will leave all this with you when I leave, but I'll go through it with you just so you know where this information is located within the files." Hank paused and stared squarely into Rube's eyes. "Are you ready for the big one?"

"Ready as I will ever get. I've been wondering since you called."

"Well, hang on 'cause here it comes." The suspense was deafening. "Ray and I have a secret weapon. An accountant who specializes in finding obscure facts in a mountain of data. He's a wizard. We asked him to look at all this and give us his opinion. It took him four days. When he called he wanted to discuss it in a secure area."

"Come on, Hank, you're killing me. What did he find?"

Hank was grinning. "Our accountant said this scam could not have worked unless someone at the top knew about it. One of two people, he said—Stackhaus or your governor, Craig Talmage. His version is that it should have come to light during the audits. It never had. Ray began to look into the auditing company. That's this file," he said pointing. "The company name is Lighthouse Audits. They are an independent company, but guess whose name is on the list of directors?" Rube shrugged. "Mr. Craig Talmage, Governor of the Great State of Alaska."

Rube nearly fell from his chair. "Are you certain? And if he is an officer in the auditing company, what makes you think he is connected directly to the thefts?"

"Here's where the plot thickens," he chuckled again. "Ms. Aliana Pedersen, whom we thought was the brains behind it all, was being used just like she used poor old Ben Gerlitz. We discovered that her little girl, the one with the learning disability, is a product of she and the honorable Craig Talmage. He promised her the world if she would quit the corporation she was working for and come to work for him as the head of a new office in the division of finance. He offered her a great salary and a free hand. What he really wanted was a fall guy, a buffer between him and this scam. We traced some of the numbered accounts and found that the money was divided in the Bahamas or somewhere and part went to Hong Kong and part went to Panama. The portion going to Hong Kong, also a numbered account, was assigned to one Craig Talmage. I'm not allowed to tell you how we know all this, but we have friends in foreign countries. Since the transfers are interstate and international, we are filing federal felony charges against your governor." Hank was looking into the perplexed eyes of Rube Hayes. "One other side note, are you ready for this one?" Hank was enjoying this way too much. "If we can get Ms. Pedersen to testify for the prosecution, we can get her immunity. Talmage is the guy we want anyway."

Rube was thinking, Ray Culp and Hank Fisk knew about him and Aliana. They were using him to provide a witness in federal court against Governor Talmage. "And you think I can get Aliana to come back to Alaska. Is that what you were thinking?"

"Along those lines, yes." He was grinning again. "You and she weren't exactly a secret, you know."

"Well, first of all I have no idea where to contact her. Second, she loves her daughter more than anything and she won't come back unless and until she is guaranteed immunity. Third, I'm not sure she would listen, even if I could find her." Rube realized he sounded as though he was negotiating a deal.

"I will guarantee a free pass from federal prosecution and from the State of Washington. I can't say what the State of Alaska will do. That will be up to your attorney general." His demeanor became serious. "Will you give it a try?"

"I'll have to think about that, but it sounds good to me."

Rube found a legal pad and the two men spent the afternoon outlining all the information in the files. It was late when they finished. Rube had taken a break and called Jim Stogsdill. They would need to be at the boat at 6 AM. Rube told him he would land on the river at Airplane Hole and asked Jim to meet them there. He then called the hangar and asked that his plane be ready to leave by 5 AM. His mood was much lighter now.

Chapter Thirty Eight

A bad day of fishing beats a good day of work, so the saying goes. Then a good day of fishing should beat almost anything. Two good days of fishing are like dying and going to heaven. For Hank Fisk it was the trip of a lifetime. The fishing had been phenomenal. A limit of coho salmon was caught the first morning, all 12 to 14 pound fish. Back at the dock, the fish were processed and frozen. Fisk had the box of fish sent to his home via FedEx. Jim Stogsdill explained to Fisk that the rainbow trout fishing would be all catch and release, and explained the reasoning behind the practice. Over and over Fisk repeated how much he was enjoying the trip.

"In the Lower-48 states, people save all their lives to be able to make a once in a lifetime fishing trip to Alaska. They seldom leave disappointed. But Jim and I are the lucky ones," explained Rube, "they pay us to be here. How can you beat a deal like that?" They were all laughing.

While Fisk napped in the afternoon, Rube called AG Woody Parsons. Once past the maze of secretaries, Rube reached Woody.

"Woody, we have to meet. Will you be in Anchorage next week?"

"No, I can't, Rube. I'm too busy with things in the office. Why, do you have something important?" he asked.

"I would judge it to be so. In fact it may be the single most important item you have dealt with since you took the office." Rube wanted his full attention, and now he had it. "I have serious information that you will have to deal with. Since you aren't coming here, I will fly down and meet you in your office on Monday morning. You had better clear your calendar for next week."

"Now wait a minute, Rube. I can't just cancel everything for next week. Things are entirely too busy here."

"Yeah? Well, Woody, they are about to get worse. I have not told Milo about this yet, but when I do he may want to come with me. I'm serious, Woody. Clear your calendar."

"If you think it's that important, Rube, I will give you Monday morning; but I can't clear the entire week."

"I think you will. See you Monday." Rube hung up, then dialed Milo.

"It's the weekend. Do you hate me so bad you wanted to ruin my day off?" Milo groused in a joking manner.

"Milo, you had better sit down for this one. I just called Woody and asked him to clear his calendar for next week. He thought I was joking, too." Rube began to explain, it took several minutes to cover all the high points. "It's no joke, Milo. Do you want to come to Juneau with me on Monday?"

Milo was silent for a few seconds. "Okay, Rube. Are you sure you have this all backed up?"

"Yes, the State of Washington is teaming with the feds on this. They're going after the governor."

"Let me change your plan a little," Milo said. "I am going with you, but I'll have the King Air fly us down tomorrow evening. I will book rooms in Juneau and we can be in Woody's office on Monday morning. What time will you be returning to Anchorage tomorrow?"

"Early afternoon," Rube replied. "Fisk has a flight late in the day. As soon as I put him on the plane, I can go with you."

"Okay, give me some time to run all this past the colonel. Call me later for the final arrangements. This is going to cause the biggest stink we have ever seen in this state," Milo said, as he hung up the phone.

Jim Stogsdill was the ultimate host. He showed Fisk the local attractions and gave him a motor tour of the local area. Fisk offered to buy dinner and the trio dined in Kenai at Louie's. The steaks were wonderful. Rube spent the evening thinking about the coming days. He hoped Aliana would call him soon. It excited him to think he may be able to get her back to Alaska. He had no illusions about how bad this was going to get before it was over.

Fisk giggled and laughed all morning. He was like a small boy, catching and releasing trout of all sizes. Small fish, a half pound or so, and large fish, some more than ten pounds. All caught on light tackle. Alaska brown bears were seen, catching their own meals, along the shores of the river. The day was a true Alaska experience for Fisk and a great day of fishing for the two Alaskans. At noon they began their final drift. The men helped Jim get the boat out of the water and they drove the twenty miles to Soldotna. Jim relaunched the boat, loaded their belongings and took the two to the airplane for the return trip to Lake Hood in Anchorage.

At the condo, while Fisk was gathering his belongings, he called Milo.

"Glad you called, Rube. There's a small change in the plan. We have the King Air, but one more passenger. The colonel will be riding with us. He asked to go along because he thinks the AG will issue an arrest warrant for the governor. The colonel thought it would only be proper for him to serve the warrant and to take the governor into custody. Any problems with that plan?"

"You two are my bosses, I'm just the messenger. I'm about to take Hank to the airport. What time are we taking off?"

"The colonel will be at the hangar at 6. Can you be there by that time?"

Rube checked the time. "Plenty of time. Once I drop Fisk, I'll go directly to the hangar. See you there, at 6."

During the trip to the airport, Hank Fisk repeatedly told Rube how much he had enjoyed the fishing trip. They discussed things regarding the case and how he was to handle things for Aliana if she returned. Rube confessed he had heard from Aliana, but had been honest about not knowing how to contact her.

Before getting out of the car, Fisk told Rube, "I have to warn you, I'm coming back, and you can count on Ray to hound you to take him fishing, too." They shook hands and Hank Fisk walked into the terminal, towing the little suitcase on wheels. Rube watched him go and tried to get his mind back to business. Before pulling from the curb, he checked the backseat for his carry-on bag and the suit bag with his clean uniform in it. Both items were where they should be. He drove to the state aircraft hangar where the King Air was kept. It was outside and the trooper/pilot was making his walk-around pre-flight check. Rube parked near the hangar. He had just opened a Coke when Milo came in.

"The colonel is on his way," he volunteered.

The flight was made at 12,000 feet and just offshore to minimize the mountain turbulence. The colonel had asked to see the files on the governor. He spent most of the trip in silence, reading the massive report. The flying weather was good, and even Juneau was having a sunny afternoon. The colonel had ordered a car to take them from the airport to the hotel. Once there he asked the driver to meet with them, here, at the Baranof Hotel at 8 AM.

In the morning the three were being driven to the office of the AG. The colonel turned around in the front seat and smiled at Rube.

"Well, Rube. This will either be the biggest day of your career or the worst, which could also mean the last."

"Thanks for making me feel better, Colonel," Rube replied

Official office hours begin at 8:30, but these three men were allowed into the building. Woody Parsons was in his office, though his receptionist was not yet on duty. The AG had purposely left his door open in anticipation of their arrival. "Come in," he called when he saw the men.

"Good morning, Woody," the colonel offered. "You know Milo and Rube, of course."

"I sure do, Colonel," Woody said, shaking hands with all three men. "Now, what the heck is all this about?"

Rube set the documents on the polished desk. "This is the file furnished to me by the State of Washington. It is a duplicate of the one the feds have. This file outlines a theft committed at SeaFirst Bank in Seattle, Washington," Rube began.

"If this took place in Washington, it is outside my jurisdiction. Why are you bringing it to me?" the AG interrupted.

"Because, during the investigation, it was discovered that the Alaska Account in that bank had been audited by a firm called Lighthouse Audits. Investigation by the Washington State Banking Commission uncovered items that should have been found in the audit. While determining why this was missed in the audit, it was discovered that one of the directors in the Lighthouse Audit Corporation, and a founding member, is an Alaska official." Rube was summarizing.

"The theft and the audit both took place in Washington and are outside my jurisdiction, as I said before," the AG repeated.

"What if this account was handling $2 billion dollars a year of Alaska's money. And what if the director of the Lighthouse Audit Corporation was a principal in the Alaska financial system. Would that make a difference?" Rube asked.

"But, as I said twice before, this alleged theft took place outside my jurisdiction," The AG said once again.

"What if the director of Lighthouse Audit Corporation, to whom the State of Alaska paid a fee for an audit of the Alaska Account at SeaFirst Bank in Seattle, Washington, was the governor of the State of Alaska? Would it be in your jurisdiction then?" Rube said coldly.

"Oh, my dear God! That's not possible." Attorney General Woody Parsons was incredulous.

"That's why we're here, Woody," the colonel said.

"Will you give me some time to review the file?" Woody asked.

Once again the colonel spoke, "Certainly, Woody, we will wait while you look at the evidence."

The three troopers sat quietly, if not patiently, for more than an hour while Woody reviewed the file. He only scanned most of the pages, but when he came to the file with the missing pages he paused and re-read the material. Finally, he looked up from the files, looking directly at Rube.

"You were right. I need to clear my calendar for the rest of the week." He punched the button on his intercom and instructed his secretary to cancel all business for the remainder of the week. Those things she couldn't cancel were to be directed to his assistant AG. "I'm not to be disturbed," he growled into the speaker.

Again the colonel took the lead. "Now that we are all on the same page, Woody, where do we go from here? They have already arrested Ben Gerlitz at the bank in Seattle. The feds will be serving warrants for conspiracy at Lighthouse Audits sometime today. We have evidence. The suspect is a flight risk and will surely hear about the other arrests soon. We need an arrest warrant we can serve on the governor this morning. Is that possible?"

"Do you want a state or a federal warrant?" the AG asked.

"That's more like it," the colonel commented. "I think, since it was state money taken, the state should prosecute him. Do you agree?"

Woody punched the intercom button again. "Send the Assistant AG in here."

Within two minutes a skinny geek-looking man arrived. The AG didn't bother to introduce anyone. "Ward, find Judge Compton quickly." Woody scrawled a short note to the judge. "Tell him I need this now. If he has any questions, have him call me. Get going." The man wheeled and left the office, nearly running.

"I don't know how long this will take," the AG said. "Can I have the secretary get some coffee and donuts?"

"We haven't eaten breakfast, that would be nice." the colonel answered for all.

The refreshments arrived while Rube and Woody talked about details of the case. The attorney general was clearly shaken by the events of this morning. Short of an hour had passed when the AG's phone rang. "Thank you," he said, finally. He made a note on his legal pad, then looked at the Colonel.

"We have a warrant for the arrest of the Governor of the State of Alaska, Craig Talmage. The charge, at this time, is conspiracy to defraud. I will get busy on the final charges after I carefully re-read this file." Woody looked sad. "Colonel, this is the worst day of my career. I don't know how to thank you for that."

"This case will make you famous, Woody. And, the state will be looking for a new governor soon." The colonel smiled. "Call my office and I will contribute to your campaign fund. I owe you."

Chapter Thirty Nine

On the street, the colonel used his cell phone to contact the local trooper commander. He ordered the trooper to locate the governor without alerting him. He also wanted two uniformed officers to meet with him at a location close to where the governor was located. All this needed to be done as soon as possible. The trooper captain said he would have it done and return his call. The trio waited beside their assigned ride. Ten minutes went by before the telephone rang.

"We have located the governor. He is at the mansion. He is in a meeting with some Eagle Scouts. This meeting will conclude in about twenty five minutes. I have two officers on their way to that location as we speak. Anything else, Colonel?"

"Thank you, nothing more at this time, but please stand by in case I need you." The colonel then turned to his two officers and said, "They have located the governor. He is in a meeting that should last another twenty to thirty minutes. Let's go." He instructed the driver to go to the governor's mansion.

They waited outside the antebellum style mansion. The home office is very large and quite beautiful. The giant columns give it a sense of elegance. Almost immediately two trooper vehicles parked behind theirs. Rube walked to the cars and talked with the two officers. He instructed them to wait and when they went inside the two troopers were to follow. He informed them that they were here to arrest the governor on a warrant. There shouldn't be any difficulty with the arrest, but you never know. The two officers said they understood. Rube returned to the lead auto. Five minutes later they saw the scouts leaving through the front door, the governor shaking hands with each of them as they departed. The troopers waited until the scouts had left the area before entering.

The colonel told Rube to take the lead and to initiate the arrest. Rube agreed. The five men climbed the steps and entered. A receptionist inside asked their business. Rube told her he needed to see the governor immediately, he didn't have an appointment.

She dialed the telephone. "Governor, there are some troopers, the colonel and some others here to see you. They don't have an appointment." She listened a moment, then spoke into the phone again. "They are due in about forty five minutes, sir." She paused again. "Yes, sir."

She stood. "If you gentlemen will follow me, I will show you to his office." With that the group made the march down the hall and into the governor's office. He excused the woman and she left, closing the door behind her.

"To what do I owe this pleasure, gentlemen?" Craig Talmage asked.

Rube stood in front of the others and answered the question. "Governor Talmage, you are under arrest on a warrant issued by the Alaska Superior Court. The charge is conspiracy to commit a felony, theft from a financial institution. The attorney general is aware of these charges. At this time I will read you your Miranda rights as required by law." He read the warning from a card. "Do you understand your right as I have read them to you?"

"Of course I understand my rights."

"Would you like to call a lawyer before we take you into custody?"

"I have no idea what this all about. Yes, I want to call my lawyer."

"We will allow you to use this telephone, or you can use the one at the booking office. Which do you prefer?"

"I will use this phone, thank you."

"We will leave to give you privacy with this conversation; however, for security reasons one trooper will remain inside the room with you."

"I won't need privacy for this call, you may all stay." He dialed the number from memory. "Lewis, I am being arrested. I need you at the jail right now." A short pause. "Hurry."

Rube thought the man was incredibly calm. "By law we must handcuff you, sir." He motioned one of the young troopers to cuff him. This was followed by a short pat-search for weapons. Rube told the arresting officer he would follow them to the jail.

At the jail Rube turned the prisoner over to the corrections people. Once he was inside the secure doors, he was just another prisoner. He was searched, fingerprinted, photographed and booked. Once all that had been accomplished, he was placed in an interview room to await his lawyer. The entire staff was abuzz with the news of the governor being arrested. He had been here on several other occasions, but never as a prisoner. The transporting officer had signed the remand slip and left the jail. The troopers had a short conference with the jail superintendent. How long the governor stayed locked up was up to the judges and courts. Under Alaska law, everyone is allowed bail. No one doubted this man would easily make bail. Of course, like Eduardo Sanchez and Larry Combs, he could flee, never to be seen again.

The colonel offered to buy lunch at the Baranof before the group flew back to Anchorage. On the way to lunch, Rube could not help wondering why the governor seemed so calm during all this. He had been surprised by the circumstance, but the arrest didn't seem to bother him.

Various aspects of the day's events were discussed by the three troopers. They all agreed that it would all go public with the 6 o'clock news. They guessed the public would know before they returned to Anchorage. The colonel suspected he would be deluged with phone calls, mostly from politicians. Milo was marveling at how smoothly things had gone.

Following a rather blah lunch, the group was driven back to the airport and the King Air. Rube was still having trouble grasping how the governor could remain so calm, given the circumstances. He asked Milo and the colonel.

"I can't answer that with certainty, Rube, but I suspect he has a plan in place to cover just this sort of event. He must have suspected this could happen," the colonel surmised.

"I guess you're right, sir, but his M.O. would suggest that he will do his best to hand off the guilt to someone else. His complicity in this scheme was well hidden. I don't trust the guy." Rube became silent again.

The words the colonel had spoken earlier were prophetic. When Rube entered his office, he found his desk stacked high with notes of calls to be returned. Looking at the names on the slips of paper, he suspected they were mostly about the arrest. It was late and he decided to let the calls wait until tomorrow. Trying to relax, he took his notebook from his shirt pocket and began to make out his daily activity report. He was thankful the regular administrative staff had gone for the day. The office was quiet. He used his cell phone to dial Aliana. No answer, out of service message.

The media frenzy over the arrest of Craig Talmage was incredible. It filled every newscast on every station. The national newscasts were now picking up the story. The investigators in Washington state were interviewed as well as some federal people. Everyone they interviewed seemed to claim credit for uncovering this crime. It seemed to Rube they were all engaged in the great American pastime: fixing the blame, not the problem.

In his office, the telephone rang endlessly. Milo called once to see how he was doing. Rube thought all he wanted was for it all to end, then realized his new position dictated he would be dealing with this kind of thing for the rest of his career. That was a depressing thought.

He returned all the calls and answered the inquiries as they came in. It seemed every other call was a reporter wanting to interview him. He declined every inquiry, citing departmental policy and referring all interviews to the colonel's office.

He had grilled some salmon for dinner and had just finished putting the dishes in the machine when the telephone rang. He was in no hurry to answer it. He picked it up on ring number six.

"Hello," he said curtly.

"Hello, Rube," the soft voice said. "Can we talk for a while?"

Rube dropped into his recliner, relaxed for the first time in days. "Aliana, I have been trying to reach you. Are you okay?"

"Oh, yes, I'm fine. I'm just lonely."

"I hope you are sitting down," he began. "I have some bad news for you. I also have some good news that I should deliver in person. Would you see me if I came to Costa Rica?"

"You know I would see you, but you shouldn't come here. You shouldn't be any where near me," Aliana said sadly.

"Have you been watching the news?" he asked.

"No, I don't get TV here. I don't have a TV set. Why?' she asked.

"We arrested Craig Talmage," he told her.

She sucked in a huge gulp of air in surprise. "You're kidding me. Is that true?"

"It's true. Now will you let me come to see you?" He was nearly pleading.

"When?" she asked.

"As soon as I can arrange it. How can I reach you?"

There was a long silence. "I am going to give you my number, here at the house. Please don't tell anyone. If anyone finds out, I will have to sell my home here and move somewhere else, and I don't want Saundra to be forced to adjust to another new home. Can you understand that?"

"Would you come back here if you had a chance?" he asked.

"You know I can't, it's too late. I wish I could come back to you, but it's impossible," she sobbed.

"Perhaps not," he said. "Don't ever give up hope."

"I wish there was hope, but I can't let myself indulge in those thoughts. I just called to tell you I love you. I wish we could be together." There was another note of sadness in her voice.

"I'm coming down there. Don't give up hope. I'll call as soon as I can make arrangements." This was the first glimmer of excitement he had felt in weeks. They said goodbye and Rube began to assemble the amnesty papers given him by Hank Fisk.

He went to the computer and began researching flights, rates, airlines and seats. How much leave time would he ask for? A week, he thought.

It was nearly 2 AM when he finally slid into bed, relaxed for the first time in a very long while.

Chapter Forty

It was mid-morning, Rube had been busy with the daily reports and his usual stack of leave requests, sick officer reports and the usual daily trivia. The telephone disturbed his routine, but he welcomed the break.

"Captain Hayes," he answered.

"Rube, it's Major Thomas," came the friendly voice. "Have you seen the news bulletins on TV this morning?"

"No, I haven't. What's happening?" Rube asked.

"I think you had better see it first hand. The governor is about to make a statement. He bailed out and is making a public statement in ten minutes. Find a TV and when it's over give me a call here at the office," Milo instructed.

"Will do," he said. He went to the officer's break room and turned on the television.

A news reporter on Channel 2 was killing time waiting for the governor to come to the podium. The scene appeared to be in the governor's mansion in Juneau. It wasn't long before Craig Talmage appeared. The voices of reporters could be heard shouting questions. He was ignoring all the voices and was turned to speak with another man at the podium. He placed his prepared statement on the stand and held up his hands, asking for quiet. As the background conversations died away, the governor stared into the camera. He was a showman and a politician.

Again he held up his hands, and cleared his throat. He smiled his familiar smile, all the while looking directly into the camera. The camera pulled back a little to give a wider view.

"Ladies and gentlemen. Good citizens of the Great State of Alaska." The room became ultra-quiet. "In the past twenty four hours there has been the greatest attack on me personally that I have ever experienced. At the advice of my lawyer, Lewis Sohms," he stepped back and turned to give an introductory wave at the man to his right, "I have come before you to explain the circumstances concerning my arrest yesterday morning. This is the most humiliating thing ever to happen to me. As far as I know, never before have the troopers come to the home of the sitting governor and arrested him. I was taken to the jail and booked like a criminal. This was done without warning and without my being offered an opportunity to defend myself. I was taken, publicly, in handcuffs, from my offices. Again I say this was an act of public humiliation." He paused and took a drink of water from a bottle on the podium.

Rube found a bottle of water in the refrigerator and opened it. He sat at the table, waiting for the punch line.

Talmage continued, "The crime of which I have been arrested and charged is conspiracy to commit a felony. My attorney thinks the state will try to add other charges in the days to come. The felony referred to in the charging warrant is theft of a great deal of money from a bank account belonging to the State of Alaska. The account is with SeaFirst Bank in Seattle, Washington."

He took another sip of water and continued. "This account was originated at my request by a person I selected and appointed as a deputy director of finance in this state. She did a marvelous job of realigning the state's losses from late fees and penalties on contracts with the State of Alaska. She built an entire staff of professional people to change the way the bills are paid by the state. The system was, and is, a tremendous success. This department handles nearly $2 billion of state assets each year. Since she took the helm at that section of finance, the savings to the state has been in the millions of dollars. She was responsible for the account at SeaFirst. During her administration, there were several millions of dollars paid to that account in interest. The fees to the bank were deducted from the total interest paid and the remainder paid to the account. Someone, in collusion with the banker in charge of the account, transferred this money out of the account to a numbered account. I knew nothing of all this. It was carefully hidden from me and state auditors by falsifying the documents that were sent to me and on file with the department of finance, here in the State of Alaska." Lawyer Sohms, standing slightly behind the governor, nodded ever so slightly.

"Ladies and gentlemen, I give you this statement not to claim my innocence, but to explain all the media hype concerning my arrest. I say to you now, I had no part in the crime except to be guilty of appointing someone capable of this crime. I am as outraged as you. This person has fled the state and, I am sure, will be hunted by authorities from this state and at the federal level. I am confident she will be found and brought to justice. I regret the dark stain this has placed on my administration. Please don't judge all the good people in my administration by the acts of one individual. I know I will be vindicated. It is my plea that all of you be patient until the final gavel falls on the outcome."

He again sipped from the water bottle.

"This concludes my statement at this time. I will not be taking questions from the gallery. I will be updating the public when new information is available. I thank you for continuing to maintain your faith in me and my administration. Good day."

With that he and his attorney left the podium and disappeared through an office door.

Rube was shocked. Now he knew the plan Talmage had devised that allowed him to be so calm when the arrest took place. He is going to lay all this off on Aliana, Rube thought. This guy is a piece of work.

He returned to his office and dialed Milo, steaming as he did.

"This guy is going to lay all this off on Aliana," Rube said, without preamble.

"Take it easy, Rube," Milo cautioned. "I just got off the phone with the AG. Right now they are debating whether he can remain in office while he is under indictment. It looks as though there will be a ruling by the Alaska Supreme Court to the effect that while he is under indictment, the lieutenant governor will sit in his place. Like I said, that is still being debated."

"How can this Sohms defend the sleaze bag?" Rube asked.

"You are letting your personal feelings rule your judgment. Step back, take a deep breath and look at the big picture. Everyone is entitled to legal representation. Everyone is entitled to the best representation his lawyer can provide. Everyone is innocent until a jury says he isn't. Everyone, that includes the governor," Milo reminded.

"You're right, Milo, but I can't help thinking he could skate and leave Aliana holding the bag. She admits she was wrong, but Talmage forced her into it," Rube steamed.

"I have to warn you, Rube. If you can't get it together, I will have to take you out of this equation. You told me you could remain objective and I took you at your word, now live up to that or I will be forced to take action."

"You are right, of course," Rube admitted, "and I will try. I needed someone to vent on and you caught it. Sorry."

"Okay, what is the plan now?" the Major asked.

"I had a call from Aliana last night. She was horrified to hear we arrested Talmage. I also told her I was coming to Costa Rica to see her. I didn't give her any information on the phone. I need to have you approve some leave time for me. I've got tickets pending," Rube said.

Milo paused a short pause, "Are you sure you can handle this without emotional input?"

"Yes, now that I have a forward-moving plan. I'm having Fisk fax me a copy of the federal immunity agreement and a list of questions he wants answered. I will take all this to her and get her to agree to come back to testify. The feds will be happy; the banking commission will be happy; and I will be happy. The only one who may not be happy is Governor Craig Talmage." Rube paused, then served his notice. "I have to tell you, Milo, if you take me off this and don't approve my leave, I'm going anyway. I have never put anything ahead of the job, but this time I would have to do it."

"I hope that isn't a threat, Rube," Milo admonished. "We have been friends a long time, but I don't take kindly to threats. I have responsibilities of my own. How much leave time do you want?"

"A week, I thought."

"Bring me the slip and I will sign it," Milo said. "Let's get this done and get back to work."

"Thanks, Milo."

Rube called Lieutenant Balfore to tell him he would be in charge beginning today and that he would be out of town for a few days. He then went to Milo's office to get his leave slip authorized. He had called Fisk and was awaiting the fax he had requested. Fisk was jubilant when Rube told him of the plan.

Rube, his mood much lighter, did his last minute paperwork and left the office. At home he packed, locked his duty weapon in a small safe, checked his cell phone for charge, pulled a beer from the refrigerator, flopped into his recliner and called Aliana. He gave her the flight numbers and times. Halfway through the beer he fell asleep. He napped for about an hour. When he awoke he picked up a light windbreaker and his bag, and called Balfore to give him a ride to the airport.

He checked in and looked for a monitor with his flight numbers. It would be on time.

The flight had been long and uncomfortable. The food didn't look appetizing, so he didn't order it. He tried to rest, but that was impossible. His mind kept returning to the speech made by the governor. Milo was right, he was having trouble being objective. It was bright and sunny when the plane landed at San Jose, Costa Rica. He had only a carry-on and his jacket, enabling him to reach the customs desk at the head of the line. The customs officer asked him to open his bag, which he did; they passed him on. They stamped his passport and he walked out of the terminal. The sun was warm, his mood was light and he was elated to see Aliana standing beside a yellow Land Rover. She waved to him, he waved back and quickened his pace.

Before she could get the car in gear, he pulled her to him and kissed her passionately. "We can go now," he said. "Did you make me a hotel reservation?"

"No," she said, breathing heavily. "You are staying at my house."

He smiled, then said, "How would you like to hear some good news?"

"That would certainly be a change," she said, keeping her eye on the road.

"I have, in my bag, an amnesty agreement from the feds and signed off by the State of Washington. It says that if you testify in the trial against Craig Talmage, you will not be prosecuted for your participation in this crime." Rube watched the expression on her face. Her mouth dropped slightly in surprise. "Are you willing to go back with me and talk with these people?"

"I just want to be sure," she said, still watching the road. "If I go back with you I won't be arrested, is that right?" She ventured a short peek at him. "Oh, Rube. I have prayed this would happen, but I couldn't see how it could possibly take place." She thought a moment, then continued, "Will I have to see Craig?"

"At the trial, yes. You can bet his lawyer will want to talk to you, but you won't have to see the governor until the trial."

"Twice that man has decimated my life. Now, and when I was in college. We were planning to be married, but when I told him I was pregnant he ran like a rabbit. I never told anyone who the father was. He never gave me any financial help. When he asked me to head the new department, he said it was to make up for all those years. Like an idiot I believed him. Then when he told me what he wanted me to do, I refused. He told me if I didn't do as he asked he would fire me and let it out that I had committed some crime. That would have destroyed my credibility and I would never have been able to work in the financial world again. I had commitments to my daughter and my sister. I felt I had no choice. It was stupid of me, I know. It only postponed the outcome. After this I will never get a position with a public corporation."

Tears streamed down her cheeks as she confessed to Rube.

"Please, stop the car, Aliana."

She pulled to the side of the road and stepped out of the car. The two embraced. They held each other for several minutes. Finally Rube looked into her sad eyes and said, "I love you, Aliana. I will stand by you for as long as it takes. Let's, the two of us, solve one problem at a time. Together we can surmount any obstacle."

"I want nothing more, Rube. What I don't want is for you to be tainted by my actions. I don't want to hurt you. I love you too much." Again her eyes glistened with tears.

He led her back to the cab of the SUV. "One problem at a time," he said, climbing into the other side. "Now, let's eat, I'm hungry."

Her home was a two story, flat roof, Spanish design. It sat atop a low hill with a view of a small valley and on the far side of that was the ocean and a white sand beach. The view was spectacular. They climbed from the car and reached into the backseat for his bag. When he turned he saw just how beautiful she was. Her smooth, dark skin accented by the sun. Her white tee shirt and white shorts and sandals, along with her long black hair, made her appear like a native of Costa Rica. Only her liquid blue eyes gave her away. He followed her to the house.

When the door opened, he was attacked and hugged and kissed by Saundra. "Oh, Senior Hayes, I am so happy to see you," she laughed and hugged him again. "I am learning Spanish, do you want me to teach you?"

"I think that would be wonderful, Saundra," He picked her up and kissed her on the cheek.

Opal stood back and waited for Saundra to finish. "Hello, Rube," she said, shaking his hand.

"Hello, Opal. You look great. This tropical living must agree with you."

She smiled and took his bag. "I will put this in your room," she said, grinning broadly.

"Come on, I'll fix something to eat." Aliana led him to the kitchen and poured a glass of Sangria cold from the refrigerator. As she handed him the wine, she asked, "How about a fruit plate for a snack? I will cook some fresh swordfish later."

"That sounds good. The Sangria is great." He sipped the drink and watched her prepare lunch. He looked out the kitchen patio door, across the little valley to the shore. "I could get used to this life," he said.

It was late when they finished dinner. Rube brought out the immunity agreements for her to inspect. She read them carefully, then read them again.

"These look wonderful, Rube. Do you think they will stick to the agreement?" She seemed hesitant.

"I've spent a lot of time with the agents from Washington. I think they are making a genuine offer. I think the feds are going along with Washington, but you can't always trust them to do what they say they will do. In this case it looks like they will follow the agreement. You have to make the choice. My advice is to take it. But, remember I am biased. I want you back in my life."

"What about Saundra and Opal? Should I take them with me now?" she asked.

"When this is over, you will want to come back and do something with the house and property. It might be best to have them wait here until the dust settles. The reporters and lawyers are not likely to bother them here. But, again, the choice is yours to make. Either way I will back you."

"You are so good to me, Rube. How soon do you want to go back?" she asked.

"I have a week of leave. It would be nice to have all this, except the trial, out of the way by the time I have to go back to work."

"I love you, Rube. And I love all you are doing for me. I have to think about Saundra and Opal, though. Can I sleep on it and give you an answer in the morning?"

He smiled and said, "Only if you kiss me before you go to sleep."

In the morning she agreed to return with him, alone. She was counting on him to protect her during this ordeal. She packed a large suitcase and let Opal and Saundra take them to the airport.

Because of the short notice, the return flight was not as direct and took much longer. It routed them through Los Angeles where the went through U.S. Customs. Aliana seemed relieved to be back on U.S. soil. The next stop would be Seattle where they would be met by Culp, Fisk and someone from the feds, treasury, Rube suspected.

Late in the day Rube and Aliana cleared customs in Los Angeles. The connecting flight to Seattle was tomorrow morning at 5 AM. They found a room at the airport Ramada Inn where they ordered dinner in the room. They both showered and slipped into bed where they renewed their courtship.

Chapter Forty Two

They returned to the airport early the next day, cleared TSA and found coffee and rolls in one of the shops on their departing concourse. The two sat close and held hands. The only conversation was the occasional rare comments about the up-coming depositions. When their flight was called, they walked to the gate hand-in-hand.

SeaTac airport was foggy when they landed. Rube was sorry he had packed his windbreaker in his bag, but it was warm enough once they were inside the terminal. Fisk was standing in the baggage area when the two got to the carousel. Rube introduced Aliana to Hank Fisk.

"Is everything still the same?" Rube asked Hank.

"The feds are so anxious over this deal I think they would pay her a reward if she asked for one." He took Aliana's suitcase. "Ray is in the car. We are parked out front."

At the car Rube introduced Aliana to Ray Culp.

"Pleased to meet you," he said. "Are you hungry? There are a couple of good breakfast places between here and Tacoma."

"We could use some breakfast, Ray. I found that the only good thing about airline food is there isn't much of it," Rube chuckled. "I must be getting old. I can remember when flying was fun."

Fifteen minutes later they pulled off Interstate 5 and stopped at a small restaurant near the top of the exit ramp. Ray was right, the food was outstanding. Once back in the car, the conversation turned to the planned schedule of events. The interviews would take place in the offices of the banking commission.

"We thought it might be more comfortable doing this on our turf rather than in the federal building," Hank explained to Aliana. "Please remember, you are a voluntary witness here. You are not under arrest and you cannot be prosecuted using any statements you make. We have Gerlitz and his statements; the feds nearly wet their pants when we showed them the text on his admissions. He didn't get immunity, by the way. I don't think they will be accusatory. They want to nail Craig Talmage. If you get tired or nervous just ask for a break, we'll see you get it. Are you okay with all that?" Hank asked in a friendly tone.

"Yes," Aliana replied, quietly. "How long do you think this will last? The interviews, I mean."

"If we stay at it all day, I think we can finish by early this evening," Ray answered. "Hank and I will spring for dinner and drinks when we finish, and that is something we seldom do." Ray chuckled, "We have to. Rube made us put it in the contract."

"We have rooms for the two of you, for three nights, at the same hotel you were in before, Rube. I hope that's okay," Hank interjected.

The conversation was light for the rest of the trip with Hank re-telling, for the umpteenth time, the story of his Kenai River fishing trip. In Olympia the first stop was the hotel where they checked in and left their luggage. Back in the car, Aliana was beginning to get nervous. Rube held her hand to comfort her. It was comforting for him also.

In the interview room where the session was to take place, she was introduced to George Findlay, the Washington State Banking Commissioner. After the introduction, Findlay returned to his office.

The next person she met was Tom Cantor. He presented his credentials and implied he would be the chief interviewer at this meeting. He then introduced Alice Miller. A square-built woman, neatly dressed, but imposing.

"How do you do," she said, holding out her hand to Aliana and then to Rube. "I will be assisting Agent Cantor today. We will be recording these proceedings, so there will be no need to take notes. We will furnish you, Captain Hayes and the Washington Banking Commission copies of the interview. You have a copy of our immunity agreement, do you not?" she asked Aliana. Aliana nodded. "Then you know that nothing you say here can be used against you in court. Once you testify you will be free as far as the State of Washington and the Treasury Department are concerned. What happens in the State of Alaska is up to them, though I understand the attorney general in Alaska has also exempted you from prosecution. These agreements are rare and I urge you to adhere strictly to the letter of this agreement."

"Don't worry about me," Aliana said, a bit incensed.

Shortly thereafter the recorders were started and the questioning began. Twice during the afternoon Aliana asked to take a break. Rube did not sit at the conference table with the others, since he had no intention of asking any question of her. Instead, he chose a soft red leather chair near the windows at the end of the room. During her breaks Rube walked with her in the halls, holding her hand, but saying nothing.

It was after 7 PM when Agent Cantor thought they had covered everything. The others all agreed and the meeting was over. Rube saw Aliana's shoulders slump with exhaustion when they finished.

"How are you doing?" Rube asked.

"I need a drink," she commented.

Cantor and Miller left and Hank had gone to make a phone call. Ray Culp met with Aliana and Rube. "It's hard to read those feds, but I think it went well." He smiled at the raven-haired Aliana. "You don't often see a treasury agent amazed, but a couple of times they sat right up. You have given us enough to nail your governor to the wall. By the way, have you heard? The AG in Alaska has made the lieutenant governor the ranking official in Alaska. He suspended all authority held by Craig Talmage. The suspension lasts until after his trial. Sohms, his lawyer, is saying it was voluntary and in the best interest of the citizens of the State of Alaska. They are continuing to place all blame on you, Aliana. And, for what it's worth, by the end of the day everyone in this room was on your side, even those two federal agents. Let's go eat. I'm starved."

The following morning the group gathered once again in the same conference room. Some poor typist had stayed up all night transcribing the entire deposition. They used the entire day reading, confirming and editing the beefy text. By late afternoon it was agreed by all that every aspect had been covered. She asked if it would be alright for her to return to Costa Rica and her family. They agreed, provided she remained in contact with all agencies involved with the case. Agents Cantor and Miller shook her hand and thanked her for her cooperation. Fisk said, "Let's go eat."

That night, in the hotel, Aliana and Rube relaxed. Talk about their future was held to a minimum. They did discuss the short term, though. Aliana would go back to Costa Rica while Rube would go back to work. The FBI would undoubtedly contact her to ascertain what she knew about El Dante and the men she flew with to Mexico. Rube advised her to be as honest with them as she was with the treasury agents. He told her to expect to be contacted by an Agent Brownfield. Rube said he could set up the interview with

Brownfield and that, possibly, it could all be done by telephone. Aliana agreed to cooperate with them.

"How soon will it be before this comes to trial," Aliana inquired.

"In Alaska the law says 120 days. In practice, and especially in federal jurisdictions, that seldom happens. There isn't really on accurate way to predict how long this will take." Rube held her face in his hands and looked into her sad eyes. "I promise I will come down to see you every chance I get; though, I don't know how often that will be. In any case I will be here waiting for you when it's all over." He kissed her gently. "I love you very much."

"Oh, Rube. I know all this is my fault, but I wish it was all over and we could be together forever. It's difficult to plan a future when you don't know if there will be a future," again sadness crept into her voice. "Have you noticed? Nobody has mentioned recovering the money I took. I don't know what will happen when they do. I have no income now. I still have to care for Opal and Saundra. I don't know what I will do."

"They never really explained it to me, but they inferred that they were going after the money though Craig Talmage. They are making him responsible for restitution. That doesn't mean he won't have his lawyers sue you civilly. I don't think a jury will listen to him once he is convicted of a felony, but juries are a fickle lot," Rube explained.

"I guess I should make arrangements to go back home, then. I'll miss you," she said.

"We have tonight," he said, kissing her again.

Fisk and Culp met them for breakfast and took them to the airport. They used their influence to arrange flights for both. Rube said goodbye to the investigators and walked Aliana to her departure gate. He kissed her again, hugged her and went to his own gate. His flight would leave a few minutes after hers.

Chapter Forty Three

It was early afternoon when Rube arrived in Anchorage, there was a feel of fall in the air. He had decided not to go into the office today. He took a cab to his condo and spent the evening there, not notifying the office he had returned. Rube was satisfied at how things had gone for Aliana. She had won almost every point and it seemed they would give her a little more if she asked for anything. Most of the negotiations of this kind leave both parties wanting.

The evening was spent laying out his uniform, cleaning his duty weapon and watching the news. The TV had nothing new to report on Craig Talmage. Rube was watching the stock report when he remembered to call Don Sears, fiance of Molita Juarez, the lady whose information had forced him so deeply into this case.

"Don, Rube Hayes, remember me?"

"Sure do, Sergeant. How have you been?"

"Great, but it's Captain now," Rube told him.

"Congratulations," Don Sears replied.

"The reason I called is to find out if you and Molita are still planning to be married. Is that still on?"

"It sure is, and I am getting impatient. Molita won't come back to Alaska until you tell her it's safe. She is really frightened. Ramon and Eddie are her nightmares."

"Well, Don, I may have some good news for the two of you." Rube could tell he had the young man's attention now. "Ramon and Eduardo have fled the country. They have some other man, from Fairbanks, running the Sombrero Restaurant. I think it is now safe for her to come back to Alaska."

"Trooper Hayes, that is the best news I've heard in a long time. I hope Molly will think it's good news and come back and get married. Wow! Thank you."

"I'm sorry it took so long, but they are a slippery bunch. We couldn't have done it without the information given us by Molita. I want you to thank her for me and tell her to come see me when she returns."

"I sure will Captain, and you are invited to the wedding, whenever that will be. Thank you again." The joy was dripping from his voice.

His next call was made to Colin James at his home number. A female voice answered the phone. Rube asked to speak with Colin.

"This is Colin James," the new voice said.

"Colin, this is Rube Hayes of the Alaska State Troopers. How are you doing?"

"Oh, hi there Rube. I'm great. I haven't heard from you in a while. Is everything going well for you?"

"Yes, very well, thank, you. I just wanted to call you and thank you again for all you did for us during the investigation. Neither of us could have known that what we learned would help to put your friend Ben behind bars. That was a terrible turn of events. Have you seen him or talked with him?"

"You know, I've tried, but he won't take my calls. I guess I was too hard on him about his drinking. He won't talk to me." There was a short pause. "Ben and I were the best of friends and after Tad Morton was killed things changed. Ben got promoted and I guess he was over his head with responsibility and began to drink excessively. I wanted to help him, but he refused to be helped. I feel bad about that. If I could, I would help him now, but he won't let me. In the end, it looks like I lost both my friends."

"Don't blame yourself, Colin. He brought all this down on himself. Now his guilt is eating him up. I've seen it before, many times. Believe me, when he can't go any lower and realizes he can't save himself, he will call you." Rube tried to lighten the conversation. "By the way, who is the lady who answered the telephone? I didn't know you were married."

"Something new in my life since I last talked with you. She is living with me now. We plan to try it for a while and if it works out we plan to get married. You should meet her, Rube. She is a sweetheart. She has been good for me. She even likes kayaking." He had the sounds of love in his voice.

"Well, the best to the both of you. What's her name?"

"Sheila Nichols. The next time you come to Seattle, we will have to get together so you can meet her."

"I'd like that. I hope to talk with you again, soon. I'll be seeing you." Rube hung up, feeling good about the call.

He made one final call.

"Hello, Mrs. Balfore. Is Leon at home? This is Rube Hayes."

A moment later Leon was on the other end. "When did you get back, Rube?"

"Today. I'll be in the office in the morning," Rube said. "Has everything been going okay at the office?"

"Smooth as can be. Someone mentioned that you must be the root of all problems, because we haven't had any since you left town." The lieutenant commented.

"That must have been Milo," Rube laughed. "Do I have any new crisis to deal with my first day back?"

"None I am aware of. Welcome back. See you in the morning, Rube."

"See you in the morning," Rube replied.

Everyone in the front office said "Hello" to him when he came in. He poured a cup of fresh coffee and strolled down the hall to his office. There was nothing on his desk. Leon was right, it appeared he was able to stop all emergency situations. However, when Leon came in he brought a mountain of work for the captain. The two men had a short conversation and Rube dove into the day's duties. It was good to be back to familiar surroundings.

Just after 8:30 Rube called Milo and filled him in on his time the past week. Milo invited him to his office where they could talk in more detail. Rube promised to do that in the afternoon.

He was just finishing the pile of duties on his desk when Stan Withers came in to pass the time of day.

"I'm glad you stopped by, Stan. I have some things I need to talk about with you. Have a seat, you want some coffee or something?"

"Nah, just finished coffee and a doughnut in my office. Thanks anyway."

Rube sat across his desk, staring at his hands. "Stan," he began, "I owe you an apology."

"What for, Rube?"

"You remember the evening of the barbeque at your place?" he asked.

"Sure, we had a great time and, as I recall, you brought that great looking lady friend."

"Well, Stan, she got enough information from that gathering to pay her way to Costa Rica. That lady was Aliana Pedersen. She is the one involved in the Craig Talmage thing. What she learned at that party from me, you and your guys, she traded with Ramon Chavez and Eduardo Sanchez. Because of what she learned, all of them boarded a private jet and went to Mexico. Aliana, her sister and her daughter went with them." Rube explained. "Except for Larry Combs and Eddie Sanchez jumping bail, we didn't lose anything.

Aliana came back and gave depositions to the feds and the Washington Banking Commission about her involvement. They gave her immunity for her testimony, for whatever it's worth. I'm sorry for bringing her to your party. The point is that she was able to get this information in the first place. She learned what she needed from us. We had all been in the beer; Aliana is a beautiful woman and you know how we men are around beautiful women, especially after a couple of beers. I trusted her and that was my mistake. I owe you for that. Someone could have been hurt over this." Rube paused. "Stan, we all need time to let off steam, but we need to learn from this and be more careful, both about who shows up and what is said."

"Since we are confessing here," Stan began, "I already knew all that. I have had a talk with my guys about it. They forgive you and so do I, but we share in the blame, all of us. You are right, it could have been much worse. Between you and me, there is enough guilt for everyone. My group has agreed to keep any partying to officers only, no girlfriends, no wives, no outsiders."

"Thanks for understanding, Stan. Still friends?"

"Of course, and thanks for the honesty." Both men stood and shook hands.

Chapter Forty Four

The next several weeks were almost boring. With the bulk of the tourists gone back to their homes, quiet seemed to be the rule of the day. Rube was beginning to enjoy the peaceful time in his office. The Craig Talmage court case was moving slowly ahead, but it only became newsworthy when he or his lawyer appeared in court. It was late September when FBI agent Brownfield notified him about the death of Eduardo Sanchez. The steroid use had finally affected his brain to the point he could no longer maintain a heartbeat or breathing. An autopsy concluded his death was the result of long term steroid use which had literally destroyed his brain function. Brownfield had also informed Rube of the rise of a new and powerful leader in the crime world in Mexico. The new leader was being trained and was now in charge of the business. Ramon Chavez was now the most powerful man in Mexico. El Dante had retired and was seldom seen outside his villa.

Instead of lunch Rube used the time to call Aliana. They spoke every week.

"Hello, Aliana," Rube greeted.

"It is so good to hear from you, Rube. I have missed you."

"I've missed you, too. How are Saundra and Opal?"

"Oh, they're just fine. This climate seems to agree with the two of them," she chuckled, "Is there any word about when we are going to court?"

"I'm sorry, there is nothing new. I spoke to the AG early this week and he said it was just the usual legal maneuvering before trial. He did say, though, that Sohms, Talmage's lawyer, hadn't filed any delays. It looked to Woody like Sohms was about ready for court. That said, I think you should be ready for a lot of negative publicity about you to appear in the papers. Woody said, and

I agree, his defense will be that you were responsible for everything. Culp and Fisk have given Woody the paper trail for the money. They say the trail splits after Bahamas or Panama at which time half the revenue goes to Hong Kong to a numbered account belonging to our esteemed governor."

"Yes, that is true. I can testify to all that, but will the jury believe me? I hope so."

"The jury will be forced to believe you, since you are only confirming what the banks have told the prosecutor." Rube tried to sound confident.

"Do you know that nobody has tried to seize my bank accounts?" she said. "I hope they leave me a little money. My own savings from working and investments is mingled with all that bank money since I left the U.S."

"I can't tell you what will happen to that and they haven't said anything about it to me." Rube thought a few seconds. "I think if the trial doesn't get scheduled soon, I am going to come down there for a few days. I have just hated being apart, I need you."

"That would be wonderful, Rube. I want to be with you, too."

At that point the conversation died off. Rube broke the silence.

"I guess we had better hang up, but I will call again in a couple of days. I love you."

"I love you, too. I just want this to be over. Bye."

Things in the office were winding down and the pace was noticeably slower. He called Milo to ask if he would like to go fishing this weekend. Milo thought it would be great and asked if his son could come along.

Rube dialed the Flourette C. The phone jingled a couple of times before a voice came on the line. She was a rough and tumble sea charter captain who had the world's biggest heart. A slim, nice looking lady who took no guff from anyone, male or female.

"Flouette C, Diane speaking."

"Diane, Rube Hayes. How are things in Seward?"

"Well, hi there, Rube. Haven't heard from you since that banker got killed up at the glacier. How was your summer?" Diane asked.

"Mostly good. I got mixed up in that flap about the governor. That has taken up most of my time lately. What I called about, Diane, if you have room on Saturday, I would like to get in on a late silver salmon fishing trip. There would be three of us, me, Milo and his son. Can you fit us in?"

"Heck, Rube, for you I would throw someone else off the boat." She chuckled at her own joke. "I only had one charter signed up for Saturday, so I can fit you in. Really glad to have more clients. It's beginning to slow down tourist-wise. You know where the boat is tied. Be there at six. Any earlier and we would be fighting darkness. We have been picking up limits out at Pony Cove. Dress warm."

"Great, Diane. I need this get-away. See you Saturday morning." He said good bye and hung up the phone. Rube called Milo and relayed the schedule.

Rube picked up Milo and his son Saturday morning at 4 in the morning. Milo sat up front while his son lounged in the back seat. He was almost immediately asleep. It was 5:30 when the trio walked down the dock to the fifty-three-foot boat. Diane kept it in immaculate condition and would immediately be on anyone's case that abused her vessel.

Once in open water, Diane asked about Ben Gerlitz, though she didn't recall his name.

"That whole thing turned into a can of worms. You remember I said I was involved in the corruption case against the governor? Well, it all started with the death of Tad Morton, the kayaker who was killed at Holgate Glacier. I can't say much about it because it hasn't come to trial yet. But, I do want to thank you again for all your help that day. You did a great job. So did your deck hand. The two of you were the heroes of the day on that occasion." The conversation went on for another hour while the boat motored out to the fishing spot. The Flourette C is not fast, but it is very comfortable, and Diane made the trip enjoyable. At daylight she pointed out wildlife on the shores and on the hillsides. She showed them eagles and identified most of the seabirds they saw.

Fishing, it turned out, was hot. They fished standing in a small steering pit at the rear of the boat. Two men fished twenty minutes and traded places with the other two. Two men kibitzing and two men fishing all day long with the kibitzers and fishermen trading off every twenty minutes. Everyone has fun fishing with Diane.

At the end of the day, with four limits in the locker, they headed back to Seward. Diane had fixed a lunch and made her famous halibut dip with crackers. Hot coffee and cocoa were served all day long. Back at the dock the fish were filleted and put into plastic bags for the clients to take home. Rube provided a large plastic tub for carrying the fish back to the city.

It was late when Rube stopped in front of Milo's house. They split up the catch, said good night and Rube went home. It took a while to cut the fillets into small pieces and bag them for the freezer. He was relaxed for the first time in several months.

He took a cold beer from the refrigerator and turned on the television to watch the 10 o'clock news. The house was lonely without Aliana. He wondered when the trial would start and she would be back. Soon I hope, he thought.

He awoke later than usual on Sunday. The phone rang while he was starting the coffee.

"Rube Hayes," he answered.

"You sound grouchy this morning, Rube." It was Aliana.

"I won't be grouchy any longer. Hearing your voice is all it takes to cheer me up. How have you been?"

"I'm fine. Missing you. Saundra and Opal both told me to say hi."

"When are you coming home?"

"That's why I called. Friday I had a call from some government lawyer to tell me the trial date is set for the end of this month. The federal case will be tried in Seattle. They say I will be in town for that at least three weeks. Will you be able to come down to Seattle to be with me?" she pleaded.

"I will do my best. I don't have anything on my plate that would stop me except the Talmage trial. They haven't set the date for that yet, but I don't see them going before the federal trial is over."

"Oh, Rube. I will be so happy when this is over and we can be together again. All this is horrible. I want to come home."

"It will all be over soon, Aliana. Just hang on a little longer." It seemed little consolation. "Have any of the lawyers from the State of Alaska or Talmage's lawyer contacted you?" he asked.

"No, but my grocer told me there has been a stranger in town asking about me. It must be one of lawyer Sohms' men. The government lawyer said I would have to testify at the state trial. The AG, Woody, has talked with the feds about it. He wants me to testify. He said that trial will be held in Juneau. It will be embarrassing, but I'll do it. After that it should all be over." Her voice was becoming sad again.

"All we can do now is wait it out." He wanted to make her feel better, but didn't know how. "I love you."

"I love you, too. I'll call you again soon." They said good bye and hung up.

Rube sipped his cold coffee and thought about her. Waiting was very hard duty.

Chapter Forty Five

The first Monday in October, 10:15 AM, Milo called Rube. "They have set a trial date on the Gerlitz trial. Can you come to my office to talk about it?"

A wave of relief struck Rube. "Are you busy now?" he asked.

"Now will be fine. I had a hunch you would like the news."

In Milo's office the tone was casual, though Rube didn't feel casual. "Want some coffee or anything, Rube?"

"No, thanks. I have a lot to do in the office and want to get back as soon as possible. I am really anxious to hear about the trial dates. I hope they will send me down for that one."

"I think we can arrange that," Milo said. "Just remember this will be state business and hanky-panky will have to be on your own time and checkbook."

"You don't have to remind me, Major." Rube laughed, wondering if this was a warning. "When is it scheduled?"

"Tuesday next week. It will be in the Federal Courthouse in Seattle." It was Milo's turn to chuckle. "Do you think you can work it in?"

"I'll try to be available," Rube was laughing again. "Have you heard anything on the Craig Talmage trial? They should be setting a date on that one soon."

"I talked to the AG on Friday and he thinks as soon as the feds finish with Gerlitz Sohms will speed up the process. Woody thinks they are just waiting for the feds to run out of bullets. Once they expose all their evidence in that trial, Sohms will know what he has to prepare for. One thing you want to remember, Talmage isn't stupid. He has been too quiet. He has a plan to beat this thing. If I had to guess, he is already making plans to re-occupy the state mansion."

Rube was nodding his head. "I get the same feeling, boss. Keep your official ear to the Juneau ground. Let me know if you hear anything new." He stood to return to his own office.

"I will have a memo and travel orders for you by this afternoon. The state will pick up the cost of travel and hotel. Meals will have to be covered out of your per diem."

Back in his office, Rube reached for his cell phone and dialed Aliana. Opal answered on the fifth ring, and called Aliana to the telephone.

"Oh, Rube, I am so glad you called. Have you heard?" she was talking very rapidly. "The trial starts next week. Will you be there?"

"I just came from Milo's office and he is making all the arrangements for me. I should have all that this afternoon. I will call you later with it. Do you know where you will be staying?"

"Not yet. The federal attorney said he would send all the information by DASH express today. They want to brief me for a couple of days before the trial starts."

"They won't book us into the same hotels, so maybe one of us won't have to get the sheets and towels changed. You can't imagine how excited I am to see you."

"Yes I can. I feel the same way," Aliana sighed.

"I will call again when I have my travel information. See you soon." He was feeling lonely already. "I love you."

The week drug on slowly. All the plans had been made by Milo's office and looked great. Rube had convinced Milo to let him leave on Friday afternoon. There were some things he wanted to do in Seattle, one of which was to contact Colin James. He wanted to get a feel for how Ben Gerlitz was doing. The other was to contact Lyda Carney. She had been the keystone for this entire case. He felt an obligation to thank her personally. There were other items on the list, not the least of which was to hope Aliana would be in Seattle for the weekend. Once again his personal feelings were overriding his sense of duty. The week wore on even more slowly.

Rube was able to contact Aliana late Saturday afternoon. He wanted to pick her up at the airport, but the feds had arranged a car to take her to the Four Seasons Hotel downtown. They made a date for dinner.

Rube was back in the Edgewater. He could walk from the hotel to the courthouse. He called Colin James and met him in south Seattle at the railroad restaurant where they had eaten before. Colin was standing on the walk in front of the restaurant when Rube arrived.

"Sorry I'm late," he said. "I sort of got lost getting here. How are you, Colin?"

"Doing fine, Rube, doing fine," he said as they walked into the diner. Colin was recognized right away and the two men were shown to a table.

"I want you to know I will be taking you up on that fishing trip in Alaska."

"Just let me know when. It's getting a little late this year, though." Colin was easy for Rube to converse with. "I went on a charter last week. We limited out on silver salmon and had a great time. The weather is beginning to cool off now." Small talk went on for several minutes, until after lunch had been ordered.

"Have you seen or talked with Ben?" Rube asked.

"He finally started talking to me again. His guilt is eating him up. He said that was why he had been drinking so heavily." Colin's eyes went sad. "There is nothing I can do to help him. His career is gone; he has no job and is about to become a convicted felon. His future doesn't look promising."

"Are you coming to the trial?"

"Ben asked me not to." Colin gave a thoughtful sigh. "I would go anyway, but there are some technical issues with the new Boeing 787 in which I am involved. My time is pretty tight right now."

Rube told him of his projected schedule, his hotel and room number, as well as his cell phone number, just in case he needed to contact the trooper. Rube promised to keep Colin posted on events at the trial.

Back in his hotel, Rube called Lyda Carney. He asked if it would be okay for him to come to her office on Monday to visit he said. They talked a few minutes before saying goodbye. Rube checked the time and decided he had time for a short nap before he would shower and change clothes for his dinner date with Aliana.

At dinner the two were equally excited, anticipating the evening ahead, they held hands across the table like two teenagers. Later the conversation got around to the trial. Aliana was nervous about it. Rube vowed to support her all the way. Aliana said the federal attorney had scheduled meetings through the weekend and for Monday. She would be very busy during the day, but evenings were going to be free. Tuesday was expected to be taken up with jury selection. Rube told her to expect him in court on Wednesday.

Later, after another bottle of red wine, the couple went to her room. He returned to his own hotel in the very early hours.

The rest of the weekend was spent in much the same manner. Monday came and after some phone business Rube visited the fifty-story bank building. Upon reaching the upper floor housing the Alaska Account section, he walked to where Lyda Carney used to have her desk. To his surprise, when he located it, Lyda was not there. Another young lady occupied the desk. She told Rube she would call Ms. Carney. A moment later she appeared. She greeted Rube with a huge hug.

"I am so glad to see you, Trooper Hayes," she began. "Come back to my desk where we can talk for a while."

Rube followed her to a desk near the outer glass wall. The desk had previously belonged to Ben Gerlitz. Rube smiled at the thought of her taking Ben's position.

"I didn't know you had been promoted. Congratulations, Lyda." he commented. "And it's Rube, remember?"

"Oh, Rube. I have you to thank for the promotion. Mr. Stackhaus said he was appointing me because of the work I did and sent to you. He said he was going to appoint me because his previous system of promotion hadn't worked well." She giggled.

"You deserve it, Lyda. This case would never have been discovered without your diligence. I showed those files to my accountant and later to the attorney general for the State of Alaska. They both said the same thing, 'This is great work.' I agree with them. You did a marvelous job without regard to your own well-being. That is the definition of a hero. And we all think you are a hero. I just came by to thank you for all you did."

"I appreciate all the kind words, but I don't feel much like a hero. All the while, I was getting the files and calling you, I was scared to death. I told you before, I didn't know who was involved and didn't know where to turn. I was so nervous even my dog didn't want to be near me." She giggled again.

Rube spent almost an hour with her, having coffee and visiting. She asked about Aliana and if he had seen Ben. She told Rube she was planning a cruise to Alaska the following summer and asked if it would it be alright if she called him when she arrived. He said he would show her around if his work load permitted. He kissed her on the cheek and said goodbye.

He called Colin and once again had lunch with him. He again promised to keep him informed about the trial.

In the early evening, he met Aliana. They went to Woodland Park and walked for miles. They sat on the grass and talked. They walked through some of the zoo hand-in-hand just enjoying each other's company. Again they had dinner together and spent a pleasant evening in her room. She had to be in court early the next morning and wanted to go to bed early. She was anxious to have this ordeal behind her.

Rube skipped the Monday jury selection, but Tuesday saw him in the courtroom. Aliana sat near the gallery rail behind a bevy of government attorneys.

The legal formalities were all addressed and the jury charged. By the time they had all been addressed, it was time to break for lunch. Aliana was to have lunch with the prosecution attorneys. Rube ate alone.

When everyone was back in court and the judge was in his high seat, he asked the prosecutor if he was ready to proceed. He said he was ready. The judge then turned to the defense attorney and asked the same question.

The defense attorney was a petite young woman whose ink on her diploma was still wet. "Yes, your honor, but the defense, at this time, would like to enter a change of plea."

The judge looked stunned, as did the table full of prosecutors.

"Are you saying your client wishes to change his plea on all charges in this case?" the judge asked.

"After reviewing the evidence with my client and after much discussion, he has asked me to change his plea to guilty and to put himself at the mercy of this court," the young lawyer said.

"Mr. Gerlitz," the judge said, "is what your attorney just said truly your wishes?"

She asked Ben to stand. "It is your honor. I am guilty and wish to plead such. There is no reason to take a lot of time and expense to come to the same conclusion via court process."

There was no objection from the prosecution. The jury was dismissed and court recessed while the judge decided Ben's fate. Except for the defense, all participants were released. The trial was over.

Rube spotted lawyer Sohms sitting in the rear of the courtroom. He, too, looked stunned as he put away his legal pad and left the court.

At dinner Aliana told Rube she was returning to Costa Rica and Saundra the first thing in the morning.

Chapter Forty Six

Life in Alaska went on. Rube briefed Milo on the Seattle trial and his time there. He relayed that he thought Sohms was disappointed by the fact Gerlitz had plead out and none of the evidence was presented in public.

Milo said he had been in contact with Woody Parsons and it appeared that very soon there was going to be a trial for Craig Talmage.

There was a flurry of legal maneuvers over the next couple of weeks. The state asked for and got a change of venue. The trial was now going to be held in Anchorage. Sohms asked the court to set a court date as soon as possible. When the date was set Rube notified Aliana. Three weeks later she arrived in Anchorage. The reunion was less than glorious, but friendly. Rube was confused by her change. She explained she was nervous and upset at having to face Talmage in court. Rube accepted that and allowed her to maintain a friendly, if not loving, relationship. Saundra and Opal remained in Costa Rica.

More than a week had gone by when a trooper came to his office and presented Rube with a subpoena to appear as a state's witness at the upcoming trial. Later the same week, Woody came to his office where he spent half a day with Rube going over the case. Rube's role was miniscule and pertained only to the discovery of the crime.

Aliana was another story, however. Woody and his assistants spent several days going over every aspect of the case against Craig Talmage. Aliana was a willing participant and, on occasion, added new tidbits of information. The state's strategy emerged from all this and soon they were ready to do battle. The preliminary court jousting had finished and the trial was scheduled for the following week. Jury selection would be on Tuesday. All the witnesses, including Rube and Aliana were required to be present. Ben Gerlitz, escorted by Agent Tom Cantor, was in court with the others. One by one jurors were selected. Twelve jurors and two alternates were seated. The judge charged the jury and released them, ordering them to return the next day to begin hearing evidence.

During the entire day, Talmage and Sohms whispered and took notes. Reporters in the gallery tried to contact them during the many recesses of the day, but Sohms advised the media his client had nothing to say until after the trial. Being news media, they would fill their news-hours with speculation, thereby keeping the trial on the front pages of the newspapers and at the top of the hour on the television.

Rube had seen little of Aliana during all this time. Each time they met, she was cordial and friendly, but there was no affection passed between them. Not once had she called him, and he had quit trying to contact her. He was totally frustrated and baffled by it all.

When things got under way for real, Woody was not present at the prosecution table. He had left this to an assistant, William David Gooch. Gooch was an old-time lawyer and ex-state senator. He wore thick glasses and a black full-length necktie. He was heavy-set and moved slowly, belying his intellect and wit. Rube speculated, the state's case was in very capable hands.

Trial is a mind-numbing process. The judge read the charges, both lawyers made their motions and voiced their objections to the other's requests. Rube was scheduled early in the trial to document the discovery of the crime. Even so, it was mid-afternoon when he was called. He was sworn in and interviewed by Gooch.

"The files, as they were sent to you, were only an inquiry, is that correct?" Gooch asked.

"Yes," Rube replied.

"Will you tell the court who sent them to you and why?" Another question by Gooch.

Rube recited the entire scenario including how Lyda Carney knew him. He related how he had met Ben Gerlitz and Aliana Pedersen. His testimony went on and on exploring every detail for which he had personal knowledge.

When Gooch finished with him, Lewis Sohms began. Surprisingly, Sohms had only a few questions to ask and seemed satisfied with the testimony he had given previously. When he told the judge he had no further questions, and Gooch had nothing further, the judge dismissed him.

He had planned to stay for all the trial, but was so confused and upset by Aliana's attitude he went back to the office. There he drank a cup of coffee and, unable to concentrate, went back to the court. After all, this was his case.

A collage of expert witnesses were presented the first day and at 4:30 in the afternoon the judge recessed the trial until 10 AM. The next day.

The following day was taken up with witnesses to the crime. One after another they testified and left the court. Late in the afternoon, William D. Gooch called Aliana Pedersen. She was sworn.

"Ms. Pedersen, you were a party to this criminal act, is that correct?"

"Yes, sir," she said, almost inaudibly.

"Please, speak up, Ms. Pedersen. Would you please tell us your entire story, starting from the beginning?"

Aliana took a deep breath and began. "I met Craig Talmage while in college. We both attended the University of Alaska Fairbanks. We lived together for a time while in school. Craig became interested in politics and had contacts through his financial institution and the contacts he made there. He was a handsome and articulate man with great ambition. Soon, he moved in the political circles and was, eventually, elected governor. One of his promises was to improve the accountability within the department of finance. When he was elected, he asked me to form a new division within the department. This division would eliminate the penalties and fees associated with the late payments to contracts with the State of Alaska. I accepted the position. The first thing I did was to hire four of the most talented and physically attractive young women I could find. Those ladies are still with the division and one of them now runs the entire financial structure. I instituted a new payment process through SeaFirst Bank in Seattle. They established an entire department devoted to the cash flow for all contracts with the state. The annual flow usually runs $2 billion a year, plus or minus a few dollars.

"It was necessary to change the individual departmental payment authorization system. This proved to be the most difficult part of the transition. Eventually, though, department heads saw the benefit of the changes and realized the end result was that more of their annual budgets remained with the department and less was paid out for late paperwork. The system is saving the State of Alaska millions of dollars each year. The cost of operation by SeaFirst Bank was paid out of the interest generated within the account by funds accumulated to pay pending completed contracts. The daily balance on this account varies greatly with the time of year and the number of capital projects taking place." She paused briefly.

"Once the system was in place, the governor contacted me with a plan to divert the interest monies from the account to his own use. He said he wouldn't be governor forever and needed to plan for his future. He said I would be included in the profits." She stared down at her hand while murmurs in the courtroom subsided. "I declined the offer, but he threatened to fire me and discredit me to the point I would never be able to get employment with any financial institution, anywhere. I have a daughter and a sister to care for and I couldn't be without income, so I told Craig I would set it up.

"It took a lot of doing. I had to find a willing official within the bank. He turned out to be Tad Morton. Tad set up the duplicate files for the account, leaving out the interest payments on the one belonging to the State of Alaska. The costs related to the account were deducted and paid to the SeaFirst Bank The remainder was paid, twice weekly, to Alaska Maritime Investments. From that account the money was transferred electronically to a number of bank accounts around the world. The final recipients were numbered accounts payable to myself and to Craig Talmage. A smaller account was set up for Tad Morton and later, after Tad's death, to Ben Gerlitz. The governor was careful not to have his name on any of these funds, only on the numbered account in Hong Kong. These banks never release the names of account holders, though in this case, I believe they did. When Lyda Carney became suspicious and found the dual files, she contacted Sergeant Reuben Hayes of the Alaska State Troopers. They had met at the bank. Ms. Carney could not determine who was involved in this conspiracy and decided to go outside the bank to have it investigated. Trooper Hayes and I had become friends at the time of the death of Tad Morton.

"Through Trooper Hayes I learned that he was investigating improper activities at SeaFirst Bank. At that time I contacted Craig Talmage and informed him we had been found out. He said don't worry about it, but I did worry. I suspected he would shuffle all the blame to me. He is pretty good at protecting himself. I had seen it before. When I learned all this, I immediately left the State of Alaska, closed the money pipeline down and withdrew all the money from my share of the account, leaving Craig's accounts as they were. I found a way to leave the U.S. on a private jet and established a home for my sister, Opal, my daughter, Saundra and myself. I have come back at this time for the trial."

Gooch picked up two files and handed one to Sohms. "That was a very good dissertation, Ms. Pedersen. I have, in my hand, the file provided by the U.S. Banking Commission and its Federal Agents. Are you familiar with this file?"

"Yes, I gave most of the depositions quoted in the files," she said.

"I will not go through this file item by item unless the defense asks me to do so. But, you say the testimony you just gave is documented in this file, is this correct?" Gooch asked.

"Yes, it is," she answered.

"Thank you, Ms. Pedersen." He looked to the bench. "Nothing further at this time, your honor."

The judge declared a short recess and upon their return asked Sohms, "So you have questions for this witness, Mr. Sohms?"

Sohms stood. "I do, Your Honor." He then turned to Aliana. "Ms. Pedersen, you tell an interesting story. I would like to clarify a few things, though. You stated you knew Craig Talmage while you were both in college, is that correct?"

"Yes, it is," she replied.

"You stated the two of you shared a room during that time. Is that true?"

"Yes, it is," again she replied.

"You claim you have a daughter. Did you become pregnant during the time you and Craig Talmage lived together?" His voice was calm and conversational.

"Yes," she answered, coldly.

"You have given a long and detailed account of this case. You have accused my client of initiating this system for stealing money from the State of Alaska. I submit your account may not be totally accurate. I submit that your account is accurate up to the point where you established this account knowing that someday it would be discovered and at that time you would blame Governor Craig Talmage for the purpose of revenge. Isn't that what really happened, Ms. Pedersen?" Sohms was speaking loudly, almost shouting at her. The jury was sitting upright in their seats.

"No, it is not, Mr. Sohms. It happened as I stated in court here today and in the depositions to the Federal Agents. I have told the truth, whether you care to believe it or not." Her voice was cold and the color had all but left her blue eyes.

"Nothing further at this time, Your Honor, but I reserve the right to recall this witness," Sohms related to the judge, leaving the last statements for the jury to digest.

Chapter Forty Seven

The following morning, when court resumed, the state rested their case. The judge asked lawyer Sohms if he was ready to present his defense. He was. He stated he had only one witness, but he might recall Ms. Aliana Pedersen. The judge agreed and left him to present his first witness, Craig Talmage.

"Mr. Talmage, what is your profession?" Sohms asked.

"I am the current governor of the State of Alaska. The lieutenant governor is acting in my stead until this trial is over."

"You have heard the testimony of Ms. Pedersen. Do you consider her testimony to be accurate?"

"Most of her statements are accurate; however, she has misrepresented some of the important facts in her statement," Talmage said.

"And, what facts do you say were misrepresented?" Sohms asked.

"In order to set things right, I will have to start at the beginning." He paused, thinking about what he would say next. "She stated that we went to college together. That much is true. That is where we met. We had a relationship for several months and lived together during that time. She claims she became pregnant during that time. If she did, I had no knowledge of it. She never told me. After we graduated, I went to work for a large bank in Fairbanks. I was fortunate enough to be promoted quite quickly. During that time I met and associated with a number of influential businessmen who asked me to assist them in several business transactions. I soon gained a certain reputation in those circles and my private consulting became more prosperous. These same clients asked if I would be interested in a career in politics. After a great deal of thought, I accepted this challenge. I was elected to the legislature where I was appointed to many important committees. During this time, Ms. Pedersen and I never saw each other and I did not know she had a child." He looked down at his hands, thinking again. "Her child was born with some learning disabilities. Tragic," he said, shaking his head.

"Some years later, I was elected governor. Through my business and banking experience, I was convinced there was a better way for the state to pay its bills. I was looking for someone to direct this new department. I knew Ms. Pedersen as a capable, intelligent and hard-working person. I thought she would be the right person for the newly created position as deputy director of finance. She did an outstanding job in that position. She never gave any indication to me that she was operating a separate agenda of her own. When this finally came to light, I was shocked. I had no idea any of this was happening. She and the head of the Alaska Account at SeaFirst Bank in Seattle had carefully kept all mention of interest payments secret from me with a second set of files. I had never been to the bank and had no reason to believe there was anything wrong with the account. I'm afraid I am guilty of trusting my employee. I should have been more diligent and less naïve." He stopped speaking, not looking at the jury.

Sohms checked his notes. "You are telling us, then, that you did not know about this child Ms. Pedersen claims is yours. Is that correct?"

"That is correct," he stated quietly.

"And you claim no knowledge of the conspiracy to defraud the state or of duplicate files that had been created for the purpose of keeping this knowledge from you, is that correct?" Sohms asked, standing near the jury box.

"That is correct, I knew nothing about her child or about the duplicate files." He lifted his head as though he had just thought of something new. "There had been many audits of the account and each time she personally briefed me on the results. Each time she produced documentation, which I signed and approved. I agree there was a conspiracy to hide the truth from the citizens of the State of Alaska. However, the truth was also hidden from me."

With that Sohms returned to his seat at the defense table and turned the witness over to prosecutors. He had not wanted his client to give much detailed information for the prosecutor to attack. Lewis Sohms was satisfied with the testimony given by Talmage and liked the reactions from the jury.

The prosecution had a team of three lawyers. They conferred in whispers, then one of them, a tall, slim man with slightly graying temples, stood. "Governor," he began, "do you expect us to believe that a man of your intelligence didn't know he had fathered a child? This, in a town as small as

Fairbanks, by a woman who worked in the same profession with some of the same people you represented?"

Talmage seemed unruffled by the question. "That is correct. I trusted this woman, both as a friend and, later, as an employee. She had never given me any reason to doubt my trust in her."

The lawyer questioned Craig Talmage for almost an hour, trying to shake his story and get him to stumble over a lie. Talmage was unshakable. His experience in public life had trained him to stay calm in all situations. The prosecution's team whispered one more time and released the witness.

Sohms rested his case. The judge gave the jury a break before final arguments were presented. It would be a long and tiring afternoon. During the final summations, each lawyer would review each and every piece of evidence and every statement by every witness. It all boiled down to which witness lied. That decision would be up to the jury.

The jury deliberated for three hours, then was taken to eat. After dinner they were sequestered in the Sheraton Hotel, a few short blocks from the courthouse. In the morning, after breakfast was served, the jury was returned to the courthouse to continue deliberation. No one outside the jury room knew what was happening inside. Deliberations went on the entire day and the jury was sequestered once again. The third morning they were, once again, taken back to the courthouse. In mid-morning the bailiff notified the judge that they had reached a verdict. The judge ordered all parties to return to the court.

Eventually everyone was reassembled and the judge called the jury. Every lawyer watched intently as they filed back into the jury box. Every face on the jury was stern and serious, but gave no indication of their vote.

"Have you reached a verdict?" the judge asked.

"We have, Your Honor," the jury foreman announced.

"On the single count of conspiracy to commit a felony, how do you find?" asked the judge.

"Guilty, Your Honor."

"Was this decision unanimous?" he inquired.

"Yes, sir."

The jury was polled as to their individual votes. When the judge was satisfied all requirements had been met, he thanked them and released the jury from duty.

The judge addressed the court. "I have checked my calendar and set the sentencing hearing for three weeks from today, 10:30 AM. All parties will return at that time. Bail will be continued until that time." With that, everyone stood and the judge left the court.

Chapter Forty Eight

Early the following week Rube was trying to catch up on some of the things he had neglected in his office. He hated to admit it to himself, but he had been in a foul mood since the trial ended. In an attempt to remedy some of that, he had, one by one, invited his trooper friends to come by his office to visit. Stan Withers had been one of the first.

Today he was having lunch with his friend Burt Fields. Over the years Fields had done his taxes and cared for his investments. Burt had made quite a lot of money through investing for Rube. Rube in turn had flown Burt to a remote camp site each year where the CPA had bagged a moose almost every year. Because of the trial and Rube's involvement with it, they had not made the annual trip this fall. Rube needed to mend his fences with the accountant.

He was finalizing his daily duty reports when the telephone rang. It was Woody Parsons, the attorney general. "Hello, Rube. Got time to talk for a minute?"

Rube welcomed the call. He leaned back and put his right foot on the partially open desk drawer. "Always have time for you, Woody. How are you?"

"I'm doing really well, even under the new governor. He loves me, says I am the one who made him governor." Woody chuckled. "I took all the credit. I didn't even mention that you helped a little."

"When you get to be the next lieutenant governor, I'll see what I can do for you," Rube laughed. "Let me know if you want to be governor."

"Hold that thought, Rube. I hadn't planned to run for lieutenant governor, but with your help I could change my mind." Now both men laughed. "In that same thought, though, I have been in contact with the pre-sentence investigators. The ex-governor is still claiming innocence. The jury said otherwise, and the investigators don't seem to have much sympathy for him. They are recommending fifteen years, seven suspended. Serve eight. Full restitution for all funds embezzled to be paid by the governor. He will forfeit all retirement benefits from the State of Alaska. They expect his lawyer to object to the terms, but the judge wants his hide also. Restitution will be in lieu of any fines. How do you like that?"

"Wow! I don't think I have ever heard of a sentence like that. He deserves it, though. When will you be in Anchorage? I want to buy you dinner."

"I'm pretty busy right now with the transition and all, but I will call you when I get time to come up there. Take care, Rube. Thanks for all you did."

"Just doing my job, Woody. Stay in touch."

Rube worked a little later than usual that evening because of some recent staffing problems. When he got home he took off the heavy duty belt and hung it in his closet. He took off his shirt and went into the kitchen. He opened the refrigerator and looked inside. He was trying to decide what to have for dinner when the telephone rang.

"Rube Hayes," he answered.

"Hi, Rube, it's Aliana. Are you busy?"

"Not since you don't want to see me any more." His voice crisp.

"I'm sorry, Rube, but I am going back to Costa Rica and I want to see you before I leave. There are some things I need to explain to you. Can I come for a little while?"

His feelings were somewhere between anger and anticipation. He wrestled with a response. "I don't know what to say, Aliana. You love me and then you leave me. You want me and then you tell me to stay away. I'm having a real problem dealing with it all."

"I know, Rube, I admit it's all my fault. I don't want what I have done to cause you any more hurt. If I stay and we try to make a life, it is only going to hurt your career. If you quit and come with me, it will take you away from the only life you know and love. No matter what I do, it will hurt you. Please let me come to your place and explain some of the reason." She was pleading. "For what it's worth, Rube, I never stopped loving you"

Against his better judgment, he said, "Okay, come on over."

Twenty minutes later she was at his front door. She seemed to get more beautiful each time he saw her. The colorful tee-shirt with a pattern of sequins on the front was an exciting sight. He invited her into the living room. He asked if she wanted a beer and she accepted. He came back with two beers and sat in his recliner across the room from her.

"This is awkward for me too, Rube. I don't want to leave here, but I must. Saundra's in Costa Rica with Opal. I have a home there. I'm afraid if I come back they will try to recover whatever money I have left. I can't get a job here with all the notoriety I've accumulated. I love you, but my first concern has to be Saundra."

"I can understand all that," Rube admitted.

"I also have to tell you that Lewis Sohms was right about one thing," she admitted.

"Right about what?" Rube asked.

"In court he speculated that I did everything and framed Craig simply for revenge."

"What do you mean, Aliana. Are you saying Craig Talmage is innocent?"

"Of the embezzlement, yes. Of not caring for his daughter, he is guilty, guilty, guilty." Her eyes were becoming cold and pale. "For all those years he refused to pay anything toward her care. He refused to pay for any of her medical expenses. He refused to publicly admit he was her father. That self-centered megalomaniac left all that for me to shoulder so he could pursue his career. Well, I fooled the fool." She was becoming more cold and bitter. "I was able to do it all. I made a career for myself; I took care of our daughter and of Opal. I provided for her all the things he refused to supply. I vowed to someday make him pay for what he had withheld from me and Saundra. Well, I accomplished that mission. He is paying. He has been publicly humiliated and disgraced. He has no job and couldn't get one now, at least not in the financial world. I have finally given that SOB what he deserved after all these years. The government has given me immunity and I intend to take advantage of it. He can now suffer like we had to do all these years. Whatever they give him, he deserves it."

"Aliana, you have distorted the meaning of the word justice beyond all reason. You can't get a man, even Craig Talmage, convicted of a crime he didn't commit and go on living with yourself. It isn't right. And to convince yourself you are doing this for Saundra is a lie, not just to her but to yourself. You have to think what you are doing; you have to make it right." Rube was completely overwhelmed by what he had just witnessed. He didn't know what to do about it.

The color returned to her eyes and softness to her face. "I can live a good life now, Rube. It would be a lot better if it were with you, but I know that can never be. I am leaving in the morning and I had to tell you this before I returned to Costa Rica. Please, Rube, don't hate me. You have my phone number if you can ever forgive me." She stood to leave. She had tears in those ice blue eyes. "I still love you."

With that she walked out the door. Rube watched her go down the walk. He was filled with negative emotions. He had to call Woody Parsons and tell him of these revelations. Rube knew he could never call Aliana. He knew he would never forget her. He knew he would always love her.